If Only

C. L. Kraemer

Published by Rogue Phoenix Press

ISBN: 978-1-62420-210-0

Credits
Cover Artist: Designs by Ms G
Editor: Christine Young

Dedication

Lori—my best friend for longer than either of us wishes to admit. I hope you recognize yourself. She was written with love and appreciation.

If Only

The blonde woman stopped in front of Barbara, tossing a fearful look Rachel's direction, before reaching out and gently lifting Barbara's hand to her, palm up, and peered at the opened extremity. She took a bejeweled, ruby-tipped finger and traced the lifeline. Her dark brown eyes peered deeply into Barbara's.

"You have recently suffered a great personal loss."

Rachel harrumphed behind Barbara.

Ignoring Rachel, she continued, "You have come home seeking a glimpse of the past to answer questions of old. You will have to make a decision between two—brothers?—which will change your living arrangements as well as your life..."

Before she could continue, Rachel grabbed Barbara's elbow and propelled her toward the front door, muttering under her breath, "Any fool can see the white circle where your wedding ring used to be and, of course, you're seeking something. You came into this bloody shop. What a fraud."

The blonde turned and softly called to the retreating backs of the two friends, "By the way, Dylan says you are headed in the right direction, and he wants to thank you. Now he can rest."

Barbara planted her feet to the floor. She whirled and, grasping her throat, whispered, "Dylan?"

The blonde approached warily, glancing at the furious face of Rachel looking over the head of her friend.

"Yes. He said you"—she pointed at Rachel—"would not believe me, but he was finding it difficult to get a message through to you. Barbara, he wanted very much for you to know the quest you have taken is the first step to setting him free. He knew he was your second choice."

Barbara gasped, tears welling in her eyes, "He never said a thing."

"He has told me to thank you for all the years of love you gave to him, and says he wants you to find your first love who also searches for answers."

One

Late 1990s

Light filtered through the fog of pain surrounding Barbara Langley. Every milliliter of her body hurt.

God, even my hair hurts. She moaned as she tried to move into a more comfortable position. *So help me, Dylan, I'll hunt you down when I make it to the Pearly Gates.* She braved opening one swollen eye. The muted light in the room blushed a gentle pink. When she had succeeded in prying her top lid from the bottom lid with no additional pain, she slowly unveiled the second eye. It took a minute to focus. Barbara looked at the one occupant in the room beside herself.

Lanky and tall, at 5' 10", with chin-length burnished copper hair complemented by piercing steel gray eyes, closed at present, snoozed Rachel Painter, Barbara's best friend. Instinctively, Barbara knew Rachel would be here, but it was still nice to see her even if she was sleeping in the only chair in the room.

"Rachel," Barbara croaked and tried to swallow.

Her parched throat needed liquid to work, and Barbara didn't want to move anything. This last operation was the worst. Two years of plastic surgery, to turn back the hands of time and regain her youth, was the price she was paying for complaining to her husband that she hated the way she had aged and wanted to look like she had at twenty-six.

Barbara hadn't thought much about her comments. Hell, everybody complained about something. Only, Dylan took her complaining to heart. He put in his last will and testament that she, Barbara Langley, was to be provided every operation needed to make her body and face appear twenty-six. She was not aware of it until his untimely death.

In all the years they had been married, she had fussed at him about drinking and driving; the irony of his death was still unbearable. He'd received a call from his brother, too drunk to drive, and Dylan had gone to the bar to give him a ride home. Another truck, driving down the wrong side of the road without lights, hit his pickup head on. Dylan, completely sober at the time, died instantly. His brother spent six months in the hospital recuperating from his injuries. The other driver, so drunk he couldn't remember his own name, suffered only a bump on his forehead.

She'd complained she wanted to look young; however, she'd wanted it for Dylan. Now that he was dead, what was the point?

The lawyer stated, at the execution of the will, she was to start her operations as soon as the funeral ended. Three months after Dylan's death, the reality of her financial situation finally dawned. The accountant had visited while she was recuperating from the first operation, and they'd gone over the numbers. She'd never have to work again—it didn't matter. She would have given it back in the beat of a hummingbird's wings to have Dylan alive and chuckling at her kvetching. The time required for her to heal left her with little to do but watch TV, and that soon lost its appeal.

Barbara tried her voice again. "Rachel?" *Better, but I still sound like a bullfrog.*

Nurse Thompson, bustling through the door, thwarted her third attempt.

"Mrs. Langley, you need your rest. You're not to speak for twenty-four hours, per the doctor's orders. I'm sure you're probably parched. Anesthesia always does that to people, so I'm going to let you have some water and ice chips if you *promise* not to talk. Do I make myself clear?"

Barbara nodded. She and Nurse Sean Thompson had become hospital friends. Sean had always been the care provider after Barbara's operations. She fussed around the bed putting a glass with a bent straw on the standup tray close by and tucked in the bed sheets around Barbara.

"I swear; Rachel could sleep through a hurricane." Sean leaned over the stretched-out body and gently shook the redhead.

"Yeah, yeah, yeah. I'm awake. What's up, Sean?" Rachel straightened up and sat in the chair running her long fingers through copper locks. Rachel and Sean had gone to high school together and played on local softball teams against each other.

"Rach, I want you to make sure Mrs. Langley does not, I repeat NOT, speak for the next twenty-four hours. I suspect her promise to me was made with her fingers crossed. Doctor's orders. It's just a precaution because the throat gets so irritated with the anesthesia. We don't want any complications from all of this. Keep her in line?" Sean's brown eyes twinkled.

"Got my word." Rachel stretched, looking even longer and lankier as she pushed her arms above her head like one of her many cats. She looked at her friend's bandaged face and smirked. "No talking for a whole twenty-four hours. Boy, the things I can say to you today. Cool."

Barbara tried to frown but found the motion caused bolts of pain to shoot across her forehead. She resorted to crossing her arms over her voluptuous, firm, new breasts and glared the best she could through her pain.

"Since you're awake and doing fairly well, I need to go home and feed my herd. If I don't, they'll shred everything I own to ribbons. I'll be back in a couple hours. I'm checking out with Sean and, if you even attempt to speak, she or I will know, and thrash you within an inch of your life. Capicé?" Rachel pushed up from the chair and walked to Barbara's bedside.

She took her friend's hand and, looking past the bandages, murmured softly, "You know he was here last night? I felt him wrap his arms around me and whisper in my ear that you should have no problem finding someone to help you move on. He thinks it's time, Barbara, and so do I."

Barbara yanked her hand from Rachel's grasp. *Damn it! I hate not being able to tell her what I think.* Gingerly, she shook her head turning away from Rachel. *No one will be able to take Dylan's place. Why can't everyone understand that? I don't want another man in my life: it's just too painful.*

"It's time you kept your promise to take me to Florida. Four years ago, for my birthday, you gave me a gift card good for one trip to Florida... destination Tampa. I'm cashing in my voucher. After I feed the herd, I'll check some travel packages. Think about it, Barbara. In six months, you'll look like you did when you left—how many years ago? Think about it real hard."

Rachel patted her lovingly on the arm and strode out the door.

I don't want to go to Tampa without Dylan. All of this was for him, and it's not the same without him to share it.

Barbara sensed a tear escaping down her swollen, bruised cheek. A sigh whisked past her puffy lips, and she gave into the overwhelming urge to sleep.

~ * ~

Diamond-shaped sunspots glinted off the cobalt ocean; waves crashed against the rocky shore thundering over the screech of seagulls swooping near the beach in search of food bits. Barbara pulled salty-tasting air into her lungs and squinted at the figure approaching her. She put her hand above her eyes, blocking out the infrequently bright sun and cerulean sky.

He was approaching; instinctively, she knew it was a he. As the figure neared, she gasped in recognition—Dylan strolling along the narrow sand in his Marine Corps dress blues. Always striking, he stole Barbara's concentration from the open book in her lap. He stood in front of her and extended his white-gloved hand in invitation. She looked up at the gleaming brass buttons decorating the midnight blue jacket piped in red. His blue woolen trousers, with their red strip down the side, held the sharpest crease she'd ever seen over his gleaming, reflective, black military-issue shoes. She brought her attention back to his ruggedly handsome face under the rigid white hat with black brim; cover was what he'd called it. Barbara's heart ached. She'd fallen so deeply in love with this Dylan: the Dylan she'd just buried.

She took his proffered hand and let him pull her to his chest, dropping her book to the sand. He held her so tight against him his buttons bit into her, leaving the Marine Corps insignia emblazoned on her skin.

"Dylan." She closed her eyes and inhaled the spicy scent that was her husband. Deep in her soul, pain began throbbing to life with her every heartbeat.

"Why...?"

He put his gloved finger to her lips and, when she'd quieted, lifted her chin to him with his finger. Lowering his mouth, he covered her lips with feather-soft kisses.

Barbara sagged into his strong chest and allowed herself to be swept away by the sweet tenderness. He held her close for an eternity and, finally, moved her back to gaze into her eyes.

"God, I miss you. Why did you leave me? When will we be together? How long do I have to wait until I can hold you again?"

A smile emerged on his lips, accenting the dimple in his right cheek. Barbara reached up and traced the line with her finger.

"Barbara?"

She heard him speak her name, but his lips had not moved. Blinking in confusion, she responded. "Yes?"

"Barbara, it's time for you to move on. Your intense love is keeping me close to you and, while I do love you, Winkie, I want to rest. We'll be together when the Creator deems the time is right, but you still have things to do and another to love. I hold you here—" He opened his gloved hand and pointed to the palm. "—and will watch over you." His tone softened. "You were always beautiful to me, no matter what the outside looked like. I hope you like the new you. I have to go now, my love. Please don't fight what the Creator has planned. He knows better than you or I. I love you, Winkie."

Barbara watched in horror as the image of Dylan faded, leaving her standing on the sand staring at the foaming waves.

~ * ~

"NO!" she shouted through raw vocal chords, the action initiating a coughing, choking fit. Rachel jumped to her friend's side. She handed Barbara the glass of water and continuously thumbed the call button for the nurse. Seconds later, a red-faced nurse huffed through the door and up to Barbara's bedside.

"What happened?" She narrowed her eyes at Rachel.

"I went home for two hours. When I came back, I slipped into the room because she was sleeping so peacefully until about five minutes ago. She started the moaning that ended with a shout and this coughing fit."

The nurse glowered at Barbara and darted a sideways glance at

Rachel. "Mrs. Langley"—acid laced her words—"you must remain quiet, or we'll have to keep you in here for another day. Do you want that?" Watching Barbara weakly shake her head, the nurse continued, "That's what I thought. Now, NO talking, whispering, shouting or anything that remotely resembles vocal communication for the next twenty hours; do I make myself clear?"

Barbara signaled her agreement. The nurse fussed around the bed and, tossing a withering glare at Rachel, stomped out of the room.

Rachel turned to Barbara, a wicked grin spread over her face. "This is going to be fun."

Barbara motioned for something to write with, her hands pantomiming in the air.

Rachel shifted her weight onto one leg, crossed her arms, and cocked one eyebrow. "Why? So you can yell at me on paper? I'd rather listen to my cats yowl." She watched Barbara's antics become agitated, as her friend opened her mouth to speak. Rachel held up her index finger. "Don't. I don't need Nurse Wicked back here scolding and berating me like a naughty five-year-old."

She rummaged in the drawer of the nightstand next to the bed, found a pad and pen, which she handed to Barbara. She watched her intently scribble on the pad and pass it back. Rachel read the message Barbara had penned. She looked at her friend, eyebrows raised. "Are you sure?"

At Barbara's nod, she continued, "Do you believe what you saw?" Another head bob. "Sure?" This time Barbara frowned, moaning at the effort, and moved her head up and down emphatically. She started to open her mouth to talk. Rachel held up her hand. "I wanted to make sure before I shared with you; you up to listening for a while?" With Barbara's anemic acknowledgement, Rachel pushed the button on the bed's control panel, moving her friend into a semi-sitting position. She dragged a chair next to the bed, flipping it around with the back facing Barbara. Flinging a long leg over the top, Rachel sat straddling the seat.

"I've wanted to share this with you for a long time, but Dylan made me promise not to say anything until the time was right."

Barbara's eyebrows shot up, a groan escaping her lips.

Again, Rachel put her hand up. "I know, I know; it sounds crazy but sometime around the second week after we buried Dylan, he started appearing to me in dreams with instructions to take care of you, and see that you followed through with the operations." She watched her friend's eyes fill with tears that slipped silently down her cheeks. "Dylan has been telling me for two years you have unfinished business in Florida, and I'm to make sure you go back to accomplish it. You just haven't been ready to let him go. He appeared last night, and said he was going to come to you and ask you to release him. He loves you with all of his soul, but he's tired and wants to rest until the time you two will be together again. This note—" Rachel waved the paper in the air. "—tells me he kept his promise, and I have to keep mine. While I was at home, I contacted my friend Sandi over at Sunshine Tours, and booked us a trip to Florida in six months. By then, if all goes well, you'll be healed. I've arranged to get a month off from work. They owe me at least a month for all the times I've saved their asses. I asked my sister to cat sit, and she's agreed. There's nothing standing in the way of us leaving for the vacation you've been promising me for the last four years." Rachel slipped her hand around her friend's. "Barbara, Dylan was a wonderful man and made you very happy, but he wants you to move on. For God's sake, woman, you have the body and face you've wanted for years. No one would put you a day past thirty. Let's go to Florida and show it off!"

Rachel saw confusion clouding Barbara's eyes. "Looks like the sleeping pills are kicking in, so I'll go home and spend some time with my kitties. Think of all the things you wanted to do *if only*. You've got the chance most people only dream about."

She stood, gently scooting the chair away, and leaned down to place a tender kiss on her friend's forehead. *I'll make sure we get to Florida, Dylan. You can count on me.* She heard a whispered *Thank you* in the back of her consciousness.

Two

Eight months later...

Barbara, arms wrapped tightly around her body for warmth, stood at the plate glass window staring across the concrete ribbons that served as landing strips. Beyond the tree-studded islands in the middle of the Columbia River, the lights of cars created a twinkling ribbon effect on Washington's Highway 14 bordering that side of the river. Steely gray clouds that had draped themselves over the Willamette Valley and Salem, crying unendingly for the last three days, turned pewter dark in Portland. The light weeping morphed into angry torrents flinging to the ground in an effort to drown all living inhabitants. Silvery droplets wended their way down the panes. She reached out a finger to trace the path.

"Barbara, come on. You've dragged your feet for the last two months. It's time to get a move on. We put this trip off once, and I'm not going to do it again. They're calling us to board. Grab your gear, and let's get the hell out of this dank dungeon." Rachel placed her hand on her best friend's shoulder and nudged gently.

Sighing herself back to the present, Barbara nodded and picked up her bag. "Let's go. As dreary as it seems, I'm going to miss this place."

"Geesh. You sound like we're never coming back. We're only going for a month. I have a job, and numerous furry roommates that will be waiting for me to get home. Now, let's get this vacation started."

Rachel barreled her way down the boarding ramp to the airplane. At the door, a uniformed, blonde flight attendant checked their tickets and pointed them to the first class cabin. They were checking the seat numbers on their tickets when a lilting tenor voice intervened, "May I help you ladies?"

Rachel turned and looked up to a face the angels carved from a corner of heaven. Dark tumbles of curly hair framed ruddy cheeks currently creased by a smile exposing blinding white teeth in perfect unison with the luscious lips surrounding them. Eyes so green the ocean must surely be jealous, ringed in thick, long, black lashes, twinkled merrily at the copper-haired beauty.

Rachel's feet grew to the spot as she stood gaping at the dark Adonis.

"Wha, what?"

The smile expanded, and dark eyes began to dance. "May I be of service? I'm Robart. I'll be one of your flight attendants today. May I help you... find your seat?"

"Uh, uh..." The normally quick-witted Rachel was reaching for a response.

Good god, Rachel. Answer the man. Barbara rolled her eyes. "Thank you, Robart. We're in seats 3a and 3b. Could you point us in the right direction?"

"How about I go you one better and take you there?" His eyes never left Rachel's face.

"Thank you. That would be terrific."

Barbara lifted her bag and poked Rachel to do the same. They followed his tight derriere to the front of the section, where he relieved them of their carry-on luggage, easily placing the two bags in the overhead compartment. Stepping back, he let the women take their seats then leaned to grab Rachel's seat belt and buckle her in, the faint aroma of musk mixed with man tickled her nose.

"I wouldn't want to see anything happen to the two of you. Buckle up. We'll be leaving in a few minutes." Winking, he flashed a radiant smile and left.

Barbara snickered. She'd never seen Rachel so bowled over by any man.

"Hello? Is anybody in there?" Barbara stared at her friend, the corners of her mouth turning up in delight.

"Oh... my... God, Barbara." Rachel strained against the seatbelt, turning to watch the hunk of manhood walk down the aisle. "Have you ever seen anyone so gorgeous in your life?"

Barbara slid her purse under the seat in front of her, grabbed a magazine from the seat pocket, and buckled her seat belt.

"I hadn't really noticed. Is he cute?" she smirked as she flipped through the pages.

"IS HE CUTE? You have to be kidding? You mean you didn't see..." Rachel whipped around to stare incredulously at her friend. She stopped when she saw the smirk on Barbara's face. "You're yanking my chain."

"Well, you deserve it, for crying out loud, Rachel. I haven't seen you react to a man like this since Gerry roared in with his motorcycle and swept you off your feet."

Rachel winced. "Don't remind me. That was lust, pure and simple."

"True and this is...?"

"Different."

"How?"

"I just know this is different. I can feel the sparks fly." Rachel's face flushed, her steely eyes dark with desire.

"Everyone within five rows felt the sparks fly. Correct me if I'm wrong, but I remember a conversation fairly similar to this one about a certain Gerry Donaldson." Barbara licked a finger and used it to flip a page.

"Oh, that was below the belt. How was I supposed to know he was married?"

"You might have asked between rutting sessions." Barbara scanned the page in front of her.

"You are in a mood, girlfriend. What is this? Pick-on-Rachel day? If you're that mad about leaving town, get off the plane, but I want to go where the sun shines more than two hours a month. I plan on enjoying this much-earned-vacation for every minute, starting right now." Rachel slumped against the seat and tested the buttons on the armrest.

"All right, all right. But, this is get-back for those days right after my last surgery when I couldn't talk. I'll give you this; Gerry was a sweet talker and good looking to boot. From the few details you gave me, I don't doubt that the last thing on your mind was asking him if he was married, but, Rachel, you didn't think at all, and that's not like you. I didn't say anything because I love you, but I was very angry at how he swooped in, broke your heart, and left without so much as a kiss-my-ass. Be careful, my friend. Just be careful. Okay, end of lecture. Let's go to Florida and soak up the sun." Barbara leaned over and gave Rachel a quick hug.

The speaker crackled to life, and an announcement followed noting the plane would soon be taxiing to the end of the runway to wait their turn in line for takeoff. Flight attendants went through the "if-the-plane-should-lose-altitude" pantomime, and the jet rumbled to life bumping along the concrete to linger interminably in line. As the engines roared with expectation, shaking the body of the plane and fueling her excitement, Rachel grabbed her friend's hand and mouthed the words *thank you* to Barbara. She leaned her head against the seat back, and smiled as the silver bird exploded with fury and leapt from the runway into the air.

Barbara recalled a similar flight that started right where she was now. *Who knows?* She might actually bump into someone she knew from her younger days. She'd loosely followed the successes of a few friends from that time. A smile played at her lips. The biggest surprise had been Billy Manetti. She'd known him as a shy, hulking figure of a kid who'd played guitar in a rock and roll band. When she left the state, she often wondered if he would survive. He'd been a big kid, 6'5" in the sixth grade, and had undergone years of cruel tormenting by his peers.

One evening, years later, when she and Dylan had gone to see an action movie, Barbara nearly fell off her seat to see "Beautiful Bronx Billy" as the featured actor. Billy had taken what he thought was a detriment and turned it to his favor. She quizzed Dylan after the movie and discovered the AWF—American Wrestling Federation—had recruited Billy into the wrestling arena shortly after she'd moved away from Florida. It had taken him fifteen years of hard work, but everyone knew Bronx Billy. His size was his infamous attribute and deadliest weapon.

One friend had become a state senator; another had written a tell-all book about the recruiting practices of the University of Florida athletic department that had landed him on several talk shows and in court. For the most part, Barbara had lost track of everyone else, including the man she'd left the state to forget—Steven Rodgers.

She glanced out the window, squinting against the sun reflecting off the opalescent cloud tops so contrasted from the sinister bottoms dumping moisture over the Northwest. As far as her eyes could make out was row upon row of billowy, cotton hills inducing her to think of a white carpet to heaven.

She returned her attention to the magazine in her lap. She was glad to be vacationing. These last two years had been hell. The surgeries had taken up most of her time during the day, not allowing her to dwell too heavily on losing Dylan. But, at night, when everything was quiet and Barbara lay in her bed, the grief consumed her, slamming her to the ground in great waves of loss and anger. She missed her husband, but was tired of the toll it was taking on her.

~ * ~

A whisper of musk tickled Barbara's nose, and she looked up to find Robart standing at the end of the aisle. He flashed a dazzling smile.

"What will you ladies be having for lunch? We have lobster in crème sauce, chicken cordon bleu, or a Caesar's salad. What's your pleasure?"

Rachel's tanned skin flushed into a crimson mask. "I'll have the Caesar's salad if you'll personally break the egg."

Robart let his eyes roam the flushing redhead's face. "I wouldn't miss the opportunity. Consider it done." He leaned down, his lips inches from Rachel's, and asked Barbara, "And for you?"

Barbara suppressed the urge to burst into laughter. "I'll have the same, and I'd like bottled water to drink."

"I can arrange that. What would you like to drink?" He'd turned and faced Rachel.

The musk combined with his masculine scent washed over her. She pulled the smell deeply into her lungs, running the tip of her tongue around her lips. Whispering so low Robart had to lean closer, she answered, "The same."

When he didn't move, Barbara thought for sure he was going to kiss Rachel, but an attendant bell went off, and he grudgingly rose up and moved away.

Rachel loosed a low groan.

"What?" Barbara shot her friend a sideways glance.

"That man makes me so hot I don't think I'll make it to Florida without changing my jeans. Whew!" She leaned back and fanned herself with her hand.

"Geez, Rachel. The man is being nice. It's his job. See, he's being nice to everyone."

"Barbara, give me a break. He's not acting like this with everyone; watch him. I think he's being, well, especially nice to me." Rachel cocked her eyebrow and crossed her arms.

Barbara observed him with several women who were making no effort to hide what they thought of the attractive flight attendant. His manner with them was polite but professional. She turned to Rachel. "All right, girlfriend. This is our vacation, right?"

"Right."

"We're not here to find husbands or boyfriends, right?"

"Yeah, but..."

"Right?"

"All right, yes."

"Okay. Then..." Barbara's eyes twinkled wickedly. "... let's make a bet. If Robart gives you his number, you win. If you have to ask for it, I win."

"What's the bet?"

"She who loses buys the first margaritas in Key West."

A lopsided smile highlighted the dimple in Rachel's left cheek. "You're on."

Three

The plane had descended over the shallow depths of Tampa Bay by the time Barbara realized she'd lost the bet. She'd watched Rachel and Robart intertwine themselves around each other's soul with each conversation. She only wondered if she would be spending this vacation alone despite the promise she'd extracted from her friend. Rachel had a bad habit of doing the exact thing she hated in others—focusing all her attention on the new man in her life to the exclusion of everyone else. As the plane's wheels screeched and bumped along the sun-warmed concrete to the terminal, Barbara started a mental itinerary for herself. It had been more than a few years since she'd been to Florida but, with a map and plenty of time on her hands, she would visit all those places that had left a warm glow in her heart—with or without Rachel.

"Hey, you coming or what?" Rachel pushed Barbara's carry-on bag at her.

"I was planning the vacation I'll be taking for the next month."

"What? I'm not part of this? I thought you were going to show me Florida." Rachel turned, her eyebrows rising, and looked down at her best friend.

"I was guessing by the disgusting public show of affection between you and Robart, you'd be keeping company with him the whole time we're here; so, I'm planning on doing what I've dreamed about for more years than I can count: visiting the state I consider my home."

"Well, smartass, you're wrong. Robart will be in town tonight and tomorrow until noon. Then he flies to England for three days where he will visit his family, France for two days, Germany for two days, finishing the last leg of the journey in Italy for two days, then, back here. While you were sleeping, and may I add you still need to rest more than you've been getting, we talked about the intense attraction we feel toward each other. We both want to pursue this relationship as more than fly-by-night, excuse the pun. He invited us both to dinner at a place in Tampa, or is it Clearwater; anyway, he's treating us to dinner at some place called Bern's Steakhouse." Rachel bumped into Barbara's rigid form stopped in the middle of the walkway.

She turned to the tall redhead, her brown eyes wide, and repeated, "Bern's Steakhouse?"

"Yeah. Why? Is it really bad or something?" Rachel dropped her carry-on to the floor and flexed her hand.

"No, no. It's a fabulous, expensive restaurant in Tampa with tremendous food and an incredible garden surrounding it; at least, it used to be. It was a quiet, romantic setting; definitely not the place for three people to have dinner, especially if only two of them are *in lust*."

"Barbara." Rachel's voice took on a dangerous tone. "I know where this is heading. Robart asked both of us to dinner so we could get to know each other and enjoy his one night in Tampa before he flies out. Not just me, but both of us."

"Look, girlfriend, you just told me you think I need to get more rest. Well, I'm taking your advice. I'll stay in the hotel tonight. You and Robart go out and enjoy the evening. I think I need some time to soak in the essence of being here, again."

"Barb? Are you sure?"

"Yes. Go. Go and enjoy the place the way I did the first time I was there; enjoy it with someone you care about a great deal. Lose all sense of time, get wrapped up in Robart, and walk through the gardens hand in hand. It is a memory you will always treasure. It needs to be a memory for the two of you, not for the three of us."

Barbara tromped down the walkway toward the luggage carousels, Rachel following behind. Once they'd retrieved their bags, they located the hotel shuttle stop and, when it finally arrived, rode in silence to their destination. The landscape had changed so dramatically Barbara felt as if she were visiting for the first time. She recognized a few buildings in the skyline but little else. Housing tracts had sprung up in areas that had been little more than swampland when she'd left the state. Many of the wild green fields she'd remembered fondly now featured strip malls with boutiques and small coffee bistros. She realized she would need some time to accept the tremendous changes that had occurred to her town while she'd been away.

The shuttle pulled under the covered archway of the hotel, and a handsome young man dashed out to open the shuttle doors. Extending a hand, his black eyes sparked with interest as he helped Barbara out.

"Welcome to Tampa, Miss. If there's anything I can do?"

Rachel stepped from the vehicle unaided and snickered as she watched the back of Barbara's neck redden.

"Uhm, uh, thank you," Barbara leaned slightly to read the nametag on the young man's uniform, "Reynaldo, but I think we'll be fine." Barbara turned away for a moment and stopped. When she turned back to face the tanned youngster, Rachel noted her eyes dancing with mischief.

"However, if we think of anything we need..." Barbara leaned toward the young man and lowered her voice to just above a whisper. "We'll call you."

~ * ~

The young porter nearly fell on his face as he watched the sway of hips walking away from him. He hurriedly grabbed the bags and loaded them on the luggage trolley to follow the enticing undulation of female entering the hotel. Barbara tossed a wink over her shoulder to Rachel, who was frowning thunderously as she brought up the rear.

Reynaldo rolled the luggage trolley to the front desk and parked it. "I'll be right back." He bolted down the hallway leading to the offices. At the final portal, he rapped his knuckles on the door, opening and entering at the same time.

The sandy haired figure behind the desk grumbled, "I don't remember saying come in."

"Oh, come on, Uncle Steven. Don't be so grumpy." The young man lounged against the wall.

"Ray-Ray, I told you not to call me Uncle Steven at work. What is so important you have to come to my office during your shift, especially when we have guests?" Steven Rodgers glanced at the bank of security monitors set up on the table next to his desk. Something about the smaller, dark-haired woman seemed familiar, but Steven couldn't quite put his finger on it. Mentally shrugging, he looked up into the chocolate brown eyes of his best friend's son. "Well?"

"I'll stop calling you Uncle Steven when you stop calling me Ray-Ray. I'm twenty-five years old and out of college now. Maybe you can start calling me Reynaldo like everyone else?"

"Fine, but that's beside the point. Why are you here in the middle of your shift?"

"Did you see the little brunette checking in?" Reynaldo pushed away from the wall and pointed to the woman at the front desk talking animatedly with her friend.

Steven sighed. Reynaldo was infamous for his dealings with women. Tampa Bay was scattered with broken hearts from his escapades.

"Reynaldo—company policy prohibits employees from fraternizing with guests. You signed paperwork acknowledging that when you were hired. I don't need to lose my franchise, and have a guest file a lawsuit, all in one day. I don't care if she's the number one box-office actress in the country; stay away from her. Do you understand?" Steven continued to enter figures in the computer. When his statement met with silence, he looked up. Reynaldo never let an opportunity go by to argue. He claimed it kept his Cuban blood flowing.

The young man stood shaking his head, light brown hair barely moving under the gelled exterior.

"Mr. Rodgers, this woman is The Madonna. She is flawless, and smells like heaven; something about her reminds me of Hawaii. She smells like those white leis you get when you graduate from college. Pohua; no that's not it, P, Pi, Pikaki! That's it. She smells like those Pikaki flowers; sweet and fresh like an ocean breeze."

Steven stopped, his fingers poised over his keyboard. *He's lost his mind. I've never heard him go on about a girl, woman, like this. Maybe I should check this girl out. No, that wouldn't be professional.*

The phone on his desk buzzed, and Steven picked it up. "Yes? Yes, he is. All right, I'll be right out."

"Well, Mr. Montez, your services are required at the front desk, and so are mine. Seems our computer has decided to act up, again. You need to get out there, and show our guests to their room. Remember—no fraternizing." Steven grabbed his suit coat from the back of his chair and slid into it. He adjusted his tie and, walking out the door behind Reynaldo, locked his office.

The young porter bounded out of the hallway and broke into a wide grin as he wrangled the luggage trolley to the elevator. "Ladies? Shall we?"

Rachel lifted her eyebrows and elbowed Barbara. "I'm sure he's talking to you."

Barbara smirked and, grabbing the card keys from the top of the counter, sauntered to the elevator, Rachel clumping along beside her.

"Whenever you're ready, Reynaldo."

The doors slid open, and Reynaldo guided the trolley into the elevator, holding the doors for the two women, and, once they were safely inside, pushed the button to their floor, flashing a smile at Donna the desk clerk.

~ * ~

Steven rounded the corner in time to catch the familiar sway of hips moving toward the elevator. Reynaldo was beaming and Donna, the daytime desk clerk, was glowering.

"That man is a total idiot when it comes to women. The way he fawned over that little one is absolutely disgusting. Steven? Steven?"

Steven watched as the two women stepped inside the elevator, turned, and the elevator doors closed. His heart began to hammer in his chest, and a light coating of sweat beaded over his forehead. *It can't be! She'd be nearly fifty by now. That young woman can't be but thirty or thirty-one. But, GOD! It looks so much like her.*

"Steven? Are you all right? You look a little pale. You want me to call someone?" Donna's brow furrowed. She'd never seen her boss lose his composure. He was pale, and his hands were shaking.

Steven cleared his throat and, facing the counter, smiled weakly. "No, I just thought I saw a ghost. Don't they say everyone has a double? A doppelganger? I think I just saw a doppelganger, that's all. Now, what was the problem you were having?"

He walked around the counter and stood conferencing with his desk clerk. The computer had hung up on the last guest's reservation—the doppelganger. Steven scrolled through to the spot where the computer had balked. He read the information and started coughing. Donna ran to get him a cup of water and, when she returned, found him sitting in the chair looking dazed. Handing the cup to him, she heard him mutter.

"A doppelganger with the same name? Can't be."

Four

Reynaldo stopped the trolley between two rooms on the eighth floor. Rachel had been so busy looking into the restaurant on the first level under the atrium she hadn't seen him stop and ran into his back. Issuing an expletive, she glared at the attractive young Cuban.

His tanned cheeks flushed. "We're here, Miss. Which suite first?"

Rachel stepped around the young man and looked at her friend, her eyes narrowing suspiciously. "What's he talking about? Suites? Barbara?"

"Rachel," Barbara said, handing Rachel one of the cards she'd picked up at the front desk, "we each have our own suite."

"Barbara! That's too damned expensive. We don't need but one... suite." Rachel pushed the card key back to her friend.

"Oh, no," Barbara pushed the card to Rachel. "I remember, very distinctly, making the mistake of sleeping on your couch one night after we'd gone out, and I was too drunk to drive home. If memory serves, Gerry showed up 'on his way through' and you two, interacted, all night long. I was drunk, not deaf."

Reynaldo turned and snickered behind his hand. Looking up to find Rachel glaring dangerously at him, he began to cough.

"Yeah, so, what's that got to do with now?"

Barbara rolled her eyes. "Robart?"

The angry lines left her friend's face, and a smile settled on the luscious ruby lips. "Oh, yeah, Robart. Okay, you win, but I'm buying the first margaritas in Key West."

"Oh? I thought he gave you his number."

"Well, it was sort of a toss-up. He handed me his number as I asked."

Rachel broke into a wide grin and inserted the card into the door lock. The door buzzed open, and she grabbed her carryon bag and suitcase from the trolley. Setting them inside, she turned to Barbara.

"I'll call you, later, in case you've changed your mind. We'd love to have you with us. By the way, why did you sign your maiden name on the register?"

Barbara stood on her toes and pecked her friend on the cheek. "I want to be sure if I have any college friends still living in the area, they can find me. None of them knew my married name and both you and... told me I need to move forward. I'm going to take your advice. I'll stay in and get more rest. Get to know your new friend without an audience. Since you'll be seeing each other in snatches of time, make each moment count." Barbara walked to the door of her room.

Reynaldo pushed the trolley to the room next door and took the card key from Barbara.

"May I?"

Barbara smiled and nodded.

The young man opened the door and pushed the trolley into the living room. He unloaded the bags onto the bed and opened them. Checking the bathroom as he passed, he stopped and turned to Barbara. "Please, let me know if there is anything I can do to make your stay here more comfortable."

Barbara grabbed her purse and began to rummage for her wallet.

Reynaldo held up his hand. "Don't. I would consider it an insult to take money from a lady. This is part of my job, and I'm happy to do it for you." He took her hand and laid the card key in it. Backing away two steps, he stopped, and bowed slightly from the waist. "I am at your beck and call. Please do not hesitate." Turning, he walked out the door closing it behind him.

Barbara smiled and moved to the bedroom. It had already been a long day. A five-hour flight, losing three hours going from the West coast to the East coast, and two and a half hours of luggage-wrangling, and hotel check-in was taking its toll on her. All she wanted to do was lay down and take a nap. She moved the suitcase to the opposite side of the bed and lay down, a nameless tune swirling in the back of her memory. The last thing she remembered was the dazzling smile on Reynaldo's tanned face.

~ * ~

Steven picked up the phone and speed-dialed #3. The cacophony of sound that greeted his ears caused him to pull the instrument away from his ear.

"Hello? Ray?" Steven found himself yelling.

"Hello? Hello? Hold on a minute."

The noise grew increasingly louder, a persistent thunk-thunk-thunk underscoring the sound of metal scraping on metal and bu-bu-bu-bu of jackhammers against concrete. Suddenly, the noise abated to background. "Hello?"

"Hey, Ray."

"What's the matter? Is it Ray-Ray?" Panic oozed from the phone.

"No. Reynaldo, as he has corrected me to call him, is just fine. Something has come up that I need to get your take on." Steven leaned back in his chair and glanced at the monitors on the side desk. He watched Reynaldo bound out of the elevator, the luggage trolley careening in front of him. Steven grimaced. "I think I've seen a ghost."

"I told you to stop drinking your lunch. What are you talking about?"

Steven heard Ray cover the phone and holler to someone.

"If this is a bad time, Ray, I'll call back." He tapped a pencil on the desk.

"No. Sorry, Steven, go ahead. You said you think you saw a ghost. Is this an old ghost or a new ghost? Should I be contacting the guys in white coats?" Ray snickered at his own joke.

"Man, you always did have the worst sense of humor. Do you remember the girl I dated when we were in college?"

"Oh, like that really narrows the suspects down. Steven, you had so many women, I'm surprised your pecker hasn't fallen off. Which beauty queen are you talking about now?"

"When we had our band, there was one gal in particular I dated, remember? Her name was Barbara Hamilton. She was a little older, and we were hot and heavy for a couple years. She left because I didn't want to settle down and get married... biggest mistake of my life," Steven ended in a mutter.

"God, how could I forget? You drove us nuts for nearly a year pining over her. When you married Lisa, we finally quit hearing about her."

"That was the second biggest mistake of my life—marrying Lisa." Steven frowned, tapping his pencil even harder on the desktop.

"Maybe so, but you wouldn't have Marcus and Alana. We tried to tell you to take that drumming gig with Cult Explosion or she'd make your life hell, but you wouldn't listen. If I remember correctly, your comment went something like, 'She loves me for who I am not what I do.' Right?"

"Bite me. I thought she was like Barbara. How was I to know she was thinking I was going to be the next Phil Collins? Anyway, that's off the subject." Steven realized he was hitting the desk so hard with the pencil the sound was echoing off his walls. He opened his desk drawer and dropped in the pencil.

"Yeah, what was the question?" Ray chuckled into the phone.

"Do you remember Barbara?" Steven glanced at the monitors. He hoped to catch a glimpse of the doppelganger before he went home.

"Yes. Do you think you saw her? What's she look like now? Must be getting pretty old, huh?"

"Actually, that's the problem. The gal I saw looks exactly the way Barbara did when she left here twenty-five years ago, and that's only part of the mystery. I figured maybe she had a daughter who came back to see Tampa, but the name on the register is Barbara Hamilton. Ray, she hasn't aged a minute since she left!" Steven leaned forward and thumped his finger on the desk to make his point.

"Man, you've lost it. I'll tell you again. Stop drinking your lunch. There is no way Barbara could have stayed the same over all these years. It's just not possible. Maybe she named her daughter the same, you know, Barbara Junior, same as I've done with Ray-Ray. I think you're lettin' Lisa get to you and daydreaming of the *old times* when things were a whole lot easier. Tell you what; why don't you meet me after work at the bar, and we'll talk about it. I'm really pushing the deadline to get this housing division built and need to rag on these guys about standing around. See ya at seven. Bye, Steven."

Ray was right. Lisa had been giving him fits about alimony and child support. She didn't want to grasp the idea the money wasn't going to be there, and she'd have to go to work to survive. Alana, their youngest, had graduated from college last year and was pursuing her doctorate with scholarships she'd won for her grades and research work. The courts had cut him loose, legally, and there wasn't a thing Lisa could do but call daily and make his life miserable. The intercom buzzed as if on cue.

"Sorry, Steven." Donna's voice quivered. "That—woman—is on the phone again. If I didn't know how awful she'd be to you, I'd hang up every time she calls. She is the rudest person I've ever met."

"Yeah, I know. Thanks for warning me." Steven pulled in a deep breath, picked up the phone, and pushed the button.

"Thank you for calling the Sheraton, this is Steven. How may I help you?"

"It's about damn time. You can help by making sure you get your ass over to the house tomorrow night to have dinner with your daughter before she leaves for England. Or have you forgotten and made a date with some new bimbo?"

Steven and Lisa had been divorced for five years, but she never missed an opportunity to harangue him about his dating life.

"I've not forgotten. How could I? You've called once a day, every day, this week and, on several occasions, twice a day to remind me of the dinner as well as several other items you seem to think life-threatening. I'll be there. I'm going to miss my daughter as much as you are, and won't throw away my chance to spend time with her."

"Oh, I see. You're coming over just to spend time with her? You don't want to see me, just her? Well, sorry, lover boy, I live in the house with her and, like it or not, you have to see me, too. Just be there at 6:00 p.m. sharp. We start eating whether you're here or not."

Steven pulled the phone from his ear when his ex-wife slammed down her end. As hard as he tried, he couldn't remember what it was about her that had made him want to marry her.

He started his computer and buried himself in the project he'd been working on when the doppelganger arrived. Occupied with entering the numbers for the monthly report due to the home office, he jumped when his cell phone rang. He groaned. *What'd she forget to bitch about now?*

"This is Steven. How may I help you?"

"Hey, buddy, where the hell are ya?" Ray was yelling over the sound of the jukebox in the background.

"Is it that late?" Steven glanced at the desk clock his father had given him. The gold hands pointed to the fact it was past seven o'clock. "I'm on my way. The ex called to complain one more time today, creating an immense need for a beer. See you in fifteen."

Steven grabbed his jacket from the back of his chair, his briefcase from the floor, and flipped the light off on his way out the door. He stopped at the desk to tell Donna he was leaving for the day when he caught sight of the familiar sway of hips exiting through the front doors on the security monitor.

Spinning around on his heels, he saw her turn to the left and walk out of his line of vision. He took a step toward the door, hesitated, and turned to face his desk clerk. She emerged from the business office red-eyed and sniffling.

"Donna? Are you okay? Is there something I can do?" Steven walked behind the check-in desk and set his briefcase on the floor.

"No. It's nothing really. Some men are just so dumb, sometimes." She grabbed a tissue from the box under the counter and blew her nose. "What are you still doing here?" Glancing at the wall clock, she turned to Steven. "You should have been gone at least an hour ago. Why are you still here?"

Smiling, and picking up his briefcase, Steven patted her shoulder gently and said, "You're right. Some men are so dumb. If you need me for anything, just call the cell."

"Get out of here," Donna pushed him in the direction of the front door. "Tell Mr. Montez I said hello."

"I will."

Steven hurried out and turned left, hoping to catch a glimpse of those undulating hips. The sidewalk in front of the building was empty, and the lot had only empty guest cars. He trudged to his sport utility vehicle, using the automatic system to unlock the doors. He tossed his briefcase in the back, and, once inside, laid his head back, closing his eyes. In forty-eight hours, the light of his life would be on her way to England for a year or more of study. *How am I going to survive Lisa without Alana to run interference?* He shook his head and leaned forward to start the SUV. Adjusting the rear view mirror, he saw the silhouette of a familiar figure. She was walking toward the Bay. He craned his neck to catch a glimpse of her and watched her form disappear behind a building.

"Damn it!" A quick glance at the dashboard clock reminded him his best friend was waiting at the bar. Steven put the vehicle in drive and, reluctantly, drove off.

~ * ~

"So, you think you saw Barbara?" Ray, beer bottle in hand, leaned against the bar looking sideways at Steven.

"Yeah. It sure seems like her. Just what I saw of her face is exactly as I remember, and those hips... man, I remember the sway of those hips. Whew, makes me hard just thinking of her now." Steven shifted in the bar stool, grimacing.

"Man, you're just getting hard because it's been what? six months? nine months? since you got yourself laid?" Ray grinned and took a swig from his beer.

"Not to hear my ex tell it. Listening to her, you'd think I was getting it every night." Steven tipped up his bottle and finished the contents. He pushed the empty to the lip of the bar and stuck six dollars under it.

Alan, the bartender, placed a fresh cold bottle in front of Steven and raised his eyes at the amount of money on the bar.

"Ray, too, and keep the change."

"Thanks, Steven." Alan walked to the cooler and retrieved another beer for Ray.

"Man, weren't you ever crazy about anybody, besides Monica? What about Sandy? From what I remember, she thought you walked on water, and for a while, you acted the same about her. What ever happened, Ray?" Steven looked over as his friend tipped his head back and drained the contents of his beer.

Slamming his bottle on the bar, Ray pulled the full one toward him and leaned his elbows on the bar. He began to peel the label off the cold container.

"Sandy. Wow. That brings back memories. She was the love of my life. Don't get me wrong, I love Monica but in a different way. Sandy was... skyrockets, man. She made me feel like I could do anything. I can't remember ever being sad around her. She lit up the room when she walked into it." Ray finished peeling the label and placed it on the bar.

"So, what the hell happened, Ray?" Steven pushed.

"I couldn't keep my dick in my pants. I loved Sandy and wanted to spend my life with her but, man, all those girls that used to come up to us when we were playing in the clubs... I'd never had my pick of women, and it was, well, more temptation than I could resist. I was going to bed with Monica, and still trying to keep things cool with Sandy. When Monica got pregnant with Reynaldo, I knew I'd shot myself in the foot. Somehow, Monica found out about Sandy, and the last gig we played at Bruno's, she walked up to Sandy and calmly announced she was having my baby. Sandy called her a liar and turned to me to back her up, but I couldn't. She ran out. The next day she came by the house and dropped off everything I'd ever given her. I tried to explain, but she just looked at me with tear-filled, red-rimmed eyes, and walked out of my life. I never saw her again. I don't even know where she went. I secretly spent three months trying to track her down. I swear, man, she fell off the face of the earth. I never found her. Eventually, I put her in a corner of my heart, and let myself begin to love Monica. It was never as white hot as with Sandy, but I do love her in my own way. After all, she's given me six beautiful kids and put up with me all these years, what more can a guy ask for?" Ray finished his beer and signaled for another.

"Yeah, Monica is definitely earning her sainthood putting up with you," Steven smiled when Ray reached over to cuff him on the side of the head. "But what would you do if Sandy showed up right now?"

"I don't know, Steven. I really don't know. I mean, things have turned out pretty good for me. I got the business, my kids, and Monica. I don't think I'd want to give up any of it."

Steven nodded. "It would be interesting to find out. I can't be sure that this person is Barbara, my Barbara, but I intend to find out."

"Then what? What if she's married and got sixteen kids and this is a vacation from them? What if this is just someone who looks like Barbara used to look? Man, you're setting yourself up for a huge disappointment.

Didn't losing her once hurt enough? Are we going to have to put up with you mooning for another year over someone who doesn't even exist anymore?" Ray frowned at Steven. "Get yourself a real live girlfriend and get laid. Make your ex-wife crazy by bringing home one of these sweeties." Ray brandished his longneck bottle at the room full of young professional women in for an after-work drink.

"Don't be an idiot. Tried that once, remember? My god, the child didn't have a clue who Jimmy Hendrix was. She thought he was some new rap singer. No, I'm not raising somebody else's kid. I have my own. I'm going to wait and see if this is the Barbara I remember, then... I'll just have to play it by ear. Listen, I have to go. I need to be sure to make it to dinner tomorrow at the old house. Alana's leaving for school in England the next day, and I want to spend as much time with her as possible, so I'm going in early to work. See you Saturday."

Steven waved at the bartender and passed several young women who cast an interested look his way. Lost in his own thoughts, he ignored them. He was plotting a way to meet the guest who had captured his attention so completely.

Five

Barbara awoke with a start, the music cycling through her memory. That song again. *I'm going to make myself crazy if I don't get that song out of my mind.* She sat up and swung her feet over the edge of the bed. A quick glance at the wall clock and she realized she'd slept for more than an hour. Standing, she moved to the window and pulled back the curtains gasping at the sight.

I'd forgotten how incredibly beautiful the sunsets are here. I have no intention of letting this one go by with me in this room. She washed her face, grabbing a sweater as she headed to the door. When she opened it, she spotted a folded piece of paper on the floor. Leaning down, she picked it up recognizing Rachel's writing on the outside.

"If you change your mind, just call. We'll come pick you up in a heartbeat."

Barbara smiled and put the note on the counter. *Not today, friend. You need to fall in love in Florida like I did. Maybe then, I can get you to move away from the Northwest to the sun.* She locked and closed her door moving to the elevator.

Barbara settled the sweater on her shoulders while she ambled through the lobby. She felt a chill run down her spine. Slowing, she glanced around furtively. No one was looking her direction, and, feeling a bit silly, she walked from the lobby into the cooling air of dusk. *Someone's watching you.* She stopped on the sidewalk in front of the hotel, scanning the area and witnessing no one behind her, gruffed at herself as she walked to the end of Cypress Street to get as close as she could to the Bay.

Her shoulders dropped and the knot in the middle of her back began to loosen. The silver-coated turquoise water of Tampa Bay mirrored the building thunderheads of the sky. Tangerine and flamingo-colored clouds edged with gold reflected off the smooth surface, doubling the heart-stopping effect. A white finger of lightning reached to the Gulf waters. Rumbling in the distance followed, warning all who would listen the evening ritual of rain was about to begin.

This is so much better than the memory.

Barbara closed her eyes and pulled air into her lungs, tasting salt and smelling the sweetness of honeysuckle tinged with jet fuel. Traffic noises from the Courtney Campbell Causeway faded as she allowed herself the moment's pleasure. Too soon, a jet roared overhead. Barbara opened her eyes. Facing the fading picture, she reached her hand to her cheek and found a tear wandering down the perfect surface.

God, it's good to be home. I didn't realize just how much I missed this place. If only...

She shook off her mood and walked back to the hotel, her stomach growling as the scent of food from a nearby restaurant wafted past her nose.

"Yeah, yeah. I know it's been awhile. Let's get something from the restaurant." Patting her complaining middle, she walked to the café located on the ground floor of the hotel. Looking up, she admired the colors splashing through the glass ceiling of the atrium. The orange and pink glow from outside warmed the salmon walls of the interior. Carefully placed trees and shrubs fed the illusion of the outdoors within the air-conditioned walls of the building. She sat at a table for two and studied the menu. An attractive, tanned young woman appeared, placed an evening paper on the table then took Barbara's order. Barbara browsed through the paper until her food arrived. The town had changed so much in the years she'd been away, she wasn't sure she'd be able to find her old haunts.

She was amazed at the changes she'd read about in Ybor City. When she'd left, it was a place to avoid. Yet now, it was thriving—alive. Barbara smiled. *Like every Cuban I've known—full of love and life. Good for you.* Raising her ice tea glass, she toasted quietly.

"To Ybor City, to Dylan, and to spirit that can't be broken. Salud!"

Finishing her dinner, and quieting her stomach, she took the elevator to her suite. Once inside, she flipped on the TV while she changed into her

PJs and crawled on the couch. The drone of the announcer, added to the relaxing effect of her walk, soon had Barbara sleeping. Tomorrow, she would begin to explore the city she had once known.

Six

Steven groaned as the alarm blasted into his ear. He reached up and silenced the offending instrument. Placing his hand on the top of his head, he tested the size of his skull. Surely, as badly as he felt, his head size must have increased two fold. He gingerly swung his legs over the edge of the bed and, moving his tongue around his mouth, decided he must've also licked the bottom of the barstools.

Why is it every time Ray and I go out for a drink, I wind up with my head the size of a watermelon and the feeling someone is tap dancing on my stomach? He groaned and shuffled to the bathroom to do his morning routine without having to open his eyes—almost. Showered, shaved, and shined, he trundled blindly into the kitchen. Munching on a piece of toast and slugging down his coffee, he took a quick look at the front page of the newspaper, then tossed it into his briefcase before heading out the door. Today, he needed to get as much work done as he could before he left the hotel office at two p.m. He had a special errand to run before he wandered over to the house for dinner with his daughter.

The early morning traffic was relatively light, and Steven made it to work in record time. He nodded to the night clerk at the front desk and strode down the hallway to unlock his office. Once inside, he settled into his schedule and was busy completing paperwork when the intercom on his desk buzzed.

"Steven here. What can I help you with?"

"Reynaldo here. There's a club on Fowler Avenue past the University called the Divine Nine. Do you know which one I mean?"

"Yes."

"Was it ever called anything else?"

Steven was intrigued. Why would Ray-Ray care about the previous name of a rock and roll club by the University? His tastes ran to salsa music.

"Yes. Before Tom Wilson bought and renamed it, the club was Big Eddie's. Why?"

"Just helping a guest, that's all. Thanks, Steven."

Steven turned to watch the monitor. Ray-Ray, behind the counter, was leaning forward to talk with a guest. As Ray moved to one side, Steven found himself looking directly into the eyes of the woman who resembled Barbara. He gasped for oxygen. This had to be Barbara, his Barbara. The woman winked before turning away and walking out of the lobby. Steven considered bolting from behind his desk and trying to catch her, but she disappeared from the view of the lobby cameras before he could free himself from his chair.

Only Barbara could know about Big Eddie's. It was one of our regular gigs back in The Day. He sat for a moment letting the feeling wash over him, jumping when the phone rang.

"Thank you for calling the Sheraton. This is Steven, how may I help you?"

"You can help by making sure you show up tonight, alone... no bimbos. This is the last night your daughter will be in the United States for a while. The least you can do is be sure she doesn't have to share you with some girl-child you met in a bar."

"Good morning to you, too, Lisa. I'm arriving solo for dinner. I'll see you at six. Goodbye, Lisa." Steven hung up the phone before his ex-wife could respond with her usual litany of vileness. He buzzed the front desk.

"Morning, Donna. This is Steven. I'm not taking any calls. Period. If my ex-wife calls back, tell her I'm in meetings, and won't be available all day. If that doesn't satisfy her, and she becomes verbally abusive, you have permission to disconnect her call. Thank you."

He finished his paperwork and, on his way out the door, picked up the messages from his slot. As he suspected, of the six messages he held in his hand, four were from his ex, one from his daughter, Alana, and the last message was from his son, Marc.

The message from his daughter was simple, just three words—

tonight, please, peace. His son's message was almost as simple-*can't make it tonight, gotta work.* Steven's irritation that his son wouldn't take the time to say goodbye to his only sister accented itself in the harsh echo of his angry footsteps. *He's over twenty-one. I can't make him behave responsibly.* He slammed the door of his SUV and stowed his briefcase before glancing at the remaining messages. Donna had noted she refused to write the actual words his ex-wife persisted in saying, but the body of the message was the usual stuff about girlfriends, money, and his lack of love for his children. He crumbled the pink pieces of paper in his hand and hurled them to the floor of his vehicle.

Looking in the mirror at himself, he muttered, "One more week; just one more week."

Leaning against the seat and, closing his eyes, he exhaled deeply. *Tonight, if necessary, I need to bite my tongue until it bleeds to keep the peace. But tomorrow, when Alana's plane leaves the tarmac, the kid gloves come off.*

Racing against traffic and time, Steven ran the errands he'd planned for this day. He parked his SUV in the garage and, glancing at his watch, uttered a swear word. The next hour, he showered and tried to decide what to wear to his daughter's farewell dinner. A long-sleeved, chambray, cotton shirt with the cuffs rolled to his elbow, relaxed jeans with razor-sharp creases down the front and back, and cordovan colored loafers completed his look. He finished styling his hair and, in a small act of defiance, reached past the Paco Raban cologne he normally wore to grab a bottle of aftershave nearly two decades old. Patting the Aramis on his face, he closed his eyes and let his mind slip to a time long past.

~ * ~

"Steven! Are you trying to make us late?" Barbara's eyes twinkled wickedly.

"Who me?" he smirked while he enveloped her within his arms.

She moaned as she deeply inhaled his scent. "You know how horny that makes me. If you don't let me go, we'll never make the gig on time."

~ * ~

The trilling of his cell phone broke the memory. Not bothering to look at the read out display, Steven answered flatly. "What, Lisa?"

"How long are we going to have to wait on you?"

"Lisa"—Steven glanced at the travel clock on the back of the toilet—"it's only 5:30. I'm on my way out the door, and will be there in less than fifteen minutes."

"Oh. Well, could you stop at the store and get some vanilla ice cream for the cake?"

"Yes."

"Thanks."

He quickly hung up and patted his shirt pocket to be sure the gift for his daughter still resided there. Grabbing the keys off the kitchen table, he headed out the door to dinner. At 5:50, his SUV slid under the trees that lined the front of the house where he'd spent his childhood. The white Spanish-styled, stucco house with red tile roof still triggered happy memories for him. Palm trees graced the front yard, and the warm, earth-toned, tile walkway evoked a welcome. He looked expectantly at the dark, iron-hinged front door, remembering the many years he'd come home from school, dragging his feet along the walkway, only to be bowled over by the exuberance of Tracy, the family dog. A smile transformed his lips. Monday, he would put the condo on the market and, when it sold, move back to the place he'd always considered his true home. He'd been paying for it all these years to ensure it would stay in his family. Although Lisa's lawyers had received adequate notice for her to move by the end of the week, he was sure she would be finagling a way to remain in the house. It had been the only reason she'd fought so hard during their divorce. The moment she'd set eyes on the Spanish-style mansion, with its pool and manicured yard, she'd obsessed about it. Only by the grace of his lawyer, and a prenuptial agreement his father, a judge, had made him draw up and demand Lisa sign, had he been able to hang on to the property willed to him by his father when he married, 'to save inheritance taxes'.

The front door swung open, wiping the smile from Steven's face.

"Did you get the ice cream?" A long-legged blonde stood holding the door.

He sighed. "Yes, Lisa." He brushed past her, walking through the terra cotta tiled entry and guest living room, and executing a right turn at the formal dining room into the country-style kitchen where he had once felt so comfortable. He placed the ice cream in the freezer and turned to face his ex-wife.

"Wow. You look really nice tonight." Steven noted Lisa's perfectly applied makeup and the cobalt blue linen slacks topped by a low-cut crème-colored blouse that emphasized her voluptuous bosom.

"Do you really think so, or are you trying to be nice for our daughter?" Lisa shook her waist-length blonde hair and unconsciously brushed it over her shoulder.

Steven turned to walk away. "I really think so, Lisa. Let's not fight tonight. Alana will be gone in twenty-four hours, and I want to spend every moment I can with her in a happy mood. Please don't spoil it. By the way, where is she?"

"Oh, so you just want to..." Lisa stopped, her light gray eyes clouded to a dangerous slate. Speaking very slowly, she continued, "As much as I hate to admit anything to you... you're right. Tonight is for our daughter, not us. I'll call a truce if you will." She raised her eyebrows in question.

Steven faced his ex-wife. At that moment, he remembered why he had married her. She was extraordinarily beautiful—full, coral-toned lips, dove-gray eyes, waist-length blonde hair, and a curvaceous full figure, even into her forties.

He pulled in a deep breath and answered, "Truce. Is she here?"

"Yeah, she's in her room. She'll be down in about ten minutes. Dinner will be ready in about twenty. You want a drink?" Lisa moved toward the refrigerator.

"I'll get a beer from the frig in the study. You still keep some in there, don't you?"

Lisa nodded.

"Great. Tell Alana I'll be out by the pool. I want to talk to her, just Dad to daughter. That okay with you?"

"Yes. I'll send her out to you when she gets down here."

"Thanks."

He walked through the house to the den area. The walls, light pine paneling and built-in bookshelves, had served many a Sunday football party for friends. Built in conjunction with the den and to the right of it was a room lined on two sides with floor-to-ceiling bookshelves. The third wall had a window where a large desk resided beneath, and directly across and parallel, the windowed fourth wall highlighted the built-in teakwood bar in the evening sun. Steven journeyed around the end of the imported bar to the refrigerator that cooled his stash of Budweiser. Opening a longneck bottle, he tipped the brown container, and took a long swig. He would need as much courage as he could muster tonight. He wandered out to the screen-enclosed patio, and plunked down on a lounge chair, staring at the turquoise pool water wavering slightly in the evening breeze. As he watched light shadows dance off the illuminated bottom, it set his mind to reminiscing.

~ * ~

"Steven, if you don't stop teasing, I'll go home." Barbara pushed her lower lip into a pout as she bobbed in the deep end of the cool water.

"I promise I'll behave—maybe." His hazel eyes twinkled. He raised a finger and, motioning for her to join him, beckoned her from the deep end of the pool to his side. "Honest."

Barbara kicked off from the wall and sluiced through the water, hair flowing behind her in a long, dark, undulating wave. Tiny droplets glistened on her black eyelashes as she fixated her smoky almond-shaped eyes on him, reflections playing in their depths. She swam to him, encircling his neck with her arms, and slowly pressed her body against his. Steven moaned low in his throat.

"Not fair," he murmured against her cheek. He wrapped his arms around her tiny form. "Do you realize my parents are gone for five days?"

"Five? Are you sure?"

"As sure as I am we're going to make love on every piece of furniture in this house." Steven feathered kisses down the side of her neck.

"Oh, Steven, if you don't stop now... I'll..." Barbara leaned her head back as he continued to kiss under her chin and down the soft indentation of her throat.

He stopped for a moment. "You'll, what?" He looked into the dark eyes he loved so much.

"I'll give in, and let you have your way." She smiled showing dimples that had won his heart.

Steven lowered his mouth to her rosy, full lips and gently caressed them with his own.

Their tongues danced lightly, urgency setting in and, before they could control their lust...

~ * ~

"Dad? Are you here?" Alana stepped into the enclosed pool area.

Steven shifted on the chaise lounge and grabbed his beer from the top of the white wrought-iron table next to the lounge.

"Yes, hon, I'm right here."

The athletic honey-blonde dragged a chair across the patio area and sat facing her father.

"You've been thinking of her, haven't you?" Her gray blue eyes searched her father's face.

Steven felt color flood his face. "How can you tell?" He shifted uncomfortably in the lounge as he took a swig of beer.

"You get this kind of goofy look on your face." Alana smiled.

"I'm sorry, hon. I didn't realize it was so—obvious." Steven stared out at the pool.

Alana reached over and put her hand over his. "Dad? I'm over twenty-one and know just how difficult Mom can be. I live with her, remember? There is nothing wrong with remembering when times were happy."

"Baby, I loved your mom once, but she killed all the feelings I had for her. I'm sorry I couldn't make it work for you kids..."

"Whoa!" Alana pushed back her chair. "Dad, if Marc and I had been able to say something you would've listened to, we'd have told you to divorce her five or six years earlier. You were miserable, we were miserable, and it wasn't going to get better any time soon. You'd decided we needed to be a family. Marc and I could've lived without the bickering, weeklong silences, and acting as go-betweens. 'Marc, tell your father...' 'Alana, tell your mother...'"

He couldn't deny what his daughter was saying.

"I'm really sorry."

"Don't worry about it now, Dad. You finally recognized there was no way to make Mom happy. She is, basically, an unhappy person who depends on the rest of the world to fill that need. Until she clues in she is responsible for her own happiness, nothing any of us does will meet her standards. Find happiness for yourself, however you can."

He stared at his daughter. *When did my little girl become so smart?*

"That reminds me, I need to talk to you, and I'd prefer not to have an audience. How about we take a walk?" He nodded his head in the direction of the intercom system located throughout the house and yard.

Alana looked into the beseeching eyes of her father. "Sure, I'll tell Mom we'll be back in about ten minutes?"

Steven nodded as he rose from the chaise lounge and moved toward the front door. Alana joined him, and they walked down the front sidewalk and around the corner of the block.

"Okay, Dad. What is it you want to tell me?" Alana reached her hand out to his arm.

He turned to look down at his daughter. "I think I've seen my old girlfriend at the hotel."

"Great. Maybe you two can get together." She started to walk away from him.

He reached out and pulled his daughter to his side. Looking deeply into her eyes, he tried to convey the intensity of his next statement. "She hasn't changed one bit since she left Tampa over twenty-five years ago."

Alana stared at her father. A small line had appeared on his forehead, worry lines framed his eyes, and his brows knit together.

"So, she's still beautiful. A lot of older women retain their beauty, Dad, you know that. Why are you so bothered by it? You're still a very handsome man. My girlfriends tell me all the time."

Steven shook his head. "No. I mean she hasn't changed one bit since she left—no age lines, no gray hair, no sagging skin; no change at all. IF, and this is a biggie, if the woman I saw is Barbara, she doesn't look a day over thirty. I know I've gotten heavier, and there's gray in my hair. I'm afraid to say anything. What if it's not Barbara? I'd feel like an idiot."

Alana stood for a moment considering what her father saw as a problem.

"Well, Dad, if it is Barbara, and you let her get away, again, none of us will hear the end of it. If it isn't Barbara, but a look-alike, why not take a chance, and make a new lady friend that will drive Mother nuts with jealousy?" Alana's eyes twinkled merrily.

He opened his mouth quickly snapping it shut. A devilish grin appeared on his face, and the worry lines relaxed around his eyes.

"You really are devious; obviously, my daughter. I hadn't considered that possibility. Your mom is always accusing me of being a playboy; I might as well milk it for all it's worth. She's the one who went ballistic when she discovered I still had pictures of Barbara. I had to hide them away so she wouldn't tear them up."

"I know. One day while you guys were fighting, Marc and I were hiding in your closet, and we discovered them."

"How could you? They were pushed to the back left-hand side of the top shelf."

Alana grinned. "Dad, we were kids on an adventure hiding from the wicked parents. We pulled a chair into the closet, climbed up, and started opening the boxes on the shelf."

Steven's eyes blazed. "I would have tanned your hides if I had known. Those pictures were private."

"We knew. We flipped through them and returned them in exactly the same place. We didn't know who she was; we just knew she was the prettiest woman we'd ever seen besides Mom. We thought maybe she was some actress or singer you'd met before you knew Mom. I didn't figure it out until years later when I heard the two of you arguing again. Now, you can substantiate the cruel things Mom has tossed in your direction. Think about it, Dad. You deserve some happiness, too."

He leaned over and kissed his daughter on the forehead. "You are something else, kid." He stood and admired the young woman. "By the way, I'm really irked at your brother. He should be here to say his goodbyes to you, too. When I get a hold of him..." Steven's eyes darkened.

"Don't. Yesterday, he called and invited me out. We went to dinner at Bern's, and stopped in at the bar. He picked up the tab for the whole night.

That's why I didn't open the door for you. I'd just gotten up from the nap I was taking. Haven't celebrated like that since graduation. Besides, Marc and Mom aren't on speaking terms right now."

Steven groaned. "What now?"

"She wants to run his life, and he won't let her—you know—the usual."

He grinned as he wrapped his arm around his daughter's waist, and they started back to the house. "Never could tell that boy what to do."

"Well, since he and Aaron Fisher moved in together, he's been behaving like a twenty-five-year-old bachelor, and it's killing Mom. She does nothing but whine about it all day long. I didn't realize what a pain she was until school let out, and I was home all day. I can't wait to get to England. I'm seriously considering have my cell number changed and not letting her know."

Alana started to walk down the sidewalk.

"Just a moment, young lady," He turned her to face him. "You will NOT change your cell number without telling your mother. I'd have to put up with the fallout the whole time you were gone. I think I can offer a solution that will help." He reached into his pocket and pulled out a plastic card.

Alana could see he held a credit card. She looked into his face and raised her eyebrows.

"What's this?"

Steven smiled and cleared his throat.

"This is a Rodgers' family tradition. Your grandfather started this tradition, and I'm continuing it." He offered the card to Alana. "When I was just a sophomore in college, my dad realized I wasn't going to give up playing the drums—well, not anytime soon, so, he got me an American Express card for emergencies. You know, like being stuck on the side of the road with a van that won't start, or in a town for an extra night we didn't expect and needing to get a hotel room... that sort of thing. I want you to have a way to come home if you need, or to get a room for a friend, or even have a night on the town after an especially difficult day of research. You'll be responsible for your charges, but if you get into a tough jam, call me, and I'll cover them. You need to let me know what your address will be as soon as you're settled, and I'll have the statements sent to you. I'm also getting a copy sent to my attention. Now, this is very important. Your mother is not to have any knowledge of this. This is just between us. If she finds out about the card, I'll have it canceled; not because I don't love you, but because the problems your mother will create are more than I want to handle."

Alana looked at the green card in her hand. A smile began to form. "What about..."

Steven held up his hand. "Marc has had one for three years now."

Alana's eyes widened. "And he didn't tell me about it? Why that little..."

He broke into a laugh. "Baby, he was sworn to secrecy. I guess he took me seriously."

"I guess."

"This is my big present to you, hon. I've got something small I'll give you after dinner so your mother doesn't kick up a fuss, but I wanted to do this with just you and me." Steven tucked a finger under his daughter's chin and raised it to look into her eyes. "I don't know how I'll survive the next year or so without you. You've grown into such a beautiful young woman; it takes my breath away every time I see you. Take care of yourself, daughter. Call collect whenever you want, day or night, and stay in touch." He choked out the last few words, allowing a tear to meander down his cheek. "I love you and will miss you terribly."

Alana choked. "Daddy, I can't thank you enough for all you've done for me. You've always been there but—" She handed the green credit card back to her father. "I can't take this. It's just too much."

He wrapped his hand around his daughter's and pushed it toward her. "Even if you never use the card, please keep it for emergencies. Give in to your old man's worrying. I'll feel better knowing you have an escape option."

Alana blinked back the tears threatening to spill over her lower lids. "Daddy, I love you so-o-o much. Promise me one thing?"

"Anything, baby."

"Please don't come to the airport tomorrow."

Steven stepped back, his face clouding as hurt filled his eyes. "Why?"

Alana wrapped her arms around her father's waist and looked up into his eyes. "Because I don't think I could stand to wave goodbye to you knowing I won't be seeing you for a year." She leaned her head against her father's chest and squeezed him.

He cradled his daughter in his arms. "I can relate to that. Well, you'll need to explain to your mother why I'm not there. Just remember, after you leave, I'm still here with her; although, I wouldn't count on not seeing me for more than a year. I don't think I can go that long without my Alana-fix. I might just surprise you and come to visit. It's been thirty years since I invaded England; I say it's time to invade, again. What do you think?"

Alana looked into her father's face, a wayward tear sliding down her cheek. "I say you'll be welcome anytime you want." She smiled wanly.

"Good. Then it's settled. Now, let's get back to the house before your mother sends out the police." Slipping his arm around his daughter's shoulders, they strolled to the Spanish-style home. Through the vestibule and into the formal dining room, they followed the aromatic smells emitting from the kitchen.

"Dad?"

"Humm?"

"I'm going to put this in my purse while I'm thinking about it... before Mom sees it," Alana held the card in her cupped hand.

Steven nodded. "Probably a good idea."

Alana left to find her purse, and Steven wandered toward the kitchen. He stopped and leaned against the threshold, watching his ex-wife glare at the clock over the window that overlooked the sinks.

"If that son-of-a-bitch stands me up, I'll..." She muttered. She stabbed the button of the intercom and barked, "Mirella! I need you here, now!"

Steven cleared his throat.

"What?"

"Why do we need Mirella tonight? Let the woman have a life."

"As long as I'm paying her..." Lisa started.

"I'm paying her." Steven crossed his arms.

"Whatever. As long as she is in my employ, she's on-call. I have a guest coming"—she turned a saccharine-sweet smile to Steven—"and I need to present the proper impression." Noting the red creeping up his neck, she continued, "I said I didn't want you bringing any of your bimbos to this dinner. I didn't say anything about me not having any guests. This is still my house, and I'll do whatever I please."

Steven's eyes flashed angrily. He clenched his fists and straightened in the doorway. As he was about to lash out at his ex-wife, the back door opened and Mirella, dressed in a black maid's outfit trimmed in white, complete with starched cap, entered.

"I'm so sorry, Mrs. Rodgers. I was detained."

"Fine. Just finish getting the table ready. Diego will be here any moment, and I want everything to be perfect. We will eat as soon as he arrives." Lisa swept past the young woman and Steven, disappearing down the hallway that led to the master bedroom. "I'll be freshening up."

Mirella, normally a robust caramel color, appeared ashen, Steven noted. Her jet-black hair, pulled into a French braid that fell below her buttocks, was straying from the neat braid she wore. Tiny tendrils wisped around her flawless face and haloed around her starched cap. Her hand trembled as she pulled the water glasses from the cabinet.

"Mirella?" Steven stepped in front of the young woman, impeding her journey to the dining room. "What's the matter? You don't look well. Is there anything I can do to help?"

"No, Mr. Rodgers. I'm fine, just a little tired, that's all." She kept her eyes downcast at the floor, her lip quivering slightly. "I guess I'm just sad that Miss Alana will be leaving."

Steven patted her gently on the shoulder as he stepped away to let her pass. "We'll all miss her, Mirella. But, she'll be back. She's just going away for a year or so."

The young woman smiled wanly. "You're right, Mr. Rodgers. She will be back. Please, excuse me. I don't wish to have Mrs. Rodgers angry at me." She moved expertly about the table, setting the glasses at each place and polishing the silverware, then hurrying into the kitchen.

Steven felt ill at ease. When he'd grown up in this house, Mirella's mother, Daniela, had been the housekeeper and part-time nanny.

Lisa breezed into the dining area, a fresh coat of lipstick on her full lips, and took a quick look at the table.

"Mirella!"

"Yes, Ms. Rodgers?"

"Please bring out the crystal salt and pepper shakers."

"Yes, ma'am."

Steven had never seen his ex-wife so rattled. Who is this guy she's so busy trying to impress? Before he could verbalize his question, the front doorbell sounded.

"Mirella, get the door." Lisa fluffed her hair and blotted her lips together. She glared at Steven, and, through gritted teeth, whispered, "Don't blow this for me. If you do, I'll never let you rest."

Steven opened his mouth to respond but a gentle squeeze on his arm stopped him.

"Dad, please."

He bit back his reply.

Mirella entered the dining room followed by a towering, deeply tanned man. Thick, wavy black hair fell into a perfect widow's peak over his forehead. It was as if it purposely pointed to his intense black eyes framed by thick black lashes, currently on the swaying hips of Mirella as she led him into the room. Steven noted the wide shoulders, muscular arms, and athletic stride of the man. *Soccer?*

"Mrs. Rodgers, Senor Diego de la Mar Montenegro has arrived." Mirella vanished into the kitchen.

Steven noted the man continued to watch the retreating form of the young housekeeper, even as he took Lisa's hand, placed it to his lips and, with a slight bow, brushed a light kiss over the top.

"Senora Rodgers. I am honored to be invited to your home for this special occasion." He strode to Alana, swept her hand into his, and passed his lips across the top. He clicked his heels together lightly and gave a small bow to her. "Senorita Rodgers. It is my pleasure to be included for this dinner." Reaching into his pocket, he produced a business card that he placed into Alana's hand. "Should you need anything while you are on the continent, please feel free to contact me. I will make sure anything you require will be at your disposal."

Alana's cheeks blazed, and she murmured, "Thank you, Senor Montenegro."

"Please, call me Diego. Senor Montenegro is my father." He flashed a dazzling white smile at her and moved to Lisa's side. "Is there anything I can help with, *cara mia*?"

Lisa smiled, "No, Diego. Mirella has everything under control. Shall we sit? Oh, yes. This is my ex-husband, Steven Rodgers." Lisa swept her hand in Steven's direction.

Diego nodded and smiled tightly. "*Con mucho gusto*, Senor Rodgers."

Steven nodded in return. "Senor Montenegro."

Lisa and Diego sat together on one side of the table while Steven and Alana occupied the opposite. Steven watched his ex-wife exude charm, batting her eyes and laughing at Diego's jokes, demurring to his opinion on everything. If he hadn't promised his daughter he'd behave, he might have taken the man aside to let him in on a thing or two. The hope his ex-wife might marry again made him pause. However, noting Diego's eyes following Mirella each time she entered the room began to concern him. He couldn't be sure his ex-wife noticed because the man was proficient at disguising his actions. Lisa continued to coo and bubble, bat her eyes, and blush at all the right times.

Mirella, her caramel colored face completely impassive, picked up the dessert plates and started toward the kitchen.

"When you have finished the dishes, you may go, Mirella." Lisa flicked her hand lightly in the young woman's direction.

"Thank you, Senora Rodgers." Mirella started for the back door.

"Thank you for your service, Senorita Alvarez." Diego nodded his head in Mirella's direction.

Lisa snapped around to glare at her dinner companion. "How do you know her last name?"

Diego turned and, catching Lisa's hands into his own, looked deeply into her eyes. "Because, *cara mia*, you told me."

Lisa's face glowed red, and she mumbled, "Oh."

He slid his hand up to cup her elbow. "Shall we take our after dinner drinks to your lovely veranda by the pool? I think that would be a wonderful way to end the evening, don't you?"

Steven watched Lisa's anger dissolve. *This man is good. What does he want?* He cleared his throat. "I think I'm going to head home. It's been a long day, and work will come very early tomorrow. Lisa, thank you for a wonderful dinner; it was superb. Senor Montenegro, a pleasure to meet you, sir. I believe I can find my way out. Alana, walk me to the car?"

"Sure, Dad."

He placed his arm around the waist of his daughter, and they strolled to his SUV.

"I wish you'd change your mind about letting me go with you to the airport."

"Dad, please. It's going to be hard enough with Mom. I just couldn't bear watching you disappear from view. I'll still have the same e-mail address, so send me a note. When I settle into a flat, I'll give you my street address. Maybe you'll just show up one day." Alana's eyes twinkled.

Steven leaned down and placed a kiss on her forehead, wrapped his arms around her, and held her tight. Minutes passed before either one dared to break their embrace.

"If you need anything, baby..."

"I'll call you first, Daddy."

"Love you."

"Love you, too."

Alana turned and sprinted to the house. Steven watched her athletic form disappear into the front entrance. He walked around his SUV and climbed into the driver's side.

Leaning his head against the seat back, he allowed the tears he'd been holding to flow. *Damn, I'll miss that ornery cuss.* A smile began to form on his lips. *Think I'll take her advice and break my own rules. I've got to know if the guest is my Barbara or some doppelganger. Either way could make things interesting.* Straightening up, he started his SUV and drove to the condominium. For the first time in longer than he could remember, he was on a mission.

Seven

Rachel asked Barbara as they walked through the front entrance into the rapidly warming Tampa morning, "What was that cheeky display all about?"

Barbara smirked. "Cheeky? So now you're talking British?"

Rachel grinned. "I guess Robart is rubbing off on me."

"Duh."

"You didn't answer my question. What was that all about?"

"What, specifically, are you talking about?" Barbara looked at her friend, widening her eyes and raising her eyebrows.

"Oh, puleeese. The winking-at-the-camera thing." Rachel rolled her eyes and stopped. "And just where in hell are we going?"

Barbara faced Rachel. "Look, everybody knows there's some geeky guy who wanted to be a cop, or some retired military guy who doesn't want to play golf all the time, sitting behind those monitor screens watching the rest of the world go by. I just wanted him to know I knew. Just wanted to make him think a little, that's all. As to where we are going... well, we're going to explore this town, at least the parts of it I still remember, in that—" Barbara pointed to a sleek, low-to-the-ground sports car. "—copper-colored convertible. You got an objection?"

Rachel's eyes followed the direction her friend was pointing, and she let out a low whistle of appreciation. "When did you arrange for this? I can't believe you had time last night."

They walked toward the low-slung beauty. Rachel circled the magnificent machine, trailing a finger along the opulent, fluid bodylines, as Barbara continued.

"I know you, and everyone else, thought I was completely despondent over Dylan's death. I can't deny my life won't be the same without him, but the pain had begun to subside while I was lying in the hospital this last time. Well, you know how much I hate watching television, and I couldn't read very long before I became exhausted, so, John brought my laptop to the hospital. He'd been clamoring to do something. Poor guy still feels it was his fault Dylan was killed that night. Nobody can convince him it was just an accident. He didn't make that idiot driver drink so much he forgot to turn on his lights. Anyway, I surfed the Internet when I was feeling up to it, to catch up on all the changes happening since I left Tampa. At that time, I set up the car and the suites. You'd already gotten the flights so the rest was easy."

Barbara unlocked the car, and the two women climbed inside, Barbara at the wheel.

"Where to, captain?" Rachel piped as she buckled her seat belt.

"I think there's a map of the area in the console, here." Barbara lifted the lid to the hidden storage unit between the seats. "And I've designated you to be the navigator. We need to get to Ybor City from here."

Rachel pulled the map out, unfolding it noisily, uhming and hmphing as her finger traced various roads. "I'm not finding anything called E boar city. None of the cities in the area start with an E." Rachel frowned as she heard her companion begin to chuckle and, before she could ask, Barbara was laughing so hard tears were streaming down her face.

"What's so damn funny?" Her eyes were narrowed so closely, her perfectly formed eyebrows nearly touched.

Barbara gasped for air between guffaws. "Now I know why I love you so much, best friend.

"What?" The thunderous expression on Rachel's face threatened to explode.

"Ybor City is a Cuban name." Barbara snickered as she gasped for breath.

"So WHAT?" Rachel glared at her friend

"Rach, when I need advice on my car or house repairs, who do I call?

"Me. What the hell has that got to do with some Cuban name?"

"Look for a city with the spelling Y-B-O-R."

Barbara watched the anger drain from her friend's face and a look of understanding replace it.

"Never was very good at Spanish. That's why the school let me take metal shop instead."

Barbara watched Rachel trying valiantly to maintain her anger, but when she dissolved into another fit of giggles her best friend folded and joined her.

"Gosh, it's good to hear you laugh. I didn't think I would ever hear that sound again." Rachel smiled.

"It feels good to laugh again. So, shall we get going? Navigator, get me to Ybor City."

"Why do we need a map? Why can't we just use the GPS System?" Rachel turned the map several directions.

"Because I like doing things the old-fashioned way. And what if the GPS goes out?"

"Fine." Rachel grumped. We need to go north on Westshore Boulevard to Interstate 275 and head east on 275 until it turns into I-4 staying east on I-4. Then we take exit 1, which is 21st street, and go south about six or seven blocks. Doesn't look like there's a lot of parking but we can figure that out when we get there. I've done my part; now it's up to you, Captain."

Less than thirty minutes later, car parked and locked, the two women found themselves strolling down the sidewalks of Seventh Avenue in Ybor City. The smell of tobacco leaves lightly scented the air in conjunction with a hint of salt, damp, and chicken and yellow rice. Rachel watched Barbara as she bounded up to each store window, amazement coloring her features.

"My, God! When I left here, hardly anyone dared to walk these streets in the daytime, let alone at night. You barreled through town as fast as you could, making sure you locked your car doors and rolled up your windows. This is fabulous! I love it! Man, the smell of food is making me realize I'm starving. Where...? Ah, yes. Carmine's Restaurant and Bar. This place has been here forever. They make some of the best chicken and rice in the world. You have to have some, Rachel. Come on."

Dragging her lanky frame along, Rachel followed Barbara to the restaurant. They asked for a table located near the window to watch the tourist traffic. Barbara ordered two plates of *arroz con pollo*, and they dug into their meal. After the main course, drinking demitasse cups of rich Cuban coffee—strong black coffee, sugar and cream—and enjoying the golden flan covered with caramelized topping, the conversation drifted toward the rest of the day's activities.

"What's on the schedule now?"

Barbara watched Rachel spoon flan into her mouth and close her eyes. "This is almost as good as an orgasm."

Barbara nodded her agreement, her own mouth full of the same sweet bit of heaven. She picked up the demitasse cup and washed the contents down with Cuban coffee. "The coffee comes pretty darn close. I've been sitting here looking at that bookstore across the street. Something about it really intrigues me. After we're done here, why don't we wander over there and see what's inside?"

Rachel agreed, and the two finished their dessert and coffee. They left the table, paying the bill and leaving a tip for the handsome waiter who'd taken their order and hovered around while they enjoyed their food; then meandered across the street to a shop called Green Dragon Books.

Rachel, eyebrow cocked, looked at Barbara. "Why this shop? You've never indulged in any of this."

She swept her hand around the room. The walls held books of different metaphysical inclinations; shelves displayed crystals, candles, tarot cards, and runes.

Barbara shrugged at her friend. "Can't explain it but I really felt the pull to come into this shop. Let's just browse for a minute, then we'll head up to the mall by the University. I want to see how much that's changed and do some major damage on my credit cards."

They strolled down the aisles, chitchatting. Near the back of the store, as the two turned up a different row, a beautiful blonde woman emerged from a door marked "Employees Only." She smiled at the visitors and started toward the front. As she passed Barbara, she gasped and turning, looked her squarely in the eye.

Barbara felt uncomfortable under the directness of the woman's stare. The woman had attired herself in a flowing, black-and-gold batiked skirt over gold sandals, and a black silk blouse with billowing sleeves, which shimmered from the gold threads woven through the material. Her blonde hair rested on her slender shoulders and, Barbara noted, she wore gold rings on every finger.

"You are the one my cards have foretold to me." She nodded at Rachel who stood behind Barbara, her mouth gaping.

"I beg your pardon?" Barbara moved back stepping on Rachel's toe.

"Ouch!"

"Sorry."

The blonde women stopped before Barbara, tossing a fearful look in Rachel's direction, before reaching out and gently lifting Barbara's hand to her, palm up, and peered at the opened extremity. She took a bejeweled, ruby-tipped finger and traced the lifeline. Her dark brown eyes peered deeply into Barbara's.

"You have recently suffered a great personal loss."

Rachel harrumphed behind Barbara.

Ignoring Rachel, she continued, "You have come home seeking a glimpse of the past to answer questions of old. You will have to make a decision between two—brothers?—which will change your living arrangements as well as your life..."

Before she could continue, Rachel grabbed Barbara's elbow and propelled her toward the front door, muttering under her breath, "Any fool can see the white circle where your wedding ring used to be and, of course, you're seeking something. You came into this bloody shop. What a fraud."

The blonde turned and softly called to the retreating backs of the two friends, "By the way, Dylan says you are headed in the right direction, and he wants to thank you. Now he can rest."

Barbara's planted her feet to the floor. She whirled and, grasping her throat, whispered, "Dylan?"

The blonde approached warily, glancing at the furious face of Rachel looking over the head of her friend.

"Yes. He said you"—she pointed at Rachel—"would not believe me, but he was finding it difficult to get a message through to you. Barbara, he wanted very much for you to know the quest you have taken is the first step to setting him free. He knew he was your second choice."

Barbara gasped, tears welling in her eyes, "He never said a thing."

"He has told me to thank you for all the years of love you gave to him, and says he wants you to find your first love who also searches for answers."

Rachel growled behind Barbara, "Let's get the hell out of this place." She turned Barbara around and shoved her out the door. Glancing back, she spotted the blonde peeking from the door as they escaped to the car.

"Barbara, you're not going to believe that garbage, are you?" Furrows creased Rachel's brow.

"Well, normally, I would've laughed in her face as we walked out, but she did mention Dylan by name. I mean, how could she know the name of, of... well, you know." Barbara had stopped on the sidewalk and was looking up at her friend.

Pulling Barbara close to the building, she tenderly grasped her friend's hand in hers.

"Winkie..."

Barbara's eyes widened.

"Yeah, I know about your pet name. He told me once when I'd just read him the riot act about his drinking and how it would end your marriage if he didn't get himself together. I hate to dump ice water on your hope but... we were talking about Dylan in there, remember?"

Rachel watched her friend's shoulders droop and the hope flicker and die from her eyes.

"Yeah, I'd forgotten about that. Well, I guess mysterious messages from those who have passed over and voodoo are the tools of their trade. I'm just feeling a little guilty, I guess. I've actually felt happier here than the last two years in Oregon. Hearing his name like that brought back all the pain."

Rachel winced. "Girlfriend, we came here so you could release some of that pain and take a breather from being 'Dylan's poor widow,' remember?" She gathered her friend under her arm, and they moved toward the parking lot.

Barbara slowed her gait and turned to look up at her friend. "I know she has a very good act going, but I never told Dylan he was my second choice. Did you?"

Rachel shook her head and with her hand crossed her heart.

"Kind of makes you wonder, doesn't it?"

Rachel picked up the pace until they stood at the doors of the convertible.

"No. The woman is good at what she does—selling the occult. Everyone who goes into her shop is looking for something, or they wouldn't stop. The white spot and indentation on your finger, where your ring used to be, indicates you were in a long relationship, which has recently ended. I hate to be the bearer of bad news, but, when you think no one is watching, you look incredibly sad. It wouldn't take a rocket scientist to figure out you might be looking for a new love. That part about two brothers, though; that was taking it just a little too far. You gotta give her this—she's a great actress."

Barbara nodded, unlocked the car, and asked, "I really look sad?"

Rachel nodded slowly. "So sad it makes me want to cry. I wish I could take some of this burden from you."

Barbara leaned over and hugged her friend. "Just being with me is more comfort than you know. Now, enough of this. Let's go shopping."

Eight

Barbara had lowered the convertible top before they left Ybor City and, with the interstate speeds, was beginning to question her actions. She wasn't overly vain, but the style the warm Florida wind was creating with her hair was not one she would have chosen herself. She gave a sidelong glance at Rachel and, snickering at the tangled stand-on-end coif she was currently sporting, asked, "You want me to put up the top?"

Rachel shook her head. "It feels great, beats the heck out of bundling up and kicking on the heater. I thought you said we were going to a mall; where are you taking me, now?"

"I thought we'd take a quick spin through the University campus, then drop by University Square shopping center, if it's still there. I want to go out to Big Eddie's tonight, and I need something spectacular to wear. The Square used to cater to the college crowd. I'm just hoping that it hasn't changed. You have any preferences?"

"Nope. I'm just along for the ride."

Taking the Fowler Avenue exit off the freeway, Barbara found herself automatically making the correct turns and getting into the lanes she needed to enter the college. Once on the campus grounds, she turned into the first parking lot she found and parked.

"This place has grown so much I wouldn't recognize it if I hadn't read the sign out front."

"You want to get out and walk around?" Rachel grabbed for her door handle.

"No. It would take half the day just to cover the main campus. It was big when I studied here, but not this big. I don't recognize any of the buildings. I couldn't find my old classrooms if you paid me."

"What you want to do?" Rachel raised her eyebrows.

"Well, I came, I saw, and decided I didn't need to 'relive' my college years. Let's go to the mall and shop." Barbara backed out of the parking spot and moved into the traffic headed to the mall.

"I sure hope they have a lingerie shop," Rachel picked at the bottom of her shirt.

"Oh?"

"Yeah, well, Robart said he wanted to go *someplace special* when he got back, and suggested I shop for some slinky underwear and nighties."

"I see." Barbara watched her fearless friend turn the most interesting shade of crimson. "Do you need swinging-from-the-chandeliers lingerie or ripping-off lingerie, because there are both kinds of stores in town? Maybe not here, but I'm sure we can locate them in one of the other malls."

"Bite me. Just park the car, and let's go shopping." Rachel growled, arms crossed over her ample chest.

Barbara laughed as she put up the top and found a parking space near the door of JC Penney. Three hours, and two shopping bags for Rachel later, the pair exited into the warm sunshine and strolled to the car.

"I don't understand why you couldn't find anything you liked beside that slinky little black dress; you can find one of those anywhere. Good heavens, there are all kinds of stores in there. Jiminy, Barbara, I've never seen you be so picky!" Rachel flung open the door of the car and tossed the bags into the back seat. Shaking her head, she sat herself in the passenger's seat, flipped down the visor, and began primping her hair.

Barbara placed the little dress encased in a plastic bag in the trunk, then entered the car and adjusted the rearview mirror.

"You, of all people, should understand what I'm going through. Yes, there were enough cute outfits in there to clean out my bank account, but I have a specific look in mind for tonight. Nothing in all of those stores was right, but you can never go wrong with a good black dress. Hmmm, I wonder?" Barbara reached into the back seat and retrieved her purse. She opened the bag and rummaged inside.

The rustling from the driver's side of the car stopped Rachel's preening. She glanced at her friend.

"What are you doing?"

"Working a hunch."

"What?"

"Give me a minute, and I'll tell you." Barbara's eyes lit up as she held up a yellowing, tattered business card. "I hope this works. Let me have your cell phone, please?"

Rachel pulled the phone from her pocket as she muttered, "This had better be good. My cell bill is going to be through the roof."

Barbara squinted at the card, held it arm's distance, then swore, "Blast. Only damn thing they couldn't fix." She reached into her bag, pulled out her glasses, and placed them on her nose as she dialed the number on the old business card.

Rachel giggled.

"Knock it off, girlfriend. Your day will come," grumped Barbara. "Yes. Is this Michael G's Clothing? It is?" Barbara chuckled. "Oh, no. It's just the card I used to dial your phone number is over twenty years old. I wasn't sure you'd still be there. Can I get an appointment in an hour? Great. This card has your number but not your address. What is it?" Barbara grabbed a pen from the jockey box between the seats and began to write. "What's the cross street?" She noted the name and set the pen on the dashboard. "That's wonderful, thank you. I have to know—do you still make your signature pants? Yes! We'll be there in an hour."

Rachel rehooked the phone to her jeans pocket. "What's so fabulous about this place?"

"The clothes at Michael G's are, normally, custom-made for the wearer. Do you remember the modeling pictures of me in a pair of tan pants with white piping and buttons all the way up the side?"

Rachel nodded.

"Those were made for Steven, and he had given them to me when he got a new pair. Unfortunately, I outgrew"—Barbara motioned quote marks with her fingers—"them, and they were given away but those are the style pants I'm looking to find. They're very unique and will look great on this new body." She smoothed her blouse over her hips as she looked up from under her eyelashes at Rachel.

The two friends started laughing.

"Let's get going. I'm not sure I still know how to get around town. I want to give myself some cushion of time. NO ONE keeps the staff at Michael G's waiting. Back in the day, some of the big name rock and rollers tried that *I'm-famous-they'll-wait-for-me* routine only to find themselves locked out of the store. I don't want to lose this chance. No matter the cost, these pants are worth every dime."

The trip down I-275 was as much an educational adventure to Barbara as it was new to Rachel. So much had changed, she found herself second-guessing where to turn. Allowing her instinct to take over, she headed off the downtown exit, took Kennedy Boulevard, turned onto Hyde Park, and was over the Davis Island Bridge before she realized what she had done. She pulled the car to the curb and dropped her head into her hands.

"Barbara?" Concern tinged Rachel's voice.

"I'm okay. I was feeling a little overwhelmed because of all the changes." Barbara chuckled softly. "But when I let the auto pilot take over, we wound up here." She waved her hand at the area.

"Great, but where is here?" Rachel looked at the white buildings where they'd parked.

"Sorry. Here, is Davis Island..." Barbara started.

"I know. That's what was printed on the sign."

Barbara narrowed her eyes at her friend.

"Sorry."

"...as I was saying," Barbara continued, "this is the road to Steven's parents' house. If I hadn't caught myself, we'd be sitting in the driveway of the house Steven lived in while we were dating."

"Oooh. Let's go see." Rachel sat up, showing more interest in the surroundings.

"That's for another day. I'm going to turn around, and we'll go down Bayshore Boulevard. The Michael G's house and shop are two down from Carolina Street and before Rubideaux Street. There's no sign out front because the shop is behind the family home. I'm not sure I can remember, but let's try it. I have the phone number, so if we get lost, we can always call."

Turning the car around, Barbara smiled. Old habits were hard to break, and she would like to have seen if there had been any changes in Steven's home. However, as she told Rachel, that would have to wait for another day.

Back over the Davis Island Bridge and to Bayshore Boulevard, Barbara allowed her excellent memory and sense of direction to lead them. Surprising even herself, she stopped the car in the driveway to admire the half-acre of green lawn and century-old cypress trees leading up to the house she'd vaguely remembered. The concrete drive ran past the two-story gray cedar shake home to a cottage in the rear. A covered porch wrapped around the entire house and, spaced evenly along the bottom eave of the whitewashed porch, were baskets of hanging fuchsia in a rainbow of colors. The white rattan table, a vase of camellias in the center, and two matching chairs added a touch of elegance to the simple front. Large, tinted picture windows on either side of the dark mahogany door contributed to the portico's image of an open, friendly face. Driving slowly, Barbara sucked in a quick breath. She'd envisioned coming back to the small shop behind the house, but had forgotten just how picturesque the little cottage was. Snuggled beneath substantial cedar trees wearing dangling tendrils of Spanish moss, the cottage hid behind great, blossoming palmetto plants. French doors with dozens of leaded glass panes peeked on to the small parking area provided. A muted glow cast amber prisms of color from behind the doors.

The delicate sound of a small bell jingled as the door opened and Barbara stepped inside, Rachel close on her heels. She closed her eyes and inhaled deeply. Sewing machine oil mixed with the fragrance of newly woven material tickled her nose. A smile snuck over her lips.

"May I help you?" A willowy brunette stepped from behind a rack of clothing.

"I called about some Michael pants." Barbara's eyes began to search the rows of clothing gracing the walls of the shop.

"Oh, yes. You were the one who asked if we still made them."

Barbara nodded.

"Well, you'll be glad to know we do. I'm Cheralyn, by the way. I'm Michael's granddaughter." The brunette held out her hand to Barbara.

Barbara coughed. "Granddaughter?"

Rachel started laughing.

"Yes." Cheralyn's brow furrowed slightly. "Something wrong with that?"

"Oh, no. I've just been away longer than I thought. I'm Barbara." She shook Cheralyn's hand. "And this is Rachel. I'm looking for an outfit that will knock everybody's socks off. The malls shops are too, well, blah. I want something that will be uniquely me. I owned a pair of Michael pants before, and was praying he was still in business."

"Well, as you can see, we're still going strong. We can make a pair of pants to order, if you want or, you can see if any of the pants on the walls strike your fancy. We have shirts, vests, and skirts of all lengths, too. I have to finish an order for some local musicians, so I'll be back at my sewing machine. When you decide what you'd like to try on, come on back, and I'll show you to the dressing room." Cheralyn moved away and disappeared into the back portion of the shop.

Rachel looked at Barbara. "I still don't get what's so special about these clothes."

"The fact is they are made one at a time and no two are alike. This is a dying art."

Rachel shrugged her shoulders and moved to the closest rack. "If you say so."

Barbara rolled her eyes and huffed, "I do."

Half an hour later, two pair of pants and two shirts over her arms, Barbara ventured to the back of the shop.

"I found some things I'd like to try on."

Cheralyn rose from her seat and directed Barbara to a stall in the back corner. A patchwork curtain served as the door. Rachel trailed behind with a pair of pants in her hands.

"You, too?" Cheralyn raised her eyebrows.

Rachel nodded, and Cheralyn escorted her to the dressing room next to Barbara's.

"Oh... my... God!"

The cry came from Rachel's dressing room.

"What? Are you okay?" Barbara flipped the curtain aside and bolted from her dressing room.

Rachel stepped out from behind her curtain and stood in front of the full-length mirror turning from side to side, a wide grin on her face. "I look fabulous!"

"Of course. These are *Michael* pants. They are designed to make you look like a rock star. Are you going to get them?"

The smile faded from Rachel's face. "I can't afford these. They cost more than I make in two weeks. I wish I could, though. These would stop Robart in his tracks; make him sorry he ever went on that jaunt to Europe." She turned and trudged into the changing booth.

Barbara located Cheralyn. One whispered conference later, she started toward her own dressing room.

"Cheralyn?"

"Yes?"

"These are nice, but I'm looking for something that will suck the air out of everybody's lungs. I've come back to Florida for, like, a class reunion. Do you have anything really spectacular tucked away that you could let me try on?"

Cheralyn thought for a moment then grabbed her tape measure. She motioned Barbara to come out of her dressing room, and when Barbara had stepped into the center of the room, she measured her bust, waist, hips, and inseam. She stood up, frowning slightly, and tapped her finger on her chin. Slowly, the frown disappeared, and a mischievous smile spread over her face.

"I'll be right back."

Barbara stepped inside the stall and stripped off the pair of pants she'd tried. They were nice, and emphasized her new figure, but didn't have the spark she needed for tonight. She'd get them for another time.

Cheralyn returned with several pieces of black material draped over her arm.

"This outfit was made for... well, let's just say it was a popular singer who decided it was too conservative for her belly baring style. See if this fits."

Cheralyn pulled back the curtain and handed the items to Barbara.

"I know you'll look fabulous in it. Call me when you're changed."

Rachel had emerged from her stall wearing a look of defeat. She started to put the trousers back when Cheralyn appeared.

"Here, let me have those. I'll hang them up." She took the pants and disappeared.

Barbara slipped into the black outfit and, pulling aside the curtain, stepped out to inspect the results in the full-length mirror.

Rachel caught her breath and dropped into the nearest chair she could find. "Woooo. That is so you. You'd better not wear that when Robart is around. I'll have to shoot you. My lord, Barbara. That outfit looks as though it was made just for you."

Cheralyn materialized and whistled. "You look better in that than the singer who ordered it. If you don't take it, you're crazy."

Rachel nodded.

Barbara turned. The laces up the back yoke of the pants was a trademark for Michael designs and added the perfect touch to the look of this outfit. She might hate herself in a month, but today, she had to have this outfit.

"I'll take this and the other outfits in the dressing room. Let me change." She flashed a grin at Rachel and handed her credit card to Cheralyn.

Changed, bill paid, and assurances to Cheralyn they would send pictures for the design album, the two friends were in the car, and on their way back to the hotel. Rachel was unusually silent as the scenery passed.

They parked the car and were in the elevator on the way to their rooms when Rachel finally voiced her thoughts.

"You know it really was unfair taking me to Michael G's and letting me try on those pants."

Barbara turned. "Unfair? How so?"

"Before, I was ignorant of what a great pair of pants could do for me. Now, I know there's a pair of pants that make me look fabulous, only, I can't afford them. I was better off not knowing."

"I see." Barbara opened her door and indicated Rachel should follow her inside. "Sit." She pointed to the couch and set the bags on the table. Rummaging through the first bag, she grabbed something, pulled it out, and held it behind her back.

"We're best friends, right?"

Rachel grimaced at her. "Of course. What's that got to do with anything?"

"Well, best friend, I had no intention of taking you to Michael G's and letting you walk away empty-handed. Remember—I know how good his pants make everyone's ass look. So, here." Barbara handed the pants to

Rachel.

Rachel's mouth dropped. She looked at the pants in Barbara's hands and pushed them back. "No way. I know how expensive these things are. I can't take them. I couldn't afford to pay you back."

"I'm not taking these back. Consider this your birthday, Halloween, Thanksgiving, and Christmas present. They're not returnable." Barbara dropped the pants into Rachel's lap.

Rachel stared at the clothing for a moment then broke into a huge smile.

"Oh boy, is Robart in trouble." She stood up and put her arms around her friend. "Thank you."

"You're welcome. Now, let's go down and get something to eat. My plans are to eat dinner, take a nap then head to the bar for dancing and playing. You've been elected to be my chaperone."

"Gee, I'm so blessed."

"Figure this as a two-way street. Neither of us will get too stupid if the other is there to slap us smart."

"I guess so. But what could possibly go wrong on a weekday?"

"Don't know but we're going to find out. Right?"

Nine

Rachel shifted on the couch. In her right hand, she held the remote control she was giving a workout, and in her left hand, she held a Diet Coke.

"How much longer is this going to take?" she hollered toward the bedroom.

"As long as it takes; I want everything to start out perfect."

"I didn't realize perfect took so much time."

"Well, for me, it does. Geez, Rachel, we'll be out until one o'clock or later. When was the last time you were out past ten?"

"All right, smartass, point taken. I'm just bored. I can't find any of my favorite programs on this television, and it's Thursday night! I'm going to miss CSI." Rachel pushed her bottom lip into a pout.

Barbara swung open the bedroom door and stepped into the living area.

"Damn! You look stunning. Where'd you get the blouse?" Rachel forgot pouting when she viewed the finished package Barbara had created.

"Remember that last shopping trip we made before we left?"

Rachel nodded.

"I saw it in one of those small boutique stores in the Nordstrom Mall. Something about it appealed to me, so I bought, didn't even try it on, just bought it. I think it works with this outfit. Don't you?"

"Like they were created for each other. Damn, Barbara. I feel frumpy, even in these pants." Rachel unfolded her long legs and stood next to her friend.

Barbara slipped her arm around Rachel's waist. "Don't. I've always envied your long, muscular legs, slender waist, and perfect bust line. What always made it worse was your ability to eat anything you want and not gain weight. I look at cookies and can feel my waist began to swell up."

"If I quit tromping around the woods hunting, and up and down the streams looking for fish, I'll be six by six. Remember my Aunt Lila?"

Barbara giggled. Rachel's aunt was, indeed, six by six. She was the biggest woman Barbara had ever met. Impressive was the word that came to mind. She brooked no guff from anybody, and her size and no-nonsense attitude had come in handy all the years she'd owned the most popular biker bar in Salem. No one with half a brain cell left started trouble at Lila's Joint. Those that thought they were tougher than the big woman behind the bar soon learned to fly—free-form.

"Yeah, she's one of a kind."

"Taught me everything I know about fighting dirty—unlike the other side of my family." Rachel rolled her eyes upward as she moved to the front door.

"We don't have enough time to talk about the other side of your family, so let's get out of here and see if Divine Nine is anything close to what Big Eddy's used to be. I need to keep this new body in shape, and dancing seems like a great way to start."

The atmosphere in the car crackled with excitement. Barbara pulled into a parking space, turned off the ignition, and sat with her hands on the wheel.

Rachel turned. "What?"

Barbara dropped her head. "This idea seemed so easy back in Oregon. Maybe we should just go back to the hotel, have a quiet drink at the bar, and call it a day."

"What in the world are you rambling about? We're just revisiting an old haunt of yours, aren't we?"

"Yes."

"If people happen to think that you're younger than you really are... don't correct them. Okay?"

"That's going to be hard. I've looked and felt so old for so long, it'll be hard not to correct them."

"Remember the time, a few years ago, when you decided to see what being a blonde was all about?"

Barbara groaned softly.

"People slowed their speech when they talked to you, acted like you weren't much older than ten, and assumed you couldn't have any intelligence because of the color of your hair."

"Yes." Barbara gritted her teeth.

"Well," Rachel continued, "Act now the way people expected back then, and you'll have no problem making people think you're twenty years younger than you are."

"Yeah, but—"

Rachel held up her hand. "I will not allow you to let that outfit go to waste. There is nobody in Oregon who would appreciate how great—no—stupendous you look in it. Now, get your butt out of this car, and let's go dancing."

"But—"

Rachel, eyes wide, glared at Barbara. "I thought I was pretty clear about this. Let's go. Barbara, what was the last thing Dylan said to you about moving on with your life? What about the gypsy in Ybor City? You can't very well get yourself involved with brothers, sitting in the room at the hotel. Now, out. All this discussion has made me thirsty. I need a beer."

Rachel exited the car. She watched as Barbara locked the car, and moved around to stand next to her friend.

"Onward."

The two walked up the ramp and entered the premises now known as the Divine Nine. A thin layer of smoke already hung in the air, and the thumping of a bass guitar and drums emanated from the three-foot by six-foot speakers hanging in the corners of the room. They strolled past a couple pool tables in use and up to the doorman. Identification at the ready, the two handed their drivers' licenses to the young man. He glanced at Rachel's, took her five dollars, and stamped her hand. He took Barbara's proffered license, glanced at the birth date, looked up at Barbara, and handed the card back.

"Is this some kind of joke?" he crossed his arms over his impressively, muscled chest.

"What?" Barbara looked at her license. Nothing appeared out of order.

"The birth date on this license would put you around fifty. If this is some kind of sick joke, you can take it down the road to Bobby's."

Barbara shot Rachel a puzzled look.

"Look—" She squinted at the nametag pinned to the young man's chest. "—Evan, I am near fifty. What's the problem? The license is correct. Why would I lie about my age?"

"Ms. Langley, I have no idea why you would try to make yourself older, given the fact most women lie about their age to the younger side, but the age on the license and, pardon my bluntness, your—" He waved his hand up and down. "—body and face, don't match."

Barbara looked at Rachel, and the two choked back the urge to laugh. She leaned into the young man and winked. "Evan, I've got a *really* good plastic surgeon. My ex-husband paid for all this work. I figured it was the least he could do when he left me for his younger secretary. Turned out pretty good, don't you think?"

The young man uncrossed his arms and, blushing a deep color of maroon, muttered, "Damn good." He took Barbara's five-dollar bill, stamped her hand, and nodded the two into the bar.

Unable to resist, Barbara leaned into him, allowing the heady fragrance of her spicy perfume to tickle his nose, and whispered into his maroon-tinted ear, "Let's just keep this our little secret. Okay?"

He twisted to find himself just millimeters from her full, sensuous lips. "Uh, uh, sure, Ms. Langley. Not a problem."

Barbara, still next to his tinged ear, watched his eyes widen with expectation as she planted a kiss on his cheek. "The name's Barbara. Ms. Langley is my ex-mother-in-law, and she's a royal bitch. Thanks again, Evan."

She turned to find Rachel, eyebrow cocked, smirking at her.

"What?"

In a mocking, little girl voice, Rachel repeated, "'Let's just go back to the hotel and have a drink at the bar then stay in for the night'. Puuuleeeese." She rolled her eyes. "Let's get a drink. I really need one, now."

She strode toward the C-shaped counter snugged up against one wall and spotted two vacant seats at the end closest to the dance floor.

Two young men moved in tandem at opposite ends of the oak and black leather bar. Wearing T-shirts with the establishment's logo emblazoned on the front, they smoothly created drink concoctions for the patrons sitting on the bar stools pulled to the counter, as well as the cocktail servers and walkup customers. The mirror on the wall behind the bar gave Rachel a bird's eye view of the action occurring behind her. She watched as Barbara, several steps behind her, moved along the barstools. A stocky, dark-haired bartender, at the far end of the bar, put down the bottle of liquor he'd been pouring to gawk at her. Men sitting at the counter turned and leered at the woman walking past them. The women frowned and shot nasty looks Barbara's way.

Rachel had to stifle the urge to snicker. She knew Barbara had no idea how good she looked.

The Michael G's outfit clung to her curves better than a second skin. Black pants, piped in red with matching mother of pearl buttons down each side from mid-hip to the hem, sported red leather tie-ups on the back of the yoke. Blood red snakeskin boots peeked out from beneath the pant leg hems. A form-fitting, ruby silk blouse with ruffled, plunging neckline and ruffled sleeves tucked into the unique pants. The corresponding black and red vest, such as it was, corseted Barbara's ribcage, the neckline curving under her breasts, emphasizing her firm mounds. A heart-shaped pendant cast in perfect rubies on a delicate gold chain hung just above her bust line drawing the eye to the spot. Matching earrings sparkled in the light cast from the beer signs on the wall. Barbara had spiked her black hair, and her makeup was flawless. A deep ruby lipstick amplified the voluptuousness of her lips. The confidence the outfit inspired had affected her usual stride. Rachel watched her friend approach the end of the bar with the walk of a fashion model. She would have laughed if Barbara hadn't done it so naturally.

The stocky bartender at the far end of the bar whipped around.

"Marc! Marc!"

A sandy-haired man busily preparing drinks straightened up.

"What, Aaron? I'm damn busy. We have fifteen minutes before the band starts and all hell breaks loose. I'd like to get as much done before deafness sets in. Booze Dogs play tonight, and you know how loud they are."

The brunette trotted over.

"You need to take a look at the vision that just floated into our life. If you don't make a move, I will. This could be the woman I'm going to marry."

Marc huffed. "Aaron, you say that about every woman. I think it's your way to justifying taking them to bed. Where is this goddess?"

Aaron moved to Marc and, placing his hands on his shoulders, turned him around to look in the mirror.

Rachel watched the exchange in front of her. She smirked when she saw the sandy-haired man's jaw drop. He stood staring at Barbara who, completely unaware of what was happening right in front of her, was gazing out at the band stand and dance floor. Barbara turned to Rachel.

"You think we'll get any dancing done tonight?"

Rachel witnessed the young bartender snap his mouth shut, say something to his co-worker, then return to his workstation.

Marc's heart stopped. Literally stopped. Aaron fell in love with every female that would give him the time of day, but he hadn't found the person he wanted to spend time with until this moment. To steal Aaron's overused phrase, this was the woman he was going to marry. She didn't know it yet, but, by this time tomorrow, he'd know everything there was to know about this woman. After all, she was going to be Mrs. Marcus Rodgers.

Ten

Rachel watched the transformation on the young bartender's face. One could almost see the wheels turning in his head as he gaped at Barbara.

Barbara turned to face Rachel. "Wow. There've been changes, of course, but for the most part, this feels just like it did when I was in college. Don't know if that's good or bad."

She grinned as she faced the bar and sat on the stool. She found herself looking into a pair of mesmerizing hazel eyes. Sandy-colored hair cut in a style known in the seventies as the "shag" framed a tanned face currently featuring a blinding white smile. Barbara sucked in a deep breath as her heart pounded. She was sure everyone around could see the palpitations under her blouse.

"Hi." The deep, velvety voice reverberated over the music and noise.

"Hi, yourself." She felt her cheeks warm and, out of the corner of her eye, saw Rachel smirking.

"My name is Marc and, tonight, I will be your personal bartender. Anything you might dream up to drink, I will create. What shall we start with first?"

Barbara's gaze was drawn to a pair of lips so inviting she had to grasp her hands on the bar railing to keep herself from leaning over and placing her mouth on his.

"I, uh, uh, I'd like a glass of Sangria, if you have it." She blushed.

"If I don't have it, I'll run to Ybor City to bring you the finest, but, I think we have some excellent Sangria in our cooler."

Barbara watched as Marc walked away. Something about the long stride of the young bartender tickled her memory; the hazel eyes, sandy hair, and luscious lips of another young man flooded her thoughts.

Not possible. Just a coincidence of coloring.

She realized what had triggered the idea when Marc walked back with a small pitcher of amber colored liquid, lemons, and oranges floating freely amongst the crushed ice.

He has on Michael G pants emphasizing his long legs and tight ass. Reminds me of Steven.

She sighed.

"You okay?" A small wrinkle creased Rachel's forehead.

"Yeah, just reliving. Maybe coming here wasn't such a good idea. It triggers some strong memories." Barbara folded the napkin several times.

"Origami?"

Barbara started at the deep voice. Looking up, she found Marc with a frosted wine glass in one hand and the pitcher of Sangria in the other.

"Uh, no. Sorry." She cast her eyes down at the bar.

"Don't be." Marc smiled kindly. "We have napkins, by the case, in the back. Just wondering if I was going to need to bring out another one—case, that is. Sangria, as ordered. If it is not the best you have ever had, it won't cost you a thing, Miss?"

Barbara allowed a small smile to form on her lips. "Langley. Barbara Langley."

She looked up into the handsome face. Warmth spread through her body, and she found herself barely breathing. The noise of the bar receded as she felt stirrings she'd long forgotten. Unconsciously, she slid her tongue out, the tip circling her plump lips. She watched as a blaze roared in the hazel eyes.

He picked up the pitcher, poured some wine into the glass, and delivered the drink to her.

Barbara noticed his fingers lingering as he touched the soft skin of her hand.

"Marc? Marc!" The cocktail server picked up a lime wedge and threw it. It landed exactly where she had intended, and her target turned, a furious expression on his face.

"What?"

"A little service here. If I gotta work, you do, too. The place is filling up fast, and Booze Dogs is about ready to start playing. I need to get this stuff out there while I can still hear."

Marc faced Barbara. "I'll be back. All you have to do tonight is think of something you need, and I'll provide it. Unfortunately, right now, I have to earn my pay, but don't disappear on me." He flashed a grin as he moved to the workstation at the end of the bar.

"Well, now, looks like this might not have been a bad idea after all. I can see you made a new friend." Rachel smirked at Barbara.

"Oh, get real. You've been a cocktail server and bartender; you know the game. Suck up to the girls or guys, as the case might be, and, if they think you're interested, they'll stay all night long and tip big. Don't tell me you didn't do it when you worked the bar. By the end of the night, he'll have found some sweet young thing to take home and impress with his abilities in the sack. I came out to do some dancing and reminiscing. I've reminisced so, now, it's time to dance; if we get great service in the bargain, so much the better." Barbara grabbed her glass of wine and turned to watch the band warming up.

Rachel leaned toward her friend. "You like him, don't you? I saw the look on your face. You like this young stud."

Barbara shot a bored look at her friend. "You just put your finger on the major problem here. This puppy can't be more than twenty-three or twenty-four. I'm old enough to be his mother, at least!"

"Didn't say anything about his age. We agreed you were going to *act* as if you were in your twenties, didn't we? If that's the case, you'd be perfect for him, only two or three years older, right?" Rachel watched Barbara blanch.

Just like Steven.

"You okay?"

"Yeah. If it'll keep you off my back, I'll play this out, tonight. But if this youngster starts getting serious, I drop the age bomb on him. Deal?" Barbara stuck her hand out.

Rachel cocked her head to one side, her mouth scrunching to the other side, and grasped Barbara's hand in a firm shake. "Deal. I'm doing this under duress, you understand. I've a feeling if you don't find someone soon; I'll be getting visits from Dylan again. How do I explain that to Robart? '*Oh, sweetheart, don't worry if in the middle of the night I scream out some other man's name. It's just my best friend's dead husband haunting me until she moves on with her life. That's all.'* I'm sure that will go over really well."

"I said I'd do it. Don't get crabby."

Rachel opened her mouth to shoot back an answer, but the band began to play, drowning out all reasonable conversation.

The music vibrated through the barstools, as the glasses behind the bar danced in place.

Barbara's head bounced up and down, and Rachel watched her body relax and move to the rhythm. A big smile spread over her face.

"Now, this is music!" Barbara shouted.

The band played for forty minutes to an empty dance floor before taking their first break. Rachel watched the lead singer jump down from the stage and move through the tables. The women sitting near the dance floor twisted in their seats to ogle as he passed by them. She didn't find him particularly stunning, but he was nice looking: blonde, athletic, and cocksure of himself. Now, the drummer was more to her liking: dark and dangerous looking. He'd fallen in step with the singer and, as they walked toward the bar, it became obvious the man was quite tall and lanky. Rachel unconsciously licked her lips as her eyes surveyed the two musicians.

"Rachel." Barbara touched her friend's arm.

"What?" The redhead bookmarked her surveillance of the band members for the moment.

"I'm heading to the bathroom. You want to go?" Barbara nodded toward the far side of the room.

"Naw, I'm fine for now. I'll hold the fort."

Barbara slid off her barstool and strode to the restrooms completely unaware of the sensation she was causing.

~ * ~

The lead singer, drummer, and Marc watched her until she turned the corner.

"Shi-i-i-t! Who is that?" the lead singer spun around and asked Marc. "She is beyond fine. She is perfection!"

The drummer shook his head and whistled lowly.

Rachel watched Marc straighten slowly. The muscle near his jaw line was flexing, and he'd clenched his teeth.

"She's a lady, not one of the groupies that follow you around, so stay away. I'm warning you. Don't bother, Dennis."

Mike, the drummer, raised his eyebrows.

Dennis leaned on the bar as he grabbed his drink and, so low Rachel nearly missed it, replied, "We'll see. I'll guarantee she winds up in my bed tonight, Mr. Smooth."

Marc glared. "She's not the trailer trash you're used to Dennis. She has class. That's not something you know how to handle. Besides, she's too smart to buy what you're trying to sell."

Mike elbowed Dennis in the ribs as Barbara came into view. Setting his drink on the bar, Dennis stepped in front of her and extended his hand.

"Hello. I'm Dennis Bozeman, the lead singer for Booze Dogs. I've not seen you in here before."

Barbara took the singer's extended hand. She jumped when Dennis brought it to his lips and softly kissed the top. Forcing herself not to smirk, she smiled sweetly as she replied, "This is my first time in the club. I'm new in town."

"If there is anything you need tonight, have Marc put it on my tab." Dennis began to stroke the top of Barbara's hand with his thumb.

She affected a blush and nodded toward Rachel. "And my friend, too?"

Dennis and Mike turned toward the direction Barbara was nodding. Rachel waved and smiled, evoking a "wow" from Mike.

Dennis returned his attention to Barbara and, smiling heroically, said, "Of course."

She slipped her hand from his. "I really must get back to my friend."

"Will you be staying for our next set? Can I come see you next break?" Dennis ran his hand down her arm.

"We'll be here for a while. If you appear next to my barstool, I guess you'll get to see me." A smile began to form enhancing her luscious lips. Stepping away, the model's walk, in conjunction with the black button pants, accented her shapely hips. At the seat next to her friend, she watched the lead singer lean over the bar and confer with the adorable, sandy-haired bartender. He glanced her way. A page over the PA system for the lead singer and drummer to join the rest of the group interrupted the heated discussion beginning to take place. The two musicians turned and walked to the stage.

~ * ~

Gazing at the men approaching the bar, Rachel noted as they stopped, turned, and gawked at the retreating ass of her friend. When they turned to stare at each other, their stunned expressions made her smile. *If only Barbara could see the effect she has on men.*

She heard the young bartender, Marc, curse under his breath before he warned the lead singer to stay away from Barbara. The singer's reply was lost in the blare of music from the jukebox.

Rachel observed the shocked look on Barbara's face as the blonde musician stepped into her path and held out his hand. His next move astonished even Rachel.

"Oh, brother. What a snake." Rachel shook her head.

Observing Barbara's performance, she noted the budding smirk on her face disappear into an affected innocent smile complete with blush. "She's not buying his act for a minute." The trio turned her way, and she waved. She could see the drummer's silent "wow," and found herself flushing from the compliment. *Just think of Robart. This pup is not worth losing him.*

Barbara finally wended her way to the stool, a smug expression on her face.

"What was that all about?"

The two caught the heated exchange between the singer and bartender and shrugged their shoulders.

"Barbara?"

"Yeah?"

Rachel leaned into her friend's ear. "You're playing with fire here. You are aware Marc has a thing for you, right?"

Barbara had to move toward her friend to keep their conversation private. "Rachel, I thought we cleared that up. He's just being nice because it's good for business. That's all."

"No, that's not all. He is smitten. I've been watching him steal glances at you when he thinks no one is looking. He's using the mirror behind the bar to keep you in sight. When you were in the bathroom, he nearly launched himself over the bar at that singer. All I could catch from the conversation was something about *Lady* and *stay away*. He's got it bad, friend."

Marc broke away from the server station and approached the two women.

Shouting over the roar of the music, he informed them, "All your drinks are compliments of the band tonight. If you need anything, let me know." He snapped around, and headed to the server station, a slight scowl marring his features.

"I think you hurt someone's feelings," Rachel picked up her wine glass and held it to the light radiating off the beer sign. "Nice color."

"I'm not here to get enmeshed into some romantic triangle. Besides, he's too young. I keep telling you that." Barbara looked away from her friend. "Maybe we should just leave."

"Again with the leaving. Let's just have a good time. We'll find some male to dance with, or maybe just each other, and forget all this drama. After all... it's free." Rachel's eyes twinkled.

Barbara laughed. "You're right. Good heavens, I'm old enough to stay out of messes like this. Let's enjoy."

The band started another song and, soon after, all types of young men were asking Barbara to dance. Rachel watched as her dazed friend moved her new body with the ease of a confident twenty-five-year-old. Rachel also noted the hostile glares Barbara was receiving from women at tables around the dance floor. Dennis, the lead singer, was overtly playing to Barbara; jumping off the stage to sing to her as she danced with her partner and dedicating songs to her. It was blatantly obvious to everyone within earshot that he fancied her. As she left the dance floor with her young partner, a brunette, barely covered in a skin-tight, plunging V-necked, midriff shirt and second-skin hip huggers sitting at a table nearby shot a comment of *tourist slut* Barbara's direction. Barbara reacted. Before the young brunette could turn and snicker to her friend, Barbara jerked her from her chair, fingers placed on the artery pulse points on either side of the young woman's neck. The woman stood on tiptoes trying not to pass out.

The room was deathly silent as every eye was riveted on the scene. Lowly, and dangerously, Barbara growled, "What did you call me?"

The woman whispered, "Nothing."

"Good, because if I press my fingers like this..." Barbara increased the pressure on the woman's arteries watching her eyes bulge fearfully. "...it will stop the flow of blood to your already addled brain. Makes it hard to breathe when your brain is off. I'm going release you to walk away. If you even think of trying to take me down, I'll finish what we started here. Are we clear?"

A weak nod of the head, and Barbara released the young woman who slithered back to her chair.

Rachel watched Barbara's dance partner stand taller and smile wider as he escorted her to the bar.

"Damn, I hate it when I react like that." She took a slug of the wine.

"What brought that on?" Rachel turned and raised an eyebrow.

"Called me a slut. Didn't even try to disguise it." Barbara shot her friend a side-glance. "You know how much I hate that word. I'm afraid I just snapped. I've noticed the dirty looks sent my way, but that was the last straw." Barbara sighed. "Uh-oh. I'm in trouble now."

Walking toward the two friends, determination evident in each stride, Evan, the doorman and bouncer, headed directly to Barbara.

Her shoulders sagged, and she gathered her purse.

"Barbara?"

"Yes, Evan?"

"I won't insult you by asking if you need my help, but is there anything further I can do for you? Do you want me to toss her out?" He started toward the dance floor.

"Evan! No!" Barbara dropped her purse onto the bar and leapt from her barstool to place a hand on his muscled arm. "I overreacted to a stupid comment made by a stupid person. I'm sorry. I promise it won't happen again."

He stopped and gave her a questioning look. "You sure?"

Barbara nodded. "I'm sure."

"We've been looking for a reason to 'eighty-six' her. Cindy's one of Booze Dogs biggest groupies—starts more fights than the Russian Navy because she thinks Dennis, the lead singer, is her personal property. We'd love an excuse to send her packing."

Barbara smiled. "No. If what you say is true, nothing you or I can do will punish her worse than when Dennis takes someone else home instead of her. Let her stew in her misery."

"If you need me, you just let me know." Evan strode back to his position at the door.

Rachel let loose a low, appreciative whistle. "Man, has he got muscles. He's got muscles in places I didn't think you could have muscles." She tenderly stroked Barbara's arm. "You going to be okay?"

Barbara shrugged.

"I think you have a new friend."

A smile began on Barbara's face. "Kinda nice, isn't it?"

~ * ~

Marc could only watch from behind his bar station as Barbara danced nearly every song. He glared at the antics of the lead singer of the band. During a lull in the stream of drink orders, he stomped to Aaron's end of the bar.

"What is he trying to prove?" Marc groused.

"That he can have any woman he wants, that he's better than you, and that he'll win any wager you two make—the usual." Aaron grabbed a toothpick, speared a lime bit, and plunked it into a rum and coke. He pushed the drink toward the cocktail server and turned to face his friend.

"Why is this chick any different than all the rest that hang out here?" He'd leaned back against the bar crossing his arms over his chest, one foot over the other.

Marc stood next to him affecting the same pose and shook his head.

"This is the first time I've ever felt sparks, physical sparks, when I touched someone. There's no doubt she's gorgeous, but there's intelligence under all that beauty. She's quick-witted and doesn't buy the line of bull these guys are trying to hand her. Aaron, she's just... different." Marc pushed off from the bar. The servers were waving orders in the air to get his attention.

~ * ~

Aaron watched Marc walk away. The slump of his shoulders and slow, measured steps told Aaron he had it bad for this girl. This wasn't going to be a couple months of mooning until everyone was tired of hearing her name. No, this was as serious as Aaron had seen his friend be about anyone. This little brunette package wrapped sexily in black and red was going to break his friend's heart.

Aaron picked up the order on his stand and began shoveling ice into the glass. He stopped, holding the glass in his hand as he realized he could hear the clinking of ice cubes into the glass receptacle. The bar was deathly quiet, anticipation hanging heavy in the air. The hair on the back of his neck prickled, and he spun around to look at Marc.

~ * ~

Marc stood, ice scoop in one hand, glass in another. He was blinking his eyes rapidly to understand the scene before him. Barbara had her hand around Cindy Rivera's throat. Cindy was barely standing on her tiptoes. Even from this distance, Marc could see the fear in Cindy's eyes. The scowl on Barbara's face, the bulge of her arm muscles, and the hard set of her mouth let Marc know Cindy was in trouble. The silence in the bar was deafening. When Barbara released Cindy, the tension wavered. Cindy slithered back to her seat, and Barbara retreated to her bar stool, her face flushed.

Out of the corner of his eye, Marc watched Evan talk with Barbara. She grabbed her handbag and looked ready to leave but something Evan said produced a big grin on her face. At that moment, he made up his mind.

~ * ~

Barbara rotated the wine glass in her hands. It scared her how quickly she'd reacted to the girl's snide comment. She and Rachel had taken this trip to escape the stress of Dylan's death and the daily reminders, but Barbara concluded it wasn't enough to fly three thousand miles away from the memories. She needed to release them from her heart. She didn't want to do that. Wouldn't that be traitorous to the life she and Dylan had together? Was there an answer to this? If only she could find Steven, and he was single, and looking for her. So many if only's.

"Hello? Anybody in there?" Concern clouded Rachel's face.

Barbara started and grinned sheepishly. "Sorry, just thinking."

"Oh, no. We took this trip so you'd stop *thinking*."

"I know, but my reaction to that little witch's comment kind of scared me. Guess I'm under more stress than I realized. I'm also thirsty for a glass of water. Being a bully makes you thirsty. Marc?"

Rachel leaned against the bar. Barbara was the most non-confrontational person she knew. She was dealing with more stress than she would admit to. The handsome young bartender appeared.

"At your service, ma'am. What can I get for you? More Sangria, ice, boxing gloves?"

His dimples deepened with the subtle jab.

Barbara blushed maroon. "I'm really sorry. I just want a glass of water then maybe we should leave."

Rachel sat up and shot a glare at the man.

~ * ~

Marc's breathe caught in his throat. He reached a hand out and gently touched Barbara's arm. An electric current tingled through his fingers, and he found himself looking into the most beautiful pair of wounded eyes he could remember.

"Please accept my apology. That was crude and uncalled for. I'm too flippant sometimes. Did you want ice in your water?" His hazel eyes searched the face before him.

Barbara nodded and began to shred her napkin.

A napkin, glass of water, and Marc appeared. Putting the napkin and water before her, Marc touched her arm. Barbara looked into his concerned eyes.

"Allow me to make up for my callousness with a dance?"

~ * ~

The band had reduced the raucous sound to a mellow slow dance. She started to hesitate but a jab in the ribs stopped her from saying no.

Marc appeared at her side, and they moved to the back of the dance floor where he slid his arms around Barbara's waist. She was struck by the sensation of how well they fit together. He moved with grace and seemed comfortable dancing, and she found herself snuggling into the safety of his arms, allowing the tension of the confrontation to leave her body. Too soon, the song ended. Barbara looked up into the intense gaze of hazel eyes. Before either of them could stop it, Marc's soft lips had captured Barbara's. Time and sensation of place evaporated. The two broke the kiss gasping for air.

Barbara gazed at the floor. "I'm sorry."

Marc broke into a wide grin. "I'm not. Whenever you're ready to do that again let me know."

They moved off the dance floor and walked toward the bar. Halfway to their destination, a leggy redhead in stiletto heels and a mini-skirt stepped in front of Barbara. She groaned. *Now I remember why I quit coming to this place unless Steven was playing.*

"You know he's used merchandise, don't you?"

The shock of the little girl voice coming from such a sexy package nearly undid Barbara.

"Sabrina, knock it off." Marc glowered at the redhead.

Barbara stepped up to the woman and leaned into her. She lowered her voice, causing the redhead to move closer.

"Aren't we all when it comes down to it?" At the shocked look on the woman's face, she turned and continued to her seat.

"What was that all about?" Rachel tilted her head in the direction of the dance floor.

"A reminder of why I quit coming into this place when Steven's group wasn't playing." Barbara drained the water glass.

"No. I meant the kiss."

"Oh. That."

"Yeah. That."

"A mistake unlikely to happen again."

"Why not? Is he a bad kisser?"

Barbara unconsciously ran her tongue around her lips and shifted in her seat. "Oh, no. On the contrary, he's a divine kisser. I can understand why the little redhead is sorry to have lost him. No, I just can't get involved with someone so young."

Rachel clucked her tongue. "Why the hell not? Dylan was younger than you."

"Not that young."

"Look at all the Hollywood women getting involved with much younger men."

"Please."

"Okay, bad example. Does he act young?"

"Not really."

"Then, what's the problem?"

Barbara turned to look at her friend. "I don't want to raise someone else's child."

Rachel looked at Barbara and turned to look Marc over head to toe.

"He looks like he's been raised just fine. Really fine. Quit making excuses. Open up and live a little, girlfriend. If something works out, great. If not, we live three thousand miles away. Who's going to know?"

Barbara started to chuckle. "Okay."

The two friends high-fived each other as Marc turned around.

"What?"

They erupted into laughter.

Eleven

Dropping his keys and briefcase on the kitchen counter, Steven took the time to check his mail. Bill, bill, bill, whoa, what's this? The expensive manila envelope set bells ringing in Steven's head. When his ex-wife, Lisa, realized he was serious about a divorce, she'd sent him an engraved invitation to their dissolution-of-property meeting with the lawyers. He'd been wary of expensive, odd-shaped letters since that time. Opening the silverware drawer, he grabbed a steak knife and slit open the envelope, pulled out the invitation, and sat down at the table.

You are cordially invited to attend the wedding and reception
Of Erik Klopffenstein and Olivia Jones on
May 29 at 6:00 P.M.
St. Theresa's Catholic Church
Tampa, Florida

Steven finished reading the invitation, leaned back, and smiled. He remembered the day Bill Klopffenstein and, then Diana Czysarski, got married in the very same church. *Has it been that long?* He got up and headed straight for his bedroom. In the upper left hand corner of the closet resided a box of memories. Steven withdrew the container from its hiding place and carried it to the dining room table. Gently, he removed the lid and, putting aside recent items, dug to the bottom. He retrieved an old picture album and placed it on the table. Reverently, he ran a finger over the front. *It's been a long time.* Taking a deep breath, he opened the cover of the album. The first sight that greeted him snatched his breath away. *The guest in my hotel is Barbara. There's no doubt.* The picture of her was the first he'd ever taken. She was smiling in the shy way that had stolen his heart, her dimples framing the lush, full lips. High cheekbones emphasized the deep brown of her eyes, and her slender form leaned against the tree that still stood out front of the house on Davis Island. Her hair was short, cropped in nearly the same style as the woman from the hotel. He turned the picture over and read the inscription on the back: *The woman I'm going to marry. Barbara Hamilton, August 25, 1976.* It was his handwriting. This picture had sent Lisa over the edge and started him hiding this box.

Steven filed through memories of Barbara and him at concerts in The Lakeland Arena, trips to Disney World, Ft. Lauderdale and Miami. He held up a picture taken at Bill and Diana's wedding and grinned. Barbara had caught the bouquet, and everyone had bugged them about when they'd be getting married. By the time of the last picture he held in his hand, most of their mutual friends had married and were starting their own families. She'd waited for him to feel comfortable committing to a relationship. He'd never fulfilled that promise. Three months after this last picture, Barbara had disappeared out of his life. A year and a half later, he married Lisa.

He decided to take the first picture to work the next day. If the hotel guest wasn't Barbara, he'd show her the picture, and she'd understand his mistaken identification. His daughter was right. If nothing else, it would drive his ex-wife nuts.

The first time Lisa had entered his room while they were dating; she walked over to his dresser and picked up the 8 x 10 framed photo of Barbara. It was one of Steven's favorites. Barbara had surprised him by having some professional photos done while he was on a road trip with the band. The picture was taken at a park full of beautiful, old trees. At the time, the length of Barbara's hair was half way down her back, and she'd been experimenting with blonde streaks in the front. The dress she and the photographer had agreed upon for the shoot was a simple black wrap with long lace sleeves. All these individual elements weren't extraordinary, but the talent and professionalism of the photographer showed in the final product. The picture featured Barbara; sitting on a fallen log, her long legs exposed to the thigh as the breeze gently blew back the skirt, hands folded delicately in her lap, and looking directly into the lens of the camera. The wind was wafting her hair away from her face, the blonde streaks in the front creating a halo effect.

Steven smirked as he remembered Lisa's reaction.

"Who is this?" she was breathless with, what he discovered later, envy.

"Oh, just a good friend," Steven took the picture from Lisa's hands and placed it into the top drawer of his dresser. That would become its home when Lisa visited. The day Lisa had stumbled across the photo where he'd written Barbara's name as the woman he was going to marry had been an ugly day. Lisa had flown into a rage that lasted a full week. She wasn't pacified until she'd thought Steven had burned all the photos. He'd made copies, of the pictures and negatives, and drove Lisa to the same park where the photography session had taken place.

In one of the barbecue pits, he threw in the photos one by one, then the negatives. Her response was to make passionate love to him all afternoon. It was the first, and last, time he'd seen her aggressively passionate. Shortly after the incident, Steven had proposed. After the wedding, Lisa's enthusiasm for lovemaking had waned considerably.

He jumped when his cell phone rang.

"Hello?"

"Hey, bud. Did you get an invitation to a wedding today?" Ray had never been one for formalities. He assumed Steven would know his voice.

"Yeah. I can't believe Erik is old enough to be getting married. But then, Bill and Diane were the first in our group to fall into the matrimonial trap, and Erik arrived a few months after the ceremony."

Ray snickered. "Yeah. Premature, my ass. Diane was as big as a house. Erik was no more premature than Ray, Jr. Still, it just doesn't seem that long ago."

"I know. Hell, Ray, I just had dinner with Alana for what will be the last time in a year. She's off to England to get her doctorate. She's not my little girl anymore. She's a woman, and a good looking one, if I say so myself."

"She sure is, Steve. Ya gotta admit you and Lisa made some nice looking kids. That reminds me, who are you going to bring to the wedding? I need to know how long to let the answering machine screen my calls."

Steven picked up the picture of Barbara and tenderly ran his finger over her face. "Somebody out of our past, I think."

"Okay, bud. Stop by the bar on your way home from work tomorrow, and I'll buy ya a cold one."

"You got it. Later."

It would only be fitting he to go to the wedding with Barbara or a Barbara look-alike. Besides, it would really piss off is ex-wife and, that in itself, would be worth any discomfort he might feel.

He got up from the table, leaving the photos spread across the top, and moved to the couch where he picked up the remote control and flicked on the television. He was actually looking forward to work. A smile crept across his face. *Oh, yeah. Tomorrow is going to be the start of a new chapter for me.*

Twelve

Rachel threw her hands up in exasperation.

"Why not?"

Barbara maneuvered the convertible into the parking space.

"Because it's not the right time yet. I'm still grappling with the age thing. I know I don't look my age, but I am, and that's not going to change anytime soon. I gave him my cell number, the real one, and told him to call during the day. If he's willing to see me in the daytime, out of the bar, then maybe, I'll take this more seriously. After all, Rachel, they can't tighten up everything."

Rachel started guffawing. "Sorry, girlfriend, but they can, and they did."

"WHAT?"

"The doctor pulled me aside one day and asked if you might be interested in having *things* tightened up. I told him since you were updating everything else, I didn't see why you wouldn't want to take advantage of that service also. So, technically, the clock has been turned back." Rachel laughed so hard she gave herself hiccups.

The trip to their rooms was punctuated with the sound of Rachel's hiccupping and trying to suppress the urge not to explode into peals of laughter.

Barbara shook her head. *Dylan if I ever see you again...*

Once she'd tucked Rachel safely into bed, she entered her own suite and dropped on to the couch. Her head was spinning madly with the events of the evening. Dennis, the lead singer for the Booze Dogs group, had waited until she'd emerged from the women's restroom to ask her, earnestly, to call him. He'd slipped his number into her palm as he swiveled his head searching for Marc. Barbara giggled. In all the years she and Steven had been together, she'd attained an insider's view of musician's games. She knew what they would say to get a girl to sleep with them. It appeared the banter hadn't changed very much. She tossed the business card on the coffee table.

"If Mr. Booze Dogs thinks he wants me, he'll pay for it. I think dinner at the Inn at Sand Key will be a good way to start." She snickered as she pushed up from the couch and wandered into the bedroom.

The song ran through her thoughts. Why was that melody haunting her now? Maybe Marc reminded her of Steven more than she realized. As she undressed and crawled into bed, she hummed the tune swirling in her memory. What she wouldn't give to see Steven now. But he was probably married with a dozen kids and a middle-age paunch. *One can always dream.*

~ * ~

Marc finished wiping down the bar, fixed himself a drink, and grabbing his tip jar, sat to count the night's take. Aaron leaned over the bar to grab a coaster and joined Marc to count his own tips.

"Well, you sure stepped into it tonight, didn't you?" He smiled at Marc.

"What are you talking about?" Marc frowned.

"First, you played that chest pounding scene with Dennis, and the next thing I know, you're out on the floor giving her mouth-to-mouth resuscitation. She didn't look like she needed it to me." The smirk never left Aaron's face even as he gulped down his beer.

"Look Mr. Take-it-when-and-where-I-can-get-it, Barbara is so different from the rest of the girls who come in here, I can't even find the words to describe her. She's so... mature. She doesn't play the coy, breathless ingénue. I want to find out everything I can about her." Marc neatly stacked the quarters in dollar piles on the bar in front of him.

"Why didn't you take her home tonight? Dennis beat you to it?" Aaron got up and moved around the bar, reaching into the cooler and retrieving another longneck beer.

"What are you talking about?" Marc leaned over and, lifting the soda gun out of its holder, filled his glass with coke.

"During the band's last break, I saw him follow her into the bathroom hallway. When he came out, he gave Michael the thumbs up sign. You know those guys as well as I do. That usually means he scored."

Marc's face clouded. The heavy silence that followed Aaron's remark made Aaron worry.

"You okay?"

"Yeah. I didn't know that last bit about Dennis. Makes me wonder why she didn't ask me to go back to her place." Marc drained his glass and put it in the dishwasher.

"Listen, Marc. I'm sorry I told you. But you said she's more mature than the usual run of chicks that come into here. Maybe she just didn't want to spend the night with someone. Who knows? You get her number?"

"Yeah."

"Call her."

"Hell, no. Not at this hour. Even I know better than that. I might call her tomorrow-maybe."

"Right. Listen, I'll finish up here. Tomorrow, you can stay late."

"Thanks. See ya tomorrow."

Marc walked out the front to his car. Unlocking the bronze-colored Camaro, he was startled to hear giggling in the nearly empty parking lot. He scanned the area until he spotted the white Dodge van owned by the lead singer of Booze Dogs.

"Oh, Dennis. Why can't we go back to your place? It's kinda spooky here in the parking lot with nobody around. Aren't you afraid we'll get caught by the police or somethin'?"

"No, baby. It's exciting thinking maybe the cops will show up. Now shut up and roll over."

Marc's shoulders relaxed. He smiled as he recognized the female voice coming through the open window of the van as Sabrina's and the male voice as Dennis's.

He began to whistle. *I think I will call Barbara tomorrow. Haven't been to Tarpon Springs in a while. Be a good way to get to know her without any pressure. Yeah, that sounds good.*

Thirteen

Steven glanced at the clock over the kitchen stove. "Damn it. I can't be late today." Picking up his pace, he grabbed his briefcase, and tore out the door to his car. He grinned as he made his way to work trying not to break land-speed records. In his naiveté as a young man looking for a career, he assumed the hotel business was quiet on weekends, and dependable, unlike the music business. He chuckled out loud. "What an idiot I was!" Fridays, Saturdays and Sundays were the landing and jumping off point of the week for most business travelers, and his business was seventy-five percent business travelers.

"Pays my bills."

He dashed inside and was relieved to find the lobby populated by the inevitable early-risers but few others. He stopped at the front desk and spoke with Tamara White, his weekend morning front desk clerk. A refreshingly sincere, honest young woman, Tamara's Jamaican mulatto good looks had created more than one scene with visiting businessmen trying to get her attention. Steven inwardly snickered. The over-amorous businessmen would've been surprised to learn Tamara's life mate was a leggy blonde female named Hakana Lindstrom. They'd met while both were flight attendants and decided to settle down in Tampa. Tamara had opted to get a day job while Hakana still flew.

"Morning, Tamara."

"Mr. Rodgers, I told you to call me Tammy."

"I know, but I really like the sound of Tamara. Have the morning papers come in?"

"Yes, sir. I distributed all but the top floor. I was going to do that before it starts to get crazy." Tamara picked up the remaining Tampa Tribune newspapers and stepped around the counter.

Steven took one from her arms. "I'd like to deliver this paper to Ms. Hamilton's room."

Tamara raised her eyebrows, but nodded, and strode to the elevator. Inside, she turned and winked at Steven as the elevator doors slid shut.

Steven pulled up the list of guest requests on the computer, and noted Room 823 had asked for a wake-up call around 10:00 a.m. The request was phoned at 2:00 a.m.

A small smile played on his lips. *This has to be Barbara. She always was a night owl. Ten o'clock it shall be.* He manned the front desk until he saw Tamara coming through the courtyard. She stopped and spoke with one of the guests then headed to the front desk.

"All done." The dazzling smile lit up her face.

"I'll be in my office if you need me. Remember, I'll be making the wake-up call for Room 823."

Tamara's dimples creased deeply. "You're the boss."

~ * ~

Barbara pulled the pillow over her head. *It can't be 10 o'clock yet.* Burying her head under the pillow, she tried to go back to sleep.

"Baby, come back..."

The song just wouldn't stop bouncing around in her head. *Player.* She threw the pillow to the other side of the bed. *Player! That's it! Been trying to remember who sang that for twenty years.* She rolled onto her back and sat up. A small groan escaped her lips.

"Oh, man. I can't remember the last time Rachel and I went out and drank that much." Her hands clutched her temples. "I'd forgotten what a kick Sangria can pack." She pulled two pillows behind her back, and slowly slid down, massaging her head.

"I will not allow a headache to ruin my vacation." Barbara rolled gingerly to her right side, and grasped her purse from the bottom of the nightstand. Squinting, she zipped open the top, felt around inside until she'd located the shape she wanted, and pulled out a bottle marked 'Migraine Relief'. Popping the lid open, she shook out three tablets. With measured caution, she plodded from the bed to the bathroom, filling a glass with enough water to wash down the pills. She maneuvered the trip back to the bed, tried to guess at the time displayed on the clock next to the bed; without her glasses, it looked like 6 a.m., and she oozed under the covers pulling a pillow over her head to screen out the ever-brightening day. Barbara felt the tension in her body drain away.

The piercing trill of her cell phone jerked her from her pain-free slumber. Throwing pillows every which way and bolting into a sitting position, she cursed as she tried to locate her phone in her half-awake state.

"This had better be damned good." She squinted at the clock radio. *It's only 9 o'clock. Not my wake up call. This idiot better have a damned good excuse for calling me so early.*

"Hello? You have five seconds to tell me who this is, and what you want, or I'm hanging up and going back to sleep."

For a second, there was no sound then a smooth, male voice stammered, "Barbara? I'm sorry I woke you. This is Marc. I wanted to catch you before you left for the day."

Barbara harrumphed. "Marc, I'm on vacation. I'm not going anywhere anytime soon. It's been a while since I was out so late, and I had thought I might sleep in."

"Oh, listen, I'm really sorry. I can call another time."

"Marc?"

"Yes?"

"Don't hang up. Like I said, it's been a while since I partied so hearty. School and everything, you know?" Barbara ran her fingers through her hair, remembering the sumptuous young man from the night before. "I don't feel as bad now as I thought I would. What was it you wanted?"

"I know you're new to town," he started.

Barbara made a coughing sound in her throat.

"You okay?"

Barbara heard real concern in Marc's voice. "Yeah. Just an early morning tickle. Go on."

"Well, I thought you might let me show you around the area. There's a great little town on the Bay side called Tarpon Springs. Greek immigrants originally settled there, and they fish and still grow sponges for a living. I thought we might wander that direction, and see what kind of trouble we could stir up. That sound all right with you?"

Barbara thought for a moment. *Why not? What have I got to lose?* "Okay, but what about my friend Rachel? I don't want to leave her alone." She smiled slightly. As the silence lengthened, she figured bringing Rachel would be the deal breaker.

"Sure; can't hurt a guy's image to be seen with two great looking ladies. Ask her to come, too. Where should I pick you up?"

"Out front of the Sheraton by the airport."

"I'll be there in about forty-five minutes."

The click of the phone was all Barbara heard. "Guess he's not going to be discouraged quite so easily. Oh, well. Better get my tukus out of bed and into the shower."

Barbara swung her legs over the edge of the bed and was on her way into the shower when she heard the hotel phone ring. She glanced at the clock. *Not ten yet. Who the hell is this?*

Picking up the phone, she heard a flurry of coughing. Rachel. "What's up, girlfriend?"

When the hacking had ceased, a sultry, rough-voiced Rachel replied. "Now I remember why I quit going to bars. Allergic to all that damn smoke. Morning, Barbara. I was awoken this morning by a call from Robart."

Barbara groaned. "I can tell I'm going to be ditched for a man—again."

"Yes and no."

"What? What kind of politician answer is that?"

"The safe kind. I'm flying out at noon to London. Robart's trip was cut short, and he's going to spend the time with his family. He wants me to meet them. Barbara, the man actually wants to introduce me to his family."

Barbara let a sigh escape her lips. "Rachel, that's great. Just don't pick some ugly color for the bridesmaid's dresses and, don't get married without me being there. If you do, don't bother coming back to the US. By the way, how are you going to fly without a passport?"

"I brought it with me."

"Why?"

"You said we were going to The Keys."

"So?"

Rachel cleared her throat. "Aren't The Keys in the Bahamas outside the US border?"

Rachel's answer caught Barbara off guard, and it took her a moment to digest what her friend had said. She started laughing, her hand reaching behind her to find a chair in which to sit.

"Oh my God, Rachel. Ms. Mensa candidate herself doesn't know that Key West is at the tip of Florida." Barbara roared with laughter, tears beginning to roll down her cheeks. When she could speak, she continued. "You owe me—big time. Call my cell, and let me know you got through Heathrow, that is where you're landing, isn't it?" She continued to snicker.

"Yes, I'm flying into Heathrow. And, Ms. Smarty Pants, beside you; how many people know The Keys are at the tip of Florida?"

Barbara stifled a giggle. "Everyone who lives in The Keys and the state of Florida."

Rachel harrumphed. "Okay. So I screwed up."

"Just let me know you got there okay. Europe has more problems with terrorism than the US could ever imagine. I might be snarfed at you right now, but I want you back in one piece—even if I have to share you with Robart. It's getting late, girlfriend, you need to get ready, and so do I. I have a date. Talk to you later."

Barbara hung up the phone, forwarded her calls to the front desk, and turned off her cell. *Let Rachel stew over that for a while.* She padded into the bathroom, and turned on the shower.

~ * ~

Rachel looked at the dead phone in her hand. *What does she mean she has a date?*

She tried dialing room to room, but the line kept diverting to the front desk. Getting up to march over to Barbara's room, the sound of her cell phone stopped her.

"Hello?"

"Hullo, luv. Is your friend really mad?"

Robart's lilting tenor drove all thoughts of Barbara out of Rachel's head.

"Not really. It's kind of weird. I mean, when you and I first got together, she was—well, irritated. She reminded me of my poor track record with guys. Now, it's like she just doesn't care. I'm feeling kind of pushed off."

"Enough you don't want to fly over?"

"Ha! Not likely. I'm jumping in the shower, and will be at the airport in time to play the hurry-up-and-wait game. After that, you'd better rest up, luv. I have plans for you."

The chuckling on the other end of the line sent goose bumps over Rachel's body.

"I hope so. I'll count the minutes until I see you. Cheerio, luv."

"Cheerio."

Rachel hummed tunelessly. The plan for this trip was to get Barbara out of her depressed funk over Dylan; but if she found her soul mate, well, who was to complain? Dylan had always been quietly devious when he was alive; she suspected he hadn't changed much when he'd crossed over.

Rachel looked up and mouthed, "thank you." A puff of warm air played over her face.

Her mouth dropped. A grin spread over her face. "You skunk."

Shedding clothing along the way, she headed to the shower. She felt sure things were falling in place exactly as Dylan had planned.

~ * ~

Steven glanced at his watch, again, and realized only five minutes had elapsed since the last time he'd checked. He pushed his paperwork to the side of the desk. He couldn't concentrate on paperwork if there was a possibility of Barbara, his Barbara, being in this very hotel. He shifted in his chair. Even now, her memory stirred parts of him that had been dormant for nearly a year. Picking up his briefcase, he snapped it open and removed the picture. Sitting back in his chair, he gazed longingly at the twenty-five-year-old snapshot.

Only Ray, his best friend, knew Steven had not been the swinging, single bachelor all the other guys imagined. The Debbie-debacle a year earlier had cured him of indulging in the wild nightlife his ex-wife so craved. *Who knew twenty-two could look so old?* If his son hadn't seen them together, followed him into the bathroom of the restaurant, and informed him Debbie had been his lab partner in college two years previously, he might have made a horrible mistake his ex-wife would have never let him live down.

Even now, he shuddered at the narrow escape. He placed the photo up against the framed pictures of Marc and Alana, and leaned over to flick on the stereo system he'd brought into the office.

The knowledge that the couch in his office also functioned as a hide-a-bed was privy to a chosen few; the floor to ceiling bookcase not only held company books and his stereo, but opened to reveal a closet, private full bathroom, and small kitchenette. When he'd bought the hotel, his marriage was already in trouble, so the architect built in certain design modifications to the plans. He'd spent more nights sleeping in his office than he cared to count.

Turning up the volume on his stereo, he leaned back in his chair, and listened to the oldies station he preferred. Every time he heard Player's 'Baby Come Back', he thought of Barbara. The month it hit the charts, he let her walk out of his life. *I wonder if she thinks of me when she hears it.* He glanced at his watch again. *Will ten o'clock ever get here?*

~ * ~

Barbara let the warm water sluice down her body, taking away any lingering pains she might have experienced. She grabbed the loofah provided by the hotel and furiously scrubbed away all traces of last night's debauchery. She drew in a deep breath, the scent of the vanilla wafting up to tickle her nose. After allowing the water to cleanse away the soap, she turned off the shower and buffed herself dry with the thick towel. A quick fluff of the hair, and she was through. Teeth scrubbed, eye drops administered and contacts carefully placed, Barbara decided to forego makeup and see if Marc's interest was in the image she'd presented last night. If he could stand her without the war paint, he might be worth...

"Get real, Barbara. If you make it through the day without telling him your true age, it will be a miracle." She looked at the image in the mirror and smiled sadly. "But it is a great ego booster to know someone that cute, and young, finds you interesting. Since I didn't make it to Tarpon Springs when I lived here, at least my reactions won't be a lie."

She padded into the bedroom and opened the dresser drawer, pulling out a pair of jeans and t-shirt from the last Def Leopard concert she and Rachel had attended. She smiled.

The group's management had been filming a documentary and spotted the two of them in line. A cameraman and commentator, complete with microphone which he stuck into Rachel's face, had asked them a few questions like—how long had they been fans, did they go to all the concerts, and were they mother and daughter. Rachel, with her usual tact, turned to the commentator and snapped, "Yeah, we're mother and daughter—I'm the mom." The camera crew quickly moved up the line.

"Has that really been four years ago?" Barbara shook her head as she slipped on the t-shirt. She stood in front of the closet looking at her shoes. Looks or comfort? Since she was foregoing makeup, she decided to err on the side of comfort by wearing her tennis shoes instead of the cute wedge sandals she'd packed. With a quick refluffing of her hair, look-see in the mirror, and, glancing at the clock, she decided she was good to go. The time showed nearly ten o'clock; she needed to head toward the lobby. She didn't want Marc knowing her room number quite yet. If things went well today... she might think about giving it to him. Right now, a little mystery wouldn't hurt.

Grabbing her cell phone, she turned at the door and hesitated. "This is ridiculous. This kid is young enough to be my son."

Probably not a bad thing, don't you think? Guarantees you won't get involved and decide to get married, right?

"Oh, sure. Marriage, ha! Not going to happen in my lifetime again."

She opened the door, and a warm puff of wind ruffled her hair.

Don't count on it. The face of Dylan flashed in front of her eyes. He was grinning impishly.

~ * ~

Marc parked his Camaro in front of the hotel. He turned and looked at the building's façade. *I can't believe she's staying at Dad's place. Hopefully, he's busy in his office with paperwork. I'm not ready to share my time with her.* He took his cell phone off his belt and punched in Barbara's number.

"Hi. I'm in the parking lot. If you give me your room number, I can come up and get you. Oh, sure. I'll wait by the front doors. I have a light blue shirt and jeans on. See you in a few."

He would like to have escorted her from her room but she'd seemed, well, terrified of the idea. Replacing the phone on his belt, Marc passed under the covered entry and entered the hotel lobby. The front desk clerk looked up and smiled in recognition.

"Marc!" The lilting tones of her Jamaican accent carried through the air. "Would you like me to call your dad?"

Marc panicked trying to remember her name—it was Candy, no; Sandy, no; Tammy!

"No thanks, Tammy. Just picking up a friend. I'll call him, later." Marc smiled.

"Oh, okay." Tammy grinned in return and answered the phone.

The elevator bell dinged, and the doors opened to reveal Barbara. She stepped into the lobby and moved toward him.

Marc moved forward and caught her hand in his. "You ready to go?"

Barbara nodded.

He frowned slightly. "Where's your purse? I thought you said your friend was coming with us, too."

A sigh unconsciously escaped Barbara's lips. "Rachel surprised me by making other plans. As far as the purse, I have everything I need, right here." She reached into the right back pocket of her jeans and pulled out a small laminated card. "Driver's license." Replacing the card in her pocket, she reached into her left back pocket and retrieved the same size card with an iridescent front. "Credit card." The card went back into its designated spot, and she moved her hand to her right front pocket. She pulled out money and another card. "Cash and room key. And finally—" She reached into her left front pocket. "Lip gloss. I've got everything I need. Oh yeah—" She snapped the cell phone out of its holder on her waistband. "—communication for police calls if you decide to get too fresh." Her eyes twinkled as she shot him an impish grin.

Marc allowed a chuckle to escape. "I've never seen any female travel so lightly."

"If I'm going to buy *souvenirs*, I don't want to be worried about juggling my purse or getting it ripped off. If I can't buy something with my credit card—I don't need it!"

Marc laughed. "Very logical. Shall we leave?"

"I'm ready when you are."

The two walked out the sliding front door.

Tammy looked up and waved.

~ * ~

Steven turned the corner to the front desk, paper and picture firmly in hand, and caught a glimpse of Tammy waving.

"I'm going to make the wake-up call for room 823. I'll be back shortly."

"Boss?"

"Yes, Tamara?"

"She just left." Tamara was pointing to the figures exiting through the front doors.

Steven whipped around to watch the familiar undulating walk of the guest he was certain was his Barbara. "Damn." Steven placed the paper on the counter. "I'm going to the café to get coffee. You need anything, Tamara?"

"Thanks, but no, boss."

Tamara watched her boss plod to the café. His slow gait and defeated expression made her think twice about telling him the guest he seemed so intent on meeting had left with his son.

Fourteen

Marc held the car door for Barbara and, after he'd settled her and himself into the car, he pulled his wallet out and handed her what looked like a business card.

"What's this?" her brow furrowed.

"Read it." The hint of a smile played at his mouth.

Barbara noted the famous figure from a child's board game on the right side of the card. "Go to Jail. Do not pass Go. Do not collect $200.00." She held the card up in her hand. "Again, what's this?"

"If at any time during this day, you feel uncomfortable or threatened, hand me the card, and I will immediately bring you back to the hotel without any questions or arguments. I want us to have a relaxed, fun day. With any luck at all, tonight, when I bring you back, you'll still have the card in your pocket." He started the engine and drove out of the parking lot.

Barbara fingered the card and slid it in her back pocket next to her driver's license. *What a great idea. I'm trying very hard not to fall for this young man, but he's definitely testing my resolve*. "This is a really great idea, Marc. You ought to patent it. I know a lot of women who would love to have the security this brings."

Marc chuckled. "I think Milton Bradley might have something to say about my using this particular card."

"Hmm. Hadn't thought about that; you're probably right. Well, I appreciate the idea behind it—a lot. Now, what is so special about Tarpon Springs that we're going to spend all day there?"

Marc launched into a spiel about the downtown area being listed on the National Register of Historic Places, and the fleet which still fished every day and, of course, the Sponge Docks. He ended by adding, "I just thought it would be a great place to wander around, window shop a little, and maybe, have lunch. There's an aquarium we can visit and, if you're still up for it, we can drive down the coast, a little, to a great bar in Indian Rocks Beach that I know. I figured we just play it by ear; see how the day goes and how tired we are by six. What do you think?"

Barbara nodded. "I think it's a great plan." She sat viewing the passing landscape with wonder. There had been so many changes since the time she'd lived in the area that she really was seeing it for the first time. Within an hour, they had arrived at the outskirts of Tarpon Springs where Marc parked in a secured lot. After he paid for the entire day, the couple meandered toward downtown, hand in hand.

"You know, I'm really quite hungry. Could we find a sandwich shop?" Barbara asked.

"I know just the place. They serve the best gyros on the East Coast." Marc led Barbara toward the center of town. They arrived at a small shop, which had several tables outside, complete with white and blue umbrellas. They chose a table close to the building. A quick glance at the menu, and he went inside and ordered.

"They'll bring out our orders when they're ready." He placed a tall glass of brown liquid and ice cubes in front of Barbara, laying packets of sugar on the table between them. "I hope you don't mind but, in lieu of Ouzo, I ordered raspberry iced tea. Since I didn't know how you wanted it, I brought the sugar along. Personally, I can't drink alcohol before five."

Barbara caught her breath. *Oh no. Here we go with the coincidences. Dylan!* She smiled shyly. "Actually, I've never been able to bring myself to drink in the middle of the day, either. I wind up getting stupid drunk or sick. Of the two, I'd rather be sick. You can recover from sick; you never live down stupid drunk."

"Isn't that the truth? Too bad more people don't realize it. We'd have a lot fewer fights in the club." Marc shook his head.

"You'd also make a lot fewer tips," she said.

"Yeah, you're right. I guess everything has its good points and drawbacks."

The waitress appeared carrying two baskets of food and placed them on the table.

"Good heavens!" Barbara stared at the heaping portions in front of her. "This would make a logger say uncle."

"That's a funny thing to say." He smiled as he sprinkled vinegar and pepper on his fries.

"Look who's talking! What are you doing to your French fries?" She wrinkled her nose. "Ugh. Vinegar on fries. The only people I know who ruin French fries with vinegar are Canadians."

Marc picked up one of the fried potato slices and popped it into his mouth. "Well, my grandparents moved to Florida from Minnesota. I guess, from what my dad says, the town where they lived is pretty close to the Canadian border. He's the one who showed me how to season my French fries so blame him for my bad taste."

"Well, in this case, I can safely say his taste is not all in his mouth."

Attacking the baskets of food, the conversation dwindled between the couple. When Marc had finished, he sat back in the chair and stole glances at Barbara.

Dabbing her mouth, she crumpled the used napkin into the basket, picked up Marc's and took them over to the waste can. She emptied the garbage, placed the plastic baskets on top and wandered back to the table.

“You know we could have done that as we were leaving? You have the reactions of a former waitress." He stirred his ice tea with his straw.

Barbara chuckled. "Busted. That's how I paid—pay for my college. My folks made it pretty clear anything past high school was going to be funded by whatever means I could arrange. I've waitressed, tended bar, cocktailed, worked retail, and temped my way through to my Bachelor's degree. It was worth every night of lost sleep."

"That would also explain the sensible shoes." Marc nodded toward her tennis shoes. "Most of the girls I know would have worn attractive, but impractical, high heels for our date. Frankly, I was glad to see you walk out of the elevator in your tennies and without a ton of makeup. It just reinforces my opinion of what a smart, beautiful woman you are."

Barbara felt herself blushing. She looked at her hands folded on the table. "Thanks."

He leaned across the table and slid his hand under hers. "Why don't we wander over to the Aquarium and see if the dolphins can come out and play?" He watched her face brighten and her luscious lips curve into a shy smile.

"You like dolphins?"

"I spent several summers earning college money by working at Sea World in Orlando. I was fortunate enough to get to know some of the dolphins. They're almost too smart for their own good but, yeah, I like them. Like people, each one had its own separate personality. I could have spent all day just watching them play. Shall we go?"

Barbara nodded and the couple strolled to the 120,000-gallon saltwater aquarium. After discovering the aquarium didn't have dolphins, they hid their disappointment while touring the Sponge Museum. Several hours, and what seemed like a hundred miles, later, Marc turned to Barbara.

"You ready to head to Indian Rocks Beach?"

With her affirmative nod, he steered them back in the direction of the parking lot and slid the Camaro from its parking place merging into the traffic moving south. Neither spoke during the next half hour. When they entered the parking lot of Don the Beachcomber's, it took her a moment to gather herself. She had the sense of having been here before, but she didn't see any familiar landmarks.

"I know the outside doesn't look like much from the road. The best feature can't be seen from here." Marc helped her out of the car and led the way down a narrow path that opened to a beach with an expansive view of the gulf.

Barbara sucked in her breath.

"Beautiful, isn't it?" Marc smiled. He plowed through the sand, holding Barbara's hand as she followed behind him to a tall table complete with an umbrella and two bar stools. Once the two were seated, a bikini-clad server appeared at his elbow.

"What would you like to drink?" She batted her eyes at Marc focusing solely on him.

He jumped, surprise registering on his face.

Barbara squelched the urge to giggle, biting the corner of her lower lip in the attempt.

He turned to her and, with exaggerated emphasis, asked, "What would you like, honey?"

A wicked smirk began to form on her lips. "Well, sugar, I'd love a blended Pina Colada."

Two quick bats of her eyelashes finished the sentence. She watched Marc turn the most intriguing shade of fuchsia she'd seen. Feeling a wave of devilishness creep over her, she leaned over and planted a loud kiss on his cheek. Her reward was another tinge of color to his cheeks, and a look of pure hatred from the server.

"What would you like, Marc?" The blonde with the voluptuous figure poured into the barest of bikinis leaned into him, grazing his arm with her bosom. She pursed collagen-enhanced lips then slid her pink tongue around the inside rim. Batting her big blue-green eyes, she brought the pencil to her lips and, slowly, snaked her tongue out to lick the tip.

Barbara was biting the inside of her cheek. If Marc didn't place his order soon, she was going to blow this girl's best attempt at being sexy by exploding in laughter.

"I, uh, uh, want a Budweiser. Thanks, Tiffany."

As the blonde undulated toward the bar, Barbara could contain herself no longer. She gasped for air between laughing bouts as Marc sat glowing red.

When she finally caught her breath, she couldn't help but ask, "What was that all about?"

He cleared his throat and, after two tries, began to speak. "Tiffany and I used to date."

"I see."

"She decided I was going to make her the perfect husband. I, on the other hand, wasn't looking to get serious. Even if I was, it wouldn't be with someone like her."

Barbara gave him a questioning look.

He quickly amended the course of his explanation, "No, it's not like that. It's just that she wanted a sugar daddy to take care of her; you know, buy her a sports car, a house on Davis Island—that's a rich suburb in Tampa—and a cigar boat to show off to her friends. We only dated for two months, but I had to break it off because I felt smothered by her neediness. She used to be a really nice kid when we went to elementary school together; she was sweet and a lot of fun, kind of a tomboy. I don't know what happened. Guess she grew into a girl." A smile touched his lips. "In light of that, I need to ask you a very big favor."

Barbara raised her eyebrows. "Oh?"

"Would you, uh, um, ah, would you pretend to be my fiancé?" Marc was drawing circles on the table with his finger.

"Why?"

"I didn't realize Tiffany was working here or I wouldn't have suggested we come. If she thinks I'm single, she'll start calling my house, coming to my job, and, in general, making my life miserable. You're so beautiful; she won't doubt that it's the truth."

Barbara thought for a moment. *It can't hurt. Anyway, who'll know? Wait a minute. He just said I'm beautiful!* She glanced at his blushing face. *He is sincere about the compliment and just as sincere about the situation he's facing. I've got nothing to lose.*

"Sure, no problem."

Marc leaned over and kissed her on the cheek. "You're a life saver. Thanks."

"It'll cost ya."

He smiled. "I was hoping you'd say that."

The server sashayed to the table thumping down Barbara's Pina Colada and moving into Marc as she placed his beer on the table in front of him. She spoke lowly into his ear, her lips inches from the curve of his earlobe.

"The beer is on the house, but that"—she nodded her head toward Barbara's drink—"will cost six-fifty."

"Tiffany, how much is the beer?" He pulled his wallet from his jeans pocket.

"I told you, darling, it's on the house." She purred, pushing her cleavage toward him.

"Tiffany, let me introduce you to my fiancé, Barbara." He looked directly into the server's eyes.

The tray slammed onto the table.

"Fiancé?"

Marc turned toward Barbara, took her hand in his, and staring into her brown eyes answered, "Yeah, fiancé. She just agreed to be my wife today at a wonderfully romantic lunch in Tarpon Springs. I'm the luckiest guy in the world, aren't I, Bunnykins?"

Barbara raised an eyebrow and silently mouthed, "Bunnykins?"

The hint of a smirk tugged at the corners of Marc's mouth.

"No. I'm the luckiest girl in the world, Snuggle Bear." She leaned forward and kissed the tip of his nose.

She was moving away. Tilting her head up, he gently pressed his mouth against her soft lips, slowly circling the warmth with his tongue. He pulled her into his embrace and held her, allowing her curves to meld with him. She relaxed into his body. The world, Tiffany, and Indian Rocks beach disappeared as the two hearts began to beat in rhythm with each other.

Marc's reaction to her flip movement surprised Barbara. She'd meant for the nose kiss to appear a bit ridiculous. When he pulled her to him and covered her mouth with his, her common sense disappeared with the moment. The softness of his lips, gentle, almost hesitant sweep of his tongue, and easy shelter of his body made her strain in response. She let herself move into his muscular form, taking comfort in his embrace. It felt good to let down her guard and react like a woman again.

"Oh, puh-lease. Get a room!" Tiffany grabbed her tray and stomped off toward the bar.

Barbara broke the seal of the kiss. She looked into the hazel eyes gently assessing her.

"Wow. That was—amazing."

Marc leaned down and tenderly kissed her forehead.

She closed her eyes and allowed the sensation of his soft lips caressing her skin to linger in her memory.

"Yes, it was, Bunnykins."

Barbara exploded into laughter. "Well, so much for ambiance. By the way, where in the world did you come up with Bunnykins?"

"It was the only thing I could think of on the spot. Which brings up, Snuggle Bear? Why that?"

"Same reason. It was the only thing I could think of on the spot."

"It's a little spooky."

Barbara frowned. "Spooky? Why spooky?"

Marc shuffled on his bar stool, coughed, then cleared his throat. "It was what Tiffany used to call me."

Barbara leaned against the back of the stool. "Who would've thought? No wonder she was so pissed. Oops!"

"No big deal. At least my problem's solved." Marc took a slug from his beer.

"Don't be so sure." Barbara swirled the contents of her Pina Colada in the glass.

"What do you mean?" He looked up at her through a veil of long, blonde lashes.

"Your problems could just be beginning."

Marc drained the contents of his bottle and looked around. His eyebrows knit together in the beginnings of a frown. "I must be dense because I don't see how there could be any problems. Where the hell is Tiffany?"

Barbara leaned forward, took a long drink from her straw, and placed her hand on top of Marc's.

"Let me give you a lesson in Woman 101. First: At this moment, you're in Tiffany's territory. Even if you didn't know she worked here, the minute you saw her, you were at a disadvantage. The management here will take her word over anyone else's if anything happens. You know that from your own bar experience. Second: You came with another woman. Again, not your fault but it gives her the right, in Woman 101, to be angry and not serve you."

Marc started to protest but stopped when Barbara put up her hand.

"This is not up for debate; this is Woman 101—the way it is. It's not logical, because it's about Women!" She popped her eyes open at him and grinned.

"Let's continue. The other problem with number two is not only did you bring another woman but it's obvious the *other* woman is not your sister. What Tiffany sees is you flaunting your new relationship in her face, even if it's been over between you two for a year or more, she still considers you her man. Third, and this is the one that's going to confuse you: she doesn't believe your engagement story. She'll send her friends to find out from your friends if you've really, truly gotten engaged. Pretty soon, all your old girlfriends will start appearing at your job asking questions about your fiancé."

Barbara watched the color drain from Marc's face. The little crease between his eyes and slightly opened mouth told her he was having a difficult time believing what she was telling him.

"Now comes the kicker. In Woman 101, if the man is lying about a relationship, i.e., not really being engaged but saying he is—it's because he still loves you and wants you to be jealous."

"You're joking, right?" Marc's gaze darted toward the bar and back to Barbara.

"Sorry, love. No joke. That's how most women view past relationships—not over until she stands in line at your wedding reception." She held up her nearly finished drink. "If we want another drink, we'll have to go inside to get it." She made a slurping sound with her straw as she finished her Pina Colada. She watched his face begin to wrinkle with worry then, suddenly, a mischievous grin appeared. His hazel eyes danced and he leaned toward her.

The smile spreading infectiously over his face, he winked as he murmured, "We'll just have to work on getting engaged for real, won't we?"

Fifteen

Back at the hotel, Barbara walked along the beach, sandals in hand. The evening had gone almost too well. Marc's closeness had sent her pulse racing and left her short of breath. She raised a hand to her lips reliving the tenderness, and heat, of his kisses. Not since Steven had she felt the lightheaded rush of lust, pure and simple. She had loved Dylan, make no mistake, but it had been a fireplace-hot cocoa-old movie kind of love; not the tear-your-clothes-off-make-love-this-instant kind of love she and Steven had experienced. Each time Marc had kissed her, she'd felt stirrings of animal passion creeping up through her body.

He'd wanted to continue their date. He'd proposed dinner and dancing, but Barbara begged off saying she was still experiencing some jet lag as well as acclimation issues from the heat. The reality was she needed time to think. She hadn't been back in Tampa for more than four days, and she was experiencing the heady rush of attraction, which, in turn, made her feel guilty.

She mulled over the immediate magnetism she felt toward Marc and realized, at some point in the near future, she would have to reveal her true age.

Why?

She stopped and turned around to find herself alone on the beach.

Why?

The question reverberated in her mind. She stopped and gazed out at the reflection of storm clouds on Tampa Bay. The illusion of continuity was perfect until a seagull landed on the water, its wake creating ripples in the scene.

Are you planning to marry him?

"Good heavens, no!" Barbara glanced around to see if she was still alone on the beach.

Then there's no need to tell him your age. He's not the one. He's close, but he's not the one.

"What do you mean close?" She whirled around and found only a seagull staring at her. It squawked and waddled down the beach.

"I must be losing my mind; hearing voices and talking to seagulls. Tomorrow, I'm lying on the beach. No phones, no dates, no talking to birds." She glanced around. "No voices."

She turned on her heel and walked back to the hotel. Stopping at the front desk, she instructed the desk clerk she was not to be disturbed.

~ * ~

Steven sipped coffee at his table in the hotel's café. This situation was beginning to feel like some stupid plot on one of those ridiculous TV shows. He just kept missing his "Barbara".

Should I take a chance and leave a note on her door?

No, he couldn't do that. While he might think about it, the rules he'd set down for his staff applied to him as well. Steven slumped in his chair. There were times he hated being the boss. If he were just an employee... He felt the vibration of his cell phone. Not checking the read out, sure it was his ex-wife complaining that Alana hadn't called yet, he answered.

"Hello."

"Hey, bud. Whatcha doin'?" Ray's voice boomed through the small phone's speaker.

Steven held the receiver away from his ear. "Where are you? I thought you didn't work on Saturdays?"

There was a burst of laughter, and a cacophony of female voices filled the air.

"Hold on a minute."

The noise began to abate. "Is that better?" Ray no longer shouted into the phone.

"Yeah. What's going on, and where the hell are you?"

"I'm at home. I forgot Monica is having a baby shower for one of her nieces today. There must be thirty women here. The noise is unbelievable. How about heading to the marina and taking the Hideout into the Bay for some skiing?"

"Well... I don't..."

"Got a hot date?"

"No."

"Meet me there in an hour. I'm bringing Ray-Ray. His eyes are beginning to glaze over. I'm afraid if I leave him here, the next baby shower will be for my grandchild. Frankly, I'm not ready yet. How about Marc? Want to bring him along?"

"I'll try, but the last time I wanted him to go out on the boat I got some lame excuse about him having to work. I don't think he's into the *dad and me* stuff anymore. See you at the marina."

Steven dialed his son's cell number and the message mode immediately kicked in. He knew with his son that meant one of two things: he was sleeping after a long night or he had a date. In either case, water skiing was the last thing he would want to do. Steven stood, left a tip on the table then walked to his office. Since he'd missed his opportunity to find out if the guest in his hotel was Barbara, he might as well water ski. Work was the last thing on his mind. He chuckled—funny how the memory of one woman could change his outlook.

When they had dated, he was the one who was always ready to play. His parents provided him the means to go to college and encouraged him to enjoy his youth. They weren't thrilled when his "little garage band" met with success. Rock Railroad kept him busier than his father felt healthy for a college student. The only verbal argument they'd had was the year Virgin Records signed Rock Railroad to a contract. Steven's father banned him from the house until he gave up his *hobby*. It wasn't until he read the contract itself that he realized Steven had cut himself a better deal than most: retaining the rights to all the songs he'd written plus ten percent of all royalties, plus retaining rights to the group name and any merchandising associated with it. When Arthur asked his son how he'd managed, Steven smiled and said he'd had an excellent teacher.

Steven packed up his briefcase and left for his condo. He'd change into his slacks and a polo shirt. The Yacht Club restaurant and bar had a strict dress code requiring its patrons to dress appropriately, even at play. Stuffing his swim trunks into his bag, he also packed toiletries. If he was at the marina, he might as well stay a night on the houseboat. The soft lapping of the Bay against the side of the boat would help him sleep. He wouldn't even mind the memories of Barbara that always haunted him when he was there.

Ray and Reynaldo met him in the parking lot, and the three took the stairs down to the berths. Along the way, Steven stored his things in the houseboat and changed into his swimming gear. They started the speedboat and observed the 5 mph speed limit enforced through the marina until they passed the seawalls. Thirty seconds later, Ray had the speedboat dancing across the tops of the small wakes left by other boaters.

Twenty minutes out found them in cool, deep water and Steven sliding over the side to strap on a water ski.

"I'd forgotten how great this feels." He bobbed in the water, his buoyant blue vest providing his lift.

Ray was letting out slack on the towrope at the back of the boat.

"Well, if you'd quit letting your ex-wife run your life, you'd find out a lot of the things we used to do feel great."

The rope was beginning to tighten as Reynaldo slowly inched the boat forward.

Steven yelled, "I don't let my ex-wife..."

Ray turned to Reynaldo and shouted, "Hit it!"

The roar of the speedboat and twang of the towrope drowned out Steven's reply. Ray grinned as he watched Steven bobble. When he regained his balance, it took him but a moment to comfortably ease into slalom skiing.

The afternoon sped by as the three friends took turns skiing and driving the boat. Around 4:30, they decided to go back to the marina. After docking the speedboat, washing off the saltwater and realizing they were starving, they stopped at Steven's houseboat to clean up for the Yacht Club dining room.

Steven made reservations while Ray and Reynaldo showered and changed. Once Steven finished, they walked to the club and sat in the bar to wait for a table. They'd just begun to drink their beers when the young hostess, conservatively dressed in a white shirt and black skirt, escorted them to a table for three along the windows that faced the darkening sky and glassy Bay. Silence fell over the table as the men looked over the expensive menu.

When the waitress arrived at the table and asked if the gentlemen were ready to order, Steven noticed a crease in Ray's forehead, and Reynaldo flipped the menu to the salad and side dish page.

"Don't worry about the cost, guys. This one's on me. You paid for the gas this afternoon. It's the least I can do."

Ray grinned. "Great. I'll have prime rib, medium rare, with rice and a salad with ranch dressing."

Reynaldo added, "Make mine the same."

Steven handed the young lady his menu. "I'll have poached salmon with rice and salad with herb dressing. Thank you."

Reynaldo craned his neck to watch the waitress walking toward the kitchen. "Wow. She is hot!"

"Do you ever stop?" Steven straightened the utensils in front of him.

Ray took a swig from his bottle of beer. "Did we?"

Chuckling, they jumped when a cell phone chirped.

Ray groaned as he reached to his waist. "Probably Monica wanting me to pick up something at the store for the party. I was hoping they'd be done by now."

Steven started to reach to his own belt, the dread of a call from his ex-wife washing over him, when Reynaldo piped up.

"Relax guys. It's for me." The young Cuban bounced up from the chair and answered his phone as he walked out to the covered deck that surrounded the Yacht Club.

The young waitress had returned with the salads for their meals, and Steven tracked her eyes as she followed Reynaldo's path outside. He was gesturing animatedly, and his face glowed with excitement. He snapped shut his phone and, with a triumphant smile, reentered the restaurant and walked jauntily to the empty chair at the table. Sliding into it, he looked into two faces with raised eyebrows.

"What?"

"That was some display." Ray speared a cherry tomato with his fork and popped it into his mouth.

Reynaldo feigned innocence. "What display?"

Steven snickered and rolled his eyes.

"What's her name?"

"Sonya Helmann, and she's the hottest chick in town. We had a business class together last year and, sort of, well, got together. Right after graduation, she got an offer from a firm in Atlanta and moved away. I bumped into her, literally, at Uncle Tito's coffee shop last week and gave her my number. When she didn't call, I was a little disappointed. She has to go to Miami on business but wants to get together tonight and hit all the clubs we used to go to when we were in school. So-o-o-o, Dad, can I borrow the car, please?"

A pair of enormous, pleading green eyes burrowed into Ray.

"How am I supposed to get home?" He quirked an eyebrow.

"Uncle Steven?" Reynaldo flashed a toothy grin.

Ray glanced at Steven. Steven gave a small nod of his head and shrugged his shoulders.

"Fine. But you had better bring it back with the tank full of gas." Ray pulled his keys from his pocket and separated out the car keys. He handed the separate ring to his son.

Dinner progressed with Reynaldo grinning from ear to ear and chattering nonstop. Steven and Ray glanced at each other and smirked. They both knew somebody was going to get lucky that night.

The bill paid and Reynaldo vanished from the scene found the two friends strolling to the houseboat.

"What were you planning to do this evening? Got a hot date?" Ray stepped aboard the boat.

"My big plans are to stay on the boat tonight. I hadn't thought beyond that. If you have to get home, I'll drive you, but, to be quite honest, I'm beat. Been a long time since I've done that much water skiing and this ole' body is beginning to complain."

Ray fell onto the couch and thought for a moment. "I know my wife, and I can bet that there are still half a dozen or more women at the house talking about babies. Mind if I crash here for the night?"

"Nope."

"I'll call Monica and tell her we've decided to have a guy's night. Hey! We can do like we used to before a gig."

Steven slid into the chair opposite Ray. He frowned. "What are you talking about?"

"You got beer?"

"Is water wet?"

"It hasn't been that long ago. Remember how we used to meet at your house on the Island, turn the TV to Channel 24 to watch the AWF matches, drink beer, then head off to the gig? Man, those were the days. Why don't we do the same thing tonight? Only, we won't be heading off to a gig but everything else can be the same."

A smile began to appear on Steven's face. How could he forget? Barbara and Sandy used to roll their eyes and laugh at the theatrics of the wrestlers. At first, they were hesitant to stay in the room with the rowdy band members but, after a few months of dating, the two girls were shouting and laughing with the rest of the group. It had been a crazy fun time.

"Sure. Why not? Here's the remote." Steven tossed the control to Ray. "And I'll get the beer. The matches still on Channel 24?"

"Yep. Every Saturday night." Ray powered up the television and entered the channel.

"How can you be so sure?" Steven handed Ray an open bottle of beer.

Ray grinned sheepishly. "I still watch them. Drives Monica crazy and keeps her out of my den for at least an hour. She'd probably cut the lines to the TV if she knew how much it brings back memories of Sandy. Well, I'll be damned. Look who's the big draw tonight."

Steven pulled on his beer. He started coughing as beer trickled down the wrong pipe. Finally, catching his breath, he choked out, "Bronx Billie. Son-of-a-bitch."

Ray smirked at his friend. "Going to be a good match tonight."

Steven leaned back in his chair, propped his legs on the coffee table, and lifted his beer in salute. "To the good ole' days."

"To the good ole' days."

~ * ~

Bacon. The smell wafted into the master cabin and brought Steven's aching head up from the pillow. He closed his eyes against the brilliant sun streaming through the porthole and drew in a deep breath. The aroma filled his lungs with its tangy essence and brought moisture to his mouth.

The sound of metal crashing to tile and angry words spit out in rapid Spanish snapped open Steven's eyes. He slipped on his shorts and padded down the narrow companionway to the galley. The picture before his eyes induced a laughing fit. Standing in the small galley in front of the stove, attired in jean shorts and one of his mother's flowery aprons, spatula in hand, stood his best friend muttering in English and Spanish.

"Good morning to you, too." Steven sauntered to the nook that served as the breakfast table.

"Aaahhhh!" Ray dropped the spatula, spun around, and glared at Steven. "You scared the hell out of me. Quit sneaking up like that. Jesus, Joseph, and Mary, you could give a man a heart attack." Ray crossed himself and picked up the spatula from the floor. He moved to the sink and washed off invisible dirt.

"And dropping something and swearing isn't a rude awakening?" Steven leaned back against the cushion.

"Oh, yeah, about that—sorry. Didn't break anything, but the pan was hotter than I thought. I grabbed it without a hot pad." He flipped an egg and, grabbing a plate from nearby, placed a couple slices of bacon on the side.

"Yes, well, one usually puts items on the stove to make them hot. At least, that's what my mom always taught me. Got any coffee made?" Steven slipped off the bench seat and moved toward the companionway. "I've got a raging headache that I'm going to fix before it gets any worse."

"There's coffee in the pot on the stove. It's pretty strong so you might want to water it down a little. Not used to making it the old-fashioned way. Monica has an espresso machine."

Steven made his way to the bathroom and opened the medicine cabinet. His parents always kept it well stocked so he knew there would be headache relief. He grabbed the extra strength pain tablets he needed and retreated to the kitchen and coffee.

"You know there's a Mr. Coffee in the cabinet under the counter top, don't you?"

Ray shrugged his shoulders. "I didn't want to seem like I was snooping."

Steven raised an eyebrow. "Ray, we've known each other for how many years?"

"About forty."

"And you've been coming to this houseboat with me for how long?"

"As long as your family has had it."

"I don't think you looking in the cabinets would be considered snooping."

"Well, yeah, but..."

"But, nothing. Were you just being lazy or is it a hangover?"

Ray grumbled. "Every time I lean over my head starts to pound."

Steven rolled his eyes. "Good grief. I'll get you some aspirin." He made his way back to the bathroom and retrieved three of the pain tablets. He returned and placed the pills next to Ray's cup of coffee. Grabbing the full plate off the counter, Steven sat at the breakfast nook and dug into his eggs, bacon, and toast. He realized, as the food began to enter his system, he was feeling more energetic, and his headache was disappearing.

Watching Ray move the food around on his plate, Steven couldn't help but comment. "When was the last time we both got that drunk?"

Ray groaned. "Don't remind me. I'm going to hear about this for the next six months. Add the fact I missed going to church with the family, and was supposed to go to my mother-in-law's about—" He glanced at his watch. "—now, I may have to rent a room in your condo to have a place to sleep."

Ray dropped his head into his hands.

Steven started laughing. Yeah, Ray's wife would be hopping mad, but kick him out? Not likely. She wasn't about to let this Cuban stallion loose on the city of Tampa.

"I doubt it. You know she'll be pissed but kick you out—I don't think so. Besides, what makes you think I want you living with me?"

The ringing of a cell phone put an end to the bantering. Ray pulled his off his waistband and shaking his head replaced the phone.

"Not mine."

"Where the hell did I lay that thing down?" Steven groused. He went into the small living room of the boat and found it on the coffee table. He answered it on the third ring without checking the readout.

Maybe, it's Alana calling from England to let me know she's arrived safely.

"Hello?"

"Hello, Steven."

He blew out an exasperated breath. "Hello, Lisa."

Ray winced at the mention of Steven's ex-wife.

"Did I catch you in the middle of someone?"

In his mind's eye, Steven could see the nasty curl of a smirk on his ex-wife's face.

"No, Lisa. Ray and I were just cleaning up from having breakfast on the boat."

That would elicit a venomous response from her; she'd fought hard to get the houseboat in the divorce settlement as well as the house on Davis Island. She'd never grasped the concept Steven's parents still owned the boat.

"Oh," the frost in her response was worthy of a winter day in the Yukon, "I'm calling to update you on your daughter's welfare."

"Good. I was beginning to worry."

"Were you really?"

"Yes, Lisa, I was."

"Well, she arrived in London after a twelve-hour flight, spent two hours getting through customs, several hours trying to locate her luggage, and, to put it in her terms, 'took the Express to Park Lane Hotel in Piccadilly'. Do you understand that last bit?"

The corners of Steven's mouth turned up slightly. Alana had used the American Express card he'd given her. Good. "Not really. Maybe she's picking up British jargon already. You know how good she was at dialects. Thank you, Lisa. I'm glad to hear Alana is safe and secure. Was there anything else?"

"She also mentioned she was going to email you with details of her flight. You'll be glad to know the movers came in yesterday and picked up my stuff. I left everything else the way it was when we moved into the house, and I told Mirella to clean the place thoroughly. The decision was yours if she was to stay on or not. All right?"

"Thanks, again, Lisa. Did you leave a note with a forwarding address?"

"Oh, you want to keep track of me in my new life?"

"Don't flatter yourself. I just want to be sure you take everything that belongs to you. If you don't want me to have the address, please give it to Mirella, so she may forward any of your stuff we come across."

"Fine."

The phone went dead.

Ray arched his brows in question. "I've never seen you smile after a phone conversation with your ex-wife. What is wrong with you?"

Steven chuckled. "I hadn't heard from Alana, yet, and was beginning to worry. Guess I'll get most of the story on my email. Lisa also mentioned she's gone from the house. She didn't say where she was going, and, to be quite honest, I don't really care, but that means—I get to move back into the house on Davis Island. I like my condo but it never really felt like a home. Now, I'm going home."

Ray let loose a whoop. "Yeah. Pool parties, Monday night football, Saturday night wrestling—yeah!"

Steven held up a hand. "Hold on, there. We're not in our twenties anymore, as is witnessed by this"—he touched his fingers to his temple—"still throbbing headache. You have a wife—a very patient wife, I might add—a houseful of kids, a construction company that has enough jobs lined up to keep you busy for the next three years, and a best friend—me—that owns a busy hotel. Your friend, me, is also trying to put his life back together after an nasty divorce that took entirely too many years to resolve itself. Frankly, I'm looking forward to setting up my drum set in the playroom and playing until my fingers bleed."

"That's it!" Ray jumped up from his seat. His immediate reaction was to clutch his head. "Ooo. Dumb move." He dropped into the chair.

"What's it?" Steven could see, in spite of Ray's pounding head, something had triggered a response from Ray. He was grinning in that goofy way he did when he thought he had a great idea. "What kind of trouble are you brewing for us, now?"

"It's an idea I've been kicking around for quite a while. Monica is always at me to find a hobby that doesn't involve sitting in a bar and drinking. I'd hoped Ray-Ray would take up the drums or guitar and we could get together a family band, but the only thing he ever took up was binoculars to watch the single neighbor across the street."

"Whew. I remember that. Got ugly."

"Yeah, well, six months of restriction and working with my construction company in his spare time only convinced him to go to college. I guess it didn't work out too badly. But I miss playing music and being on stage. Now, with you back in the Davis Island house, we can put the band back together and do weekend gigs."

Ray beamed at Steven.

"Ray, who the hell wants to listen to a bunch of old guys playing music from the seventies? We only had two hits, if you can call them hits, and two so-so songs that made it on the charts. Nobody wants to hear that stuff."

"Geez, Steven, where the hell have you been—living under a rock? Haven't you paid any attention at all to what's happening in music? Have you seen what the kids are wearing these days? Michael G pants are back in fashion, and, if they're vintage—you know, from the seventies—they're selling for three to four hundred dollars each. I was driving Reynaldo to work the other day and let him choose the music in the truck. We nearly had an accident because I swerved when I heard our song '*Left Behind*' on his radio station."

"Oh, come on, Ray, it was just an oldies day. Every so often, when I listen to the Oldies station, what is it—WXGL 107.3—I'll hear '*Revenge*' being played. You know those two songs did pretty good for us. Let me finally pay Mom and Dad something for the house on Davis Island and helped you start up your construction company."

"That's just it, Steven. This wasn't an oldies station. It's WLLD 98.7, the station all my kids listen to and, if they thought for one moment I'd like the music, they'd change it. I asked Ray-Ray if he knew who the band was playing the song. He told me it was a group from Europe called Rock Railroad. Steven—that's us."

"Was Reynaldo impressed?"

Ray cleared his throat and coughed. "Well, it's like this..."

Steven watched his friend squirm in his seat. "Like what, Ray?"

"Uh... I never told the kids about my time in the band. Monica and I agreed it would undermine our authority as parents. I took all my pictures and gave them to my mom to hold until I thought the time was right. I just never got around to it."

"So, Reynaldo has no idea that you played guitar in a rock and roll group who released four albums?"

"No."

Steven started laughing. He laughed so hard he wound up with the hiccups.

"It would—" hic "—be worth starting—" hic "—the band just to—" hic "—watch the reaction—" hic "—of your kids!" Steven stood, picking up their plates, and took the dishes to the sink. "Where's—" hic "—the rest of the—" hic "—dishes?"

Ray shrugged. "I always clean up as I go, makes cooking a lot easier."

"Great. Then—" hic "—all I'll have to wash—" hic "—is these few in the sink."

"Right. Steven, you should really think about starting the band again. You need something to get you out of your house and back into life. You really haven't dated in what?"

He murmured quietly, "A year."

Ray leaned back in his chair, his fingers interlaced behind his head. "A year. Do you know how many girlfriends Ray-Ray has had in one year?"

"No. Wouldn't even venture a guess."

"Well, too many to count. The point is you need to quit moping around."

He turned from the sink to face his friend. "I'm not moping. I'm just waiting to find the right person. I jumped from Barbara to Lisa, and looked what happened. In between the two, I was miserable. I'm not a Casanova like Reynaldo. Dating just for the sake of dating is not my thing. Besides, I have the hotel. The more time I spend there, the more successful the business."

Ray leaned the chair back on two legs. "Your hiccups are gone."

"Good."

"About you spending so much time at the hotel... let me give you a head's up. Your employees' nerves are frazzled."

Steven pulled out a chair and slid down. "Why?"

"They think you don't trust them. They do a job you ask them to do then you come behind them and double-check everything they have done."

"I... I don't. Not really. I'm just..." Steven rested his head in his hands.

"Oh, no. That is what it looks like. I've finally got the crew I want working, and they think I don't trust them." He slapped his forehead. "What an idiot! Reynaldo tell you this?"

"Yeah. He wasn't sure how to handle telling you. He didn't want to appear to *suck up*, but all the employees were beginning to grumble and talk about leaving; even though you pay the best in town and give them benefits, the hovering is getting under their skin. Steven?"

"What?"

"You need to start the band again; to focus on something besides your job. Allow your employees to succeed or fail on their own. I'll bet you still practice and still write songs."

A smile spread across Steven's face. "Uh-huh. One hour every day. Thank God for storage unit rentals." He sighed. "I really do miss the music. When I didn't sign the contract with Cult Explosion, Lisa forbade me to play or tell her about any writing I might be doing. Said if I wasn't going to pursue it professionally, it was just an expensive hobby she didn't want to hear about. I don't think she ever knew I rented a storage unit just to practice. I've had it for twenty years. And yes, I've written hundreds of songs since the break-up of the band. Don't know if they're good or not. Just something I needed to do for myself."

Ray brought the chair down with a thump and slapped his hands on the table, making Steven jump. "Then, it's decided. As of this Sunday in May, Rock Railroad is officially reunited."

"Don't be so fast. It wouldn't be the same without Marcus and Ricky. If memory serves me correctly, Ricky was killed last year in the Nassau-to-Miami cigar boat races, remember?" Steve lifted a brow to emphasize his point.

Ray smirked. "You think you've got this all figured out, don't you?"

"What?"

"Marc has been sitting in on some jam sessions held at the Devine Nine Club every Sunday. Think you know the place, don't ya?"

Steven nodded.

"Well, last week, Ray-Ray and I went to visit your son, Marc, and listen. Seems our old lead player taught his son how to play. Carl plays a killer jazz bass line and holds his own on basic rock and roll songs, too. I went up to say hello, and we, of course, got to talking about the old days of Rock Railroad. Marcus would like to start playing again, and his son wouldn't object to playing with a bunch of old farts. It's all there, Steven. All you have to do is say yes. We can start by playing at the jam sessions on Sundays, then see how things go from there. I'm betting we still have a following."

Steven threw up his hands. "Okay. We'll start practicing at my house on the Island after I get moved in next week. Say a week from Wednesday. Since I own the name Rock Railroad, we can use that or decide on another name. You win, Ray. Now, I need to get back to the condo and start getting it ready for the move, call somebody to put it on the market, and put my stuff together for work on Monday. Is that okay with you?"

Ray jumped up from the table. "Cool! I can't wait." He started singing.

Revenge is a dish best served cold,
Said a man from times of very old,
I've replaced your cold lips
With her warm tender kiss,
Your cold eyes
With her warm loving sighs,

Steven stood up and, throwing an arm around his friend's shoulder, joined in.

The best revenge I know
Is just to let you go,
To start my life anew
Loving her and not you.

The two men high-fived each other and laughed.

"You know, Steven, getting the band back together will drive Lisa crazy."

Letting an evil grin spread across his face, Steven replied, "Yeah. You might call it *Revenge*."

Sixteen

Barbara spread the beach towel over the chaise lounge. Making sure there was no webbing to tattoo her skin, she arranged herself on the supple terry cloth. She drew in a deep breath, tasting the salt in the air. The last vivid memory she had of her previous life in Florida consisted of standing on the snow white sand of Indian Rocks Beach cocooned in warmth, a light breeze dancing across her body, watching the silver Bay reflect a cloud-filled sunset in hues of orange and pink. The recollection had warmed her on many a cold, damp night in Oregon.

Here she was, again, gazing over the turquoise sea, listening to the gentle lapping of waves, and allowing the tendrils of sun to caress her. Her lips curved, and a contented sigh escaped her lips.

"Home again."

Barbara started. Had she really said that out loud? *I guess I did. Oregon was supposed to be a stopover, never a stop. I have always thought of Florida as home.*

Reaching underneath the chaise lounge, she located her bottle of water, the radio-CD player, and her tanning lotion. She slathered herself thoroughly with burn protection, took a swig of her water, and fiddled with the radio. When she'd found the station she'd listened to previously, she plugged in the earphones and leaned back to enjoy the sun. Commercials over, the station started its normal block of music. Barbara rose up from the lounge and tore out the earphones.

"Whoa! Darn it." *Can't expect anything to be the same. I'm not listening to Rap. Not today.*

She plugged the earphones in and started searching the radio waves for a station with music she could tolerate. She stopped when a velvet-toned voice announced, "You're listening to WARM 94.9. Playing today's hits and yesterday's best memories. I'm Don Barber, the voice of Tampa Bay, and today is Dedication Sunday. Got an apology to make? Maybe, you want to send a message to a new friend. Just give us a call here at WARM 94.9 and we'll try our best to play your song and get your dedication out to the one who needs to hear it.

"This next song is from Roger to Christina. He wants you to listen to the words and give him a call. Here's Player with '*Baby Come Back*.'"

Barbara quit her search for a station and lay back in the lounge. The song, which had been haunting her since she and Rachel had started to plan this trip, began to play. Barbara closed her eyes and listened. *Call him, Chris. That's an apology if ever I heard one.*

~*~

Ray put his hand over the phone. "You sure about this, mi corazon?"

Monica slipped her hand around his waist and rose up on her toes to place a delicate kiss on his cheek. "Yes, Papi. I've not seen you this excited since you bought your new boat. Just remember what you have waiting at home." Walking away, Monica slapped Ray on the ass and winked.

Ray sighed. *Yes, things had worked out for the best. Monica was everything he could have hoped for and more.* He turned his attention back to the phone.

"Don. Yeah, it's Ray. How about playing *Left Behind* and dedicate it to Sandy from the one she left behind? And, just a word-up about Rock Railroad—we might be getting back together."

"Are you serious?"

"Yeah, but don't make any major announcements just yet. I've got to convince Steven it would be a mistake not to reform the group. Maybe a little help on your part? Say, asking the public to call in or email their support?"

"Consider it done."

"I owe you, Don."

"Yeah, you do. Trust me. I'll take you up on it if the group gets back together."

"Great. Talk to you later."

Ray hung up the phone and bounced into his garage. Monica was right. He hadn't felt this good since he'd bought the ski boat. Ray put on his headphones, picked up his guitar, and began to limber up his fingers with scales. He'd never stopped playing, but now there was a purpose to his practice. He closed his eyes and let the music direct his fingers.

~ * ~

After the Player song, another tune began and, before she realized it, Barbara was singing along with the radio.

Barbara felt moisture on her arm. She looked into the sky but saw only cerulean openness.

"That song was dedicated to Sandy from the one she left behind. For those of you who have lived in a cave for the last twenty-five years, that was *Left Behind* from Rock Railroad, written by Steven Rodgers, one of our own Tampa residents and a friend of mine. Say Steven—when are you going to resurrect Rock Railroad? A lot of fans have been asking.

"Hey guys! I have an idea. Why don't we let Steven know how much we'd like to see them in concert again? Maybe a new album. After all, if Duran Duran can get back together after twenty years; why not Rock Railroad? Call me at 247-5222 and let me know if you want to see Rock Railroad reunite. Or email me here at the station; that's DonB at WARM nine-four-nine dot com with your replies. Maybe, if we all work together, we can get our own Rock Railroad back in the studio."

Barbara couldn't believe her ears. Steven was still in the area! Should she look him up? *Naw, he's surely married by now. Should just leave well enough alone. After all, it was over twenty years ago.* Barbara shuddered. *He could look like any or all of the Rolling Stones.*

She wiped the unbidden tears from her eyes and reapplied lotion to her face. Maybe she would just lie here and snooze a bit. She was still feeling tired and had told Rachel she was going to rest. Speaking of which—Barbara hadn't heard from her best friend. *If she doesn't call today, I'm getting a hold of her tonight no matter the time.* The sun tugged at her eyes, and she gave into the urge to sleep.

~*~

Steven stepped out of his SUV mindlessly humming a familiar tune. He gathered up his belongings and entered his condo.

"I need to make a list." He walked into the kitchen tossing his gym bag on the couch as he walked past. Opening the catch-all drawer, he pulled out a pad of a paper and a pen.

"Let's see: thoroughly clean condo." He looked around. "It needs it, then call Maria Gutierrez at Coldwell Banker to do the listing, start packing up my stuff." He began to tap the pen on the counter. "...and get over to the storage unit. I want to spend a couple hours on my drums finishing that song. Seeing Barbara, or her look-alike, has given me the push I need to get it completed. I'll finish doing the recording and give Ray a copy. See what he thinks. Maybe, just maybe, if Rock Railroad gets back together, we can put it on an album."

He put down the pen and leaned against the kitchen counter. A smile spread across his face. *The thought of playing again with the group really revs my jets. I didn't realize how much I missed the band; Hell, how much I missed playing in front of an audience. Now, if the guest in my hotel is Barbara, and we could share this together that would be frosting on the cake.*

Pulling his wallet from his pocket, he retrieved an embossed business card. He dialed the number shown and left a message for Maria Gutierrez. He'd just replaced the phone in its cradle when it rang.

"Hello?"

"Steven?"

"Yes."

"This is Maria Gutierrez. I heard your message on my answering machine and was desperately trying to pick up before the machine did. Spilled my coffee in the process. What can I do for you? You're not going to put the house on Davis Island on the market, are you?"

Maria sounded so hopeful Steven was almost sorry to tell her no—almost.

"No, Maria. I'm going to put the condo on the market. I've finally gotten my home back and will start moving on Monday."

"Steven, that's wonderful. Eduardo always spoke so highly of that house and the fact you had your own music room next to your bedroom."

Steven chuckled. Eduardo Gutierrez was one of the most talented keyboard players in the Southeast. During a six-month hiatus from Rock Railroad, Steven had stretched his music wings and played with the Cuban Nights Dance Band that Eduardo led. They'd had more than one practice in his music room at the house on Davis Island.

"What do you want to ask for the condo, Steven?"

"Exactly what I paid."

"You're joking, right?" Disbelief vibrated through the phone.

Steven smiled. "No, Maria, I'm not."

"Steven, you've been in that condo for five, no six, years and, frankly, the value has skyrocketed. Why wouldn't you take advantage of the market?"

"I can't explain it, but, I know I don't want to increase the price. Just add enough to make a good commission, and put it on the market as soon as you possibly can. Do you still have the pictures from when you sold it to me?"

"Somewhere."

"Use those. I haven't made any major changes except to have the unit repainted last year, and I used the same colors that were here. Maria?"

"Yes?"

"I'd appreciate anything you could do to move this quickly. I'll even dedicate the next gold record to you."

"Did I hear you say gold record?"

"Uhm, yes."

"Steven? Are you putting the band back together?"

"I'm thinking about it."

"Well, that's the best news I've heard in a long time. Wait until I tell Eduardo. He'll be jazzed. He always liked Rock Railroad. Said there was a lot of Cuban influence in the music, and we all know where that came from." Maria laughed.

"At this point, I'm just thinking about it so hold off on telling Eduardo. I will be sure you two are among the first to know when I make the final decision."

"Ohhh! Just like a man! Tell me something then tell me to keep it a secret! Aaahh!"

Steven heard her sigh.

"All right, but only because I want this sale, and I want that dedication when you make the final decision to get back together—and you will."

"Thanks, Maria."

"You're welcome, I guess. But I expect the dedication to be in bold print. If I have any questions, I'll call you. Do you want me to call you before I show your unit?"

"No, just bring them in. I'll be at work during most of the time you'll be showing. I would prefer no one come after eight in the evening, if you don't mind. You know I usually work weekends so that won't be an issue. Again, thanks, Maria."

"You're welcome, Steven. I'll be in touch."

Steven whistled as he began to clean. *I can't believe how much better I feel.* He grabbed the vacuum cleaner and, with a vengeance, started in the living room.

~ * ~

Barbara started awake. *Oh my gosh, I've been sleeping! I hope I didn't snore*. She giggled. *If I did, anybody close by would just push me back in the water and tell me to swim free.* Looking down at her slim body, she thought. *Well, maybe not.* Barbara glanced up and down the beach. A few people were strolling along the sand looking at the shoreline and toeing the sand in search of the perfect shell, but she couldn't see anyone else sunbathing. *I've been in Oregon too long. Most of the folks around here think it's too cold to lie out. Good! Means I don't have to fight for a spot.*

The faint trilling of her cell phone interrupted her thoughts and initiated her in a frantic search through her beach bag. Finally locating her phone, she answered just before the signal would have dropped the caller into the message mode.

"Hello?"

"Cheerio!"

"Rachel! I was about to send out the seals to locate you."

"The Navy Seals?"

"No. Real seals. I figured you and Robart would be sitting in some fish and chips place that real seals would be able to track better than the Navy boys. Besides, they're cheaper to hire. Just promise them a few free meals, and they work fairly hard. Where the heck have you been, girlfriend? I was beginning to worry. It's been over twenty-four hours."

There was a slight hesitation before Rachel replied.

"I almost got on a plane and came right back. I made it through customs in record time according to several travelers at the airport, retrieved my luggage and headed for the curb to wait for Robart. Now, I had no idea what he'd be driving but I'd know those eyes anywhere, so I figured I'd be able to spot him a quarter mile away. Well... I sat, and I sat, and I sat. Finally, when my bones froze clear through, I went inside and sat on my bag. Two hours later, he showed up in a two-seater sports car. Found out later it's a 1969 MGB. Robart apologized profusely, and stored my bag in the smallest trunk I've ever seen. Excuse me, boot—smallest boot I've ever seen. Thank God, I decided to pack light and use my credit card if I needed anything."

"Rachel, this is beginning to sound like a familiar bad pattern."

"Hold on before you make any rash decisions."

Barbara literally bit her tongue. Rachel was a fully grown woman and her best friend. She'd watch this passion play unfold and, when it was over, pick up the pieces—as usual.

"All right."

"We drove from the airport around London then out to his home in a town called Wennington in the Borough of Havering. When I get settled in, I'll send you a detailed email about his house and the history of the town and the borough. It took us two hours just to get past London, and another hour to get through the narrow streets in the town where he lives. Barbara, the town has been around since the twelfth century!

"Close to downtown London, they're jammed into every conceivable spot they can find to build. I was dreading the thought of Robart living in that sardine can but when we sailed past the turnoffs and into the countryside, I started to breathe easier. He lives in an area called 'The Green Belt.' It means that the Borough Council Members must approve all building. Barbara, it was like being back in Oregon."

"Then, does this mean you're not coming back to Florida? Should I ship all your stuff to you from here?"

Barbara could hear Rachel roll her eyes.

"Give me a break. I've worked on you for ten years to get you to take me to Florida. I guess I'm thrilled that England isn't too different from what I'm used to seeing. Since Robart and I settled in, he's been everything I had hoped he would be. I'm falling hopelessly in like. I plan to enjoy every minute with him I have. This time next week, we'll be flying into Tampa, and you'll be stuck with me, again. I'll call you the night before we leave and let you know what time I'll be getting back. I want an explanation of the last comment you made before I left."

Barbara smirked. She knew Rachel hated being in the dark about anything.

"Well, girlfriend, that's a conversation we'll have when you get back to Florida and not before. Besides, I'm guessing your cell bill is going to be astronomical if we keep talking. Call me when you have a definite date and time of your arrival."

"Hmph. Always with the trump card, huh? Okay. But just to spite you, I'm going to enjoy every single minute I'm here."

"Fine. And Rachel?"

"Yes?"

"Be careful. I don't mind losing you to Robart, but I don't want to lose you permanently."

"I promise. Barbara?"

"What?"

"Love you, girlfriend."

"Love you, too. Now go be with your beau. Bye."

"Cheerio."

Barbara grinned at her friend. She was picking up the jargon and would drive Barbara nuts when she returned. Well, she had a week to explore old haunts that would bore Rachel so she'd just make the best of the situation. She turned over to lie on her stomach and plan the next few days. The sun caressed her back and soon Barbara found herself giving into the urge to sleep.

Go house hunting.

Barbara's eyes snapped open. She lifted her head and looked around to see who had the nerve to invade her section of beach. No one was within a hundred yards of her.

Go house hunting.

"What!" She popped her head up again to stare down a deserted beach. She pushed up on her elbows. "What's going on?"

Barbara. Go house hunting. You always considered Florida your home so buy yourself a place to live.

"Dylan?" Barbara whispered the name.

Yes, Winkie. Your life in Oregon is over. If you stay in Salem, my brother John will never heal because of his guilt over my death and his love for you, his sister-in-law. Find your happiness here in the place you've missed for so long. Go house hunting, Barbara.

"But..."

We will always be connected, my love, but as I told you before, it's time for me to move beyond this plane. We'll meet again when the time is right. But that won't be for a long time. Enjoy living, Barbara.

"But Dylan, where will I start to look?" Barbara's eyes scanned the top of the small dune behind which she had chosen to sunbathe.

Open the phone book, Winkie. You'll know when you see the name that the agent is the right one. The next time you see me will be at your wedding.

"I'm never getting married again."

Never is a very long time, love. Not even I know how long. Find your home.

"There are so many realtors..." Barbara stopped. The sound of her voice echoed back to her hollowly from the small rise of sand.

"Dylan? Dylan?"

There was no reply, no warming sensation in the back of her mind. Barbara shivered as a cool breeze wafted over her skin. Looking up, she saw a single, white, cotton ball of a cloud hovering over the sun. She glanced at the read out on her cell phone and realized it was nearly three o'clock. By the time she gathered her belongings, drove back to Tampa, and cleaned up, it would be nearly five thirty. The growling of her stomach convinced her it was time to pack up and leave. Besides, she had to start hunting for the perfect house.

Seventeen

Marc sat back in his office chair. He'd just read the email from his sister, who was adjusting, quite well, to England and the English way of life. He knew she would. Alana was able to fit into any situation with ease. Marc had been a bit jealous of her ability to master her surroundings; he was usually tongue-tied and awkward.

He slipped his hands behind his head and interlocked his fingers as he leaned back.

"But Barbara..." A smile played across his lips. "Yesterday was... amazing."

"What was amazing?" Aaron, coming through the office door, had heard the last of Marc's statement and, seeing the computer screen lit, leaned over Marc's shoulder to read the email from Alana. "Nice to see Alana has things well in hand, as usual. What was amazing?"

"My date with Barbara."

"Did you get lucky?"

Marc dropped forward in his chair and reached out to punch Aaron in the arm.

"No. Barbara's not that kind of girl. She's... she's a lady. And I treat her as such. Who's holding on line one?"

Aaron smirked. "Oh, yeah. A very rude, cranky Tiffany is demanding to speak to you."

Marc groaned. "Barbara told me this would happen."

"Is there something I should know?" Aaron's smirk widened.

"I'll explain later." Marc sighed. "Can't put this off. Better handle it now."

He picked up the phone and punched line one. "Devine Nine, this is Marc speaking. How can I help you?"

"Why is it your roommate, and best friend, doesn't seem to know a thing about your... engagement?"

Marc grimaced. Barbara had warned him but, in all honesty, he thought she was just being silly. He'd been sure telling Tiffany of his engagement would put an end to his problems with her, not open up a new set. "Since we've been broken up for over two years, Tiffany, I don't see how that's any concern of yours."

The frosty silence at the other end of the phone seemed interminable.

"If there's nothing else, I have a business to run."

"I think the reason you lied to me is because you still care. This isn't over, yet. You haven't seen the last of me, Marc Rodgers." Tiffany slammed the phone down.

Marc sighed as he leaned back in his chair. It was uncanny how Barbara had predicted everything that had just happened. Now, a parade of Tiffany's friends and all his old girlfriends would be coming to the bar to ask if he was off the market. He'd have to enlist his staff to be accomplices in this ruse. With any luck, he could make this rumor a fact.

Marc went into the bar and sat on a stool. "Aaron? I need to talk to you."

The brunette bartender finished washing the glass then leaned against the back bar crossing his arms. A lopsided smirk spread over his tanned face.

"I'm listening. I wondered when I'd get the full story."

"Yesterday when Barbara and I were out," Marc started.

Aaron's eyebrows shot up.

He frowned slightly as he continued, "As I was saying, we spent the day in Tarpon Springs. Near the end of the afternoon, I asked if she wanted to see Don the Beachcombers. She thought it sounded like fun, and we drove to Indian Rocks Beach. It was a great day to sit at the outside bar so we headed through the sand to the table where we always sit. You know the one."

Aaron nodded as he shifted his weight from one foot to another.

"Well, we're sitting at the table commenting on the beautiful sunset..."

Aaron bit his lip to suppress a smile.

Marc glared at him as he moved on with the story, "Anyway, Tiffany shows up in the *uniform* all starry-eyed and breathless."

"Uh-oh."

"Tell me about it."

Aaron leaned forward and placed his elbows on the bar. "What'd you do then?"

Marc shrugged. "What could I do? I ordered for both of us because Tiffany was being a bitch and ignoring Barbara, and, when she left to fill the orders, I asked Barbara to do me a favor. I asked her to play along with anything I might say when Tiffany returned. She agreed. So-o-o, I introduced Barbara to Tiffany as my fiancé. Told her we'd spent the day in Tarpon Springs, and Barbara had said yes when I'd asked her to marry me during lunch."

Aaron rolled his eyes and started chuckling. "This was your brilliant solution?"

Marc shrugged. "I thought it would get her off my back. It was very spooky when Barbara called me by the same nickname Tiffany had always used. Needless to say, Tiffany was breathing fire by the time she left the table. I had to go get our next round of drinks because she'd disappeared. Barbara told me she'd call to verify if I was telling the truth or lying. She also said all my old girlfriends will probably be coming in to check on the rumor. So, I need your help, too. Just tell everyone on staff if anyone asks about the engagement, they're to say they don't mettle in the boss' business, and if the patron needs the information, they should come in first thing in the morning or on my Friday night shift to talk to me about it. It's going to be a bit hairy for a while."

Aaron couldn't contain himself any longer. He started guffawing, doubled over, and clutched his sides. "Man, you blew it this time, didn't you?"

Marc frowned thunderously. "Will you help or won't you?"

Aaron nodded still clasping his sides and shaking. "How long do we have to keep up this charade?"

"Until I can get her to say yes for real."

"This is still part of the joke, right?" Straightening up, the smirk had disappeared from Aaron's face.

"No. We spent all day together, and, spare me the laughter; I missed her the minute I dropped her off. She's intelligent, sure of herself, easy to talk to, and when we kissed... skyrockets. My insides turned to jelly, and I couldn't have walked across the beach if you'd held a gun to my head. This sounds crazy, but I think I might be falling in love. It's like we've known each other all our lives, it's so easy being with her. I don't want the feeling to stop."

Aaron leaned over the bar and looked directly into his friend's face. "What kiss?"

"I think it started out as a way to make Tiffany disappear. We were at the Beachcomber's, Tiffany was being—unwelcoming—and Barbara leaned over and kissed me on the nose. I just pushed it a little further and moved my lips into the place of my nose. At that point, I couldn't have told you where I was. Everything disappeared." Marc's eyes misted over, and his face softened.

Aaron stood up. "You've got it bad. I'll make sure everyone tells the same story. And Marc?"

"Yeah?"

"I don't want to hear about it for the next three years if she doesn't say yes."

"I swear." Marc held up a hand, his eyes twinkling. "However, I don't think it'll be a problem."

"Yeah, whatever. We need to start putting this place together for the jam session. I heard Carl Dillman say he and his dad were going to show up tonight." Aaron began to stack small drink glasses on the bar in front of the mirror.

"That'll bring in business. If their friends come to watch like they did last time, I may do better business tonight than I did Friday night." Marc stood up and maneuvered his way around to the working side of the bar. "I'm headed into the cooler to see what we need. I may have to make a trip to the store for beer. We're not due for a delivery until Monday."

The two friends busied themselves. Jam night had been an idea Marc hit upon when he first bought the bar. The slowest night of the bar business had always been the night the band wasn't playing, and, while it was a refreshing break for the bartenders and waitresses, it cost money to keep the bar open; closing it would lose important clientele—musicians and their groupies. Marc noticed, on the few Sundays when he had gone to other clubs that were holding jam sessions, even when the musicians played six days a week, they came out to play just for fun on the seventh. So he tried it at his own club and found, when the word got out, business was as good or on occasion better than during the weeknights when the band played.

Marc emerged from the frosty cooler. "Aaron!"

"What?" He popped his head up as he stood.

"I'm heading to the store for more beer. Do we need anything else? I don't want any surprises tonight."

"Lemons. We're nearly out. If Dennis shows up tonight with Cindy, we'll be making Long Island Ice Teas until our fingers bleed. You know how she gets if everything isn't 'just right.'" He moved to the drain area and started slicing the lemon he held in his hand.

"Good lord, yes. I don't want a repeat of the scene she made two weeks ago. Okay, beer and lemons. Anything else?"

Aaron shook his head and wiped his forehead. Marc was right. The scene Cindy had pitched two Sundays earlier because there were no lemons for her drink was classic. He didn't want a replay, either.

~ * ~

Ray looked at Monica, guitar case in hand. "You're sure you won't be mad?"

"Listen, Papi, if Rock Railroad gets back together, you'll owe me one helluva kid-free vacation to anywhere I want to go. Got it?" Monica stood with her arms crossed, a smile lighting her face.

"Count on it, Corazon." Ray leaned down and kissed the tip of her nose. "Count on it."

He placed the guitar case in the back seat of the car and got in the front. Pulling into the street, he waved at his wife standing in the doorway. *I did make the right decision all those years ago. I don't think I could live my life without her.*

He turned the radio station from the Cuban music Monica had it on to WARM 94.9 in time to catch StevO Z asking the listening audience to email their answers to the question, "Do you think Rock Railroad should reunite?" Ray smiled. This idea was picking up like a speeding train. There was no stopping them now. He punched in the speed dial number he wanted and pulled over to the side of the road.

"Hey, it's Ray. That rhymes; guess I'm still a poet. Listen, I know you have to work tomorrow, but I don't think I want to wait until next week to start playing. How about meeting me at Divine Nine? It's jam night. Might be fun to get up and play with some of the kids—see if they can hack playing with *real* musicians. Starts at eight. Call me if you're not going to be there, otherwise, I'll expect to see you." He hung up and, swinging back into traffic, began to whistle.

~ * ~

Steven listened to the message on his voice mail. Yeah, he did have to work Monday, but it wasn't like he hadn't put in a few all-nighters in his time; besides, he was bored with cleaning. He doubted Maria would have anyone to show the condo to before his cleaning lady came in on Tuesday.

"I'll just pay Lenore double and have her clean like my mother was coming to visit. I was going to practice at the storage unit, anyway; playing in front of people again will sharpen my riffs. If we put Rock Railroad together, I'll need to get used to seeing and hearing a crowd. Now, where did I put those Michael G pants? Hope I can still get into them."

He showered, washing the cleaning grime from his body, and, as he buffed his body dry, walked toward his bedroom whistling. Things were looking up. He was moving into his family home, and he was going to be playing in front of live listeners, even if only for a few minutes. He was determined to find out this week if the guest in his hotel was his Barbara or not. It was time he moved forward.

"Aha!" He took the pair of black button pants from their cellophane-covered hanger and held them to his body. "Now, if they still fit." Dropping his towel, he slipped his form into the tight pants. He squatted, then stood looking into the mirrored closet doors. He lifted each leg to his chest then sat on the bed. Easily getting up, he grinned at his reflection.

"They still fit. Guess all this recent debauchery is helping me slim down. Well, I'm not Flea from the Chili Peppers so I'd better find a shirt to put on over this." He went to the bathroom and quickly dried his hair, shaved the stubble of two days off his face, and lightly splashed on some Aramis cologne. Back in his room, he moved to the back of his closet and located the black shirt he'd always worn with the pants. His black ankle boots completed the look. Going to his jewelry box, he opened the top and, with extra care, removed a delicate gold chain with a filigreed Aquarius figurine. He placed it around his neck, a sad smile touching his lips.

"I wish you were going to be there, Barbara." He fingered the golden form that rested above the tuft of silver and blonde chest hair at the base of his throat. "This necklace always brought me good luck. Maybe it will help me get over the 'has-been' jitters."

Stopping by his home office, he pulled open a drawer in his bookcase-storage unit and retrieved the drumsticks he'd been practicing with as well as a new set still in their wrapper.

"Might as well be prepared." Grabbing his keys from the kitchen counter, he started humming "Revenge" as he started the car. He adjusted the rearview mirror and winked at the image. He hadn't felt this exhilarated in a long time. He just hoped Marc wouldn't be too surprised. Oh well. He was old enough to get over it.

Steven backed the car into the street and started warming up his voice by singing *Revenge* all the way to the club. Exiting the SUV, he felt his stomach begin to flutter.

"Suck it up, old man. You're just sitting in on a jam session. No one will know who you are." He strode through the door of the club, nodding at Evan and searching the room for Ray. The size of the crowd surprised him. Clinking of ice in glasses, voices rising in volume, and the cocktail servers yelling at the bartenders sent a wave of reminiscence over him. He began to unconsciously twirl the drumsticks in his hand.

"Dad! What are you doing here on a Sunday night?" Marc held a bottle mid-air as he looked in shock at his father.

Aaron let loose a low whistle. "Whoa, Mr. Rodgers. You are stylin'. I'm bettin' you'll be getting lucky tonight."

Steven smiled as he nodded at Aaron. "Thanks, Aaron. I'm not here to get lucky. Just dropped by to sit in on the jam session."

Marc's mouth, which had been open in surprise, snapped shut. "Sit in on the jam session? What are you going to do? Sing?" The grimace on his face made Steven laugh.

"Maybe, I'll sing if the guys play something I know. Mostly what I'll do is play the drums." He twirled the drumsticks in his hand. Seeing Ray waving near the dance floor, he ambled toward the table.

Aaron turned to Marc. "Drums? He plays the drums and sings? Why didn't you ever tell me?"

Marc finished making the drink, tossed the order form on the server's tray and turned to Aaron. "Because I never knew he could play drums or sing. I remember lullabies as a kid but as we got older, Dad started working a lot more. There was never any music in our house except what played on the radio.

"The grand piano in the formal living room was for looks only. Neither Alana nor I took music lessons and, I don't know about Alana, but I can't carry a tune in a bucket. I just hope he doesn't make a fool of himself."

Marc turned toward the sound of a small ruckus near the dance floor. His father, Ray, Carl Dillman and his father, Marcus Dillman, were lustily greeting each other; shaking hands, slapping each other on the back and man-hugging. He shook his head. Maybe he could pull one of the cocktail waitresses to tend bar and hide in the office.

The lights dimmed, and the musicians on stage began to tune up. Marc watched as Carl and Marcus Dillman clambered on stage, opened their instrument cases, and pulled out their guitars. Carl was playing a Fender Jazz Bass, and Marcus was tuning a seventies' model Flying V six-string guitar. The band started with several Allman Brother tunes and followed with a couple of Leonard Skynyrd songs. Marc found himself leaning on the bar, tapping his toes, and watching as the audience did the same.

At a break in the first group of songs, Marcus stepped to the microphone and announced, "I'm going to bring up some old rock and roll buddies of mine to play a few tunes you older folks might remember. Would Steven and Ray come up to the stage?"

Marc felt his shoulders tighten and his stomach roll. His father walked across the floor with his Uncle Ray, up the steps, and entered the stage. A gasp went up from the audience.

An older blonde sitting at a stool at the bar exclaimed. "It can't be! It is!"

Her brunette companion answered, "No, you can't be right. I thought he died last year in the boat races to the Bahamas."

The blonde turned, "That was Ricky Thompson, the bass player."

Taking a sip from her drink, the brunette responded, "Well, when they start playing, we'll know. No one could sing *Left Behind* like Steven Rodgers."

Marc stumbled, catching himself on the back bar. *My dad, a singer? Not possible!*

The group hit a few chords, retuning when the audience groaned at the sour notes. Marcus leaned to the mike. "We'll start with a little tune that helped some of us pay our mortgage. Steven?"

Steven started the beat with his drumsticks in the air and the group, now just the three original members of Rock Railroad plus Marcus's son on bass, opened their part of the session with *Revenge*. They followed with *Money Man*, *Rock Hard*, and ended with *Left Behind*. Finishing the songs which had put them on the charts, they continued with a set that had been their staple when they were playing the club circuit.

Marc leaned against the back bar, his arms crossed. *I can't believe this. My dad plays drums and sings.* The realization made him angry. *Why didn't he ever tell me?*

Aaron stood next to his friend, adopting the same pose. "They're pretty damn good, aren't they?"

~ * ~

When the set ended, no one in the audience moved. Steven grabbed a bar towel provided and wiped his forehead. He was about to tell Ray 'I-told-you-so' when the audience started clapping. The sound exploded throughout the room. He climbed from behind his drums and came out front to stand next to Ray. Everyone in the place was on their feet whistling and clapping.

"I don't believe it." Steven shook his head.

Ray turned, a lopsided smirk covering his face. "I told you so."

Steven rolled his eyes. *The words right out of my mouth*. He tried to come back with a snappy reply but found the words drowned out by the audience chant.

"Rail-road, Rail-road, Rail-road."

Steven put his hand up. Five minutes later, the audience silenced. He motioned for them to sit down, and they complied.

"So you think this is Rock Railroad?"

The crowd roared.

"You sure?"

Another roar.

"Would you like to see Rock Railroad come out of retirement?"

The whistling, foot-stomping, and clapping made any attempt at talking impossible. Steven held up his hand again. "Okay, okay guys. It's been a long time, and I suspect we'll have to start from the bottom, BUT we'll give it a shot. Happy?"

The crowd's response was enthusiastically loud.

"We need to take a break because we're old men, guys, but if you want, we'll come back and jam some more."

Marc had never seen any band get the response his father and godfather were receiving. He turned to Aaron.

"Who the hell is Rock Railroad?"

Aaron grinned. "Apparently, your father and uncle."

Eighteen

Barbara walked into the living room fluffing her short hair with the towel. Showering after a day at the beach always made her feel squeaky-clean. She plopped down on the sofa and pulled the room service menu from the end table. After she phoned in her order, she flicked on the TV and channel surfed. In her memory, she recalled seeing a real estate station. Finally, locating what she was looking for, she watched for the forty-five minutes it took her meal to arrive. Signing for her chicken Caesar salad, she continued to watch the homes for sale parade across the television screen. Just as she was about to turn the station, the face of an agent caught her attention.

"Hi, I'm Maria Gutierrez. I grew up in Tampa, and knowing the town makes me feel I can help you locate whatever your real estate needs dictate. Contact me at 245-3111. Let me help you find the perfect home for your family, whether it be one person or many. I can locate the best property and negotiate the best price. Call me."

Barbara's hand had stopped, fork in air, romaine lettuce and chicken dangling mid-bite. The face was so familiar. She put down her food and picked up the phone and dialed the number on the screen. When the recorded message ended, Barbara found herself speechless. *What do I say?*

That you're looking to buy a place to live.

"Hi. This is Barbara Hamilton Langley. I saw your ad on the TV and would like to speak with you regarding the possibility of looking at some places to buy. I'd like to discuss the particulars: price, size, etc. when we meet. I'm available anytime after nine in the morning. I'll be at this number for the next three and a half weeks." Barbara gave the number of the hotel and her room number. Putting the phone back on the hook, she sat on the couch and finished her meal. Her skin was tingling, and a flutter began in the pit of her stomach. She smiled as she surfed through the channels on the television.

I'm coming home.

~ * ~

Maria called the office to check her voice mail. It was a ritual she'd started four years ago when the first TV showings had begun. She'd come back from a weekend away and found sixty voice messages relating to the homes featured on the show. From that point forward, Maria checked her office message machine every two hours. Being successful did have its down points. The first two calls were Looky-Lou's probably trying to fix a price on their own house; Maria could tell by the wording of their messages. The third call intrigued her. A possible client, Barbara Hamilton Langley, was looking to buy in the area. The fact she was trying to buy in the area wasn't intriguing; it was the name. Something about the name niggled at her memory. She picked up the phone and dialed the number given by the woman.

"Thank you for calling the Sheraton. This is Tamara. How may I help you?"

"Room 823, please."

When the front desk connected the line to the room, it took a moment before someone picked up the phone. The instant she heard the voice, Maria knew why the name was so familiar.

"Hello?"

"Yes. This is Maria Gutierrez from Coldwell Banker returning your call. I understand you're interested in looking at a place to buy here in Tampa?"

"Wow. That was fast. Yes, Ms. Gutierrez, I am." Barbara felt a tug at her memory

"Well, Ms. Langley, can you give me an idea of where you might be looking to buy? How large a home are you interested in seeing? Is money an issue? I'll be able to set up a few places for tomorrow with that information."

"That soon?"

"Yes."

"Well, I was hoping to look on Bayshore Boulevard or Davis Island. I can go seven figures but am hoping to keep it below that. It will be just me, I'm a widow, and maybe a critter or two, but a comfortable size home anywhere from twelve hundred square feet to three thousand square feet will do. I don't need a pool, but I won't say no if the property already has one. Outside of that, I really don't care."

"Let me make some calls, and I'll get back to you tomorrow. Let's meet at my office at ten. I have a home I'd like to show you that's just off Bayshore Boulevard in the Hyde Park area."

Barbara's breath caught in her throat. "Has it deteriorated since the 1970s?"

That's it! This is the Barbara Hamilton I thought it was, and she said she's a widow!

"Actually, Ms. Langley, the area has improved since the seventies. The local businessmen have put in a great deal of money to upgrade their establishments and pushed for city ordinances to keep the area green. The shops are small and fit in with the neighborhood look of the twenties. The homes are sprawling the closer you get to Bayshore Boulevard, and there are yard size requirements. I just had a condominium unit become available in a gated community. Would you be interested?"

Barbara thought about trying to mow a sizeable chunk of grass in the blazing Florida heat. "That sounds fine. Is the community quiet?"

"It's pricey enough that there are very few families within the gates, and they're in the larger units at the back of the property."

"Excellent. I'll meet you at your office at ten in the morning."

"Until that time, Ms. Langley."

"Goodbye, Ms. Gutierrez."

~ * ~

Steven parked in the garage and entered the condo through the kitchen, flipping on lights as he walked through rooms. His head was buzzing from the compliments and reaction of the audience tonight. He hadn't realized so many people still listened to rock and roll. Walking into the living room, he knelt on one knee to open the stereo cabinet doors. His hand automatically went to the record he was searching for, and he loaded it on to the player. Setting the needle on the first track, he lifted the headphones to his ears, pulled up his papasan listening chair and leaned back to bask in the past. The soft tsk, tsk, tsk of the high hat cymbal was joined by the guttural notes of the bass line. Four measures of quiet introduction exploded into the beginning lines of *Revenge*. Steven leaned into the chair and played air drums along with the song. This had truly been the best night he'd experienced in over twenty years.

He couldn't remember falling asleep but was awoken by the sh, sh, sh sound of a record that had ended. He stretched his arms, the smile still on his lips, and looked at the clock.

"Damn, I'm not going to make it by eight this morning. I'll call and tell them to start the morning ritual without me. Time to let them stand or fall on their own." Picking up the phone, he called the front desk of his hotel.

"Hi, Anne, this is Steven. Yeah, it is late for me. I'm not going to be in at eight so would you leave a note for Donna to start the morning routine without me? Thanks. Just tell her I'll get in before noon but exactly when, I'm not sure. She has my cell number if there is an emergency. Oh, and Anne? You're doing a really great job. Thanks."

By the bewildered tone in her voice, Steven guessed his graveyard-shift front desk supervisor suspected he might have been drinking. A tired smile still graced his face as he trudged up to his bed.

"Let 'em wonder."

~ * ~

Marc grabbed Ray's arm as he walked past.

"Since when did you and Dad..." He swept his hand toward the stage. "Why didn't he tell me? And when was he going to..."

Ray could see the confusion on his godson's face. "Let me say goodbye to Marcus and Carl, and I'll tell you the whole story if you keep the beer cold and full." Ray walked away.

Aaron moved to Marc's side. "So what's the story?"

Marc shrugged his shoulders. "I don't know yet, but Uncle Ray is saying goodbye, then said he'd tell me. I'm going to talk to him in the office..."

Aaron started to complain. Marc held up his hand. "You'll get the story later, but right now..." He looked at his watch. "...it's nearly one o'clock. Geez, I didn't realize it was so late, anyway, if you'll cover things here until we close, I'll come out and help you clean up. Deal?"

Aaron frowned but acquiesced.

~ * ~

Ray had walked Marcus and his son to the door to say his goodbyes.

What the hell am I going to say to Marc? Should I sugar-coat it? He thought as he walked to the end of the bar where Marc stood waiting. *Hell, no.* His mother has hidden the truth from him for long enough. *It's about time he found out what his father has been hiding all these years.*

Ray leaned against the bar.

Marc handed him a dark, long-necked bottle. "Cold beer as promised. Let's go into my office. It's quieter." He indicated the group of musicians tuning up for the last set of the night.

"Lead the way." Ray followed the young man into a small, neat room that held a bank of cameras on one wall, roll-top desk and two matching chairs in the middle, and on the opposite wall was a bulletin board with schedules, notes asking for time off, and invoices from distributors. The cacophony from the bar provided a dull, thudding background.

Marc indicated Ray should take one chair while he sat opposite.

"Okay. What is Rock Railroad, and what have you and Dad got to do with it? And when did you guys start playing instruments?"

Ray held up his hand. "I'll get to all of it but give me a minute to breathe. I used to be able to play all night and go to work at five the next morning, but that was when I was your age. I'm getting a little too old to do it now." Ray took a swig from his beer, settled in his chair, and looked at the young man who called him Uncle.

"I've known your father since we were both about nine years old."

"What's that got to do with...?"

Ray raised his eyebrows at Marc. "I'm telling this, and I'm going to tell it my way. So, relax and listen. Your dad and I met when we were taking music lessons from the same teacher. We both started on piano…"

Marc's mouth dropped open. "Dad plays piano?"

Ray glared at him. "Yes and several other instruments. Don't interrupt again, or I won't tell you anything."

"I promise. Not a word until you're done."

"Fine. Anyway, as I was saying, we met at piano lessons, and it didn't take too long for us to become friends. We both came to the conclusion we didn't want to be concert pianists but did want to play rock and roll. So, we made a pact to hound our parents until they let us learn to play the instruments we wanted. The deal we made was we had to continue to take piano lessons, and do well, but we also had to take lessons for the other instruments. Your dad chose the drums, and I chose guitar. By the time we hit seventh grade, we were doing fairly well at mimicking the popular songs played on the radio. We had two friends from school, Marcus Dillman and Ricky Thompson, who had been taking lessons, too. We decided to start a band. Our first name was The Cherries, you know like The Hollies, but we got so much flak for it we changed our name to Rock Railroad. It sounded more rock and roll.

"We started playing for school functions and, pretty soon, we had gigs for birthday parties, bar mitzvahs, weddings, and, finally, we were playing in clubs. We had to step out the back door during the breaks because we weren't old enough to be in the club, but when we all turned eighteen, things changed. Soon, there were groupies hanging around and things got pretty wild.

"Your grandparents put their foot down and told your dad that he would go to college and get his degree because '*music isn't going to pay your mortgage*.' Little did they know." Ray snickered.

"We all had day jobs and played on the weekends for fun, but your dad started getting serious about his music. He'd met a gal that helped him get focused. They dated for five years, but when he wouldn't commit to marriage, she left. She'd inspired him to write about a dozen songs, and we began to add original music at our gigs. Shortly after she left, your mom appeared on the scene, and your parents started dating.

"All of a sudden, our music took off. We had offers from two or three record labels we had to consider. Because he was getting his degree in business at college, we left it to Steven to handle that end of things. He listened to the offers, chose the best label, and before we knew it, we were recording the first of four number-one hits. We made four albums, did four promotion tours, and were doing really well when Marcus and Ricky decided they wanted to go a different direction. We talked and agreed it was time to split up.

"Your dad was offered the drummer position with Cult Explosion but turned it down because he wanted to settle down. He'd seen what being on the road could do to family life, and he didn't want that for his family. When he turned down the job, your mother pitched a fit and told him to never speak about his music or play again as long as they were together.

"Your dad has rented a storage unit for all these years and practices his drums five to six hours a week."

"Who would have thought?" Marc shook his head. "All these years I thought he had another woman. That's what mom always said."

Ray snorted. "Your mom would. Sorry, Marc."

"Don't worry about it, Uncle Ray. I'm old enough to see what kind of a person she is. That's why I stay away from the house as much as possible. Listen—do you have a CD of the albums you guys recorded? And what about Reynaldo, does he know?"

Ray chuckled as he stood. "Marc, rock and roll is a bullet train as far as groups and popularity goes so our albums were never made into CDs. I do, however, have the records at the house somewhere. I can lend you a player and the albums if you want, and, no, Ray-Ray doesn't know about me being in the group. His mom and I decided if the kids knew I was in a top-ten rock and roll group, they'd think they could get away with anything. I was going to tell him when the time was right. I just never found the right time. Now, I'm dying of thirst. How about another beer?"

The quiet of the bar struck both men as they exited the office. Marc checked his watch.

"I didn't realize it was that late. Sorry for keeping you up so long, Uncle Ray. Still want another beer?"

"It's free, right?"

Marc nodded.

"You bet I want another beer. This is the beauty of owning your company. If my job is on schedule, nobody will yell at me if I don't go to work." Ray took the offered beer and grinned.

Aaron joined the two men at the far end of the bar. "Hey, dude. You owe me big time for bailing. What's the story?"

Marc turned. "You're right. I do owe you. Thanks for picking up the slack. I'll fill you in later. Why don't you head on out, and I'll lock up?"

Aaron raised an eyebrow. He moved to the exit tossing over his shoulder, "See you later."

Marc leaned on the bar. "Is there anything else I should know, Uncle Ray?"

Ray pulled on his beer. He sat playing with the label then looked at Marc. "Grab a chair. This might take some time. What I'm about to tell you, your father doesn't even know."

~ * ~

Barbara stretched all over, reaching to turn off the alarm clock. "Oh, oh, oh. Even with all that time in the tanning booth, I'm still too tender to fall asleep on the beach. I should've remembered how brutal Florida sun can be. I wonder how badly I'm burnt." She got out of bed and, gingerly lifting her T-shirt, looked at her back.

"That's going to leave a mark. I'd better get the aloe vera on it now." She padded barefoot into the bathroom, and opening the drawer, gazed at the array of medicine tubes lying before her. "Maybe, I'll shower first, lotion after."

When she had run a cool shower over her body, taking special care with the tender sun-burnt area, Barbara slathered herself with aloe gel. It was the one item she had been careful to pack. One sunburn, which had left her sick years ago when she'd first come to Florida, had convinced her she didn't want to share that experience again. She always kept a bottle of aloe gel in her purse—at all times.

Barbara dressed in Florida business casual. Linen slacks topped with a silk blouse and open-toed pumps gave her the professional, yet comfortable, appearance she wanted to present.

She brushed on mascara and chose a neutral-toned lipstick. Double-checking herself in the mirror, she decided she was as ready as she could get. A quick glance at the time revealed she had forty minutes to find the realtor's office.

Barbara smiled and gave a quick wave to the young lady at the desk as she darted through the lobby toward the exit. Inside her rental car, she checked to be sure she had her phone and checkbook. If something caught her eye today, she wanted to be able to put enough money on the place to hold it until she could pull the funds from her savings account.

She'd thought about weaving through the surface streets to get a feel of the neighborhoods but opted to take the Tampa Expressway to the realtor's office. Exiting at the South Armenia off ramp, she traveled southwards until she came to Swann Avenue. Barbara shivered as a sense of deja vu crept over her. How many nights had she taken this same route after leaving one of Steven's gigs? She passed the TGI Friday's, and the sensation hit her. *I'm home.* She hadn't realized how tense she was until that moment. Shoulders relaxing, the back of her neck loosening, Barbara let the glow of homecoming wash over her. *Today is going to be a great day. I just know it.*

~ * ~

Maria rummaged through the file drawer. "I know I put those pictures in here someplace." Turning to her credenza, she found Steven's paperwork from the original sale of his condominium.

"Aha! I knew they were here—somewhere. I think I'll show this client the condominium first, then we'll look at houses afterward. Let's see, here's one on Palm Drive then one on DeSoto Avenue and, oh yes, that overpriced white elephant on Bayshore Boulevard. After that, we can go to lunch at TGI Fridays; I'll reserve the company table, and see if she wants to look further." Maria leaned back in her chair and smiled. All in all, it looked to be a promising day. Maybe, she'd be able to make a sale and take the rest of the week at a leisurely pace. Her intercom buzzed.

"Yes?"

"Miss Langley is here."

"I'll come get her. Please ask her to take a seat."

Maria pulled out her compact and checked her lipstick. Taking a deep breath, she walked into the lobby to retrieve her client. She rounded the corner, nodded at the receptionist, and extended her hand toward the solitary woman sitting in the leather chair.

"Hello, Ms. Langley, I'm Maria Gutierrez."

Barbara stood and took the proffered hand, looking into a familiar pair of deep brown eyes.

Maria stumbled as she clutched the delicate hand in her own. "Barbara! It is you. Barbara Hamilton! You haven't aged a day in, what, twenty-five years? You look fabulous. You have to tell me your secret."

Barbara grinned, squeezing the hand of an old friend. "Maria, you should talk. You don't look much older than the day I saw you and Eduardo walk down the aisle. Speaking of which, are you two still married?"

Maria nodded.

"That's good news. It's so hard to find people that stick it out these days. As for my secret to these looks? Great plastic surgeons, but it's just that—a secret. I doubt I'll run into any of the old crowd. Do you see many of them?"

Maria smirked. *I'll make sure you see, at least, one from the old crowd. Steven, dear friend, your single days are coming to an end.*

"I see a few of them. You remember Ray and Monica?"

Barbara smiled in recognition of the names of old friends. "Yeah. What ever happened with them? The last I knew was Monica was pregnant, and Ray was making noises like he was going to make an honest woman of her. I didn't really believe it because he was such a playboy."

Maria guided Barbara toward her office. Inside, she offered her the chair opposite her desk. "Well, believe it. They're still married."

Barbara allowed a lopsided smile, emphasizing the dimple in her left cheek, to crease her face.

"And they have six kids."

Barbara's eyes popped. "You're joking, right?"

Maria shook her head.

"Well, I'll be. Who would've thought that scoundrel would settle down and be a family man?" Barbara continued. "I'm glad to hear that. I was very fond of Sandy, the girl he was dating when I was living here. We always kept each other company at the band's table when the guys played. It really irritated me to find out Ray was catting around behind her back. But... since it has worked out for him and Monica, I guess it was meant to be.

"I've decided to relocate back to the Tampa area and would like to buy a home. What can you show me?"

Marie spread out the pictures she'd collected before Barbara's arrival. She touted the benefits of each of the homes and sat back, letting Barbara peruse the photos. Barbara pulled the pictures of the condo toward her. She rummaged in her purse.

"The only thing the doctors couldn't put back to original were my eyes. I still need to wear reading glasses."

"I know what you mean." Maria pulled a set of half glasses from her suit pocket.

Barbara looked at each photo, examining them closely.

"You know, if it's possible, I'd like to see this one first. I like the layout, and it appears to have a fairly nice view. Would that be doable?"

Maria hid the smile fighting to emerge on her lips.

"I don't think there'll be a problem. I know the seller is anxious to move out..."

"Is there something wrong with the place?"

"No, no, it's just the seller has had an opportunity to take over a family property and doesn't want to be a landlord. I don't think the community allows rentals, anyway, and they would like to move this quickly. I have permission to show it at any time. Would you like to go now?"

Barbara picked up the picture of the front of the condo. Large picture windows reflected a view of the Hillsborough Bay, and she could see the old trees that lined most of Bayshore Boulevard surrounding the building. "Yes. I'd like that."

The two women exited the office and walked toward the lobby. Maria left her location with the receptionist, instructing her that unless there was a national disaster she was not to be bothered.

Outside, in the sleek, dark green Mercedes, Barbara allowed the soft leather to surround her body. Watching the scenery pass by, she felt more "at home" here than she had in all her years in Oregon. Maybe Dylan was right.

~ * ~

Steven rolled over and looked at his alarm clock.

"Damn it!"

He jumped from the bed and dashed into the shower. Allowing the warm water to cascade over his body, he closed his eyes and slowed his heart rate.

"I'm not going to rush. They know I'm coming in late so I'm not going to panic." *After all, what's the big hurry? I can send my weekly stats from home.*

Slowing his pace, Steven reveled in the stolen time. He took his time shaving and blew dry his hair. Deciding he might not go into the office at all, he sat at his desk and fired up his computer. He pulled information from his work files, let the program do its magic, and sent the necessary reports to the regional offices.

A noise from downstairs stopped him. Rising slowly from his chair, he heard voices. A line formed on his forehead, and he moved around his desk to grab the tennis racket leaning against the bookcase.

Won't kill them but sure give them a scare.

He raised the racket above his head and crept toward the office door.

"Right now, the owner is using this room as an office but it could be a sewing room or a... aaahhh!"

Maria and Barbara came face to face with a shirtless, barefoot, racket-welding Steven lunging in their direction.

"Barbara!"

"Steven?"

The racket clattered to the floor as Steven's face blanched. "Oh my God, I nearly hit you."

He stumbled backwards until he plopped into his chair. "Is it really you or are you her daughter?"

Barbara had instinctively moved to his side and was holding his hand, looking into his face. She reached up and stroked the still lean jaw line.

Steven reacted by covering her hand with his own.

Barbara jerked her hand back. "It's really me, Steven. What are you doing here?"

"This is my condo... I live here."

Barbara turned to Maria.

"You knew, didn't you?"

The dark-haired realtor grinned. "Of course. Does this mean you're not interested in the condo?"

Startled by the woman's question, Barbara stared at her. Noting the beginnings of a smile on Maria's face, she felt joy bubble from deep inside her. She burst out laughing, catching the other two off guard.

Maria and Steven exchanged glances. Seeing the absurdity in the situation, they too, started to chuckle. Maria was the first to talk.

"Well, Barbara, did you want to look at the other houses?" She raised an eyebrow.

"Actually, when you showed me the pictures of this place, I had pretty well decided if it lived up to the photos, I would purchase it. I like the layout and how the sun and shade give it warm and cool spots. I remember being in Tampa during the summer and know shade and coolness is as important as view. This has it all. The garage is the right size for my vehicle, and there isn't much yard work to do. Hopefully, I can get one of the local young men to mow the grass for me..."

"Well, how would you like to proceed? Do you want to go back to the office and draw up a contract or put down earnest money? We'll go forward as you wish."

"Since we never discussed it, I'd like to see what the asking price is."

Maria pulled a small note pad from her briefcase, retrieved her glasses and put them on the end of her perky nose, and scribbled down a figure, which she handed to Barbara. Barbara looked at the numbers.

"You're joking, right?"

Maria shrugged her shoulders and looked at Steven.

"Not according to the owner."

Barbara turned to Steven. "Are you serious about this price?"

Steven, who'd been watching the exchange between the two lovely ladies as one would watch a tennis match, smirked.

"You're right. The price is a bit too low."

Maria narrowed her eyes at him. *You dog. Don't blow this sale for me.*

"Maria left out one detail in the asking price—dinner, tonight."

She rolled her eyes. "You two work out the details. I'm going to check in with my office. I'll be downstairs in the kitchen when you're ready, Barbara."

Exiting out the office door, she let the grin she'd been hiding spread slowly across her face. *That sly devil is being more aggressive than I remember. At this rate, I'll have the condo sold, Steven matched, and a wedding invitation in the mail to boot.* Without consciously thinking about it, Maria started humming *Left Behind* as she called her office.

~ * ~

Steven held his breath. There was something about the touch of her hand on his face... He couldn't remember the last time he'd felt goose bumps all over his body. It was a good thing he hadn't needed to stand up because it would have been evident that Barbara's touch still affected him the way it had over twenty some years ago. His arousal was beginning to subside when those big, brown eyes ringed with long, dark lashes that had always gone straight to his heart gazed at him. She could have asked him to give her the condo at this moment, and he would have signed the papers without hesitation.

Barbara cleared her throat. "What about your wife?

"I've been divorced for six years."

"Children?"

"Two fully-grown and living-on-their-own children: one son, who owns his own business, and one daughter, who is currently in England studying for her doctorate."

Barbara's nose crinkled as she asked the next question. "Your father and mother?"

Steven's father had always treated Barbara as if she were one of the household servants, making it abundantly clear she was not of an "acceptable" social level to be involved with his son.

He sighed. "When someone of the *right* class came along and I married her, while she provided me two beautiful children, she made my life miserable. So much for 'socially acceptable.' Mom and Dad built a home in Indian Rocks Beach. The kids used to visit, but I don't often go there. After I decided to stay with Rock Railroad, my father pretty much ignored me."

"Speaking of which..."

"Barbara?"

"Yes?"

"...will you have dinner with me, tonight?"

Barbara felt the blood rushing to her face. Her chest was pounding so hard she was sure Steven could hear it. *Don't blow this chance, Winkie.*

Barbara swallowed her trepidation. She peered into green-flecked, hazel eyes that had always turned her resolve into jelly. Time had sprinkled laugh lines around the edges adding a touch of distinction to a face she felt had always been handsome.

"Okay. On one condition."

"What's that?"

"I bring my car, you bring yours."

"Are you afraid of me?"

"No. I'm afraid of myself."

~ * ~

Maria dialed her secretary's number. "Lola. Put together a contract for the condominium I'm showing on Bayshore Boulevard. I think I've got it sold. I should be back in the office by one o'clock with the buyer to sign papers. Thanks."

She browsed through the numbers of received calls on her cell, stopping at the one she wanted. A sleepy voice answered before the answering machine kicked in.

"Hello? This had better be good."

"Good morning to you too, Ray. This is Maria Gutierrez."

"Morning. What can I do for you, Maria? I'm happy with the house I have, and the company hasn't finished the subdivision in Thononasassa, yet." Ray's gravelly voice hesitated. "Everything all right with you and Eduardo?"

"Yes. I just thought you'd like to know, we might all be getting invitations to a wedding soon."

Ray groaned. Last night's session at Devine Nine had reminded him why he hadn't minded giving up playing in bars. His head hurt, his eyes felt as though someone had tossed sand in his face, and his lungs ached with second-hand smoke residue.

"Who's your victim this time, Maria?"

Infamous for her passion to match-make, Maria had been responsible for more than a few marriages and almost marriages.

"What would you say if I told you Steven Rodgers might be getting married in the near future?"

"I'd say you've been drinking your breakfast. If that's all, I need to take some aspirin and get back to bed."

"Not working today?"

"No. As the boss, I'm giving myself a day off. I had a rough night."

"Oh, out with the boys."

"In a manner of speaking. Remember, last night was jam night at Devine Nine?"

"So?"

"I got Steven to come out and jam with me and Marcus and Carl."

Ray listened to the silence as time ticked by. Finally, Maria caught on to what he was telling her.

"That's right, you told me Rock Railroad might be getting back together again."

"I think so. I haven't seen Steven that happy in a long time."

"Well, I just added to that."

"What are you talking about?"

"I just showed Barbara Hamilton his condo. She's looking to buy a place in Tampa."

Ray's eyes snapped open. He sat up in his bed, his senses tingling. "Are you sure it was *the* Barbara Hamilton? The one that got away?"

"Yes. And she doesn't look a day older. The two of them were talking when I left them—she still cares for him. I can tell."

Ray ran his hand over his aching head. "Where's she staying now?" He heard paper shuffling.

"At the Sheraton. Why?"

He whistled lowly. "Because Steven owns the Sheraton. He has a strict rule about employees dating the guests. Boy, does this open a can of worms. He thought he'd seen her but couldn't say anything." A wicked grin began to curl at the corners of Ray's mouth.

"Ray?"

"Yes?"

"You still there?"

"Yes."

"What's going on?"

"I'm going to love to see him get out of this. Man! This is too sweet; if Steven puts Rock Railroad back together and gets back together with Barbara, his ex-wife will have a cow. And there's nothing she can do about it. Keep me posted, Maria."

"Not a problem. You'll be one of the first to get a wedding invitation."

Nineteen

Marc paced through the apartment flipping open his cell phone and snapping it shut. After the fourth pass through the living room, Aaron blocked his way.

"You're wearing a trail in the carpet. What's going on?"

"It's her."

"Her—who?"

"Barbara. I can't get her out of my mind. I want to see her again, but I don't want to seem too pushy or too anxious. I start to call, then decide I'm rushing things, so, I stop. It's making me crazy."

Aaron sat down on the couch, flipping one long leg over the arm. "You? I'm getting dizzy just watching you. At least it's good to know you still have your man-sense."

Marc turned to his roommate and raised an eyebrow. "Man-sense?"

"Yeah, man-sense. Show 'em you're a little bit interested and wait. They'll come running to you, and you won't have to do any of that flower-dinner-spend-all-your-cash stuff. If she's one of those liberated types then you don't have to waste your time." Aaron grinned smugly.

"Gee... and you wonder why you can't keep a girlfriend. Go figure." Marc sat at the other end of the couch. "She's different, Aaron. She's the take-home-to-Mom type. I don't get the impression she needs to have a man in her life. She doesn't have that clingy, can't-get-out-of-her-sight feel most of the other girls I've dated have. She seemed a little uncomfortable with me paying for our date. And, she insisted on paying for the gas it took to wander all over the coast. She didn't latch on to me. I like that. I just can't stop thinking about her and how much fun we had together."

Aaron flipped his leg off the arm of the couch and onto the floor. "She's also easy on the eyes, roomie. Listen, I've got a date with one of those other types. Somebody from the club. If I'm lucky, I won't be home tonight. Call your new friend and see if she wants to come over. Maybe, just maybe, you'll get lucky." Aaron pushed up from the couch and bounced down the hallway to his room.

Marc realized there was no way Aaron was going to understand how he felt.

"BY THE WAY, ROOMIE, WHAT WAS YOUR UNCLE TELLING YOU LAST NIGHT?" Aaron had poked his head out of his room as he yelled.

Marc walked down the hallway and stood in the doorframe while Aaron changed.

"Seems my uncle Ray and Dad are Rock Railroad."

"Shut up." Aaron stood mouth open, eyes wide, with one jean leg dangling. "Those guys had like, four big hits, and, like, four or five albums when they broke up—for no good reason. Whoa, this is so tight!"

Aaron had finished dressing in his jeans and favorite light green Izod shirt. Slipping his bare feet into a pair of beige loafers, he slipped past Marc to finish his routine in the bathroom.

"How is it you know so much about a group of guys my dad's age?"

"My dad was a huge fan. He has all the albums they recorded. Want me to bring them over?"

"Yeah. I'd like to hear what they sounded like."

"If that's all you want, listen to WARM at 94.9. They're doing some call-in thing to get Rock Railroad back together. They play one song an hour by the group. Are you going to the club, later?"

"If I can't get a hold of Barbara, yeah, why not?"

"Maybe, I'll see you there."

Marc ambled into the living room and dropped on to the couch. *I should just call. After all, what's the worst she can do—tell me no?* Once again, he flipped open his phone, and this time; he called the number he had programmed into the memory.

"Hello?"

He almost hung up. The soft voice at the other end of the phone startled him; he'd been expecting to get her voice mail.

"Barbara?"

"Yes?"

"This is Marc. I was wondering if you'd like to have dinner with me tonight."

Silence.

~ * ~

Back in her suite, the butterflies in Barbara's stomach were threatening to explode out of her mouth. She had hoped to bump into Steven, but to find him, and find out he was single, was more than she had dreamed possible. It was a sad fact that most of her generation had been married and divorced at least once, but Steven wasn't just anybody.

She and her husband, Dylan, had grown to love each other very much, but they knew their love wasn't the take-your-breath-away kind. Both of them had been recovering from heartbreak when they'd met. What had started as friendship had grown into comfortable, enduring love. She knew if the drunk driver hadn't killed Dylan, she would still be in Oregon washing his shirts and hugging him close on those cold winter days. But life had intervened. Being able to come back to Florida, and find the man who'd stolen her heart so many years ago, had been a fairytale, a fleeting wish she'd held deep in her heart when she and Dylan would fight.

She looked to the sky and mouthed the words "thank you." Smiling as she pondered over what to wear tonight, Barbara jumped when her cell phone rang.

He's calling to cancel. I just know it. I knew it was too good to be true. Oh, well, I'll just go to The Shops on Harbor Island, find a little bistro, and have dinner by myself.

"I'm coming, I'm coming." Picking up her cell, she sucked in a calming breath, and, tentatively, answered. "Yes?"

"This is Marc. I was wondering if you'd like to have dinner with me tonight."

Her lips tingled with the memory of his tender kiss and, lightly, she touched them with her fingertips.

Barbara was stunned beyond speech. In all the excitement of finding a single Steven, she'd put Marc in the back of her mind. A little voice deep inside told her to hang on to this young man; Steven might not work out. After all, it had been twenty-plus years since they'd been together.

"Barbara, are you there?"

"Yes, Marc. Sorry. You caught me off guard. I guess I wasn't expecting to hear from you quite so soon."

"Is that a no?"

"I'm afraid so. I have other plans for this evening. May I take a rain check?"

"Yes. A rain check would be fine. Maybe, I can arrange for us to watch one of the baseball teams at spring training. I have a friend who works for the Cincinnati Reds. He'd be able to get us in to one of the practices."

Barbara smiled. She wasn't a big sports fan and baseball bored her, but Marc seemed to be trying very hard to find something they could do that wasn't threatening.

"You know Marc that sounds like a good time. Why don't we say Thursday?"

"Thursday, it is. I'll call my friend, and I'll let you know what time I'll pick you up. And Barbara?"

"Yes?"

"Wear your tennis shoes. Until Thursday."

Giggling, she said goodbye. She wrote herself a note and, with a piece of tape she'd found at the desk, she taped the paper with date and time on the bathroom mirror. *Should be able to remember it that way.*

Fussing through several changes, Barbara finally settled on a cotton blend skort—skirt short combination—and a short-sleeved cotton blouse in lavender tones that emphasized her golden tan and dark hair. Single-strapped, two-and-a-half-inch heels and matching clutch bag completed her outfit. She accessorized with silver button earrings and a single silver necklace at her neck. A quick glance in the mirror, and she was satisfied that she appeared cool, calm and collected. If anyone knew how many thousands of butterflies were kicking up a fuss in her stomach...

"I'm as ready as I'm going to get. Just a touch of lipstick, and I'm out the door."

Once in the car, she looked at the address Steven had given her. She input it into the GPS system, foregoing a map this time, and ran through the directions. Something about them set off bells in her memory. It seemed so recognizable, and yet...

"I'll know when I see it. So much has changed about Tampa that even familiar places take me a minute to remember."

Her cell phone chirped, and Barbara pulled to the side of the road to answer.

"Yes?"

"Barbara?"

Chills danced on her arms and her heart began to thud in her chest. Barbara closed her eyes and pulled in a deep breath before answering.

"Steven. Is something wrong?"

"No. I was just checking to see if you were ready to go."

"Actually, I pulled over to take your call. I'm on my way now and, according to my GPS, I should be there in ten minutes."

"Great. I'm going out the door now and will meet you there. Bye."

"Goodbye."

She sat for a moment centering her thoughts and trying to control her raging heartbeat and hormones. *That man still sets my body on fire! Maybe having dinner wasn't such a good idea.*

In the back of her mind, she heard a voice. *Don't second-guess yourself, Winkie. Let things happen naturally.* With a deep breath, and a quick smile, she moved back into the flow of traffic and continued on her way. Once again, Dylan's rational thinking was guiding her along.

How will I live without you?

You will.

Barbara pulled into the parking lot of the destination given on the GPS locator. She parked the convertible and locked the door. Turning to look at the front of the restaurant, she broke into a wide grin. *Steven, you devil. Steak and Ale.* How many times had they enjoyed a great prime rib meal here, rushing back to the house on Davis Island to make passionate love in his room, then on to one of his gigs? Barbara blushed at the memories.

"I hope this is all right?"

The sound of Steven's smooth voice behind her took Barbara by surprise, and she jumped.

"This is fine." Barbara looked up into the twinkling hazel eyes that had swept her away so many years ago. Her heart skipped a beat and, unconsciously, she slipped her tongue out to run the tip around her dry lips.

"Shall we?" He offered his arm, and Barbara slipped her hand through the crook.

Entering the restaurant, she couldn't contain the smile her heart was feeling. "We had some wonderful times here, didn't we?"

"Yes we did." He smiled and walked up to the podium. "Reservations for Rodgers."

The host escorted them down the walkway and around the corner to a booth hidden in the back, placed menus in front of them, and told them Eric, their waiter, would be with them momentarily.

A thin, young man sporting a dark tan and blonde hair approached the table.

"Hi, I'm Eric. Welcome to Steak and Ale. May I bring you something to drink?"

Steven looked up from his menu. "Yes. I'll have a Bud bottle and the lady will have...?"

Barbara glanced up into a pair of twinkling eyes so blue she envisioned Key West. "I'll, uh, I'll have iced tea, no lemon, thank you."

The young waiter winked and whisked away.

Steven put his menu at the edge of the table and turned to look at Barbara. "I can't believe it's really you." His eyes surveyed the face he'd spent so many nights recalling. "Smokette, you haven't changed a bit since the day you drove out of my life."

Barbara stared. "Steven?"

"Hmmm?"

"Do you realize you just called me Smokette?" She watched as his face turned crimson.

"I, I'm sorry. It just slipped out. Maybe coming here wasn't such a great idea." He began to slip out of the booth.

Barbara reached out and placed her hand on his arm. "It's all right. This is a wonderful idea."

He slid into the booth reassured by her tender smile as the waiter brought drinks.

"Are you ready to order?" He stood pencil in hand.

Steven nodded. "I'll have a ten-ounce steak, medium rare, baked potato with everything and salad with ranch dressing. And"—he looked at Barbara eyebrows raised in question—"May I?"

Barbara nodded, a lopsided smirk creeping over her face.

"The lady will have a small prime rib, baked potato—plain with butter and sour cream on the side—and a salad with Italian dressing."

"Thank you." Eric gathered the menus and sped off to the kitchen.

"That was phenomenal. How could you remember something so trivial after so long?"

Steven grinned. "As you said, we spent a lot of nights here, and you usually had the same thing every time. It wasn't hard to remember. I'm curious, Barbara. If you don't mind me asking, why are you in Tampa buying a place to live? I thought you'd gotten married. That was the last thing I'd heard."

Steven watched as Barbara's face changed, a sadness drawing her mouth down and hooding her brown eyes.

"That was tactless. I'm sorry; it's really none of my business."

"No, that's okay. When I left here, I was devastated. My heart had been broken into a million pieces, and I could barely breathe. I had an aunt living in Salem, Oregon, and she insisted I come live with her for a while. She's an amazing woman, my Aunt Lori. After a month of not leaving my room except for quick meals, she flung open the door one day, and told me to get off my dead ass and get a job. The free ride was over. If I was going to live in her house, I was going to contribute to the house payment. I had no idea, at the time, she owned the house, but it got me moving. I put my resume together, went out, and got a job as a secretary with the State of Oregon. I'd been working at the DMV for about a year when one of my co-workers invited me to join her pool league team. The first night we had a game, she brought her brother along. He was recovering from a breakup with his fiancé who left him for his best friend and was not in the best of moods. We sat at the table and started commiserating. Soon, Dylan was coming to every game to cheer us on. After about nine months, we realized we had a lot in common and really did like each other. On a weekend trip to the Oregon Coast, sitting in a restaurant called Moe's in Lincoln City, he asked me to marry him, and I said yes. We would have celebrated our twenty-sixth wedding anniversary this June."

"Would have?" Steven watched pain flicker in Barbara's eyes.

"Three years ago, while coming home after picking up his brother, John—who had called Dylan to get him because he was too blasted to walk, let alone drive—a drunk, driving with no lights at 2:30 a.m., hit my husband's pickup truck and instantly killed my husband and injured my brother-in-law. John spent six months in the hospital relearning to walk."

Steven extended his hand and covered Barbara's. He found her fingers cold and shaking.

She took in a deep breath and continued. "To answer your question about my buying a house... I met a quirky, irrepressible, redhead at a second job I was working who became my best friend. For years, I'd raved about Florida and all the great times I had when I lived here. She and my husband didn't hit it off immediately, but, eventually, decided being friends was easier on all of us. When Dylan died, Rachel, my friend, was as devastated as I was. She stood by me through all my medical procedures and, with the final process completed, announced she was holding me to a promise I'd made five or six years previous. She wanted to come to Florida to lie in the sun and party until we dropped."

Steven raised an eyebrow. "Where is she? I would have been happy to have her along with us tonight."

The dimple in Barbara's face deepened as she smirked. "My best friend did to me what she hated other people doing to her. On the trip down here, she met an airline attendant who swept her off her feet. From the moment they laid eyes on each other, she was smitten. He took her to dinner at Bern's..."

Steven flinched slightly. He'd contemplated asking Barbara to dinner at Bern's but decided Steak and Ale was safer.

"...then he called to tell her he missed her and couldn't stand not being near her, et cetera, and he was sending her a ticket to fly to England to meet his family. I told her she owes me drinks in Key West before she gets married."

The waiter arrived with the salads and darted back in the direction of the kitchen. After a few moments of silence, broken only by the sound of forks scraping against the wooden salad bowls, Barbara continued.

"I found myself more relaxed and happier than I'd felt in years. Of all the places I'd lived, Tampa represented home to me. So, lying on the beach at Indian Rocks, I decided to sell my house in Oregon and buy a place here. I suspect my best friend will be making a similar decision about living in the US or moving to England.

"It was by chance I saw Maria's name on the TV and called. I told her what I needed, and she said she had the perfect place for me. When we met, she recognized me right away. I'm just guessing she's been in her matchmaking mode, again. If I remember correctly, she set up several of our friends."

Steven laughed. "Yeah, she did, quite successfully. Her rate is about eighty percent. Most of the folks she 'arraigned' are still married. You have to admit—she has a knack."

"With an eighty percent success rate, 'a knack' is an understatement. Maybe she should reconsider her career."

"I think Maria would be fine matchmaking but Eduardo would go crazy. From some of the conversations we've had, I gathered his grandmother was a matchmaker in Cuba. That's how Eduardo's parents met. But it drove his grandfather to distraction; too much drama." Chuckling, Steven allowed the waiter to remove the empty salad plates.

"We've spent a good deal of time talking about me; what about you, Steven? What happened after I left? I know Rock Railroad did well, for a time, and quite suddenly broke up. I kept watching the music scene to see if you'd gone to another group but couldn't find your name anywhere. Did you go behind the scenes?" Barbara sipped her tea.

Steven shifted on the plank bench seat. It was ridiculous to feel uncomfortable talking about his past. After all, Barbara had driven out of his life. It had been her choice to leave, sort of. He had to admit, if only to himself, that his lack of commitment might have had something to do with making her leave.

"When you left, I played the field for a while but it didn't take me long to realize just how much I loved and missed you. Every time I heard Player's 'Baby Come Back,' I thought of you."

Barbara coughed into her napkin and stared at him. "It made me think of you, too."

A sad smile touched Steven's lips. "After a gig at the Devine Nine one night—it was still Big Eddy's at that time—about nine months after you'd left, I wrote *Left Behind*. A girl had shown up at the club that resembled you—a lot. I thought you'd come back to Tampa, and my heart danced. I felt happier than I'd been since before I'd watched the taillights of your car drive away from me. When I first spotted her, I was on stage and couldn't get close enough to see if it was you or not. It wasn't until the second break someone brought her to our table and introduced her. When I observed her up close, I realized the only resemblance to you was in her long, dark hair and the clothes she chose to wear. My heart felt like you'd just walked out of my life, again.

"After the gig, I went home and spent all night pouring my heart into the song. As you know, around 1980 or so, we got picked up by a record label and *Left Behind* was our first single. The reason I wrote the song was the anticipation you'd hear it, someday, and contact me. When you didn't, I gave up hope. Lisa had entered my life, Marc had been born, and things were cooking with the band.

"I wrote *Money Man* when we discovered our manager was liberally dipping his hand into the pot. As you can guess, we fired him, and I took on managing the band as well as writing and playing. People starting calling us has-beens and we wrote *Back Again* to show them we still had punch.

"By this time, I saw my marriage was looking pretty rocky and, with thoughts of you dancing around in my head, I wrote *Revenge*. Not too long after the release of our fourth album, Marcus and Ricky started balking at doing the tours. The fun had gone out of playing and we decided, collectively, to disband.

"Ray started up his construction company..."

Barbara grinned. Ray had always worked construction with his dad and swore he would never do it on his own. *So much for swearing.*

"...Marcus went back to college and got his law degree, and Ricky started racing cigar boats." A shadow of pain crossed Steven's face. "He was killed last year when his engine was sabotaged by a member of another team on the Bahamas to Miami race."

"I read about that. I'm really sorry, Steven."

The waiter brought the main course, setting the dishes in front of them. "Is there anything I can get for you?"

Steven and Barbara shook their heads.

"Enjoy."

"Thank you." Barbara cut a small portion of her prime rib and placed the tender meat in her mouth. Oral sensations from years earlier flooded her memory. She closed her eyes and allowed the flavor to dance across her taste buds. Opening her eyes, she found herself looking into the amused face of her companion.

"What?"

"You look like you got lost, for a moment."

"I did. This is a one-of-a-kind experience, and, trust me, I've tried, unsuccessfully, to find someplace else that makes prime rib this tasty. Well, Steven, you've told me things I could have looked up on the Internet if I had wanted to, but you haven't told me what you're doing now."

He pushed around a piece of steak, chewing slowly and turning over what he wanted to say.

"Well, my ex-wife chased me for six months before I gave in and took her out on a date. Dad knew her father, a local lawyer, which gave her the right connections, and wanted me to settle down and get a real job. He figured if I married then I'd give up the band and give him grandkids.

"When the band broke up, I floated a while since money really wasn't an issue. I allowed Lisa to talk me into going to a few auditions, and when Cult Explosion called me back to offer me a position, I said yes, at first. It took only one month of the drugs, sex, and rock-n-roll lifestyle to convince me we didn't mesh. I talked with the guys in the group, and they understood why I wanted to leave, but my ex-wife exploded into a rage when I tried to explain it to her. She screamed, called me every name in the book, plus a few I hadn't heard before, and stomped out of our apartment. She was gone for a week. When she finally returned, she told me she would come back into my life on one condition."

Barbara raised her eyebrows. "And that was?"

Steven pulled in a deep breath then slowly released the air. "I was never to play, speak about, or otherwise infer I had ever had anything to do with the music business again. I had no idea where you were or if you were married, so I agreed."

Barbara had stopped eating and stared at Steven. "She was just mad, right? You were able to practice and play at home, weren't you?"

Steven shook his head. "No mention of music was ever made in the house again. When my parents built the house on Indian Rocks Beach, they let me buy the one on Davis Island from them for a dollar to avoid the inheritance taxes. In the formal living room, there is a grand piano. Without thinking one day, I sat down and began to play as I had when I was a kid. Lisa walked over and slammed the lid down on my hands. It took two months for all the bruises to disappear."

Barbara's eyes widened in horror. "Good lord, Steven. Why did you stay with her?"

"By that time, she was seven months pregnant with my son. I wouldn't leave her. I decided I couldn't live without making music so, covertly, I rented a storage unit near MacDill Air Force Base and practiced there. I let her think whatever she wanted about where I was going. It was the only thing that kept me sane while the kids were growing up. Neither of my children knows I played drums or was involved in a band."

"You still haven't told me what you do now?" Barbara pushed the nearly empty plate away from her.

"I own a hotel."

"Oh, which one?" She picked up her drink and took a sip.

"The Sheraton by the airport."

Barbara started coughing.

Steven slid out of his seat, moved next to Barbara, and gently stroked her back. "I... I'm sorry. I didn't mean to upset you."

"When were you going to tell me?"

"I wasn't sure. It's a complex situation. I have a strict rule about my employees dating any of the guests. But Barbara..." He turned her chin toward him and gazed deeply into her eyes. "I couldn't let you get away again. I'll sell the hotel before I let you disappear out of my life."

"Then, it's a good thing I put down earnest money on the condo and signed the papers, isn't it? Technically, I'm now a prospective home owner." She watched as his face brightened.

"That's right. I'll be out of the condo by the middle of next week, and you can move in. If you want, I can leave some basic furniture in the unit until you get yours here from Oregon."

"That would be wonderful. I'm going to stay in the hotel until Rachel, my friend, flies back from England and either stays here or returns with her new beau, but I'd prefer to start my life here as soon as possible."

"Then it's settled. I need to go to the Davis Island house and see what, if any, repairs I might need to make. Would you like to follow?"

Barbara smiled. *Would I like to see the house on Davis Island? Does it rain in Oregon?*

"I'd love to."

Steven paid the bill and escorted Barbara to her car.

"Do you think you can find the house or would you like to follow me?"

"I think I should probably follow you. It has been a few years since I was there, and so much has changed. I'd hate to get lost."

"I won't let that happen."

Steven pulled her to him and captured her lips with his own.

Barbara felt herself meld into his body as easily as she had twenty years previously. Her toes curled, and the butterflies, which had quieted for dinner, now buzzed her stomach with enthusiasm. When Steven let her go, she found herself breathless.

"I've waited over twenty years to do that." A quick kiss to her forehead and he opened the door to his SUV.

"Shall we?"

Barbara moved to the rental car and pulled in a deep breath.

"We shall." She smiled at Steven and started her vehicle. She followed the SUV down streets that began to feel familiar, and when she pulled in front of the Spanish-style home, the sensation of homecoming swept over her body. She turned off the engine and stared at the white two-story home with maroon and white awnings and red tile roof.

"Welcome home," she whispered.

Twenty

Steven opened her door and held his hand out. Barbara grasped it and felt herself drawn from the car. They strolled down the driveway under the porticoed entry toward the kitchen door. As Steven placed the key in the lock, a scream pierced the evening. He whipped around, his ears straining to follow the sound. Another panicked yell came from the apartment over the garage.

"Mirella!"

Steven dashed over the lawn and up the stairway leading to the apartment, Barbara close on his heels. Slamming open the door, he quickly surveyed the scene.

Mirella, pinned to the bed by a large figure, was struggling against the hand held over her mouth. Her clothes were torn and partially off her body, and she was kicking to free herself from the attacker.

Steven bolted to the bed and grabbed the back of the person's neck. Once the assailant was upright, Steven threw his arm around the neck and stepped back into the small kitchen area.

Mirella rolled off the bed, clutching the comforter to her body, sobbing loudly.

"Barbara."

"Yes?"

"Take her into the house." He tossed the keys to her. The attacker began to squirm. Steven tightened his grip. "If you so much as move one muscle, I'll break your neck. You're trespassing on my property and assaulting my staff. Relax or die."

Barbara gathered the shaken young woman into her arms, and the two skirted past Steven and the man he held. Mirella's sobs shook her body.

Barbara opened the door of the main house and instinctively reached for the light switch, turning on the kitchen lights.

"I think we need to get you to the bathroom and check out your injuries."

The shaken girl nodded.

~ * ~

Steven leaned close to the ear of the assailant he held in a chokehold.

"I have no idea what you think you were doing here, and I don't care. If I ever see you on my property, or find out you've been skulking around here, I'll have you thrown in jail. Your diplomatic immunity will get you released, Senor de la Mar Montenegro, but you'll spend at least twenty-four hours in the American penal system.

"I'm going to release you, and, if I were you, I'd take the opportunity to get as far away from this house as possible. I won't be responsible for my actions after five minutes."

Steven relaxed the hold he had on the man.

Senor de la Mar Montenegro slid his trousers up his body and buckled his belt, rebuttoning his shirt, he turned to Steven. "This has been an unfortunate misunderstanding. I'm sure when you speak to the young Senorita she will explain what occurred here. You will see how very wrong you have been. I will not speak of this to your ex-wife."

As he turned to walk out the door, Steven spoke. "Of course, you won't speak of this to Lisa. She'd cut your balls off and hand them to you. I don't know what you perceive happened here, but in my eyes and the eyes of the local authorities, I interrupted a rape. Your government may not take immediate action, but I suspect you'd find yourself transferred to some other lovely location in the world.

"You now have three minutes to leave my property before I call the cops. Get out and don't come back here." He watched the diplomat grab his jacket off the back of the small couch and registered steps descending the staircase. Steven pulled in deep breaths of air in an attempt to calm the anger boiling inside. He heard the start-up of a vehicle down the street and tires screech as it left. Exhaling deeply, he closed the door and went inside the main house.

~*~

Barbara held the young woman close. Mirella was shaking uncontrollably and sobbing lightly.

"I don't understand why he did this. I didn't give him any reason to think I was interested in him." Mirella snugged into the safe haven of Barbara's arms. They had moved to the den and were sitting on the overstuffed couches in the comfortable, wood paneled room.

"Rape is not about sex. It's about power." Barbara rocked gently back and forth.

"Rape? That's not what he called it." Mirella lifted her head and looked into the dark eyes of her protector.

"What did he tell you he was doing?"

The thunderous frown on Barbara's face made Mirella hesitate. Barbara realized she was frightening the young woman and she softened her expression.

"I'm sorry. Why did the man say he was there?"

Mirella let loose a deep sigh and sat against the back of the couch. "Senor de la Mar Montenegro is Ms. Rodgers new... friend."

Steven slipped quietly into the den area, retreating to the wet bar to hear what Mirella had to say without embarrassing her.

"He said he was worried about me being by myself in this big house. He said Ms. Rodgers had sent him to make sure I was safe. Then, he said since Ms. Rodgers was his new lady, anything that was hers was his, and I was her maid, so I was his to do with as he pleased. He grabbed me and smashed his mouth on mine. Then his hands started grabbing me all over my body. I kept telling him to stop, that Ms. Rodgers would be very angry, but he wouldn't listen. It was awful. He ripped my blouse and put his mouth..." Mirella broke into a sob.

Barbara rocked her until the weeping stopped.

"That's considered rape. If he tried to have sex with you against your will, and you told him to stop or fought him, it's rape. We can file a report with the police so it won't happen again."

"No! He said he would have my family deported back to Spain."

The terror in Mirella's eyes tore at Barbara's heart.

Steven had heard enough. "I'll kill him."

His outburst startled the two women. They shrieked and clutched at each other.

Steven moved into the den area and sat on the couch opposite them.

"I'm sorry. It rankles me the man thinks he is bullet-proof. Mirella, where were you born?"

The young woman frowned at him. "You know, Mr. Rodgers. My mom said you waited outside in the waiting room until I was born. Here in the Tampa General Hospital."

"Exactly my point. You are an American, Mirella. You can't be deported, and I'm certain my father arranged for your parents to get their citizenship. As a judge, he couldn't afford the scandal undocumented workers would provide to his opponents. All of your family is in this country legally. Senor de la Mar Montenegro was using his position and power to try to get you to do what he wanted."

Steven watched as the young Spanish girl contemplated what he had just told her. Her expression went from one of fear to anger. The black eyes flashed and her body straightened with rage.

"Then I wish to make a complaint to the police. I want him punished for what he did to me."

"I'll make the call. By the way, have you two met?"

With both of the women shaking their heads, Steven continued. "Mirella, this is a friend from long ago, Barbara Hamilton...?"

"Langley."

"Langley. Barbara this is Mirella Alvarez, Daniela's daughter."

Steven watched the expression on Barbara's face. Daniela had treated her with as much love as she had lavished on Steven.

"I'm very pleased to meet you, Mirella. I was very fond of your mother. She was very good to me when things got very tough around here." Barbara threw a glance at Steven.

"I'm pleased to meet you, Ms. Langley. I just wish it had been under better circumstances."

"Speaking of... Steven? Please call the police. Do we have a way to find this creep?" Her eyes clouded with angry uncertainty.

"I, I have his address here. It is the same as Mrs. Rodgers. It is at the Tampa Bay Yacht Club. The consulate has a boat there the staff is allowed to use. Senor Montenegro is living there with Ms. Rodgers until she sells the house and buys a new one. He told me that when they moved into the house, I would have to move in with them since I was Ms. Rodgers employee."

Tears began to course down Mirella's cheeks.

Barbara slipped an arm around the young woman. "Over my dead body."

Steven bent down on his knee to speak face-to-face with the young woman. He slipped his hand under hers and looked her directly in the eye.

"First, Ms. Rodgers doesn't own this house and never did. When we got married, the senior Mr. Rodgers made her sign a prenuptial agreement which stated if anything were to happen to my marriage, the house was to revert to the family if I wasn't living, and I would own it if I was still alive. There's no way she can sell this place. I'm afraid Senor de la Mar Montenegro is in for a big shock when he makes that discovery.

"Second, if anything, you are my employee, although I hate the idea. As you said, I was in the lobby of the hospital with everyone else the day you were born hoping everything was going to be all right. Your mother had been very sick during her pregnancy, and we were concerned there might be complications. You are more a daughter to me than an employee. You're my *familia*, Mirella. I won't allow anyone to treat you as a second-class citizen."

Steven rose from his knees and placed a gentle kiss on the forehead of the young Spanish girl. "I'm calling the police."

Three hours later, the police had taken everyone's statements, given Steven instructions on how to swear out a restraining order for Senor de la Mar Montenegro and Ms. Rodgers, and left their card. Steven and Barbara had convinced Mirella to stay in the upstairs bedroom that had once been his daughter's. They sat outside by the pool and, in an eerie shadowing of years previous, sipped on sodas and discussed the situation.

"I'm so sorry you had to come back to this." Steven caressed Barbara's hand on the arm of the chaise lounge next to his own.

"Don't be. I'm just glad to see you so compassionate." She took a swig off the can of soda she held. "Rape has nothing to do with sex and everything to do with power. We need to make sure Mirella talks with a kind and understanding psychologist. Do you know anyone that would fit that bill?"

"I think I'll be able to find someone that can be gentle and give her the care she'll need. Like I said, Mirella is family. I've watched that young woman grow up. When Daniela retired, she asked if we would allow Mirella to continue to work in the house to help pay for college. Dad agreed and, without Daniela or Mirella's knowledge, set up a college fund. As philanthropic as that may sound, it was my father taking advantage of the tax laws. He wrote it off his taxes as charitable donations for the fourteen years it took to accrue."

Steven grimaced as he spoke of his father's manipulation of the tax rules.

Barbara remembered how the two had fought over Steven's involvement in the band. It wasn't a wise financial investment, according to Steven's father, and would lead the business community in Tampa not to take Steven seriously. There had been several nights when Steven had stayed with Barbara because he'd been thrown out of his house after a fight with his father about Steven's "future in the business world."

Steven continued. "Every bit of money she's spent on college has been set aside so when she graduates, she'll have something to fall back on if she needs it. Staying in the apartment just seemed logical and gave her freedom to buy a car to get back and forth.

"It's as though my own daughter has been attacked. I don't want to leave her alone, but I have to go into work tomorrow. I haven't lived in this house for six years; consequently, I don't have a change of clothes here. Everything I own is at the condo."

Barbara watched Steven's face screw up in anguish. It was evident he cared deeply for the young lady whose safety had been compromised in his home.

"Do you know anyone who could stay until tomorrow? Then, you'd be able to get some of your things moved over and start setting up your household. You were going to do that anyway, weren't you?"

He narrowed his eyes and appeared to stare at the bottom of the turquoise pool.

"You're right. I do know someone. I'm going to give them a call. Do you mind waiting here a little longer?"

"Not at all."

"I'll be right back."

"I'll be here."

~ * ~

Marc shifted on the couch and flipped through the channels. There was nothing to watch on television. *Maybe I'll go into the bar and do paperwork. There's always something that has to be done.*

He turned off the big screen and wandered down the hallway to his bedroom. He was rummaging in his closet when the house phone rang. Sticking his head out, he frowned. Not too many people had his house number. *What now?* He moved to his bed and, sitting on the edge, answered the phone on his nightstand.

"Hello?"

"Marc? It's your dad."

"What's wrong? Is Alana all right? What about Mom?"

"Alana is fine, and I have no idea if your mother is fine but, to my knowledge, she's not hurt. I need your help."

"You need my help? What's up?"

"Are you available tonight?"

"What did you have in mind?"

"I'd like to ask you to come to the house on Davis Island and, well, for lack of better terms, baby-sit Mirella."

"Why? What's wrong with Mirella?" Marc's frown deepened. The pit of his stomach was beginning to roll.

"She was attacked in her apartment tonight, and, before you fly off the handle, we've handled it. I've convinced her to stay in the big house in your sister's old room. I'd feel better if there was someone here to act as a watchdog. I'd do it myself, but I don't have clothes with me, and I really don't want her to be alone for any amount of time right now. Would you be able to do this for me? I'd appreciate it."

Marc had jumped up when his father had explained the reason he was calling. *Mirella, attacked? What idiot...*

"Sure, Dad. I'll grab some clothes and be over in about twenty minutes. Will that be okay?"

"Thanks, Marc."

~ * ~

Steven walked to the enclosed patio, finding Barbara at the edge of the pool gazing into the crystal depths. He cleared his throat.

Barbara looked up at the sound. "Hi. Any luck?"

"Yeah. My son is coming over to stay. He and Mirella grew up and played together as kids. I only hope I can keep him from going off the deep end. She's like a sister to him, and I wouldn't want to be Senor de la Mar Montenegro if he is foolish enough to come back. My son is young enough not to fear jail.

"He should be here in less than half an hour. I'd like you to stay until he comes but understand if you're too tired. It has been a long day, and this evening did not end as I had hoped."

Barbara smiled wanly. "I would have preferred a little less explosive excitement. I'll stay until your son arrives, but I need to start putting together a plan for moving and figure a way to tell Rachel. As always, Steven, this has been a memorable evening."

Steven started to apologize until he spotted the twinkle in Barbara's eye. He moved to her side and turned her to face him. "I can't let you walk out of my life again, Smokette. You do know that, don't you?"

Tucking a finger under her chin, he lifted her face up and lowered his lips gently to encompass hers.

Barbara reached up on her toes, allowing the passion of the moment to sweep her away. She felt him pull her to his body, imprinting her upon his still muscled form. His arousal was becoming rigidly evident when he, reluctantly, pulled away.

"I, I, won't rush this. You've said you're moving back, and I'll know where you'll be living, so I'm going to slow this down. I don't want to push, shove, chase, or scare you away, Barbara." He trailed a finger down the side of her face. "You're just too important to me. Last time, I found out *how* important too late. This time, no screw-ups." His hazel eyes crinkled at the edges, and he allowed a lazy smile to cover his face. "I have plans for you, Barbara Hamilton Langley."

"Dad! Dad!"

Steven turned to the sound of the shouting.

"Sounds like my son is here. I'll explain the situation and try to cool the explosion I know will occur when he hears what happened. Don't leave before I have a chance to say goodnight. Please?"

Nodding, Barbara took her empty soda can to the bar then escaped out the front door. The shadow of a figure flit past her peripheral vision. She hurried to her rental car and climbed in the driver's side. Running into Steven after all these years was a fantasy come true. Facing, and possibly meeting, his flesh-and-blood son was more realism than she wanted at the moment. She knew he'd married and had children; they'd discussed it, but to stand face to face with the child he'd created with another woman—it was more than Barbara was ready to accept. If she and Steven became an item, she'd find a way to get past her unrealistic feelings of hurt. A tap on the window made her jump. Barbara jerked around to see Steven standing next to her car.

She rolled the window down.

"Where'd you go? I came back to the pool and you'd disappeared. I took a chance you hadn't left, and, when I saw your car, I sprinted out here to be sure I got to say goodbye."

Barbara blushed although she was sure, in the darkness, Steven couldn't tell. "I figured it would be best for me to fade out of the scene."

"I wanted to introduce you to my son." Steven leaned down, crossing his arms over the window. "Maybe another time."

He leaned in, and Barbara met his lips. The parting kiss lingered, soft and beckoning.

Grudgingly, Barbara pulled back. "I would love to continue this line of... thought?" She giggled. "But we both have a busy day tomorrow. I need to get my beauty sleep. I've got a lot to get started." Kissing her forefinger, she placed it on his lips.

Steven held her hand to his mouth. It was hard to release her. She'd just walked back into his life, and he didn't want to let her out of his sight. He let her finger slip through his and stepped back as she started the car.

"May I see you again?"

"Sure." Barbara turned on the inside light and opened the console between the front seats. "I know there's a notepad in here, somewhere." She spotted the small lined tablet and, rummaging in her purse, located a pen. She wrote her number on a sheet of paper, which she handed to Steven.

"Call me. We can figure out a way to get together without arousing the suspicions of your employees." She flashed him a grin and started to move away from the curb. Glancing in the driveway, she noted the Camaro parked there. Something about the car seemed familiar.

All Camaros look alike, silly.

A small cloud of doubt passed through her mind but could not stop her from starting to grin. She turned on the radio.

"This is Lex Lord. I have to say—you guys have blown my mind. I can't believe how many of you have responded to our request about whether Rock Railroad should get back together. Seems Rock n' Roll is alive and well. I've had almost a thousand 'yes' emails in the last week. There are a few of you who have sent me some off-the-wall responses, but, frankly, I think you're listening to the wrong radio station. So what do we do now, guys? Do you want me to tell Steve and the guys we want them back? Our phone lines will be open for the next two hours for your answers. If there are enough yes's, we'll get Steve Rodgers on the line and interview him. See if, maybe, we can convince them to reunite. Now, to get everyone in the mood; I'm going to play a little tune called *Back Again* by Rock Railroad."

Barbara hummed along with the music. Finding Steven had been a nice surprise, but to have him playing in the band again? She glanced upwards. *Dylan.* She felt a chuckle whisper down her back. *You skunk.*

~ * ~

Ray sat in the family room, his fingers flying over the strings of the guitar. His head was down, and he was concentrating on keeping up with the song coming from the radio. When the song ended, the announcer started talking about Rock Railroad reuniting.

"Monica! Monica! I need you in the den, now!"

The petite, dark woman burst into the room, dishtowel between her hands. "What? What's the matter? Are you okay?" She looked at her husband; he didn't appear to be bleeding, yet.

"Listen."

She sat on the couch next to him, and the two listened as the announcer pleaded with the audience for a response to his request of Rock Railroad reuniting. Ray turned to look at his wife. His eyes sparkled as they had when they'd first met.

"You really miss it, don't you?"

"Well, yeah, but we decided, together, it would be better not to continue in the music business while we raised a family. But now, well, the kids are pretty much grown, and my construction company is successful. I'd like to get back into music again."

His face glowed so hopefully, Monica could only laugh. She got up, kissed his forehead, and, throwing the dishtowel over her shoulder, walked into the kitchen as she tossed over her shoulder. "Go for it, Papi. Go for it."

Ray pumped his fist in the air then picking up the guitar, easily fell into the riff from the Rock Railroad song playing on the radio.

Reynaldo, Jr., strolled into the kitchen, lifted the lid of the pot on the stove, and asked his mom, "What's for dinner? Where's Dad?"

Monica slapped his hand, the pot lid clattering back into place. "Beef stew is for dinner, and your father is in the den."

The young man wandered through the dining room. Monica watched as he stopped in the doorway of the den. He stood motionless.

Reynaldo stared at his father sitting on the couch, guitar in hand, plugged into an amplifier, playing along, note for note, with the group on the radio. This couldn't be his dad. His dad was the owner of a construction company, worked with his hands building things. When did he learn to play guitar and so well?

Ray looked up to see Ray-Ray gaping at him. Ray started to smile. *Now's as good a time as any.* "Junior... we need to talk."

Twenty-one

Rachel sat in the teashop and gazed out the window. The powder blue sky, checkered with clouds in various shades of gray and white, cast beams of sunlight to the damp streets. The city park across the street spread its emerald green carpet of thick grass over rolling hills dotted with trees bursting in spring foliage. She sighed and leaned against the high back chair. *I could easily live here.*

"Are you all right, luv?" Robart had returned from his foray to the men's room, the loo as he called it. He sat next to the redhead who'd won a permanent place in his heart and swept her hand into his own. "Not homesick, are you?"

Rachel, her tan skin standing out in the crowd of pale faces within the small shop, answered. "No, I, uh, I was just thinking how easily it would be for me to live here." She lowered her eyes to the table.

Robart leaned forward and pulled her hand closer to him.

Rachel looked up.

"That's good to hear. I was afraid you'd hate the cold, rainy weather. No one believes the sun ever shines in England." Spreading his other hand in the direction of the park. "As you can see, we do have our sunny days." A devilish grin touched his lips.

Rachel huffed. "Please, Robart. I'm from Oregon, remember? I'll bet we can beat you on the number of rainy days we have. Besides, I knew what the weather would be like when I agreed to visit. What I didn't count on was..."

"What?"

"Falling in love with the countryside, the small villages and towns, and..." Rachel lowered her voice to a whisper and dropped her gaze to the bone china cup with primrose pattern in front of her. "... you."

Leaning in, so they nearly touched noses, Robart allowed a smile to slowly spread over his face and tilted her head so she looked directly into his deep green eyes, a dark, curly lock of hair resting on his forehead. "I was hoping all of those things would make you fall in love with me. I'm a practical man. That's why I haven't become involved to this point, but when you walked into my section on the plane... well, Rachel, it was love at first sight. Something I would have sworn did not exist three months ago. Why is that making you so unhappy? Don't you want me to love you?"

Rachel's eyes widened. "No, I mean yes. Oh, jiminy. I want you to care for me the way I care for you, but this trip was about helping my friend Barbara get over the death of her husband and... look at me! I'm here in England with you, happier than I've ever been, and she's, well, she's in Florida, alone, I think."

Robart shook his head. "Whew. That was confusing. Did she forbid you to come see me? Did she seem unhappy you were leaving her?"

Rachel tilted her head to one side and narrowed her eyes. "Actually, she didn't seem unhappy at all. She said she had a date. She did tell me, however, if I got married without her she would never speak to me again." Realizing what she had just let slip, Rachel blushed crimson and rolled her eyes. "I never was very good at being covert."

Robart started laughing, a deep bubbling sound that seemed to originate from his toes. Rachel couldn't help herself and started to giggle. Stern stares from the surrounding patrons muffled the two.

Rising, Robart asked. "Are you ready to go for a walk?"

Rachel nodded and took his proffered hand. The stately couple strolled out of the small tearoom and meandered down the sidewalk looking through the shop windows facing the roadway. When they'd walked past a jeweler's, Robart halted and turned to look at Rachel.

"Shall we browse through the engagement section?"

Grinning broadly, she slipped her hand through the crook of his arm. "Yes. And yes I will."

~ * ~

Steven closed the door to his garage and headed directly to his refrigerator. Tonight held more excitement than he'd bargained for. Having Barbara, his Barbara, back in his life was a dream come true. He took his soda can upstairs and sat at his desk. Starting his computer, he received the announcement, "You have mail." Going through the motions to open his email account, Steven recalled those times when Lisa had made his life so miserable with her accusations and screaming; in his imagination, he would watch her fade away, and Barbara would replace her. His daydreams always involved finding Barbara, reuniting and creating the life he'd pushed away.

His email account opened; the message he had was from his daughter.

"About time."

He opened the mail. Alana had written how tedious the trip had been. She'd thought she'd lost her bags, only to find a professor at the college whose luggage was identical to hers had mistakenly picked them up. His name was Geoffrey Townsend and, as luck would have it, he was one of her Literature professors. She went on to describe his comfortable tweedy appearance and fascinating accent.

Steven groaned. His little girl was exhibiting signs of being love-struck. Oh, well. He supposed he could tolerate an English son-in-law.

Steven replied he was glad she'd found a friend to help her get to know the college and England, and things were going okay back in the States. He hadn't wanted to alarm her about the situation with Mirella but would tell her at another time; maybe when he went to visit. He sent the reply and shut down his computer. It was late, and he was tired.

~ * ~

Marc softly closed the door to the room where Mirella was staying. His father had finally convinced the young woman to take three aspirin to help her sleep. It would relax her but not create the after-effects sleeping pills left. As he passed through the entry hall, he peered out the floor to ceiling windows facing the street and noticed his dad leaning down and talking into the window of a convertible parked at the curb in front of the house. He couldn't make out the figure inside but, if his dad's body language was any indication, the driver was a woman. *Helluva way to end a date. Date!*

Marc spread himself on the couch in the den, flipped on the TV, and pulled out his wallet.

"I know I have Lenny's number in here somewhere." He rummaged through the leather holder until he found the business card for which he was searching. Picking up his cell phone, he punched in the numbers.

"Hey, Lenny. Marc Rodgers here. I know it's been a long time since we talked, but I need to ask a favor. I would like to bring a friend..."

There was a click on the line, and a voice said, "Hold on. Give me a minute."

Sounds of paper shuffling and the clatter of dishes filled the background. Finally, a voice answered. "Hey Marc. It has been a long time. Is this friend pretty?" Chuckling.

"Actually, Lenny, she's an absolute knockout. You know, now that I think about it, maybe I shouldn't bring her to the stadium. She's so good looking; the guys on the field won't be able to concentrate on their game."

"I've gotta see this one. I'll leave tickets to my box at the front gate, and I'll throw in on-field passes so you can meet the players. I figure that will make us pretty much even. I couldn't have afforded the kind of reception you gave Kandi and me. I don't think I can thank you enough for that, Marc."

"Let's not get into that. Like I said before, you covered my back so many times at the frat house, I'm not sure there are enough favors I can perform to make us even. It looks like we have a stand-off. Why don't we mark it up to friendship?"

"Done. What day do you need the box?"

"Is the team practicing on Thursday?"

"Let me see."

Marc heard the sound of papers shuffling, again.

"Thursday at seven p.m. they have a pre-season game with the Mets. Should be a good one. From the looks of the lineup, they're playing this game as if it were the regular season, using all the first stringers. If you're trying to impress her, this game should do it."

"Great. Thanks again, Lenny."

"Just send me an invitation to the wedding."

"Consider it done."

Marc hung up the phone. "I guess we'll just have to find something to do until the game at seven." He smirked as he flipped through the TV channels. "Oh, darn."

A blood-curling scream pierced the air and ripped Marc from his comfortable position on the couch. Dashing through the house, he took the steps two at a time up to the second floor where the sound seemed to originate. He stopped at the closed door to his sister's old room and, fisting his hand, pounded on the door.

"Mirella! Mirella! Are you all right?" Marc stepped to the door and placed his ear against the wood. Soft shuffling and quiet sobbing filtered through the thickness. "Mirella!"

"Just a moment."

The sobbing had stopped and Marc heard the shuffling move in the direction of the door. He took two steps backward. His stomach rolled in anticipation, and he knit his eyebrows together in worry. The handle twisted, and the door fractioned open.

A pair of ebony eyes peered around the barely opened portal as strands of long, dark hair swung around the opening. "Marc. Why are you here? What's the matter?"

He blew out a breath. "Mirella, you screamed. Is everything all right?"

The door opened a little wider, and the slender young woman stepped forward.

"Oh, that."

"Yes, that." He reached his hand out and gently covered hers. "I was worried. Dad called and asked me to stay here at the house tonight. When you screamed, well, I thought the worst. Are you okay?"

The caramel face of the young woman flushed pink. She lowered her eyes, and Marc watched as an unbidden tear slipped down her cheek.

"I woke up, didn't recognize the room, and panicked. I'm so sorry. Maybe I should just go to my mom's in Ybor City." Mirella stepped back into the room and started to make the bed.

Marc followed her into the room and, lightly touching her shoulder, stopped her. "Mirella. How sensible would it be for you to go to your mom's? Of course, you'd be confused waking up in Alana's room. Even after all the years I lived here, if I slept in my old room, I'd probably be confused waking up there, too. Tonight has been a nightmare. Dad filled me in with the details, and I'm here to make sure nothing else happens. First thing in the morning, we'll go to my grandfather's legal firm and get the restraining order completed. By tomorrow evening, you'll have the order in effect."

Mirella sat on the bed and dropped her head into her hands. "I hate confrontation, and I know that was what he was depending upon." She raised her head to look into his eyes. "Marc?"

"Yes?"

"I really need to get some things from the apartment, but I don't think I can face it alone. Will you go with me so I can get a change of clothes? I have one last class to attend before the end of school, and I really don't want to wear what I have on to school."

Marc offered his hand. Mirella reached up and allowed him to raise her off the bed. She slipped on her shoes, and the two walked down the stairs and through the kitchen toward the back door. As they crossed the yard to the outside steps of the apartment, Mirella hesitated, slowing the closer they came to the stairs. Marc turned and slipped her hand into his. He watched as she lifted her chin, and marched up the steps with determination. He was a step behind her when she opened the door, flipped on the light and let out a small groan.

The disaster that was her bed stuck out in the neat room—comforter thrown to the floor, sheets crumpled and bunched, and her robe tossed on the ground in a heap. The pillows had been thrown around, and Mirella's torn blouse hung off the end of the bed.

Marc felt her form start to slide to the floor. He stepped behind her and placed his arms around her waist, holding her to him and allowing her to slump her body against his own. A groan from deep within the slender woman escaped into the semi-darkness.

"Do you want me to do this for you?"

She shook her head and straightened up. "I need to get over this. I don't want that animal to control my life in any way, shape, or form. If I allow this to haunt me, he wins, and I lose. I won't lose."

Mirella allowed herself to lean into the comforting arms of her childhood friend. "Thank you for being here, Marc."

"You're welcome." At that moment, he realized she'd grown into a lovely young woman, the closeness of her body to his emphasizing the point. He bit his lip as the hint of spice tickled his nose. The silky texture of her flowing black hair made the idea of running his hands through it difficult to stop. Marc became painfully conscious if he didn't remove himself from his closeness to Mirella, he would compound the problem she'd faced earlier. He stepped back and cleared his throat.

"Why don't we turn on all the lights? I'll help you throw the bed together, and we'll get what you need and get the heck out of here. How's that sound?"

"Like a great idea."

The two turned on all the lights in the small apartment and went about putting the place as much in order as they could. Mirella pulled a small valise from the closet and tossed in clothes and toiletries for several days. She handed the bag to Marc then grabbed all her schoolbooks. As quickly as they had entered the apartment, they turned out lights and locked the door, sprinting across the yard to the big house.

Upstairs in the bedroom, Marc set the valise on the floor and turned to leave. Mirella placed her hand on his arm. "I do feel safe with you here, Marc. Thank you. I know this is probably the last thing you wanted to do..."

Putting his finger on her lips, Marc smiled. "Mirella, you're family. This is the first thing I would do if it were Alana. I'm just glad you're allowing me to help. I only wish I could get my hands on the son of a—"

Removing his hand, she said, "Suffice it to say, the law will see that he is taken care of. I only hope his diplomatic immunity will not stop his punishment. If it does, I'm not sure what I'll do."

Marc acknowledged there was going to be nothing easy about this situation. "Let's just take this one step at a time."

"You're right. Thanks, again." Mirella stood on her tiptoes and placed a delicate kiss on Marc's lips.

He stumbled backward and sprinted down the stairs into the den. He grabbed a beer from the refrigerator and, flipping on the TV, dropped onto the couch. Slugging down a shot from his beer, he sat, dazed by what had just happened. He put his hand to his lips and traced where Mirella had just kissed him. The charge he'd felt when she'd delicately brushed her mouth over his was making his lips tingle. The impish tomboy he'd grown up with had turned into a ravishing beauty that set his blood on fire. He'd been unable to find anyone he wanted to be near for years, and now, two women, in less than two weeks, had his head spinning and his hormones racing.

He groaned. Like he'd told Mirella, he was going to have to take this one day at a time. Getting off the couch, he made his way to the linen closet and grabbed a blanket. He had planned on sleeping in his old room across the hall from where Mirella was spending the night, but after that kiss... he placed his hand on his lips again; there was no way he could trust himself so close to her. He patrolled the house, securely locking all the ground floor windows and doors. Then, he retired to the den. When his grandparents had owned the house, his grandfather had practically lived in the den. There was a wet bar and a bathroom. Marc was set. He flipped through the channels until something caught his attention and he settled on the couch.

It was going to be a long night.

Twenty-two

Barbara finished tying her tennis shoes. Standing up from the bed, she made a final check in the mirror over the dresser.

"Looks okay to me."

She grabbed her driver's license and credit card, shoving them into her pockets, and stood contemplating whether she should take her cell phone or not. She hadn't heard from Rachel, yet, and was beginning to get worried.

"To heck with it. She's done it to me, one more time and after firmly swearing she wouldn't ditch me for a man. I'll leave the phone here and, if she calls, she can leave a message. I'm sure Robart knows enough people here, since he flies in and out of this hub, to hitch a ride to her room. But she's going to get a piece of my mind, that's for sure."

She bounded out her door and to the elevator. The last two days had been filled with long distance calls to family, friends, her realtor, and the bank officials setting everything up in Oregon so she could buy the condo here in Tampa. Frankly, she was tired of being on the phone and thankful Marc had promised a day in the sunlight.

A brief call Tuesday morning explaining how wildly insane things had gone at his father's law firm with the restraining order sworn out against Mirella's attacker was the only contact Barbara had experienced from Steven. There appeared to be some issue concerning diplomatic immunity for the man. Steven was going to try to approach the problem from a different angle.

Barbara rolled her eyes at the thought. Twenty-some years ago, she could have guaranteed there would be some bloodshed involved. She couldn't be sure it wouldn't happen that way today. Outside of the brief call, communication with Steven had been nil.

She strolled through the lobby and popped through the sliding entry doors just as Marc drove up.

He parked the Camaro and jumped out to open the door for her.

Barbara stood surveying the car. *I'm sure this is exactly like the one parked in Steven's driveway the other night.* She felt the skin on her arms rise in goose bumps, and she shivered.

"You, okay?" A small line formed between Marc's eyes as his brows furrowed.

"Yeah. I think it was just a gust of air conditioning. Compared with the air out here, it's chilly." Barbara slid into the car and smiled at Marc. She saw the disbelief in his eyes. "It's okay, really."

He walked around to his side of the car and started it up.

"Ready?"

Barbara leaned against the soft leather and nodded. "Oh yes. I'm ready."

An hour later, as they passed through Bradenton, Barbara sighed. "This was always such a pretty town."

Marc shot a side-glance her way. "Always?"

Realizing she'd slipped, she amended her statement. "Yeah, my aunt and uncle used to vacation here near the beach somewhere, and they always took hundreds of pictures. Do you ever recall those northern tourists with the bright flowered shorts and cameras around their necks? It seemed like they took pictures of everything. You know—palm trees, stop signs, the locals?"

"Oh yeah. Down around this area, Bradenton and Sarasota, they're everywhere; especially in the winter. Although, I have to admit, the last couple of years, the hurricanes have kept all but the most dedicated snowbirds from heading our direction."

Barbara wasn't sure if Marc bought her "aunt and uncle" story but it seemed to ease the suspicion from his voice. The landscape had changed so much since she was last here. Her Florida didn't exist anymore. She was going to have to decide, and fairly soon, if she liked this new place as much as she had loved the old. Buying a home in Tampa was a big step. Maybe, she should call the realtor and her banker and stop things before they got too far.

"You're awfully quiet." Marc, slowing for a red light, had moved into the right turn lane.

"Just enjoying the scenery. There seems to be a lot of building since my aunt and uncle vacationed here."

He turned on to Hwy 64 and was heading west. "Yes. There has been somewhat of a boom, then again, some of this building is repair from the hurricanes last season."

"How stupid of me, of course. I'm sure they're going put up better buildings than were destroyed. It's still a little sad. There was such 'character' in the old town of their pictures. By the way, where are we going?" Barbara looked around and found she didn't recognize the scenery—old or new.

"I thought we might spend some time on Long Boat Key. We can park the car, stroll along the beach, and look for shells. Spend some time getting to know each other before the game tonight. There are shops we can look through and, when you get hungry, you can decide where you want to eat.

"We have box seats so we don't have to worry about someone taking our place, and the game doesn't start until seven. I hope you don't mind."

The hopeful lilt in Marc's voice made Barbara smile. "It sounds like a perfectly wonderful day. Lead the way."

Long Boat Key was one of those places Barbara had always planned on going, but she had never made the short trip from Tampa. Life had always interrupted and, when Steven had been playing in the Bradenton and Sarasota area, they lived the life of musicians: getting up at noon or one o'clock, doing a little sightseeing or lying by the pool, going to dinner, then going to the gig until two or three in the morning. Usually, everyone in the group, and the "new" girlfriends, would go to breakfast until five or six in the morning. Real sightseeing hadn't been their priority.

Barbara marveled at how much she'd missed.

At seven fifteen, when Marc and Barbara slid into the box seats located on the first base line, her nose was a tender pink color that matched her cheeks. She was thrilled to sit in one place. She and Marc had walked for hours on the beach talking. He was a smart, funny man she was sure she'd have fallen for had she been closer to his age. But the truth was she was old enough to be his mother. Several times, she'd nearly given away her true age.

"Penny for your thoughts." He tipped the popcorn bucket in her direction.

"Just recalling what a great day this has been." She grabbed a handful of popcorn and popped the lightly buttered kernels into her mouth. "I've had a really good time."

"Well, I hope this game lives up to the hype my friend gave it. I like football because it moves so fast. Baseball, however, bores me—too slow."

Barbara placed her hand above her eyes to shadow out the field lights. The glare was in such a position at the moment; she was unable to see the home plate and the batter. "I agree. TV baseball makes a great sleeping pill. But I find that true of all sports on TV. Everything is much better in person."

The crack of the bat signaled the batter had been successful, and the couple watched as the baseball sailed over the back fence. Barbara rose to her feet and found herself clapping and laughing with the rest of the stadium. Marc turned and high-fived her.

"This could be a good game, yet!" He leaned down and placed a kiss on her slippery lips. "Hmm. Love that buttery taste."

Barbara stood on her tiptoes and returned the kiss. Her heart was pounding, and she found herself losing the battle to stay detached. He pulled her to him. The thin material of her t-shirt let her know his heart was hammering as quickly as her own was.

"Whoa. We are, after all, here to watch the game." She placed her hand on his thumping chest and, pushing gently, put distance between them.

As they sat down, a groan rose from the crowd. Looking to the monitors, the couple realized they'd been on camera. They looked to the field and found all the ballplayers looking at them, applauding and whistling. A man in the box above them leaned down and clapped Marc on the shoulder.

"You've got a real beauty there, kid. Don't let her go."

Barbara felt heat wash over her body. She couldn't be sure how much was embarrassment and how much was from Marc's touch. *This is getting waaay out of hand. I can't fall for this kid, not with Steven back in my life. Or is he? I haven't heard from him since Tuesday. It's been two days of silence. This is too much like the first time we met when it took him a week to get back in touch with me. Damn! I'm not twenty-two, and I don't have to wait around for anyone*. Barbara crossed her arms over her chest, the expression on her face darkening.

"Did I do something wrong?" Marc knit his eyebrows together and bit his lower lip.

She relaxed her face into a smile and dropped her arms, putting her hand lightly on his knee.

"No. Just remembering I haven't heard from my friend since Sunday. After you dropped me back at the hotel, she called to let me know she'd be returning from England this week. She hasn't called to let me know exactly what day, and it irritates me. I didn't mean to take it out on you. Sorry, Marc." She watched him relax and lean back against the seat. "Why don't we concentrate on the game? I'd like to see Cincinnati win. How about you?"

Marc slipped his arm around the back of her chair. "I would, too."

~ * ~

Steven paced in his office. When he'd come to work this morning, his intention was not to call Barbara. She was, after all, a guest in his hotel. It would be unethical and against every rule he'd set down for everyone else. But the urge to pick up the phone and dial her room was becoming overwhelming. Sometimes being the boss stank.

For the umpteenth time, he checked the monitors then decided to chuck all his common sense. He picked up his phone and buzzed the front desk.

"Front desk. This is Donna. How may I help you?"

"Hi, Donna. This is Steve."

"Mr. Rodgers. What can I do for you?" Donna looked at the receiver in her hand. Mr. Rodgers was a great boss, a little obsessive compulsive but, for the most part, a good man to have as a boss. Lately, he'd been telling everyone what a good job they were doing and staying home more often to let the staff manage the day-to-day running of the hotel.

"Will you please ring room 823? I need to speak with the resident."

Her eyes widened in panic. She dialed the number then remembered. "Oh, she left about two hours ago..."

Steven checked his watch. It was 9:30. She'd gone before he'd arrived at work.

"Thank you, Donna. I'll contact her later."

"Do you want me to leave her a message to call you when she arrives back in the hotel?"

"No. I'll drop a note in an envelope and have housekeeping put it in her room when they clean. Thank you. Oh, and Donna?"

"Yes, sir?"

"You're doing a terrific job."

"Thank you, sir."

She pressed the #3 on her cell and stood waiting as the line rang.

"Come on, come on, finally. Reynaldo? This is Donna. I need you to be honest with me, is Mr. Rodgers selling the hotel?"

~ * ~

Ray hummed as he finished checking the blueprints on the last house he was constructing in this division. The owners had liked the basic plan but wanted to add touches of their own to make their home unique. As Ray perused their sketches, he realized there wouldn't be any additional workload for his crew, and the changes the owners had designed were simple but added elegance the other homes in the subdivision lacked.

"Amazing what some people can see."

He rolled the plans and, grabbing his walkie-talkie, contacted the foreman of this project.

"Alan? Where are you? I need you in the office trailer."

"On my way, boss. Be there in five."

Ray turned up the radio as he caught bits and pieces of Rock Railroad's song *Money Man.* He was singing, a bit off key, when Alan entered the trailer. Ray handed the rolled blueprints to his foreman with a few instructions and sent him to the job site. As he leaned over to turn down the radio, his cell trilled. He flipped open the lid and smiled at the name displayed.

"Don! What can I do for you?"

"Have you been listening to my show?"

Ray pulled the phone from his ear and pointed it in the direction of the blaring radio. "Yeah, and if you don't mind, I'm going to turn it down so we can talk." He reached over and flipped the off button. "What's so important you have to call me at work during your show?"

"Let me have your email address. I want to send you some of the responses we got to our 'Get Rock Railroad Back Together' survey last week. I'll be honest with you. I haven't had this much action on one of our surveys since we ran the Duran Duran debate; that one was split down the middle with most of the yes answers being from women.

"This one, Ray... you guys have got to get back together. This Bay is screaming for some good ol' rock and roll and they seem to like the kind your band created. I've had requests for songs from all the albums, not just the hits. You're not out strokin' the numbers, are you?"

Ray chuckled. "No, Don. I haven't been strokin' the numbers, although, that's not a bad idea."

"Don't! There's no need. Listen, when can I get you and Steve in the studio to do an interview?"

Ray leaned back in his chair and propped his feet on his desk. "Let me work on him, Don. I'll get back to you before the end of the day."

"Don't forget to call me, Ray."

"Not a chance." Ray rattled off his email address and clicked off his cell. Interlacing his fingers behind his head, he stared into space. If Rock Railroad got back together and started touring and recording again, another 'what if' of his life would be completed. Monica had all but pushed him to get back into music, and he did miss playing with the band—drinking, second-hand smoke, and hangovers aside. He was a successful businessman with a beautiful, loving wife and family. He'd proven to himself and his family he could make it in the real world. No—he'd like to try the insane world of music, again. He gazed dreamily at the ceiling in his trailer. When the phone rang, he started, dropping his feet to the floor and grabbing for the receiver.

"Montez Construction."

"Dad, it's me, Reynaldo."

"What's up? Aren't you at work?"

"Not yet. I go in late today. Dad, I need to ask you a question."

"What Ray-Ray?"

"Reynaldo."

"Excuse me, Reynaldo."

"Dad, is Uncle Steve selling the hotel?"

"What! Where'd you get that idea?"

"Well, he's been complimenting everybody and kind of staying out of our way. He's not been in the office for two days in a row, and we were just kind of wondering."

Ray snickered then broke into laughter. "So, he doesn't show up for two days, and you guys think he's selling the hotel. Oh, yes, and he's complimenting you on how well you're doing your job. Isn't this what you told me you hoped he would do? I thought you felt he was looking over your shoulders too much and didn't appreciate how much work you were doing and how well."

"Yeah, but..."

"Look, Reynaldo, you can't have it both ways. As far as him selling, well, he hasn't said anything to me. Just enjoy the change. Who knows? He could go back to being the way he was before. Is that what you want?"

"No."

"Then don't complain. And tell your mother I might be late for dinner. I'll call her later and let her know for certain. Bye, Reynaldo."

Ray continued to chuckle. It looked as though Barbara had gotten to the untouchable Steven Rodgers. Now was as good a time as any to call him about reforming the band, but first, he wanted to see what some of the emails Don sent were saying. If they were positive enough, he'd print them up to show Steven. One thing he knew about his best friend; he had the instincts of a lawyer so a person had better have proof in black-and-white if they wanted to win an argument with him.

Ray opened his email and sat back in his chair. The system had slowed to a crawl because of the volume of the attachment. Fifteen minutes later, he was able to open the first email.

"YES!!!! Please reunite Rock Railroad. The crap that's on the radio now isn't fit to listen to. Please ask the guys to get back together and start making 'real' music for the world to hear. I'd give up eating to buy a CD of theirs. Becky."

Ray read and printed out responses like Becky's for the next hour and still his email was blinking at him that it was too full. He'd have to get his daughter Estrella to do it at home.

Right now, he had a handful of requests he wanted Steven to see. If he worked this right, he could get an interview with Don by tomorrow and talk with Marc about the jam session on Sunday. The radio airplay could guarantee more business at the bar on Sunday. Maybe Marc should set up a small cover charge. If the guys got paid, even fifty each, that would mean they were back in business again. Ray began to whistle. He hadn't been this happy in a long time.

Rock Railroad was on track again. He chuckled at his own pun.

Twenty-three

Steven clicked shut his phone. This was the fourth, no, fifth message he'd left on Barbara's cell. He'd tried not to call but the thought of never seeing her because he was being *manly* was more than he could stand. He'd just have to wait for her to call back.

When his cell rang, he didn't check the digital readout; he just answered.

"Hello?"

"You low-life, scum sucking, piece of..."

"Stop right there. If all you're going to do is swear at me, Lisa, I'm hanging up. I don't have to listen to this. In fact, I can have you locked up for harassment. Now... what is it you want?" Steven ground his teeth together to keep from hurling back to his ex-wife the insults for which she was so fond.

"How could you have Diego thrown into jail? He is a man of quality-something of which I'm sure you have no concept. It was humiliating and degrading to a man of his stature. How could you have a restraining order placed against him and myself? What have we done? Nothing! That's what! How could you..."

Before Lisa could tear in to him full steam, Steven knew he had to nip this harangue in the bud.

"Lisa? Lisa! Did Senor de la Mar Montenegro bother to tell you why he was a guest of the county?"

"No, he didn't. I know it's because you're jealous that I've moved on to someone of a higher quality and status in life. You need to get over the idea we will ever be together again. It just won't happen. Now you need to have the restraining order removed. Thank goodness, Diego has diplomatic immunity. He was only forced to endure a couple hours of inconvenience."

"So, Senor Diego didn't tell you I walked in on him trying to rape Mirella? I don't doubt it. I warned him to stay away from the property and Mirella. As you are now his concubine, and no longer have access to the Davis Island house because of the legal document you signed before we got married, you are included in the restraining order as well. Don't come stomping around the house expecting to receive any kind of welcome. I'm sure you'll recall we had security cameras installed when the kids were young. I've made sure the cameras are all in good working order, the codes updated and redone, the locks on the doors rekeyed, and the local police are aware there is a possibility of a recurrence of the attack.

"Your choice to stay with the Senor is just that—your choice. Don't expect me to fall into line anymore, Lisa. Your ego has always been large, but this delusion that I want you back is enormous, even for you. I love the children we had but don't miss one thing about our marriage. Don't fool yourself into thinking I care for you; I don't.

"You've been warned, twice. If you show up or approach me, Mirella, or the house, you will be arrested. Am I clear?"

"Crystal. You haven't heard the last of this."

The silence on the other end of his phone told Steven his ex-wife had hung up. She just didn't get it. He wasn't interested in her, anymore, and worse for her, the man with whom she was choosing to align herself was a controlling, inconsiderate chauvinist who viewed women as objects and vessels for his own pleasure.

While Steven didn't care for his ex-wife, Senor de la Mar Montenegro was the lowest form of man alive, and Steven wouldn't wish that on his worst enemy, or his ex-wife.

~ * ~

Barbara barely felt her feet touching the elevator's carpet. Marc was an incredible man. Every time he touched her, her skin tingled, and his kisses... it had been a long time since she'd been with a man, and her hormones were in overdrive. She was going to have to revert to taking cold showers. Sliding through the door into her suite, she hummed softly. *Hmmm.*

Let's see how this fits, Mrs. Marc—? Stopping in the center of the living area, Barbara realized she had no idea what Marc's last name was. *I can't believe I'm doing exactly what I yell at Rachel about. I have no clue what his last name is. I know he works at the Devine Nine, but I'd feel like an idiot calling up and asking for his last name.*

Picking up her phone from the dresser top where she left it, she wandered back into the living room and plopped down on the couch. She had twelve messages. The first three messages were from her brother-in-law John, the realtor, and the banker in Oregon about tying up details for selling her house. The details were going to be handled so she would just have to sign paperwork, pack up, and move when she returned. John was interested. He felt it was time to settle down and thought being in Dylan's house would help him heal.

Barbara wasn't so sure. It seemed like a bad idea, but if John wanted the house, she wasn't going to discourage him. Maybe, he'd propose to his girlfriend of ten years, finally.

The next three messages were from Rachel. The first one sounded normal saying she'd call back later. By the third message, Rachel's voice was sounding strained and panicked. Barbara smiled. She'd call back but not tonight. It was too late.

Rachel would just have to wait one more day. The next five messages surprised her. Steven—somewhat casual at first then, by the fifth message, a tone in his voice Barbara could only describe as desperate. His last message said, "I can't bear the thought of not having you around. I won't be an idiot like last time. Please, call me at your earliest convenience, no matter the time. I just need to hear your voice."

Barbara couldn't hide the smile spreading throughout her body. So, he'd realized he'd been a fool all those years ago. The admission was over twenty years late, but the satisfaction felt good, anyway. She entered his number in her phone. She was reveling in the glow of Steven's disclosure when she realized she had one more message. She pushed the retrieve button.

"Hi, beautiful lady, it's Marc. I know it's only been ten minutes since I dropped you at your door, but I miss you already. Can we get together again? How about Monday night? I have to work all weekend, and, while I don't want to wait that long to see you, sitting in the bar watching me work is booorrring. I'll leave my number, so you can call at your convenience. Hope to hear from you soon. By the way, I had a great day."

What a delicious dilemma: two men who wanted her company. A pang of guilt slid across her heart. She shouldn't be feeling so—happy.

Don't be silly, Winkie. I always knew I was a lucky man. Don't feel guilty for moving on with your life. It's been nearly three years since I left you. I know you'll always love me just like I'll always love you, but it's time to move forward.

A deep sigh pushed through Barbara's lips. "I always hated it when you were right, Dylan." She picked up her phone and made her first call—to Steven.

She closed her eyes when the silky voice answered the phone.

"Hi. This is Barbara. You called?"

~ * ~

Ray pushed his speed dial. The breathless greeting was more than he expected.

"Well, hello to you, too."

"Oh, it's you."

"I think I'm insulted, now."

"I was expecting someone else."

"Would this someone be female and back in town after a twenty year absence?"

"You might say that."

"I would say that. Under those circumstances, I'm not insulted."

"How kind of you. What do you want, Ray?"

"I'm on my way over..."

"It's late and I..."

"Have stayed up later than this on many an occasion. You'll live. There's something you need to see then we need to talk."

"I'll leave the front door open. I'll be in my study emailing my daughter to see how she's holding up after the first day of classes. Oh, yeah, my security code for the front gate is 081975."

Steven could hear Ray muttering the numbers as he wrote them down.

"Hey, isn't that..."

"Yeah. The first day I met Barbara. See you in thirty minutes."

When Ray walked into the study, thirty-one minutes later, Steven glanced from the computer screen suspiciously. "What do you want? You are never on time unless you want something. What is it, Ray?"

The tanned Cuban slapped down a stack of papers two inches thick. "I want you to read at least half of these."

Steven pulled several sheets off the top, reading the pages and letting the ones he'd finished slip to the floor. "Are they all like these?"

Ray nodded. He dropped into the leather chair in front of the desk and, grabbing a handful of pages, started reading aloud.

"Can't get together soon enough. When's the new album to be released?"

"What took you so long?"

"Please send tickets for the first concert to me at the address below."

"Yes, yes, yes. If Steven Rodgers looks half as good now as he did then..."

Ray put down the stack. "Steven, what are we waiting for? Your kids are grown adults; mine aren't too far behind, and we're successful in the real world. What more do you need to see before you realize there is a place for us in the business? So what if we're only popular in Florida? We'll be playing music again. And, frankly, I've missed it, haven't you?"

Steven leaned back in his chair and swiveled it from side to side. The pile of papers on his desk was impressive but...

"This is only a fraction of the responses Don got. I've got Estrella printing out the rest, in case you need further convincing."

What had he to lose? Planting his feet on the floor, he leaned down and opened a desk drawer.

Ray watched as he rummaged in his files and pulled out several long forms.

"These are the legal forms that everyone needs to sign. If Marcus and Carl agree, I'll have them notarized at work, and we can officially call ourselves Rock Railroad again. You willing to fill it out and scratch your signature on it, now?"

Ray pulled the form to himself, grabbed a pen from the cup on the desk, and, with a flourish, autographed his name to the bottom of the legal form.

"You didn't read it."

"I know you wouldn't hand me a form that would screw me over. That's why you always did the legal mumbo jumbo. When it comes to business, you're so honest you squeak."

Steven had to agree. He'd made sure every contract the group had been given was thoroughly read and clarified to him by the paralegals in his dad's office. He wasn't sure if his father had been aware of it or not. He sat and filled out a form for himself.

"How do we get Marcus and Carl to sign, and do they want to?"

Ray smirked. "You've been the only hold-out since the idea started two years ago. I'll get them to sign on Sunday at the jam session at Devine Nine. Now, Don Baker has done a lot of promotion to get us to re-form, and I promised him the first shot when it became a reality. We'll call him and do a phone interview. He's going to promote the jam session on Sunday to see how well the public will receive us. We're on our way. Maybe we should practice on Saturday and put together a couple of sets of old stuff and throw in a new tune or so? Think we can do it?"

"Didn't stop us before, shouldn't now."

Steven's cell trilled and he looked at the readout. "If you don't mind, this is private."

Ray stood, a lopsided smirk tattooed on his face. Maybe Maria was right. They'd all be getting wedding invitations soon.

~ * ~

Steven felt his stomach roll and his nether regions began to remind him he was still human. Barbara had always had this effect on him.

"Hi."

"Hi, yourself. What's up, Steven? Is Mirella all right? Your daughter? Your son?"

"Don't panic. Everyone is okay. I, uh, I..."

"What?" Barbara could feel the hesitation.

"Look, I know I said I was going to take things slow but, to be quite honest, I lied. I can't risk losing you again. When you didn't answer your phone, well, I thought you'd left town without telling me. I sort of lost it."

Barbara couldn't help but smile. Her heart felt as if it were doing handsprings in her chest.

"I'd really like to see you as soon as possible. I know it's late but would you be willing to come to my place? I would like your input on a project that has come up. I'll be a gentleman and take you for a drink in a public place, okay?" Hope had replaced the hesitation in Steven's voice.

She let him wait for a moment before she answered. Twenty years earlier, he would've known the answer before she said it, but time seemed to have robbed him of his cockiness.

"All right, Steven. Are we going dressy public or casual public?"

"Dressy public. The place I have in mind is quiet and private but does require its clientele to be properly dressed. That won't cause a problem, will it?"

"No, but it will take me forty-five minutes before I can get to your place on Bayshore."

"No problem. I'll see you when you get here. Call me before you get to the gate, and I'll meet you. We can take your car. That way, should anything happen, you won't feel trapped. Until then."

~ * ~

Barbara bolted up from the couch and dashed to the bathroom. She'd been trying to sound casual when she'd told Steven she could be ready in forty-five minutes. She hated when she put herself in a bind. To be calling him at the gate to his community in that amount of time, she was going to have to fly through her routine. She needed a shower, anyway, since she had sand on her feet and a thin layer of baseball dust all over her body.

Boy, what a day! She'd been to the beach and gone to a baseball game with a great looking young guy, and, now, was going for a drink with a drop dead gorgeous older man. This was almost like being twenty-five again. *I could get used to this.*

Barbara hummed as she turned on the water, stripped down and stepped into the shower. That little black dress she bought at University

Square would be perfect for this evening. *Look out, Steven Rodgers. If I lose you this time, it won't be without a one helluva fight.*

~ * ~

Steven dialed the number of the Yacht Club Bar. When he'd hung up from the conversation, a small, candlelit table in a secluded corner complete with the club's best bottle of champagne in a chilling bucket had a reservation sign on it with his name. Now, he had to hustle to be ready by the time Barbara showed up at the front gate. He wanted to discuss her thoughts about him going back into the band, and what he should do about the hotel. She'd always had a fairly good head on her shoulders when it had come to business, but, most of all, he wanted to sweep her off her feet and guarantee she wouldn't leave.

For nearly six years, he'd been a single man, and while he'd tried the dating scene, he'd found himself comparing every woman to Barbara. Now, she was here, and he wasn't going to let her slip through his hands. Tonight was the start of his campaign to get Barbara to marry him.

~ * ~

When Barbara spied the sign for the community where Steven lived, she dialed his number. "I'm about two minutes away."

"I'll meet you in front of the gate." He stood gazing at the lights reflecting off the Bay. He'd traveled some with Rock Railroad and had seen some pretty amazing places in the world, but he'd always been relieved when the plane landed at Tampa International. Car lights swept across the lawn and spotlighted him. Stopping, the driver door opened and a figure rose from the vehicle.

"Steven?"

"Hi."

"Why don't you drive? There's been so many changes I wouldn't feel comfortable behind the wheel, just yet."

Steven moved to open the passenger door, holding Barbara's hand as she lowered herself into the car. He walked around and tried to slip into the driver's seat. "Aaahh! Who drove this last—a munchkin?" He moved the seat back and slipped the car into the lane heading toward Davis Island.

Barbara giggled. "Sorry about that. I keep forgetting most of the world lives above five foot one. Where are we going that I had to get so duded up?"

"It's a surprise. I suspect you'll guess before we get there."

"Is what you want to discuss a surprise, too?"

Steven shot her a side-glance. The city lights silhouetted the straight line of her nose and full lips. He caught his breath. *I can't believe she's really here.* He reached across the console and took her hand in his. Without hesitation, she shifted herself toward him and leaned on the console, her hand slipping easily into his. It was a move from twenty years earlier but accomplished as if no time had passed at all.

"It's not a surprise but I'd like to discuss it when we're face to face. Your opinion is very important to me." He heard Barbara suck in a breath.

"The Yacht Club." Her soft voice was barely audible. "I don't suppose you still have the houseboat?"

Steven chuckled and felt the heat rising to his face. "Yes, Mom and Dad still keep the houseboat here. They've upgraded from the last one. It's much bigger and has more toys, but is still berthed in the same slip."

"That's not where we're going, is it?"

Steven felt a pang of hurt. "Would that be so bad?"

Barbara heard the wounded sound in his voice. "No. But I'd like to see it during the daytime first before we attempt any nighttime maneuvers." She could almost hear the smile on his face.

"Okay. No, we're going to the Yacht Club. I thought we could sit in peace and quiet and enjoy the view of the Bay. As I said, I want to ask your opinion of something I need to decide this evening. Quiet and calm seemed more appropriate."

He slid the car into the parking space labeled with the family's name and helped Barbara out. She stopped for a moment and took in the changes time had painted over the landscape.

The couple walked into the club lounge, and the host escorted them to a table by the window. A linen cloth covered the small table and a matching set of rose-colored candles glowed warmly in their matching silver holders bearing the club crest. A bucket filled with ice and a champagne bottle stood next to the table. The bartender retrieved two champagne glasses from the cooler and, with a practiced hand that displayed the expertise of his profession, quietly opened the champagne bottle with no spillage. He filled both chilled glasses, wrapped the bottle with a cooled towel, and melted away to the bar.

Steven lifted his glass. "To fulfilling a dream I thought had died—to us."

Barbara lifted her glass and touched the rim to Steven's. "To us."

They gazed out the window at the twinkling skyline of Tampa. The harbor water, unbroken by waves, mirrored the scene. To the side were the boat docks. Their silent sentinels bobbing in the quiet evening.

"I've missed this more than I realized." Barbara sighed.

Steven slipped his hand under hers and squeezed. "Welcome home, Barbara Hamilton."

She turned her gaze to the man who's first captured her heart. Muted candlelight danced in his hazel eyes; the few laugh lines around them adding warmth to his face. She felt a lump forming in her throat. Coughing to push back the emotion, she asked, "What is it that needs my input?"

Steve leaned against the back of his chair, his eyes staring at a point above the sparkling skyline, and started to speak. "When we were together, I never thought it would be any different. I was pretty blind to anything but my view of the situation. I figured you'd hang around, indefinitely. It was a huge shock when you left. I was certain you'd come to your senses and come back. It never occurred to me to ask you to come back."

Barbara bit her lower lip. Even twenty some years later, the thought of what had happened that summer made her heart ache.

Steven continued. "I stumbled around for a while pretending it didn't matter, but Ray busted me. He told me to call you, write you; do whatever was necessary for me to stop mooning over you. But I wasn't about to give in. I didn't realize something as important as our being together wasn't a contest. Sad to say, I probably wrote my best music during that period.

"Six months later, Lisa showed up, and you know the rest. I've spent the last few years what ifing—about us, about music, pretty much about my life."

"But an opportunity has dropped into my lap, and I want to see what you think." Steven turned his gaze to the dark brown eyes regarding him. "I'm thinking of re-starting Rock Railroad. There's been a little hype about us getting together, again..."

"I know. I've been listening to WARM 94.9, too," Barbara smiled.

"...and I'm not sure. Last time we did this, we were in our twenties, and it was new and exciting. I'm not in my twenties, anymore, and I know how much work this could be. I have to think if I want to give up my hotel, free time, any social life I might have..."

"Whoa. I think you're jumping the gun." Barbara leaned forward and caught Steven's hand in hers, locking her eyes onto his. "First, do you still love playing music?"

"Yes."

"Do you want to play in the band again?"

"I've dreamed of it since I promised to quit all those years ago."

"The rest is just semantics, isn't it?"

"True."

"I'm guessing you have an assistant manager at the hotel that must be doing a good job or he or she wouldn't still be there. So, promote him or her. Do you have to be at the hotel every day? If you own it, can't you be a silent owner? Let your people do their jobs. As far as free time and social life, well, you are older now. Demand the time you want. You have enough legal savvy to be able to write it into any contract a recording company may offer the group. If that doesn't work, get Ray to build a recording studio; record on your own timetable and with your own musicians. Hire a manager that knows the group and is willing to book nightclub gigs or a tour on your terms.

"Steven, take charge of things this time. Make your years of experience in the business world work for you."

He sat back in his chair and grinned. The twinkle in his eyes told Barbara he'd baited her.

"You dog. You had this all figured out all ready, didn't you?"

"Well, not completely, but hearing you reiterate what I was thinking helped to put it in concrete. Now for the real reason I asked you here. Would you go with me to a jam session on Sunday night?" He was drawing circles on the tabletop with his fingertip.

"I'm not sure."

The finger stopped. He looked up into the dark eyes to find a twinkle dancing with the candlelight. She was trying hard to hide a smirk and wasn't being very successful. He leaned forward taking his finger and running it down the side of her soft face.

"Please."

"Well, okay. What time should I be there?"

"Do you mind if I pick you up? I'll pull my SUV out front around seven thirty. Remember, it takes us about an hour to set up, and the jam session starts at nine."

Barbara rolled her eyes. "How could I forget? I think I still remember how to set up and break down your drum set. Do I dress up as a band *groupie* or go for comfort?"

He raised her fingers to his lips and gently brushed his lips across the top. "Whatever strikes your fancy. I would hope you'd consider yourself my lady, but maybe that's going to take some time. I can't apologize enough for being the idiot I was to let you go, but I can try to convince you to come back into my life. With any luck, permanently."

Barbara started. He'd just said permanently. "You do realize what you've said to me?"

Steven looked at the face of the woman who'd lived in his dreams for over two decades. "Yes. But I'm not about to rush anything and chase you away. You've said you're moving back into town, and, hopefully, into my life. This time, I want you to be one hundred percent sure of the answer when I ask you."

Barbara gazed across the table at the man she thought she knew. Her heart thudded in her chest. She didn't know why she should be so surprised at the change in him. After all, she'd matured and grown in the years they'd been apart, why shouldn't he? What she hadn't counted on was falling in love with this mature Steven. His touch sent her blood pressure soaring, and parts of her body she'd thought long dead were making themselves known—loudly, lustfully, and urgently. It was going to be difficult to keep her hands to herself. Just like old times. Barbara grinned. What was the line from that song—"You had me from hello."

So he did, so he did.

~ * ~

Barbara floated to sleep dreaming of Steven and lovemaking in the bedroom of the house on Davis Island. Light streamed through the windows as she looked down from her seated position on his stretched-out, naked body to his lightly furred chest. He ran his hands up her taunt stomach and cupped her breasts in each of his palms, running his thumbs back and forth over her nipples until they pebbled in response. Rising up, he brought his tongue to her breast and flicked the brown end, sending rushes of pleasure through her. His warm lips covered the end, and he pulled the hard nipple into the heat of his mouth. Barbara squirmed in delight, a moan escaping her throat. The sunlight glint off the blond streaks of his head as he moved down her stomach to her wet, throbbing triangle. His tongue traced circles above the curly black patch of hair before he targeted the hardened nub in the center. The moment his wet, warm tongue touched her...

...the cell phone was ringing annoyingly.

"Hello," Barbara gruffed into the irritating instrument.

"Yeah, well, same to you. Sorry to call so late but you told me to let you know when I'd be flying into Tampa."

It took Barbara a moment to recognize the voice. Rachel had a bad habit of expecting everyone to know her voice when she called. "Well, you've woken me up from a very hot dream. What time do I need to pick you up?"

Rachel started to giggle.

Oh great. This isn't good. She never giggles unless she's nervous and about to lay a bomb on me. "What time, Rachel?"

"Oh, hell. I might as well just tell you. Robart got called back early, and we're sitting at the airport waiting for the flight. We'll be leaving in about two hours. The flight is projected to land at Tampa International at three p.m. It'll be landing at the United Terminal, the two p.m. flight out of Heathrow. Sorry for the short notice but Robart didn't get the call until a little while ago."

"I'll be there, Rachel. I'll want you to tell me the date of the wedding and what god-awful color dress I'm going to have to wear."

There was silence at the other end of the phone.

"Rachel? You still there?"

"How, how did you know?"

"I could feel the connection between the two of you the moment you met. I knew it was just a matter of time. There's something a little different in your voice, and you giggled. You never giggle when it's lust."

"Please don't say anything to Robart. He wants to take us both to dinner and make the announcement at that time. He knows how special you are to me, and he wants to do it right. Okay?"

"Rachel, I promise I won't let something slip out. You are my best friend and I'm just thrilled you've finally found someone this special. I'll see you at the airport. Now, go away and let me get back to my dream."

Twenty-four

Barbara watched the 747 United flight from London taxi into the berth. The size of the plane, and the fact it could get off the ground and into the air, still amazed her. She'd had to watch it from the restaurant, as the security restrictions were still tight at the airport. Finishing her coffee, she started the walk to the baggage area. Deplaning would probably take forty-five minutes to an hour so she had no need to hurry. She hadn't been standing by the baggage carousel for more than fifteen minutes when she spotted Rachel heading her direction. Barbara checked her watch.

"Jiminy. You got out of there in record time. How'd you arrange that?"

Rachel dropped her carry-on and sat on the edge of the motionless luggage conveyor.

"I guess when the flight attendants are called up to work they get to fly first class if there are any available seats. We were the first to get off the plane. Robart had to report in to his supervisor. He'll meet us to pick up his luggage. Oh, Barbara," Rachel grabbed her friend's hands, "I love the town he lives in, and his parents, and his brothers and sisters, and everything about him. But what am I going to do about my cats? If my sister won't take them, I know they won't survive quarantine."

"Aren't you getting a little ahead of yourself?" Barbara squeezed her friend's hand.

"What do you mean?" A small line formed between Rachel's eyes.

"What if Robart wants to live in the United States? Have you thought about that? Have you asked him?"

The two woman jumped as the conveyor belt began moving.

"Not really. I just figured we'd live in England. Maybe you're right. I'd better hold off panicking until I ask. But what if he doesn't want to live here and my sister doesn't want the cats? What am I going to do?"

Barbara grinned at her friend. "You just can't leave it alone, can you?"

"What?"

"You know I'll take your babies if your sister says she can't so stop worrying."

Barbara watched as Rachel's face lit up. Turning, Barbara spotted Robart, head and shoulders above the crowd, moving in their direction, happiness beaming from every pore on his face. There was no doubt in Barbara's mind, now. *He looked like a man in love.* A sear of pain stabbed Barbara's heart. *How will I live without Rachel in my life?*

She listened as the couple chatted easily about everyday things. The drive from the airport felt comfortable and relaxing, and when they arrived in front of the hotel, Robart helped Rachel carry her bags to her room. As they moved to open the door, they looked at each other and turned to Barbara. Robart spoke for the first time since disembarking.

"You know, don't you?" his hand rested on the doorknob.

"It's a little hard to miss. I'm thrilled you two found each other. After you've cleaned and rested up, why don't we order room service, and you can fill me in on the details?"

"Sounds like a wonderful idea. We'll ring you before we arrive." Robart smiled down at Rachel, and the couple disappeared into the suite.

Barbara wasn't counting on seeing them before Saturday morning, which suited her just fine, because she wanted to call Michael G's and set an appointment for the morning. She only hoped they had an opening. Rummaging in her wallet, she pulled out the card with the number and called.

She was in luck. Cheralyn answered the phone and remembered Barbara. They agreed to meet around noon. Barbara then called a tanning salon and set herself two appointments. She would be leaving in half an hour to keep the one tonight and her second appointment was at eleven on Saturday morning. She was going to knock Steven's socks off. He liked the little black dress and heels but she wanted him to be completely speechless. What she had planned for Sunday night would remind him of what he had thrown away.

She phoned Rachel's room and, as expected, got the front desk.

"Yes, can you please leave a message for Ms. Painter? Thank you. Tell her I'll meet her and her beau in the café for breakfast at eight tomorrow morning. We'll talk then."

She sauntered through the lobby. Slipping on her sunglasses, she stopped and smiled. It was so good to be home in the sunshine.

~ * ~

Rachel absently stirred a cup of tea as she watched Barbara walk to the table and sit down. "You're up bright and early. What's the occasion?"

"I figured it would be the only way to get to see you. Where's Robart?"

Rachel sighed and, with a clatter, dropped the spoon onto her saucer. "He had to take a flight out at six this morning. He sends his apologies and promises he'll take us to dinner when he gets back next week."

"Rachel? Is he going to continue to fly with the airlines or does he have another job skill?" Barbara furrowed her brow.

"Believe it or not, his dad is a police officer in Wennington and he's got a brother on the force, too. But Robart didn't want to follow in that particular family tradition which is why he went to airline steward training after college. He's actually got a degree in business. He said he was only going to fly for a couple years then go into the other family business. He found he liked flying more than he thought he would. Since he didn't have a wife, he didn't see any reason to settle down in one place. After we met the family and made our announcement, we discussed our future.

"His maternal side of the family has a hunting lodge with attached pub outside of Cambridge. Right now, a sister and her husband are the proprietors, but have asked to be relieved of the duty because the husband has received his doctorate and an offer to teach at the college there. Robart has decided to give his notice to the airlines, take his retirement, and settle in the lodge. I'll start making arrangements at my end of the world and move into one of the guest rooms until we get married in September."

Barbara, who'd been sipping her coffee and picking at her cinnamon roll, raised her eyebrows. "You're going to stay in another room?"

"It's a promise I made Robart's mother. Oh, Barbara, she is the sweetest woman I've ever met. I was so afraid that, being English, the family would turn up their nose at me. You know, because I'm American. The second reason I was afraid is because this happened so fast. When he told them at dinner our last night there, no one seemed to flinch. We took our tea into the lounge and talked for hours. She came up to me, grabbed my hands, and told me 'if Robart loves you then we love you.' We agreed to a six-month engagement and to live apart before the ceremony. We'll be married in the church where his parents got married and live in the lodge's apartment."

The stricken look on Rachel's face startled Barbara.

"What's the matter?" she leaned forward and grabbed her friend's hand.

"I'll miss the football season!"

Twenty-five

The bright, warm cocoon of the tanning booth was lulling Barbara into sleep. Just as she let herself slide down the relaxed path toward slumber, the lights turned off and a chill of air conditioning swept into her private shelter. She rose and, wiping off perspiration and tanning lotion, dressed. Thirty-five minutes in a tanning booth was as effective as an hour massage for Barbara. She glanced at the wall clock and hurried to make her appointment at Michael G's. Lying in the tanning bed, she'd decided on the color and style outfit she wanted for tomorrow's date.

Her phone trilled as she started to pull out of the parking slot. Driving back in and parking, she looked at the read out and smiled. Steven was not being patient.

"Hello. What is it that I can do for you, today?"

"Hello, beautiful. I'm a desperately lonely man whose about to go into a marathon practice session, but before I do, I'd like to have the company of a beautiful woman for a late lunch. Could we meet at two o'clock at Mama Leoni's on Dale Mabry?"

"My god, Steven. Are they still there?"

"You bet."

"Consider it a date. See you at two."

Barbara clicked off, a lopsided smile forming. She glanced at the digital readout on the vehicle's clock and uttered a swear word. She was on the borderline of being late and didn't want to lose this chance to find the perfect outfit.

After barely keeping the legal speed limit, and buzzing through a couple of yellow traffic lights, Barbara pulled into the small parking lot with five minutes to spare.

"Thank god." She dashed from the car to the door, and Cheralyn greeted her with a smile and a glass of sweet tea.

"You look like you could use this. Let's go into the sewing area and discuss what you might be looking to find. I got the impression during our phone conversation that you had something specific in mind."

Barbara took a long drink from the iced tea. She was thirstier than she'd realized. Moving behind the slender Cheralyn, she took a seat next to one of the sewing machines.

"Do you have something in mind?"

Barbara nodded. "I'd like to see something in a powder blue color and the sexier the better. I'm out to capture the one that got away."

"Are we talking bedroom-look-then-rip-off or are we talking out-in-public-eat-your-heart-out sexy?"

Barbara burst out laughing. "I knew there was a reason I liked you. You're as devious a thinker as I am. I'm looking for out-in-public sexy. Enough skin showing to elicit stares and drooling but enough coverage to pretend to be modest." She watched a wicked twinkle enter Cheralyn's deep blue eyes and a sinister smile began to spread over her face.

"He's in so-o-o much trouble. Let me see if the outfit I'm thinking about is still here."

She got up from the sewing machine and left the small shop.

Barbara watched her cross the jade lawn into the big house. Feeling too restless to sit, she rose and started browsing through the racks of clothing hanging from the ceiling. She'd found a pair of stone-washed pants she thought might be close to what she was looking to achieve but they weren't perfect for the mission she had in mind. She was beginning to feel hopeless when Cheralyn came back into the shop. She carried something on a plastic draped hanger and wore an enormous smile.

"It was still here in the storage area in the house. I think with the proper shoes, and I have a friend who can help with that, this will be perfect." She put the hanger on a T-stand next to the sewing machine then pulled up the opaque white plastic.

Barbara gasped and, grabbing the chair behind her, plopped down. "It's perfect!"

There, on the hanger, was a powder blue outfit so delicate and sexy Barbara could barely breathe just looking at it.

Cheralyn stood back a smug smile on her face. "Let's see how it looks on you. If there are some simple alterations, I can make them before," she raised her eyebrow, "tomorrow?"

Barbara nodded.

"However, if they're too complicated, we'll have to find something else."

I don't want something else. This is exactly what I'm looking to find and will accomplish everything I have in mind, and then some. She reverently took the outfit from the T-stand and into the changing booth.

Cheralyn turned on the radio and SteveO Z, from WARM 94.9, was gushing through the speakers. "We've done it boys and girls. I'm so cranked I can hardly sit still. We, the majority rule, have spoken, and Rock Railroad has listened. I'm going to play an interview Don Barber, our night DJ and personal friend of the leader of Rock Railroad, taped last night."

Barbara heard Steven's voice over the speakers but it had faded into the background. She gazed at the vision in the mirror. *This outfit is so perfect.*

Cheralyn coaxed. "Come on, this isn't like a wedding dress. I am allowed to see you before you wear it out."

The moment Barbara stepped from the dressing room, she heard Cheralyn's sharp intake of breath. "Oh my God. You look—amazing. Where are you going?"

The radio was nothing more than background noise.

"I'm not sure exactly but he said it was a jam session. If memory serves me, several clubs in town hold jam sessions on Sunday. We could hit one or all of them, for all I know right now."

"I just wanted to be sure to stay away from wherever you're going to be. My boyfriend won't pay one wit of attention to me if he sees you in this."

Barbara's dimples deepened as she grinned. "It is perfect, isn't it?"

"What's not to like? The trousers slit up the side to high thigh, laced with powder blue leather strips, front V-ing to just below your, might I add, quite tan belly button. The top cups your breasts like a second skin while the neckline plunges dangerously toward the trousers. See, you can insert lace here or use the leather strips to close this opening," Cheralyn was showing

Barbara how the two inch space between her breasts could be closed or left open to display her ample cleavage. "What I really think is neat about this top is the stand-up collar. It's a seventies style that the group, La Belle, made popular, but we downsized the height. I think it's really cool. What do you think about these sleeves?"

Barbara looked at the fitted-to-the-elbow sleeves and nodded. They would do fine. Laced from shoulder to above the elbow on the top of her arm, they gave the wearer the freedom of movement with the look of skintight. The ruffle, as such, went from above the elbow to the wrist in a soft flourish, rippling with movement.

"They won't get in my way. Cheralyn, this is perfect. I'm afraid to ask what the price is on it, but I have to know how far in debt I'm going."

The slender young woman stood with her finger tapping her chin. "Well, the gal we designed it for was an imitator, you can guess who she was imitating, and had this made for a big show. The day she came in to try it on, she had to admit that she wasn't going to be able to buy it because she'd gotten pregnant and wouldn't be able to fit into the outfit. I can't remember the exact date we designed it, but let me say, she's now a plump grandmother." She tapped her finger on her chin again. "It is one of a kind, but... I'll charge you what I did for the black outfit you bought earlier in the week. Sound fair?"

Barbara's eyes grew wide. "More than fair. I'll take it. But what am I going to do about shoes? I'd love to be able to match the shoes to the outfit but this is so unique I don't think there's anything close." She watched as Cheralyn's eyes twinkled and a wicked little grin appeared on her face.

"Don't bet on it. What size shoe do you wear?"

"Seven and a half."

The young designer flipped open her cell phone and pressed a button. Placing the phone to her ear, she hummed along with the tune on the radio. "Hello? Didi! Listen, do you remember that pair of powder blue platforms you created way-back-when for the Cher outfit? Do you still have them? Great! What size are they? This is going to be so cool. Listen, I have someone I'm sending over to look at them. If she doesn't like those, can you pull some heels that are the same color or close? You're a lifesaver. I owe you. Thanks."

She turned to Barbara. "Didi sells the kind of clothes I like to wear. She has a shop down the road behind her house like we do. I'll give you the address. If you find a pair of shoes that you like, will you put on the outfit and let her take a picture? We've been waiting a long time to have this one included in our album."

"Of course, now let me change and I'll head over to her shop." Barbara removed the Blue Heaven, that's what she'd decided to call it, and hung it carefully on the hanger, pulling the plastic over to protect it. Once she left the dressing room, she settled with Cheralyn, got specific instructions to the shop that had the shoes and was on her way.

Four blocks from Michael G's, in front of another thirties-style mansion with stately pines and weeping willows, was a tastefully designed sign, "Vintage clothing and accessories for Vintage people." Barbara turned her car into the driveway and drove around back to the small parking area. She followed the flagstone path to a cottage complete with front porch. Inside the door, she found an eclectic array of items spanning several decades. A woman in her fifties sporting a large flowered print painter shirt and black bell-bottoms swept up to her.

"Did Cheralyn send you over?"

Barbara nodded a smile creeping over her lips.

"I have the shoes back in our footwear area. If you'll follow me."

She had to admit that Didi had kept her figure and could wear the bell-bottoms with style, but it was still a shock to see anyone in the sixties fashion. The proprietor indicated she should sit in a wing-backed chair. Barbara acquiesced.

When Didi presented the shoes, Barbara found herself having difficulty breathing. They were exquisite; made of soft leather dyed the identical shade of her outfit, the sandals sported a heel only three inches in height, small in comparison with some of the other creations of the time. The thin straps buckled at the ankle and one strip of leather crossed mid-foot to join the two straps over the toes. Frankly, they were more practical and stylish than some of the creations she'd seen in the stores lately. Holding her breath, she tried them on and stood. They fit as if made for her. Blowing out her breath, she grinned.

"I'll take them. Cheralyn says I have to put on the outfit with the shoes and have you take a picture."

Didi directed Barbara to a dressing room where she changed and reappeared in the room. She dropped into the chair Barbara had just occupied.

"It's been nearly thirty years since that outfit was created, but it looks as though it was created for you. It's unbelievable. Let me get the camera." Bolting from the chair through a curtain in the back, she returned with video cam in hand and had Barbara turn and strike several poses for her. Dropping the video cam to her side, she stood frowning.

Barbara panicked. "What's the matter? Did I rip it somewhere?"

Didi chuckled. "No, dear. It's just something is missing. If I remember correctly, a cape went with that outfit. Let me call Cheralyn." She picked up the rotary phone on the 1920s end table and dialed the number.

Barbara was surprised the old phone worked properly, however, this was a vintage store.

"Cher, my love, I know the outfit was designed with a cape. Is it there?" Didi plunged ahead. "I thought so. I'll send her over as soon as we're done here. Oh, yes. Absolutely perfect and they fit. I'll bring the video over tomorrow. *Ciao, bella*." Didi turned to Barbara. "You need to stop by the Michael G's shop for the cape. It completes the outfit."

Barbara nodded. "Thanks, I will."

Two customers, hearing the commotion, had appeared from somewhere in the recesses of the small cottage and were oohing and aahing.

Barbara asked, "Do you think this will get a man's attention?"

The consensus was unanimous—he'd have to be deaf, dumb, blind, and stupid not to notice. Exactly what Barbara was hoping. She changed, purchased the matching shoes and left to pick up the final piece to complete the look, as Didi had said. When she entered Michael G's shop, Cheralyn greeted her.

"I'd completely forgotten about the cape. It's a good thing Didi remembered. She would, though. She designed the outfit. Now, this is the finishing touch to this look."

Cheralyn swung open a powder blue lace cape on top of a cutting table. Intricately woven, the lace shimmered in the lights. Barbara stroked a finger across the fine material.

"It's called a peek-a-boo cape because of the cut out material between the lace patterns. As you can see when you put it on," Cheralyn swung the cape around Barbara's shoulders, "it allows the wearer to show as much or as little of the outfit underneath as they desire. Believe it or not, it also provides some warmth if you're in a situation where the air conditioning is cold or the breeze off the Bay is a little too chilly."

Barbara gazed at the final piece. She was going to set Steven's imagination, among other things, on fire. She watched as Cheralyn folded and placed the item in a tissue-lined box.

"I'm so glad to see this finally worn. I hope you enjoy it."

Barbara's eyes twinkled wickedly. "Oh, we will."

Twenty-six

Barbara sat in the booth at the Italian restaurant where she and Steven had shared their first meal together. She wasn't sure but thought the cook in the kitchen was the same as nearly two and a half decades ago. She giggled. The door opened and she looked up. Steven held his hands behind his back and tried to hold back a grin beginning to crease his handsome features.

"I see you remember *our* booth." He slid into the opposite side, hands still out of sight.

One corner of Barbara's mouth turned up. "Yes, I do. There's a lot of things I still remember. What are you up to?" She turned a mock frown toward him.

Gently lifting a single pink carnation from his lap, he placed it on the table in front of her.

"I believe this was also part of our first meeting." He watched the mock frown leave and a tender smile spread over her lips.

"Oh my. I wasn't sure you'd remember. It's beautiful, Steven." Barbara felt tears begin to well in her eyes, and there was a lump the size of Texas in her throat. She lifted the carnation to her nose and pulled in the fragrance. The smell still brought forth the memory of her grandfather on Sunday mornings; the last thing he did before church was to put a carnation in his lapel.

"Thank you." Reaching across the table, she slipped her hand into his and squeezed.

Steven ordered for them when the waiter appeared: antipasto salad and garlic bread. He hesitated for a moment, glancing at Barbara. "Is that going to be all?"

She giggled. "I've gotten a second lease on life, and if I want this new body to stay in this shape, and I do, I have to be careful what I put into it. I'm not as... active as I was at twenty-three." She realized the heat she felt was from the blush rising to her cheeks. *Get serious! This is the man who saw you naked more than once in five years.*

Steven chuckled. "I think your form looks just fine. I, on the other hand"—he patted his stomach—"need a little more fuel so I think I'll have one of the individual lasagnas."

"If the group gets going again, and you play as much as you used to, you won't have to worry about working out and watching your weight. I remember a pair of very muscular legs and a very flat stomach." She felt herself blush again. *Jiminy! Quit acting like a fifteen-year-old virgin.*

He waited until the waiter, snickering, had walked into the kitchen before continuing. "I had a very interesting phone call before I came over."

Barbara raised her eyebrows in question.

"Seems my son wants to talk to me about my 'rock and roll days' as he put it. He wants to get together before tomorrow night. I hope you don't mind if I have to leave a little early."

"Good heavens, no. Family comes first, always."

Steven gazed at her, his eyes shining in appreciation. "You are amazing. I don't think most women would have been so generous."

Barbara blew a puff of air through her lips. "Then you've been hanging around with the wrong women."

"That's obvious. I would've said no, but I'm hoping we've already started the beginning of a long association between Mr. Steven Rodgers and Ms. Barbara Hamilton..."

"... Langley."

"Langley. Food's here."

The two chit-chatted through their meal, and Steven wrestled Barbara for the check when it came time to pay the bill. As they stood in the parking lot next to their vehicles, Steven drew her to him, gently covering her lips with his. The traffic noise of Dale Mabry's four lanes disappeared as Barbara felt heat building from her toes to the top of her head. She slipped her hands around his neck and drew herself to his form. She teased his tongue with her own and allowed his hands to roam over her backside until he'd cupped it in both hands and snugged her into his body. His arousal pushed against her stomach. She withdrew her tongue, and, leaning her head against his chest, sighed.

"I'd love to continue this, but, you have a meeting with your son and practice, and I need to get back to the hotel." She gazed into his smoldering hazel eyes watching the glaze of lust slowly dissipating. "I'm sorry."

"No. I shouldn't have let things get this heated. I intend to continue this when we have the time and are in the right place. Until tomorrow." Steven raised her hand to his lips and kissed the back then placed a delicate kiss on top of her head. He got into his car and, with a wave of the hand, left the parking lot.

Barbara really had wanted to let things go farther, but, in front of Mama Leoni's, on Dale Mabry boulevard, within sight of the Tampa Stadium, was not the optimum spot. Steven was right. If the relationship got to that point, she wanted romance and comfort. She was past the back-seat-of-a-car days; although, Steven's SUV might have been fun.

She giggled. He made her feel twenty-three again. *Horny as hell and devilishly wicked.*

~ * ~

Marc stared at the television not seeing what was moving across the screen.

"You watching this?" Aaron's scrunched face made Marc focus on the screen. An infomercial for thigh cream was featuring before and after pictures.

He shook his head. "No. Just waiting for my dad to get here. We're going to have a talk we should have had years ago. Would you mind if I had the apartment to myself?"

"Hell, no. Tiffany and I have a date over at Don the Beachcomber's."

Marc's eyes widened in surprise. "Be careful, dude. She's looking for a sugar daddy."

"Yeah, I know. But you want to hear the down side of this?"

Marc nodded.

"She was like that the first time we went out. Then, all of a sudden, this really nice girl broke through the phony bimbo routine. We've seen each other every day this week. I guess hearing you were getting married last weekend really shook her up. She came storming in after she called last Sunday, but you'd already gone to the store for beer. I sat and talked with her for about forty-five minutes, and, when we closed, she and I met at the House of Pancakes for breakfast. We talked until six in the morning. I, uh, I think I'm falling in like. She admitted the same to me last night. We're going to talk about it, today and, maybe, I might be moving out. I'll let you know tomorrow after the jam session." Aaron glanced at his watch. "Gotta go. Good luck with your dad."

"Same to you." *You just can't tell. I hope she doesn't screw him over. Well, he's a big boy and can make his own decisions.*

There was a knocking at the front door, and Marc got up wondering why Aaron didn't just come in or use his key. Swinging open the door, Marc faced his dad, a silly grin brightening his face.

"You look like you've been drinking your lunch." They walked into the living room. Marc flipped off the TV and sat on the couch. Steven sat on the matching love seat.

"No. Just got a new lady; somebody very special."

"Is she somebody I know?" Marc nervously tapped the arm of the couch.

"No, someone from my past who's come back to town. And before you ask, she's my age. What was it you wanted to talk about? Should I guess?"

Marc leaned forward, clasped his hands in front of him with his elbows resting on his knees, and looked at the floor. "No. I just wanted to know about Rock Railroad. Why didn't you tell me? Were you ever going to?"

Steven knew this day would come but there was no easy way to put the truth into words. "I'll tell you but you have to understand, this is my point of view."

Marc nodded and looked his father in the eyes.

"You and your sister got into my pictures when you were little so you are aware of The Lady. When she and I met, I was in a hometown rock and roll band called Rock Railroad. We were playing local clubs in Tampa, St.

Pete, Clearwater, and the Sarasota area. All of us were going to college, and the band was a way to meet chicks and play music, emphasis on the meet chicks part.

"Most of my non-music friends were beginning to settle down, get married, and have kids, and The Lady wanted to do the same. I was hesitant to commit. After five years, she told me she was leaving because she wanted marriage and to start a family. I thought she was bluffing. I mean, she'd already waited this long, I was sure she'd be back. I was wrong. She disappeared from Florida. I looked everywhere I could think of and still couldn't find her. It brought me to my knees. For months, I went through the motions of living. Your Uncle Ray finally suggested I use the pain to write. What came out of the experience was the song *Left Behind*. It became such a big hit that all of us in the group were able to pay some bills and buy a few toys.

"At a concert, where we were opening for a group called Cult Explosion, I met your mother. I was pretty miserable, and she sat and listened to me whine. She told me later that your grandfathers had set up the meeting. They thought we were a perfect match, and, we were—for a while. After Rock Railroad's success begin to dwindle, and the guys decided to go their separate ways, Cult Explosion offered me the job of drummer in their band. Your mom had just informed me she thought she might be pregnant, and I knew I needed a gig to help support the family I was about to have, whether I was ready to commit or not. I played with them for about a month and decided I wasn't happy being just another drummer; so I thanked them and left the group. Your mom went ballistic. Told me I'd better find a job to support her and the baby, and I was never to speak about or play music around her or our children, *ever*. A week later, she announced because of the stress of the situation, she'd lost the baby she'd been carrying. It was six months before she became pregnant with you.

"I did what I could. Music is, now and always, my saving grace. In the beginning, I rented a storage unit on the sly and practiced two or three times a week. When things started falling apart, every time your mother and I would fight, I'd go to the storage unit and practice. I've had the same place for, well, as long as you've been alive.

"I guess that's most of it except that I've been playing music since I was old enough to sit at a piano bench. Anything else you want to know?"

Marc shoved himself to the back of the couch and laid his arm across the top. He cleared his throat and began. "Well, last Sunday, Uncle Ray pretty much filled me in on most of what you just told me."

Steven narrowed his eyes at his son. "Then why did you ask me to tell you?"

"I wanted to hear it from you. There is one other thing he told me I don't think you know. My grandfathers had no idea about the meeting between you and mom. She was hanging around backstage trying to make Isaiah Yeltsin, the lead singer of Cult Explosion, jealous. He'd just divorced her for a younger, blonder groupie."

"Your mother was married before?" Steven's eyes flashed. "She left out that little piece of information."

Marc crossed his arms over his chest. "May I continue?"

Steven nodded. "Sorry."

"Mom was furious and out to get even. When she saw you, and how unhappy you were, she jumped at the opportunity to use you. Isaiah had seen the two of you together, and it worked. According to Uncle Ray, he was livid—for two reasons. First, that she had the bravado to show up at one of his concerts; and second, that she would flaunt her relationship with you in his face. Seems she told him you two were an item before it happened."

Steven muttered, "Sounds like your mother."

Marc continued, "Apparently, he continued to see Mom while the two of you were dating. When Rock Railroad broke up, she told him she thought she might be pregnant with his child, and if he ever wanted to see it, he'd put you in his band. She must have told you the same thing because Uncle Ray says you proposed, as he put it, 'out of the blue'. When you made the decision not to play with Cult Explosion, she told Isaiah the baby she was carrying was not his but yours. According to Uncle Ray, Isaiah laughed in her face, told her good luck, and took off.

"That's when she told you never to speak about or play music again."

Steven sat against the back of the love seat and absorbed the information his son has just imparted. So many mysteries in his marriage to Lisa were now clear. If only he had just married Barbara... he wouldn't have Marc and Alana. *So much for regrets.*

"I'm sorry I didn't tell you sooner, but your mother was adamant I not destroy our image of respectability in your eyes. I only wish you would have wanted to play an instrument."

"But I did, Dad. I wanted to play drums so badly I drove mom crazy my sixth grade year trying to get her to let me play in the band. She was vehement I not play an instrument. Now, I know why."

Steven stood and moved to the door. "I hate to leave so soon, but I've got to practice tonight. If you're still interested in playing the drums, son, it's never too late to learn. I think I might know someone who'd be willing to show you how."

Marc rose from the couch and stood in front of his father. He extended his hand. "Thanks, Dad. I might take you up on that."

Steven pulled his son into an embrace. "I hope you realize I love you, Marc. I always have and always will."

Marc stepped back still clasping his father's hand. "I know, Dad. I love you, too."

"I'll see you tomorrow at the club. Later, Marc."

"Tomorrow, Dad."

Twenty-seven

Barbara put one final swipe of mascara on her lashes. Stepping back from the bathroom mirror, she squinted to see if she'd achieved the effect she wanted.

"Damn." She reached to the back of the toilet and grabbed her glasses. Slipping them on, she surveyed the finished product. "Should work just fine."

She hadn't put on much makeup, except her eyes, and had the glow of healthy skin accomplished by soaking up the Florida sun. She opted not to wear her contacts tonight because the smoke in the bar would create so many problems. As she finished dressing, her mind wandered over events that had occurred since her late lunch with Steven.

She'd come back to the hotel to find Rachel burrowed in her suite. Barbara forcibly dragged the tall redhead out to the nearest bookstore. When Rachel was moping, a book always brought her around. Since they'd been close to the airport, Barbara decided to take Rachel for a drink at the revolving restaurant on the top—CK's.

They rode up the elevator and sat at the bar watching the outer rim slowly rotate.

"I was a hostess the first day this place opened." Barbara smiled at the memory. "It was a nightmare. The powers that be had set the rotation of the outer ring a little too fast, and several of the customers that had wandered in for dinner had gotten very ill. It took a week of adjusting to find the right speed."

Rachel had turned on her barstool and was gazing out at the runway. "It must have been fun watching the planes landing and taking off. I could be happy working here."

The bartender, who had been wiping glasses, leaned toward her. "I'd be happy to get you an application. We can always use tall, good-looking... bartenders. Do you know how to make mixed drinks?"

Rachel turned to the blonde, still holding his towel in hand, and leaned in toward him holding the gaze of his blue eyes.

"You name it; I'll mix it."

Barbara was glad she'd convinced her friend to change out of her shorts and t-shirt and into a body-hugging miniskirt with clinging silk tank top. With a pair of heels that put her well over six feet tall, Rachel was a stunner.

A smirk blossomed on the bartender's face. "Come back behind the bar."

Turning to Barbara, Rachel's steely eyes held a wicked twinkle. "I think I'm going to enjoy this." She walked to the end of the bar and slipped under the leaf to the working side.

The bartender stuck out his hand. "Tony."

She reciprocated. "Rachel."

He crossed his arms. "I'll call out orders like we get them during Friday night dinner."

Rachel raised an eyebrow. "How's your boss going to like wasting all this booze?"

Tony chuckled. "We need the write off. I'll call it marketing. Are you ready?"

Rachel turned to Barbara and flexed her fingers. "I haven't done this in a long time. Hope I can remember them all."

"I have every faith in you, girlfriend. Kick some booty."

"Long Island ice tea, margarita on the rocks-no salt, surfer on acid, Polynesian passion- blended, Manhattan, Perfect Smirnoff's martini, coke, ice tea and a Budweiser draft." Tony watched as the long-legged, busty redhead moved effortlessly behind his well. She mixed drinks as though she had read his mind. By the time he'd finished saying the drink, she was waiting for his next order.

Two businessmen moved up and sat at the bar. Tony nodded for Rachel to handle their order. She walked over and, flashing a million-watt smile, asked for their order. Tony snickered as the men sat slack jawed, gaping at the statuesque beauty. After a minute of silent staring, they ordered: a Manhattan and a Perfect Smirnoff martini. Rachel undulated back to the well and grabbed the two drinks she'd just made. She turned to Tony. "You knew they were coming in, didn't you?"

His grin was his reply.

As Rachel ambled back toward the pair, Barbara watched the two men hold their breath until Rachel had placed the drinks in front of them. Both men blew out slow, low whistles as she walked away. The younger man frantically waved Tony over.

"Who is that?"

"Somebody I'm thinking of hiring."

"Don't let her get away. Whoooooeee!" He took a sip from his Manhattan and slipped Tony a twenty. "This is the most perfect Manhattan I've ever tasted. Not only is she a knockout, but she's a helluva bartender, too. George, how's your martini?" His partner raised a thumb up.

"She's earned that tip, and Tony?"

"Yeah.

"Don't blow this by trying to sleep with the help."

"Screw you, Bob."

The businessmen laughed as Tony walked back to Rachel. "The job is yours. Here's a tip from the boys. If Bob and George don't complain about their drinks, you've passed the toughest test in this place. Those two are regulars here; they'll pay your rent if they like you. The last bartender thought she was above the clientele, and they complained loudly enough to management to get her fired. When can you start?"

Rachel laughed, taking the twenty and placing it between her ample breasts. She watched as Tony's eyes widened and his tongue snaked out and ran around the inner rim of his lips.

"Let me have an application, and I'll get back to you. I'm here on vacation for the next three weeks. I don't plan on doing any working while I'm here, but, I'll fill out the form, in case I change my mind." Rachel walked past the businessmen, winked, and blew a kiss. Lifting the bar leaf, she returned to her barstool next to Barbara.

Barbara shook her head. "You are something else, girlfriend."

Rachel leaned back and rotated her glass in her hands. "I like my job at the warehouse but I really miss being a bartender. This wouldn't be a bad place to work. Being able to watch the planes coming and going, I'd feel close to Robart. I could work here and rent a small studio somewhere until he quit working with the airline."

"What about your cats and the house?" Barbara signaled Tony for two more drinks.

"I called my sister earlier today and hinted I might be moving. She told me she wants first crack at the house and, when I said I might be going overseas, she informed me the cats were staying with her. I was not to put them in quarantine and take them to some foreign country where they'd get sick eating the local cat food."

Barbara's eyes popped. "She what?"

Tony brought over two drinks and indicated they'd been bought by the businessmen.

Both girls thanked Bob and George.

Rachel rolled her eyes. "She has some cockamamie idea that, like people, the cats will get 'Montezuma's revenge' by eating anything but American cat food."

Barbara looked at her friend. "She's not really serious, is she?"

"Unfortunately, she is. But the good news is the cats have a home, and I have a buyer for my house, if I want it. I just hate having to search for a place to put all my stuff until Robart and I move into the Lodge."

"What if you had a place?"

"Well, it would sure make things a lot easier but, Barbara, leaving my stuff at your place in Oregon wouldn't make much sense, would it?"

"It would make sense if you had a place to stay and store your stuff here in Tampa."

Rachel turned to Barbara and narrowed her eyes. "What have you done?"

"Uh, bought a condo?"

The surprised look in Rachel's eyes confused Barbara. "You did know that Oregon was just a stopping spot for me, didn't you? I'm sure I told you this before, I was just pulling myself together after Steven and I broke up. But then... I met Dylan and things just sort of happened. While you and Robart were in England getting to know and love each other, I had two dates with the young bartender from Devine Nine and... bought Steven's condo."

"What? Go back over that again. You bought Steven's condo?" A confused expression clouded Rachel's face.

"Yes. Dylan had been at me again..."

Rachel smirked.

"...and made me realize I wanted to move back here. I've always considered this my home and, quite frankly, when you went off to the British Isles with your knight in shining armor, I suspected you'd be staying permanently. Dylan made me realize as long as I live in Oregon, his brother John will never move on with his life. He feels obligated to make sure I'm happy. So, I found a realtor featured on the Real Estate Channel who looked familiar. I realized she's someone I knew from the first time I lived here. She had a condominium listed the day before and, when we toured the place, I discovered it belonged to Steven. He's getting the house back on Davis Island so he's selling the condo. It's in a perfect location and large enough for both of us to stay there and keep out of each other's hair. What do you say?"

"That you have this pretty well planned out, don't you Ms. Langley?"

Barbara smiled at her friend. "Yes, I do, Ms. Painter. But it will work, won't it?"

"Yes. It will. Hey, Tony?"

"Yeah, Rachel?"

"Could you use a good bartender in about two months?"

Bob and George looked at each other and grinned.

Tony looked at the pair and turned to Rachel, "I'll make a spot for you. Just fill out the application and get it back to me. Don't forget to leave a number where I can reach you."

The wicked look in his eyes made Rachel smirk. A place to work close to where Robart flew in and out, a place to stay until he left the airline, her house sold and cats with a home... she wasn't sure who Dylan was manipulating, her or Barbara.

The two women finished their drinks and drove back to the hotel. When Barbara invited Rachel to accompany her on Sunday night, Rachel politely declined citing the way the smoke had affected her the last time. Besides, she had a new book she wanted to start reading. They agreed to go to the beach for several hours Sunday, and after sharing lunch at the hotel café, they'd go their separate ways connecting Monday to catch up.

Barbara hadn't mentioned the Rock Railroad connection to Rachel, yet. She wanted to see where her feelings lie with Steven. If things didn't work out, she'd tell Rachel his connection to the group later.

~ * ~

Barbara grabbed a small silver bag she'd bought on her shopping safari. She hated carrying one but the Michael G outfit had no room for anything but imagination. A quick survey of the room and she was satisfied she had all she was going to need for the night.

The elevator doors opened on the sixth level and two women, about Barbara's age, stepped into the car and moved toward the back. Barbara watched the scene below as the glass room quietly slid to the ground floor.

"It's her. I tell you, it's her." One of the voices behind her stage whispered to the other.

"Is not. She's too short."

"How the hell would you know how tall she is?"

"I read it in the Enquirer."

"Oh, and that's full of truthful information. Why don't you ask her?"

"Why don't you?"

By the time the two had worked up the courage to ask Barbara if she was who they thought, the elevator door had opened. In her best imitation of Cher, Barbara turned, "You ladies have a great night." She hurried out through the lobby and, peering at the two white SUVs parked out front, moved to the one where the driver had waved at her. She could only hope it was Steven. By the time she reached the car door, he had moved around and was holding open the passenger side. Giggling, she vanished inside the vehicle at the same time the two women stepped out the front door.

"I told you it was her, Marge. Wait until I tell Edgar we saw Cher!"

Barbara could hold her laughter no more, and, while Steven started driving, she told him about the incident in the elevator, concluding, "It has to be the color of this outfit and my dark hair. I no more look like Cher than the man in the moon." She started giggling.

"Actually, Smokette..."

Barbara smiled at the two-decade-old nickname.

"...you do look a lot like her in that outfit. Maybe we should call you—Barbra."

"Can't."

"Why not?

"Barbra Streisand has that locked up."

"Uhm. You're right. How about Miss B?"

"That sounds too much like a teacher."

"Okay, how about B or maybe Queen B?"

"I like Queen B. Piss me off, and I'll rap until your eyes roll back in your head, or I'll sting you. Steven?"

"Hmm?"

"Where are we going?"

"To a club on the north side of town. They have jam sessions on Sunday night. We practiced last night and this morning. Even though it's been a number of years since we all played together, I was really pleased at how easily we slipped into our music. Marcus's son has the bass down. I hate to say it, but he plays a lot better than Ricky ever did. Marcus still has the best guitar riffs in town, and Ray doesn't sound like he put his guitar down at all during the last twenty years. Although there is one small problem I was hoping you might be able to solve."

Barbara glanced at him and saw the beginnings of a worry line forming over his eyes.

"What do you need?"

"Do you remember the harmony to any of our songs?"

Chuckling, she answered. "All of them. Why? What's the problem?"

Sighing, Steven left the questions hanging as he turned off the freeway onto the side streets.

Barbara recognized the area. They were in the University District. Her stomach began to quiver. *Please, not the Devine Nine. I don't want a confrontation tonight.*

Once Steven had made several turns and seemed to be on the right path, he continued. "Ray has practiced his guitar all these years but he hasn't kept up on his singing. He's okay but forgets some of the harmonies. Marcus's son is still learning our music and, if you remember, we never asked

Marcus to do anything but be amazing on the guitar.

"Would you sing backup next to Ray? He'll be more confident when he hears the music from someone else. You'd share the same microphone."

Barbara swallowed. Singing in the shower at the top of your lungs was one thing but singing on stage in front of who-knows-how-many people was another.

"I'll try but I've never been very good at being in front of a lot of people."

A lopsided grin touched his lips. "Thanks for the vote of confidence, but this is just a local club with a bunch of wannabe musicians and a group of old rock and rollers. I doubt there'll be very many people there. Will you help out? If we're going to put Rock Railroad back together, we need practice in front of small venues like this." Steven slowed the SUV and turned into the parking lot.

Barbara's stomach knotted. The sign out front announced, "The Devine Nine Club is proud to feature Rock Railroad and Don Barber from WARM 94.9 at tonight's Jam session. All musicians welcome."

Steven stopped the car. "What time does your watch say?"

"I didn't wear one, tonight, but the dashboard clock readout says seven twenty."

"Would you look at this parking lot? I'll be lucky to get my car near the back entrance so I can unload my drums."

She had to agree. The last time she'd seen the parking lot this full was the weekend before she left. Rock Railroad's schedule put them into the studio for four months to cut their first album and they had decided to play one last gig at the club. At that time, it was Big Eddie's and Eddie Van Houtan owned it. He'd been a big supporter of local groups and was pleased when Rock Railroad began to make it big. The memories of that night were bittersweet. At the end of the night, when everyone else had gone home, Barbara had told Steven of her decision to leave. He'd made all the right comments but she could tell he thought she was bluffing.

She felt a lump in her throat and a wayward tear make its way down her cheek. She quickly swiped it away from her face. As if sensing her memory, Steven turned her face to him and captured her lips with his own.

"I'll never be as stupid as I was the last time we were here." He tilted her face up to look directly into his eyes. "I love you, Barbara."

She tried to swallow over the lump in her throat. She whispered, "I love you, too, Steven."

"Good. Then let's make some good memories." He backed the SUV up to the side door and pounded on it. When it opened, Barbara watched a cloud of smoke roll out the opening. She cringed knowing, by the end of the night, not only would she look like Cher, she'd probably sound like her, too. Steven helped her out of the vehicle and escorted her to a chair on the backside of the stage. He leaned down. "Will you sing backup?"

She bobbed her head in agreement. She might make a fool of herself but this was one of those if-I-ever-get-a-chance-again moments.

~* ~

Ray unrolled a sound cord and plugged it in to a power strip near her chair. He stopped and did a double take. "Barbara? Is it really you?" He pulled her out of the chair and into a bear hug. "Steven said you were in town, and he said you didn't look a day older than when you left." He pushed her arm's length away and looked her up and down. "He was right. You look spectacular. Are you staying? How long?"

"Whoa!" Steven had walked up behind the pair. "Give her a chance to answer, Ray. If I have anything to say about it, she'll be staying indefinitely. I'm working on it. Listen, I'm going to have Barbara sing backup with you, do you mind?"

She watched Ray's face relax. "Thank God. I was worried about it. I don't mind having the company and, if I remember correctly, Barbara knows some of these songs better than I do. Great. Well, I need to finish getting this PA system put together, tune my guitar, and, most importantly, get a beer." He leaned over and placed a delicate kiss on her cheek. "Welcome home, Barbara. You have been missed more than you know." Winking, he turned and grabbed a box full of cords and began sorting them out.

Steven stopped. "I don't know if I've told you, yet, but you look phenomenal tonight. That outfit is—dangerous. At least, what I can see of it. If the jam session turns out to be as slow as I think it will be, we'll be leaving early." His eyes flashed and he grinned.

"I was going to give you a sneak peek, but I think I'll wait until I'm on stage. Then, you can't do anything until the set is over." Barbara shot him a wicked smile as she pulled the peek-a-boo cape around her.

They bantered back and forth until eight thirty when the noise level beyond the closed curtains began to overtake all conversation. Steven had finished setting up his drums and helping get the PA system up and in working order. He decided to see what the crowd looked like by getting himself a beer and bringing Barbara a Tom Collins. He started out the side of the curtains. A hand pushed him back. The hand was followed by Don Barber, Marcus, and Carl Dillman. The Dillmans nodded to Steven and moved to their amplifiers. Unlocking their guitar cases, they pulled out their instruments, plugged in, and began tuning up.

Don beamed. "You are not going to believe the crowd out there."

"Hello to you, too, Don. But I'm thirsty and would like a beer before we start playing. Why are you here, tonight? This is just the usual Sunday night jam session."

"Steven, where have you been? I've been advertising all week long that you guys would be playing tonight. There's a standing-room-only crowd out there. Unless you're in the mood to be mobbed and get your clothes ripped off, I wouldn't go out there if I was you. I'll send my assistant to get you what you need."

"You're joking, right?" Steven arched one eyebrow.

Don grasped his arm and led him to the edge of the curtain. Don stuck his head out and motioned for his assistant to come back stage. Steven snuck a peek out front. Quickly, he pulled his head back and pushed himself against the wall.

"I, I'm not sure I can do this. I haven't played to a group this large in over twenty years. Don? What have you gotten us into?"

Don chuckled. "What you should have been doing all along. You'll do just fine. My assistant will be back with your drinks. Who's drinking Tom Collins?"

Steven walked him back toward the chair where Barbara sat, her leg bouncing nervously.

Don looked at Steven. "Is that who I think?"

Steven let a small smile blossom.

"She looks as good as the last time I saw her over twenty years ago."

"Barbara?"

She looked up. Standing in front of her with Steven was one of the guys who'd been in the inner circle of friends she and Steven had shared. "Well, I'll be." She stood up and threw her arms around Don's neck. He leaned down to hug her.

"When did you get back in town?"

"About a week ago."

"Sure didn't take this guy long to find you." Standing, Don held Barbara's hand in his. "Man, it's good to see you. I never did figure out why this clown let you get away. Hopefully, he won't let it happen again."

"I have no intention of letting her slip away, so, don't get any ideas." Steven stood behind Barbara, his hands on her waist.

Behind the group, Marcus and Carl Dillman had walked up. Barbara recognized Marcus but said nothing. The first three months she and Steven had dated Marcus had actively pursued her—to the point of asking her to marry him. When she'd made it abundantly clear she wasn't interested, they'd agreed not to say anything to Steven and to maintain a friendship only. His hesitancy to approach her indicated to Barbara he hadn't forgotten their agreement.

He nodded at Barbara. "Barbara. Nice to see you again. This is my son Carl."

The young man had the same penetrating blue eyes of his father. "Pleasure, ma'am."

Barbara snickered. No one had called her ma'am in a very long time. "It's just Barbara."

Don checked his watch as his assistant slipped through the curtain bringing Steven and Barbara's drinks. "Got about ten minutes, guys. I'm going to warm up the crowd. I'd like to introduce everyone so if there's anything I need to know..."

"Yeah. Barbara is going to sing backup with Ray but don't introduce her by that name."

Steven had a twinkle in his eye that made Barbara feel she was going to regret his next statement.

Don raised an eyebrow. "Oh? What do I call her then?"

"Queen B."

Don looked at Barbara, who pantomimed innocence, batting her wide opened eyes.

"Whatever suits your fancy. Good luck, guys. I think the train is going to leave the station, tonight. You ready for it?"

Nods all around sent Don through the center opening of the curtain to monstrous applause.

"How is everyone?" More applause and whistling.

"Well, just in case a few of you in here have not been listening, I'll clear up what this little party is about."

Steve pulled Barbara to him and tilted her head. He placed a gentle kiss on her lips then winked. "Break a leg, Smokette."

"You, too, Smokey Bear."

The two grinned and took deep breaths. Tonight was their new beginning.

Twenty-eight

Thunderous applause rolled back to the bar.

Marc stood still for a moment and watched as the curtains opened. Don Barber was introducing the members of the group. He squinted to see who the girl was. She looked familiar but was too far away for him to see her face. When she stepped to the microphone, she was cocooned in some sort of light colored cape. Marc could hear people whispering that it was Cher. He looked again and could see the confusion; the dark hair, lithe figure and dramatic clothing. Don introduced her as Queen B, and the girl flung the cape off stage revealing an outfit only the diva could possibly have worn. Plunging in all the right places, the men in the audience started catcalling and stomping their feet, while the women were sneering and whispering it must be Cher using a fake name. No one else could possibly wear something that skimpy and daring and get away with it. Marc frowned and went back to mixing drinks. Uncle Ray had been wise when he'd told him to institute a cover charge at the door. His doorman, Evan, had come back three times to drop money into the floor safe, saying people seemed to be expecting to pay ten to fifteen dollars at the door. The five-dollar charge Marc had put in place was making him some lifelong customers.

"Hello-o-o-o? These animals are drinking like it's a frat party. A little service."

The server was waving to get Marc's attention. Moving to his well, he started on her drink order. No sense is making the natives more restless than necessary. He heard Don announce his father's name and felt stunned by the crowd's reaction. The audience cheered, applauded, and whistled—and there was even some screaming from the ladies. The glasses on his shelves rattled from the noise. With each member of the band, the audience response was the same. Marc signaled Evan to come to the bar.

"Have Tommy take over at the door. I want you to bartend tonight. I've got to see what makes these guys so special." Untying his white apron, he swapped places with the muscular doorman. He motioned to Tommy to watch the door and recruited a couple regulars to act as temporary bouncers. He didn't need trouble tonight. He walked to the end of the bar and stood in the hallway to his office, leaning against the doorframe.

He was able to pick out a few familiar faces. The guys in Booze Dogs were sitting in the second row of tables; there were the members of Devil in Red and... once he started looking, he realized every group he'd booked into the club was represented by one or more members of the band. All these other people knew and liked Rock Railroad. How could his mom have done this to his dad?

Don asked the audience if they wanted to hear the group play. A roar went up. He said he couldn't hear them; a louder roar went up, and when he put his hand to his ear, the third roar was deafening. Marc watched his servers and bartenders throw their hands up in defeat.

There was a tap, tap, tapping of drumsticks and the group began to sing *Money Man*. The crowd went ballistic. Marc stood in amazement as the people sang along, word for word. Even his servers seemed to know the song. Anger gnawed at him.

The building shook with the vibration of so many voices. Rock Railroad went into another song that brought silence almost as deafening as the raucous singing and foot-stomping of fifteen seconds earlier.

"Something new from Rock Railroad. We call it *Older and Wiser*; hope you like it." Steven slowed the beat and the spotlights softened to rose and blue. The girl faded off stage and Marc watched the crowd sway to the beat. He'd never seen a group hold the attention of the crowd like his father's group. He stormed into his office, picked up a sponge basketball, and threw it across the room.

"You bitch!" He sat fuming at his desk. His mother had filled him full of so many lies, Marc wasn't sure if anything she had said was true. He knew his Uncle Ray wouldn't lie to him, and his father had been honest, but he needed some kind of candor from his mother.

"I'm not sure she's capable of telling or even recognizing the truth," he muttered.

The crowd began to get rowdy again, and Marc could tell the music was shifting to fast, furious and rock. He went to stand in the doorway. He had a direct view of his father. The group was gearing up for a song that even he had heard—*Revenge*. The brunette had come back on stage, and several guys had rushed the dance floor to get close. Marc watched his father come alive behind the drum set. His hands flew over the snare and high hat. He smiled and sang into the microphone with such feeling that women in the audience were letting out little screams. Marc was stunned. This was the man he considered dull and boring, someone he hadn't wanted to grow up and emulate. How could he have been so wrong?

~ * ~

Barbara panicked the minute the curtains had opened. She could feel the warmth radiating off the crush of bodies, and the air hung thick with a cloud of smoke, aftershaves, and perfumes. If it hadn't been for the blinding spotlights, she might have turned and run back behind the stage.

Suck it up. Pretend. People think you're Cher then play to their fantasies. When Don introduced her as Queen B, she unclipped the cape and tossed it to a chair just off stage right. She heard Steven suck in air and murmur, "Oh my God." A wicked smile touched her lips, and the audience responded. *This is going to be fun.* After the group had been introduced, Don riled the audience to a frenzy. It took two starts for everyone to hear the lead in from Steven. Once Marcus, Ray, and Carl had picked up the lead, Barbara felt a calm take over. Ray tentatively leaned into the mike and, so lowly his voice disappeared, faked the harmony of the first line. Barbara snaked up to him. Vocal memory kicked in and she slinked to the mike adding her strong alto to his hesitant tenor. By the second verse, Ray and she were playing off each other and providing a strong backup. She glanced up at Steven, who winked at her and licked his lips. She felt a stirring of lust. Tonight, she didn't think they'd be getting away early, not with this crowd.

When they finished *Money Man*, the group slid into a song Barbara didn't recognize.

She faded behind the curtain and stood watching Steven. It still set her heart to pounding and her senses reeling when she watched him play the drums. She giggled. *I feel twenty-two again.*

She listened as the words of the song reached her through the monitors. *How true they were for all of them—Older and Wiser*. As the song neared its end, Steven motioned her to move up front. Hand signals they'd invented over twenty years ago began to flash. He was moving into *Revenge* then they'd do three more from the same album and take a break. After the first chord from *Revenge*, the crowd exploded. People moved from their tables to the edge of the stage, singing and clapping their hands above their heads to the beat. Barbara allowed the sensations of the moment to wash over her. It was intoxicating and empowering. Each time she leaned in to the microphone, she could hear several guys near the stage moan. Executed dance steps brought undisguised lust from the males in the audience. She found herself playing to get the responses. No wonder Steven had gone through such a difficult time chilling down after each gig. The power of the experience was addicting.

She pulled back on the next three songs, and, when the group announced they'd be taking a break, a groan rippled through the building.

"Don't worry. We'll be back." Steven waved and the curtains closed. He leapt from behind the drums, picked her up, and spun her around. "You were outrageous. I love it. Why weren't you like this before?"

Barbara wiggled an eyebrow and replied, "Because I'm older and wiser."

Steven pulled her into a kiss.

Don Barber cleared his throat. "Too soon for a room guys. Hey, that would make a great song... too soon for a room, la la la..."

Steven rolled his eyes. "Work on it, Don. Can you still get your assistant to get us some drinks?"

"I think so."

"I'd actually like some ice water. Barbara?"

She nodded emphatically. Her throat felt thrashed from singing so much and from the cigarette smoke.

"Consider it done. Angie!"

The college student sporting a University of South Florida T-shirt and jeans listened to Don's instructions and bolted from the stage.

"I don't think we're going to get to leave early. Sorry, Smokette," Steven whispered across Barbara's ear.

She turned and ran a finger down his smooth cheek. "I think you're right. We'll just have to make another date."

The second set went off without a hitch, and Barbara found herself enjoying her time on stage. The fans were enthusiastic and roared their approval of the familiar old songs. Rock Railroad ended the second set by playing a new tune called *Ain't Dead, Yet.*

When they relinquished the stage, communal grumbling started.

"It's been twenty years since you guys played—just one more set!"

"Rail-road, rail-road, rail-road."

Steven stood in front of the microphone and held up his hand for silence. When there was more quiet than noise, he spoke.

"Thank you. We, I, needed to know you wanted us back again." He raised his hand as the level of noise began to rise. "With all of the latest music, we weren't sure our brand of rock and roll had an audience, anymore. For that—we thank you. But now, show the musicians who've been providing you with great sounds and dance music all these years the same appreciation. After all, Rock Railroad started out as just another club group. You never know—next week one of these groups could become the next superstars. Make sure you can say you supported these guys 'way back when...'"

The applause started sporadically, and, soon, everyone in the place was on their feet clapping. Steven motioned the other members of the group to the front of the stage for the standing ovation. Barbara had slipped behind the curtain, retrieved her cape, and was watching with unconcealed admiration.

Don Barber took the microphone. "Steven?"

"Yes?"

"How soon can we expect to see the next album; excuse me, folks, my age is showing. How soon can we expect to see the new DVD?"

Steven glanced at the other members of the group. They nodded their approval.

"As soon as I can find a label that wants to give four old musicians a chance to make music again."

The crowd responded loudly and enthusiastically.

Don raised his hand for silence. "I think we can make that happen. Now, boys and girls, these guys have to pack up their gear and let the next group of players come up and set up their instruments, so, the break will be a little bit longer. Please don't go away. There's a lot more music on the way."

Barbara saw the group gathered around Don's assistant and headed over to see what was happening. When she got close she realized, the young lady had taped the show and was playing it back for them to see. She peeked over Ray's shoulder and let loose a moan. "I look like an idiot."

"I think you look sexy." Steven moved up behind her and wrapped his hands around her waist. "You smell good, too. Perfume mixed with sweat. Can't beat that for an aphrodisiac."

"I think you look sexy, too." Marcus, the lead guitar, walked away and began to tear down his equipment.

Steven turned her to face him. "Marcus doesn't say things like that very often. I'd take it as a very high compliment. Maybe we should consider using you all the time?" He wiggled his eyebrows at her.

Barbara rolled her eyes. "Please. First things first. Contract with record company then touring. You're going to be so busy in the studio, this foolish," she nodded her head toward the video the assistant was showing, "yes, foolish idea will disappear."

"I'm not so sure it's foolish. Ray sang better than I've ever heard him, and that includes when we were kids. He seems to feel comfortable with you sharing his mike. I think I want to explore this idea with the guys. Listen, I need to talk to them about practicing next week. Why don't you have a seat, and when we're through tearing down, we can try to find a place to sit. We have to schmooze, just like before."

Barbara nodded her head. "I remember. But be advised—if I feel like you're schmoozing too much with one young lady, I'll have no compunction about calling a taxi for a ride back to the hotel."

Placing a soft kiss on her forehead, he said, "I have only one lady on my mind. There is nothing short of dynamite that will take me from your side. Don't worry." He trotted over to the other members of the group.

Barbara sat in the nearest available chair and let the nostalgia of a time past wash over her. The scene could have been from any gig they'd played in the seventies. The guys were busy giving each other a hard time as they expertly disassembled the equipment. Except for the lack of groupies hanging around hoping to be chosen for the night, it felt as though no time had passed at all.

She headed to the ladies' room, catching Steven's eye and pantomiming her intentions. Slipping through the curtain, Barbara stumbled back from the heat. There was a continual buzz of voices, and smoke hung in a slowly descending curtain over the room. As quickly as she could navigate the burgeoning crowd, she worked her way to the back of the bar and the restrooms. Up the steps she climbed and hesitated, her stomach rebelling. She tossed a quick glance in the direction of the bar but couldn't see Marc. Momentarily assuaged, she continued.

As she exited the stall, the next person in line, a young blonde, eyed her up and down.

"Wal-Mart special?"

"Yeah. Got it right next to where you picked up your personality."

A few titters passed through the line. At the sink, she peered at the reflection in front of her as she washed her hands. *Nope. Don't need to fluff. Eye makeup is smudged just right.*

She stopped at the door and pulled in a calming breath. Tonight had been a dream come true. If she could make it out of the bar without running into Marc, everything would be perfect. She liked the young man and didn't want to hurt his feelings, but there was no choice between him and Steven. Steven had been her world more than twenty years ago, and she now had a chance to end the "if only" she'd been wishing most of her adult life.

She found a circuitous route back to the stage that kept her away from the bar. As she slipped back stage, she let go of the breath she hadn't realized she was holding.

Steven moved next to her. "You okay?"

She nodded.

"Let's see if we can find a place to sit for the next set. After that, I've got to say goodbye to someone and we'll go home. How's that sound?"

"Like a great idea."

~ * ~

Marc watched the brunette wend her way through the crowd. He'd be sure when she got to the steps and was close enough for him to see her face clearly if it was who he thought.

"Ma-a-a-r-c."

He closed his eyes and gritted his teeth. *Maybe, if I pretend I didn't hear her, she'll go away.*

"Ma-a-a-a-r-r-c."

Sighing, he turned to the bar. "What, Stephanie?"

Lowering her eyes to look up through her lashes, she bat them as she asked. "Would you hand me a cherry for my coke? And my name is Steffy."

"Well, Steffy, why didn't you just reach over and grab yourself one like everyone else does?" Marc watched the little blonde's face distort into anger.

"How rude. Would you at least keep an eye on my coke while I go to the bathroom?"

"Whatever."

Barbara's prediction fulfilled itself. Steffy was Tiffany's best friend and had been in the club all weekend asking about Marc's fiancé. He'd had it with her coyness. He looked up to see if he could see the brunette. He scanned what he could see of the crowd in the main room and did a quick visual survey of the bar area. Walking to Aaron's end of the bar, he peeked around the corner to the game room. She was nowhere in sight.

"Damn."

"A little service here. These cretins aren't slowing down."

Marc channeled his frustration into filling the orders that were furiously coming at him from his servers. He'd pull Evan behind the bar again, later, and take himself a break. Maybe he could find her then.

~ * ~

Dennis Bozeman, the leader of Booze Dogs, stood and waved frantically at Steven and Barbara. He sent a couple people from the table and indicated they should come over and sit.

Steven looked at Barbara. "What do you think?"

"I think if we don't go over, there could be an ugly backlash. I've seen this guy work. He's got the tongue of a snake and the manners of a baboon."

Steven raised an eyebrow. "Oh? When was that?"

Barbara pulled herself tall. "It's really none of your business, but, last weekend, when my friend Rachel and I first got to town, I wanted to see if this place was still in business. I had asked one of the young men at the hotel if Big Eddie's was still around. He took a few minutes, came back, and told me Big Eddie's was now Devine Nine. So we did some shopping and came out to enjoy the music. Booze Dogs were playing. He—" Barbara nodded in the direction of the table Dennis was sitting. "—acted like every musician I remembered. Promising the world to get what he wanted. He struck out but I don't think he realized it. Okay?"

Steven squeezed her hand. "I was just teasing. We're both beyond that foolishness. I was just curious how you could be familiar with the local music scene after being in town only a week. Now I know. By the way, that young man you spoke with at the hotel?"

Barbara nodded. "Yes?"

"That's Ray's oldest."

She stopped and turned to face Steven directly. "No way!"

"Yes. He's my godson and my son is Ray's godson. Here we are." He pulled out the chair for her and made sure he sat directly at her side.

"Thanks. I was wondering where we were going to find a place."

Dennis eyed Barbara. "Haven't we met before?"

"Yes, last weekend. I was here with my tall red-haired friend. I believe one of your—groupies—tried to rearrange my face. As I recall, I stopped her cold. Right?"

Dennis' face flushed. "Yeah. That was Cindy. She's a little possessive when it comes to us. Don't know why; none of us gives her the time of day."

Barbara turned and looked up at him from under her lashes. "Maybe you should. Someone that devoted deserves respect. She'll be there for you when no one else shows up at the gig; she'll drive hundreds of miles to make sure you have a friendly face in the audience, and she won't allow anyone to talk badly about you. Sounds like a devoted fan to me. In this life, true devotion deserves some respect. If I remember correctly, she's not bad to look at, either. You could do worse."

"And he has." Michael, the drummer of the group, walked up and placed a beer in front of the singer. "The stories I could tell..." Dennis glared at him. "...but won't." He nodded at Barbara. "Nice to see you again. You look"—his eyes traveled the length of her—"stunning, again. Dennis. We have to get up there and put our stuff together, now. Mr. Rodgers, I have to let you know that listening to your records—my parents were huge fans—is what started me drumming. It was an honor to see you in person tonight."

Michael held his hand out to Steven who shook it. "I only hope when I get as old as you that I can still be playing half as good." Once the statement had left his mouth, Michael realized how it sounded. The stricken look on his face was priceless.

Barbara turned and coughed to keep from bursting into laughter, and Dennis rolled his eyes heavenward.

"God, you're such an idiot. Come on Michael. Let's get on stage before you make a bigger fool of yourself." The two musicians crossed the dance floor and ascended the steps, disappearing behind the curtain. Spotlights flashed back and forth and guitars were tuned. The people milling around began to find their seats and a lowering of the noise level ensued.

Barbara surveyed the room. Quite a few people had left but there were still no available seats at any of the nearby tables. She was relieved they were sharing Dennis' table. The set seemed to drag interminably and guitarists, drummers, and various singers took the stage. When the announcement that it was break time came from the stage, she relaxed. While the outer form might look to be in its twenties, the inner Barbara was in her fifties and more tired than she could remember. She put her hand on Steven's arm.

"Can we go now?"

He nodded, looking as exhausted as she felt. "Been a lot of years since I played that much for that long. I'm beat! I need to talk with someone before we go."

"Oh?"

"Yeah, my son works here and would be highly insulted if I didn't say goodbye. I'd like to introduce you." Steven stood and extended his hand to her. "You ready?"

She could no longer put off facing the truth. Steven had moved on with his life after she left, just as she had. It was time to quit pretending and face reality. "Sure. Lead the way." She accepted his hand, and they walked toward the bar. Barbara ran through her mind the young men she'd seen working here. Evan? No, too stocky. Aaron? Well, there was some resemblance in the light hair and pale eyes. If Steven's wife had been blonde and blue eyed, Aaron was a possibility. Marc. She stopped. He had the fair hair and the hazel eyes that had drawn her to Steven when they were younger. And the dimples—the dimples were so similar to Steven's it would be a miracle if Marc was not his son. This is going to be uncomfortable. She lagged behind, allowing Steven to take the lead.

The bar side was quiet. Steven moved up to the rail.

"Marc!"

Barbara's heart sank.

The handsome young man finished his conversation with the customer at the other end and walked toward his father. When he spotted Barbara, he hesitated and slowed his progress.

"Hey, Dad. You guys really packed the place tonight. Thanks."

"Not a problem. Thank your Uncle Ray. He was the one who came up with the idea. I'm heading out. I'm bushed, but I wanted to you to meet someone very special in my life."

"Oh?"

Steven tugged at Barbara's hand bringing her to the bar. "Marc, I'd like you to meet..."

"Barbara."

"You two know each other?"

Barbara shifted from one foot to the other not sure what to say.

Marc spoke up. "I believe she was in here last weekend, weren't you?" His eyes looked at her coolly. "With that amazing, tall redhead, right?"

"Yes, that was us."

"How is Rachel?" Marc smiled but there was no warmth in the gesture.

Steven interrupted. "Listen, I need to make a pit stop before we leave. I wanted to introduce you two and say good-bye before we left. I'll be back." He turned and placed a kiss on Barbara's forehead.

Marc watched him walk away. "Well, isn't this cozy. So you have a thing for older men, is that it?" He glared at her.

Oh, boy. This is going to be sticky. "No, Marc. I have a thing for the love of my life." She watched confusion cloud his eyes.

"What are you talking about? My dad is in his fifties."

"Yes, and he's younger than I am." She stood waiting for the truth to dawn on him.

Bewilderment and distrust crossed his face, but, finally, his eyes registered what she was trying to tell him.

"When were you going to slip that little bit of information to me?" he spit out.

"I didn't think the situation would get that far. I'm sorry for deceiving you, but I believed you'd be like most young men at your age—unwilling to think beyond the moment. I lied to you when I didn't divulge my true age at the beginning. For that, I'm sorry. But I'm not sorry for spending time with you. I really do enjoy your company."

"You said my dad is the love of your life."

"Yes."

"How can that be unless you'd been here in Tampa before? Was anything you told me true?" Marc had leaned against the back bar and was scowling, his arms crossed over his chest defensively.

"I lived and went to school here for five years. I dated your father when he was your age, but I'd never made it to Tarpon Springs or Longboat Key. We never saw a Reds training game because, at the time, your dad was going to school and playing in the band. Most of our off time we would go and listen to other groups or just hang out by the pool.

"I wasn't lying about not having been those places before. The things we talked about and my feelings at the time were truthful. I just let you think I was as young as this body looks. For that, I apologize again. I can't ask you to like me, but I'll let you know, I'm not about to walk away from your dad without a fight. I lost him once—never again."

Barbara watched the grim expression on Marc's face soften. "You're that Barbara."

"Yes, I am."

He uncrossed his arms and stood away from the back bar as he watched his father move toward them. "I'm not sure how long it will take before I trust you, but, if my dad wants you in his life, I'll try to be civil. I can't make any guarantees. Here he comes." Marc pasted a smile on his face. "Welcome back to Tampa, Barbara. I hope you enjoy your stay. Listen, Dad. I'm going to stay at the Davis Island house for a couple more nights. Mirella is still kind of spooked, and I'd feel better just being there for her. I'll see you around."

Steven tried to hide his surprise. "Sure. See you, son." He waved at Aaron and grabbed Barbara's hand. "Shall we?"

They walked passed the dance floor and to the stage steps. Steven handed the keys to Barbara. "Could you back the car up to the door?"

She nodded and stepped into the parking lot to retrieve his white SUV. She looked to the sky. *Please, don't let me have blown this.*

As they closed the back of the vehicle, Barbara handed Steven his keys. She slid into the passenger's side and leaned against the back of the seat.

"How about we go to my place, have coffee, and you can fill me in on what just happened?" Steven reached his hand out and covered Barbara's squeezing gently.

"Good idea."

The rest of the ride passed in contemplative silence. Once in the condo, Steven changed into jeans and a t-shirt. He found a pair of shorts he said he'd grown out of and a t-shirt for Barbara to wear.

They sat together on the couch in the living room, Steven's arm around her shoulders, gazing at the lights along the Bay. Barbara shifted away from him.

"I told you my friend and I went to the bar last weekend."

"Um-hmm."

"What I left out was the fact that Marc became... enamored with me. He asked me out, and Rachel pushed me to accept. I had no idea if you were married with ten children, single, dead, or alive, so, at that time, I was just a single girl in a new city. Sort of. We had one date—no sex—then you came back into my life. I'd already accepted a second date with Marc. I still wasn't sure what your intentions were. For all I knew, you had soured on relationships and didn't want anything more than a quick roll-in-the-hay. Let's be honest, I loved you years ago, but how could I be sure that what I was feeling was love?

"After the second date with Marc, I knew he was an exciting, handsome young man but, by that time, I realized my feeling for you were as strong as when I'd left all those years before. I didn't want anything to jeopardize any relationship we might have. Guess that's kind of selfish, isn't it?"

Steven let a smile flicker over his mouth. "Yes and I'm glad. I can say one thing about my son—he's got good taste. I've always put my kids ahead of everything else in my life, but, this time, I'm being selfish. I love you, Barbara, and I won't let anything or anyone take you from me. Marc is at the age that, yes, he'll hurt for a while, but, he'll recover and move on quickly.

"I, on the other hand, have a chance at the happy life I let walk away all those years ago. I'm not going to bungle it." Steven lowered his head to within inches of Barbara's and as he feathered her mouth with soft kisses, he whispered. "Please say you'll marry me?"

She pulled away, eyes wide. "What did you say?"

He got off the couch and dropped to one knee. Gently lifting her hand, he looked her directly in the eyes and repeated. "Barbara Hamilton Langley, will you marry me? As soon as we possibly can?"

She stared at the figure before her. This was what she had dreamed for so many years. Why wouldn't her voice work? She saw anxiety begin to build in Steven's eyes.

This is right, Barbara. I'll always love you, but the time has come for you to fall in love again, marry, and move on. Say yes!

"Yes," she croaked. "Yes!"

Steven stood up and pulled her to him. He covered her lips with his own and kissed her with a passion she hadn't felt in many years. She opened her mouth slightly allowing him to explore her warmth with his tongue. Feelings and sensations long forgotten washed over her.

Steven broke the seal. "I hate to be the meanie, but I've got to go into work tomorrow and start putting together a plan for the hotel and the band. Why don't you stay here tonight?"

She gave him a wary look.

"We'll... just sleep. I don't think, even as much as I love you, that I could do justice to lovemaking tonight. We'll save that for a time when we're both rested and ready. Okay?"

She smiled. "Getting old really sucks sometimes, doesn't it?"

He grinned. "Yeah, but we're going to get old together. And that's best of all."

Epilogue

Standing in the small church, next to Rachel, Barbara felt at peace for the first time in several years. She was the maid of honor at her best friend's wedding in a small chapel near Oxford. Rachel was radiant and Robart handsome in his tuxedo. The vows taken and given, the couple announced to the world as Mr. and Mrs., and the wedding moved to the lodge Rachel and Robart now operated.

As they sat next to the newlyweds, Steven and Barbara smiled at each other.

"Just two more weeks until we do this," he whispered in her ear.

"Yeah, but not quite so noisily." She snuggled into the crook of his arm.

Rock Railroad had spent the last four months sequestered in the recording studio putting together the first of a four-record deal. Rachel's wedding had proven a good excuse to take a vacation. The couple had secretly flown into the London area, and Rachel and Robart had picked them up and spirited them away to the lodge. Once the announcement Rock Railroad was reuniting had hit the airwaves, privacy had become a fleeting memory so plans for a quiet wedding had moved to the British Isles.

Alana, Steven's daughter, had been overjoyed at meeting the woman who'd captured her father's heart and used the opportunity to introduce the couple to her Literature professor friend.

Marc had sequestered himself for three weeks after discovering the woman he thought he would marry was to become his stepmother. He took solace in the arms of his childhood friend, Mirella, and it became evident to Steven and Barbara, at the May wedding of Erik Klopffenstein and Olivia

Jones, that he was healing quite well.

Steven's ex-wife, Lisa, discovered her Latin beau had been asked to leave several countries because of "indiscretions." The incident at the Davis Island house brought unwanted attention to the embassy and emphasized they had a growing problem with the Lothario. Senor de la Mar Montenegro became a private citizen in June, and the consulate deported him back to Spain at the end of the month. Lisa moved to Miami and started a modeling career. Her good looks, natural thinness and towering stature kept her in the lifestyle to which she'd become accustomed.

Steven watched Barbara's friend dance with her new husband. He leaned over and kissed Barbara's forehead.

"I'm so glad you came back"

She wiggled into his warmth. "So am I."

About the Author

C. L. Kraemer
Fantasy, Sci Fi and Mystery writer

C. L. Kraemer has been a gypsy all her life. From her military child beginnings to her might-not-get-this-chance-again attitude after she left home, she's seen most of the continental United States as well as Hawaii and Alaska.

Three contemporary romance novels *Old Enough*; *Moon in Mazatlan*, and *If Only* are being rereleased by Rogue Phoenix Press as well as *Cats in the Cradle of Civilization.*

Healthy Homicide, the October 2008 launch book for Rogue Phoenix Press picks up the torch in the mystery world. In February 2010, she contributed to two Valentine's anthologies at Rogue Phoenix Press: *A Valentine Anthology*, with a story titled, "Lending Library," and *A Different Kind of Valentine* with a story titled, "The Prize."

She has completed the base story for a Dragon Fantasy series, *Dragons Among Us*, which was released August 2010 by Rogue Phoenix Press and the first follow up in the series, *Dragons Among the Eagles*, released in 2011.

"Meadows of Gold" is another faerie story released by Rogue Phoenix Press in the March 2011's anthology, *A St. Patrick's Day Tale*. A third story featuring the Fae of the valley outside Eugene, Oregon, "Defying the Odds" was included in the *May Day Anthology,* May 2013. "Boots and Blades" will be included in a Christmas 2016 collection.

August 2011 saw the release of *Shattered Tomorrows*, a

mystery/crime novel loosely based on the May 7, 1981 shooting at the Oregon Museum Tavern in Salem, Oregon where four lost their lives and twenty were wounded.

A motorcycle poker run is featured in her March 2013 release, *Joker's Wild* and the third in the dragon series, *Dragons Among the Ice*, is yet to be released.

For detailed information, visit her Web sites for background on her books: www.clkraemer.com

Other books by C. L. Kraemer
Available at Rogue Phoenix Press

Healthy Homicide

Two murders have occurred at the Barrel Springs Day Spa. Police hurry to find the method and reason before anyone else is murdered.

MANIC READER REVIEWS says: Healthy Homicide by C.L. Kraemer is an intriguing plot driven mystery. The plot is well written and pretty much carries the whole story...

Dragons Among Us

In a world full of anomalies such as the platypus and self reproducing Komodo dragon, is the human race willing to accept that dragons may be real?

Sapien Draconi-human-dragon shape shifters-all over the world face this dilemma every day. The question has become life and death as their species is plagued with unexpected and unwanted shifting in the most unlikely of places.

The Ancient Ones-full-blooded dragons-can offer advice, but few seem to put forward workable solutions to the problem.

The fate of the shape shifters hangs in the balance, and an answer must be found before the Homo Sapiens find, dissect, and hunt Sapien Draconi to extinction.

Dragons Among The Eagles

Aleda Sable faces the toughest decision of her life--to stay in dragon form, live as a two-legged or put one foot in the human world and one talon in the dragon world.

An urgent call from her newspaper editor sends Aleda to report on an accident whose driver appears to be a dragon. Authorities have the scene locked down and aren't allowing access to anyone. Television broadcasts flash pictures of scaly legs hanging from a crashed car. However, the bodies disappear into thin air. When the stations try follow-up reports, all they find are state highway workers busily tearing up the roads.

In determining the truth of the shifter disappearances, Aleda finds the truth of her own dilemma.

Shattered Tomorrows

Lucy Daniels has a secret--a deeply guarded secret.

Her life was going along just fine until she accompanied her best friend, Cassie, to her attorney's suite on top of the Equitable Building in downtown Salem, Oregon.

Once inside the lawyer's office, the world turned upside down and Lucy was forced to face a demon from her past. Thirty years ago, life had been different. Lucy had discovered Prince Charming and was headed to her happily ever after.

That's when the devil intervened and because of her brush with the devil, innocent people died.

Joker's Wild

Four brothers raised in the Northwest.

Two choose to stay and pursue life in Oregon. Two are seduced by the promise of Hollywood.

Life throws the Palmer brothers an ugly curve when two are killed in preventable accidents. Even more upsetting is the lack of justice in the trials of the perpetrators.

The remaining brothers will find justice using a shared passion of all the participants--motorcycle poker runs.

Cats in the Cradle of Civilization

Glenda Nagel, editor for Getty Museum's monthly magazine loves her home in the Juniper Hills and her cats. When an ivory and emerald statuette of the cat goddess Bastet makes its way to her home and sets her cats on edge, Glenda is panicked.

Who knows about his and why has the darkly handsome, new Director of Egyptian Antiquities become so determined to visit her high desert home? Doesn't Egypt have enough sand?

Moon in Mazatlan

Detective Corey Williams is content with his small town Virginia home. Normally, his busiest night is Saturday, but when his best friend's ex-wife attempts to have him killed, Corey gives his promise to ensure justice is served. Meeting a red-haired, Harley riding goddess has thrown a wrench in his quiet staid life. Only one hiccup in this situation; the goddess is a reporter. When the ex-wife of his friend flees the country, the reporter makes sure she is right behind Detective Williams. He is oath bound to bring the fugitive ex-wife back for trial. What he hadn't counted on was falling for the Harley riding reporter.

Old Enough

She was looking to escape her past in the quiet little town. He was recovering from a bad marriage and trying to get custody of his daughter. The last thing she needed was a younger man complicating her life, but fate threw them a curve and sparks flew.

C. L. Kraemer
is also featured in these anthologies available at
Rogue Phoenix Press

A Different Kind of Valentine

A collection of four short stories:

Witness by k. J. Dahlen

When Colten finds an injured woman the police are looking for her, should he trust his own judgment about keeping her hidden from the law even if it means she might kill him?

The Prize by C. L. Kraemer

A computer geek learns valuable life lessons when he is given his dream car as well as a condo and the perfect job.

Crazy 'bout You by Clay Renick

Can a psychologist and a romance writer find true love in time for Valentines Day?

Time Changes by Nicolette Zamora

Laurie is just about ready to give up on love when she spies Rob Hender, her high school sweetheart's older brother.

A St. Patrick's Day Tale

By Christine Young, C. L. Kraemer, Genene Valleau

Tumble through time…

…to Ireland in 1817, when tensions are high between Protestants and Catholics and fae people guide the fate of villagers. A lovely Catholic lass stumbles upon the weakly ritual fisticuffing between Irish lads. She falls into the lap of a handsome young Protestant. Family ties, grudges, and two conniving faeries threaten their budding love. But the faeries outsmart themselves when they hijack a time machine that has mysteriously appeared in their forest and are whisked to…

…Eugene, Oregon in the 20th century, amid a property feud between the local faeries and night elves. The conniving faeries from Olde Ireland try to stir up more mischief. However, a warrior gnome convinces the magic folk to control their own destiny, and forces the intruding faeries to take refuge in the time machine again, spinning their way toward…

…A modern day castle in western Oregon. An eccentric inventor is determined to reclaim his wayward time machine and save his beloved wife from her latest misadventure. If only they can travel safely past the black hole…

A Valentine's Anthology

The Lending Library-a fantasy by C. L. Kraemer

Faeries try to fit into the human world when the forest where they make their home is destroyed by a mysterious enemy.

Chasing Rainbows-a contemporary romance by Genene Valleau

An eccentric aunt, an inventive uncle, a mother who wears poodle skirts, and a brother who wears pearls provide a hilarious backdrop for the courtship of a young woman who yearns for a "normal" family.

The Gift-an historical romance by Christine Young

A man and a woman on opposite sides of the Civil War get a second chance at love after one final battle returns soldiers to their war-torn homes to rebuild their lives.

www.ingramcontent.com/pod-product-compliance
Lightning Source LLC
Chambersburg PA
CBHW051420170626
46809CB00006B/2246

* 9 7 8 1 6 2 4 2 0 2 1 0 0 *